THE RUGGED RANCHER

BY

DONNA ALWARD

AND

SOLDIER ON HER DOORSTEP

BY

SORAYA LANE

MILLS & BOON®

Dear Reader,

Before I was blessed to turn writing stories into a career, I was a stay-at-home mom. It has been the toughest—and best—job I've ever had. I have never regretted having those precious years at home. And I am very fortunate to have a husband who supported me one hundred percent.

But every now and then I wondered—what would happen if suddenly I was left to provide for our children on my own? I was employed before they were born, but how difficult would it be to get back into the workforce, make ends meet, and still be there for them in the way I wanted? That's exactly what happens to Emily in *A Family for the Rugged Rancher*. I like Emily. Yes, she's been hurt, but she's pulled up her socks to do what's best for her son. She's a good mother. She does what I hope I would have done if I'd found myself in those circumstances. Cope—with a smile.

Of course Luke is dealing with his own issues, and one many of us face as time ticks on: aging parents. He needs someone to bring him out of his shell. To show him all the rich possibilities of the future. And that someone is Emily.

I often hear people say that romance novels are unrealistic fairy tales, but I don't agree. My characters aren't just characters—they're people trying to deal with issues we all face in our lives. And when life gets bad sometimes it's nice to know—just for a while—that the sun is going to peek from beneath that cloud. I'm here to say that fairy tales happen. There *are* such things as happy endings.

I hope you find your happy ending too!

Warm wishes,

Donna

A FAMILY FOR THE RUGGED RANCHER

BY
DONNA ALWARD

All the characters in this book have no existence outside the imagination of
the author, and have no relation whatsoever to anyone bearing the same name
or names. They are not even distantly inspired by any individual known or
unknown to the author, and all the incidents are pure invention.

First published in Great Britain 2011
by Mills & Boon, an imprint of Harlequin (UK) Limited,
Eton House, 18-24 Paradise Road, Richmond, Surrey TW9 1SR

© Donna Alward 2011

ISBN: 978 0 263 88887 4

23-0611

Harlequin (UK) policy is to use papers that are natural, renewable and
recyclable products and made from wood grown in sustainable forests. The
logging and manufacturing processes conform to the legal environmental
regulations of the country of origin.

Printed and bound in Spain
by Blackprint CPI, Barcelona

A busy wife and mother of three (two daughters and the family dog), **Donna Alward** believes hers is the best job in the world: a combination of stay-at-home mum and romance novelist. An avid reader since childhood, Donna always made up her own stories. She completed her Arts Degree in English Literature in 1994, but it wasn't until 2001 that she penned her first full-length novel and found herself hooked on writing romance. In 2006 she sold her first manuscript, and now writes warm, emotional stories for Mills & Boon's Cherish line.

In her new home office in Nova Scotia, Donna loves being back on the east coast of Canada after nearly twelve years in Alberta, where her career began, writing about cowboys and the west. Donna's debut Romance, *Hired by the Cowboy,* was awarded the Booksellers Best Award in 2008 for Best Traditional Romance.

With the Atlantic Ocean only minutes from her doorstep, Donna has found a fresh take on life and promises even more great romances in the near future!

Donna loves to hear from readers. You can contact her through her website at www.donnaalward.com or her page at www.myspace.com/dalward.

A great editor is worth her weight in gold.

To Sally, for her constant faith that I'm up to the task. It means more than you know.

CHAPTER ONE

"ARE WE HERE, Mama? Is Daddy here?"

Emily smiled, though Sam's innocent question made her heart quiver. Sam looked for Rob everywhere, never giving up hope no matter how often he was disappointed. "Yes," she replied, "we're here. But Daddy's not coming, remember? I'm here to start a brand-new job."

She touched the brake pedal as she entered the farmyard of Evans and Son. It was bigger than she'd imagined, sprawling across several acres criss-crossed with fence lines and dotted with leafy green poplar trees. She slowed as she approached the plain white two-story house that rested at the end of the drive. It was flanked on one side by a gigantic barn and on the other by a large workshop with two oversized garage doors. More outbuildings were interspersed throughout the yard, all of them tidy and well-kept. The grass around them was newly clipped and the bits of peeling paint made for a broken-in look rather than broken-down.

Evans and Son looked to be doing all right in the overall scheme of things—which was more than Emily could say for her family. But she was going to change all that. Starting today.

She parked to the right of the house, inhaling deeply and letting out a slow breath, trying to steady herself. When she looked into the back seat, she saw Sam's eyes opening, taking a moment to focus and realize the vehicle had stopped.

"But I want to see Daddy."

"I know, baby." Emily told herself to be patient, he was only five. "Once we're settled, I'll help you write a letter. Maybe you can draw him a picture. What do you think?"

Sam's eyes still held that trace of confusion and sadness that had the power to hurt Emily more than anything else. Sam had been clingier than usual lately. It was hardly a surprise. She'd put the house up for sale and their things in storage. She'd announced that they were leaving the city, which also meant leaving playschool friends and everything familiar, and a five-year-old couldn't be expected to understand her reasons. But the house in Calgary held too many memories—happy and devastating by turns. Both Emily and Sam were stuck in wishing for the past—a past that was long over. Rob had moved on, withdrawing not only his financial support but, more importantly, severing emotional ties with both of them.

Emily would never understand that, especially where his son was concerned. But now it was time to let go and build a new life. One where they could be happy. One where Emily could support her son and find her own way rather than wishing for what should have been. There was a certain freedom to be found in knowing she could make her own decisions now. Her choices were hers to make and hers alone. A massive responsibility, but a liberating one, too.

She reminded herself that a happier life for the two of them was why she was here. "Wait here for just a moment while I knock on the door, okay? Then we'll get settled, I promise."

"It's quiet here."

"I know." Emily smiled, trying to be encouraging. "But there is still sound. Listen closely, Sam, and when I get back you can tell me what you heard."

Sam had only ever lived in the city, with the sounds of traffic and sirens and voices his usual background music. But Emily remembered what it was like to live outside the metropolitan area, where the morning song wasn't honking horns but birds warbling in the caragana bushes and the shush of the breeze through poplar leaves. For the first time in months, she was starting to feel hope that this was all going to turn out all right.

"Wait here, okay? Let me talk to Mr. Evans first, and then I'll come for you."

"Okay, Mama." Sam reached over and picked up his favorite storybook, the Dr. Seuss one with the tongue twisters that he'd practically memorized. Emily paused, her tender smile wavering just a little. Sometimes Sam seemed to see and understand too much. Had the breakdown of her marriage forced her son to grow up too soon?

"I won't be long, sweetie." Emily blew him a kiss, shut the car door and straightened her T-shirt, smoothing it over the hips of her denim capris. It was really important that everything got off on the right foot, so she practiced smiling, wanting it to seem natural and not show her nervousness. She climbed the few steps to the front porch, gathered her courage and rapped sharply on the door.

No one answered.

This was not a great beginning, and doubts crept in, making her wonder if it was a sign that she was making a big mistake with this whole idea. Selling the house and uprooting the two of them was a bit of a radical move, she knew that. She glanced back at the car only feet away and saw Sam's dark head still bent over his book. No, this was best. Her experience as a mom and homemaker was what made her perfect for this job, she realized. She'd loved being a stay-at-home mom, and being with Sam was the most important thing.

Maybe Mr. Evans simply hadn't heard her. She knocked

again, folding her hands. It was a bit nerve-wracking being hired for a job sight unseen. She'd interviewed at the agency but this was different. She'd have to pass Mr. Evans's tests, too. He had the final say. When was the last time she'd had a real interview? All of her résumés over the last year had been sent out without so much as a nibble in return. No one wanted to hire a lab tech who'd been out of the work force for the past five years.

She forced herself to stay calm, stave off the disappointment she felt as her second knock also went unanswered.

"Can I help you?"

The voice came from her right and her stomach twisted into knots as a man approached from the shop, wiping dirty hands on a rag. This was Mr. Evans? He looked younger than she was, for heaven's sake. He wore faded jeans and dusty roper boots, his long stride eating up the ground between them. His baseball cap shaded his eyes so that she couldn't quite see them. The dark T-shirt he wore was stained with grease, stretched taut over a muscled chest. All in all he had the look of honest work about him. And honest work ranked high on her list of attributes lately, she thought bitterly. Good looks didn't.

"I...I'm Emily Northcott. I'm here from the agency?" She hated how uncertain that sounded, so she amended, "From Maid on Demand."

There was a slight pause in his stride while Emily went back down the steps. They met at the bottom, the grass tickling Emily's toes in her sandals as she held out her hand.

The man held up his right hand. "Luke Evans. I'd better not. You don't want to get grease on your hands."

Embarrassment crept hotly up her cheeks, both because she knew she should have realized his hands would be dirty and because of his flat tone. Emily dropped her hand to her side and tried a smile. "Oh, right. I hope we...I...haven't come at a bad time."

"Just fixing some machinery in the shed. I heard the car pull up. Wasn't expecting you though."

"Didn't the agency call?"

"I'm not often in the house to answer the phone." He stated it as if it were something obvious that she'd missed.

Emily frowned. His communication skills could use some work. Didn't he have a cell phone like most normal people? Or voice mail? Or was he being deliberately difficult?

"I was specifically given today as a start date and directions to your place, Mr. Evans."

He tucked the rag into the back pocket of his jeans. "They probably called my sister. She's the one who placed the ad."

"Your sister?"

"My sister Cait. They might have tried there, but she's in the hospital."

"Oh, I'm sorry. I hope it's nothing serious." His answers were so clipped they merely prompted more questions, but his stance and attitude didn't exactly inspire her to ask them.

Finally he gave in and smiled. Just a little, and it looked like it pained him to do so. But pain or not, the look changed his face completely. The icy blue of his eyes thawed a tad and when he smiled, matching creases formed on either side of his mouth. "Nothing too serious," he replied. "She's having a baby."

The news made his smile contagious and Emily smiled back, then caught herself. She clenched her fingers, nervous all over again. She hadn't really given a thought to age...or to the fact that the rancher looking for a housekeeper might be somewhat attractive. What surprised her most was that she noticed at all. Those thoughts had no place in her head right now, considering the scars left from her last relationship and her determination not to put herself through that again.

And Evans wasn't a looker, not in a classic turn-your-head handsome sort of way. But there was something about the tilt of his smile, as though he was telling a joke. Or the way that his cornflower-blue eyes seemed to see right into her. He had inordinately pretty eyes for a man, she thought ridiculously. Had she really thought "somewhat" attractive? She swallowed. He was long, lean and muscled, and his voice held a delicious bit of grit. His strength made up for the lack of pretty. More than made up for it.

Suddenly, being a housekeeper to a single man in the middle of nowhere didn't seem like the bright idea it had been a week ago.

"The agency hired me," she repeated.

He let out a short laugh. "So you said."

Emily resisted the urge to close her eyes, wondering if he'd seen clear through to her last thoughts. Maybe the prairie could just open up and swallow her, and save her more embarrassment. "Right."

"You're able to start today?"

Hope surged as she opened her eyes and found him watching her steadily. He wasn't giving her the brush-off straight away after all. "Yes, sir." She forced a smile. "I can start today."

"Mom, can't I come out now? It's hot in here."

The nerves in Emily's stomach froze as Sam's soft voice came from the car. Luke's head swiveled in the direction of the car, and Emily gave in and sighed. Dammit. She hadn't even had a chance to talk to Evans about their arrangements or anything. A muscle ticked in Luke's jaw and he looked back at her, the smile gone now, the edges of his jaw hard and forbidding.

"My son, Sam," she said weakly.

"You have children."

"Child—just Sam. He's five and no trouble, I promise.

Good as gold." That was stretching it a bit; Sam was a typical five-year-old who was as prone to curiosity and frustrations as any child his age. She looked again at Evans and knew she had to convince him. He was the one who'd advertised. She'd gone through the agency screening and they had hired her for the job. If this didn't work out she had nowhere to go. And she wanted to stay here. She'd liked the look of the place straight off.

Another moment and he'd have her begging. She straightened her shoulders. She would not beg. Not ever again. She could always go to her parents. It wasn't what she wanted, and there'd be a fair amount of told-you-so. Her parents had never quite taken to Rob, and the divorce hadn't come as a big surprise to them. It wasn't that they didn't love her or would deny her help. It was just…

She needed to do this herself. To prove to herself she could and to be the parent that Sam deserved. She couldn't rely on other people to make this right. Not even her parents.

"Mrs. Northcott, this is a ranch, not a day care." The smile that had captivated her only moments before had disappeared, making his face a frozen mask. The warm crinkles around his lips and eyes were now frown marks and Emily felt her good intentions go spiraling down the proverbial drain.

"It's Ms.," she pointed out tartly. It wasn't her fault that there'd been a mix-up. "And Sam is five, hardly a toddler who needs following around all the time." She raised an eyebrow. "Mothers have been cleaning and cooking *and* raising children since the beginning of time, Mr. Evans."

She heard the vinegar in her voice and felt badly for speaking so sharply, but she was a package deal and the annoyance that had marked his face when he heard Sam's voice put her back up.

"I'm well aware of that. However, I didn't advertise for a family. I advertised for a housekeeper."

"Your *sister*—" she made sure to point out the distinction "—advertised with Maid on Demand Domestics. If any part of that ad wasn't clear, perhaps you need to speak to them. The agency is aware I have a son, so perhaps there was a flaw with the ad. I interviewed for the job and I got it." She lifted her chin. "Perhaps you would have been better off going without an agency?"

She knew her sharp tongue was probably shooting her chances in the foot, but she couldn't help it. She was hardly to blame. Nor would she be made to feel guilty or be bullied, not anymore. If he didn't want her services, he could just say so.

"It's not that…I tried putting an ad in the paper and around town…oh, why am I explaining this to you?" he asked, shoving his hands into his pockets despite any grease remaining on his fingers.

"If it's that you don't like children…" That would make her decision much easier. She wouldn't make Sam stay in an unfriendly environment. No job was worth that. She backed up a step and felt her hands tightening into anxious fists.

"I didn't say that." His brow wrinkled. He was clearly exasperated.

She caught a hint of desperation in his voice and thought perhaps all wasn't lost. "Then your objection to my son is…"

"Mom!" The impatient call came from the car and Emily gritted her teeth.

"Excuse me just a moment," she muttered, going to the car to speak to Sam.

It was hot inside the car, and Emily figured she had nothing to lose now. "You can get out," she said gently, opening the door. "Sorry I made you wait so long."

"Are we staying here?"

"I'm not sure."

Sam held his mother's hand…something he rarely did any more since he'd started preschool and considered himself a big boy. Perhaps Evans simply needed to meet Sam and talk to him. It had to be harder to say no to children, right? It wasn't Sam's fault his life had been turned upside down. Emily was trying to do the right thing for him. A summer in the country had sounded perfect. This place was new and different with no history, no bad memories. She just needed to show Evans that Sam would be no extra trouble.

"Mr. Evans, this is my son, Sam."

Evans never cracked a smile. "Sam."

"Sir," Sam replied. Emily was vastly proud that Sam lifted his chin the tiniest bit, though his voice was absolutely respectful.

Emily put a hand on Sam's shoulder. "The agency did know about him, Mr. Evans. I'm not trying to pull a fast one here. If it's a deal-breaker, tell me now and take it up with them. But you should know that I'm fully qualified for this job. I know how to cook and clean and garden. I'm not afraid of hard work and you won't be sorry you hired me."

He shook his head, and Emily noticed again the color of his eyes, a brilliant shade of blue that seemed to pierce straight through her. Straightforward, honest eyes. She liked that. Except for the fact that his gaze made her want to straighten her hair or fuss with the hem of her shirt. She did neither.

"I'm sorry," he replied.

That was it, then. Maybe he had a kind side somewhere but it didn't extend to giving her the job. She would not let him see the disappointment sinking through her body to her toes, making the weight of her situation that much heavier to carry. She wouldn't let it matter. She'd bounced back from worse over the last year. She'd find something else.

"I'm sorry I've taken up your time," she said politely. She took Sam's hand and turned back towards her car.

"Where are you going?"

His surprised voice made her halt and turn back. He'd taken off his cap and was now running his hand over his short-clipped hair. It was sandy-brown, she noticed. The same color as his T-shirt.

"I never said the job wasn't yours. I was apologizing."

Is that what that was? Emily wanted to ask but sensed things were at a delicate balance right now and could go either way. She simply nodded, holding her breath.

"The job description said room and board included." She was pushing it, but this had to be settled before either of them agreed to anything. She felt Sam's small hand in hers. She wanted to give him a summer like the ones she remembered. Open spaces and simple pleasures. Some peace and quiet and new adventures rather than the reminders of their once happy life as a whole family. Life wasn't going to be the same again, and Emily didn't know what to do to make it better anymore. And this farm—it was perfect. She could smell the sweet fragrance of lilacs in the air. The lawn was huge, more than big enough for a child to play. She'd glimpsed a garden on the way in, and she imagined showing Sam how to tell weeds from vegetables and picking peas and beans later in the summer when they were plump and ripe.

"I offered room and board, but only for one. Adding an extra is unexpected."

"I'll make sure he doesn't get in your way," she assured him quickly, hearing the edge of desperation in her voice, knowing she was *this* close to hearing him say yes. "And we can adjust my pay if that helps." She wished she weren't so transparent. She didn't want him to know how badly she wanted this to work out. She was willing to compromise. Was he?

Pride warred with want at this moment. She didn't want to tell Luke Evans how much it would mean for them to stay here, but seeing the look of wonder on Sam's face as he spotted a hawk circling above, following its movements until it settled on a fence post, searching for mice or prairie dogs... She'd do anything to keep that going. Even if it meant sacrificing her pride just a little bit.

"Little boys probably don't eat much. If you're sure to keep him out of the way... I have a farm to run, Ms. Northcott."

He put a slight emphasis on the Ms., but she ignored it as excitement rushed through her. He was doing it! He was giving her the job, kid and all. For the first time in five years she would be earning her own money. She was making a first step towards self-reliance, and she'd done it all on her own. Today keeping house for Luke Evans...who knew what the future would hold? She reveled in the feeling of optimism, something that had been gone for a long time. She offered a small smile and wondered what he was thinking. She would make sure he didn't regret it and that Sam would mean little disruption to his house. "You mean we can stay?"

"You're a housekeeper, aren't you? The agency did hire you."

The acid tone was back, so she merely nodded, the curl at her temple flopping.

"And you did say you could cook and clean. I'm counting on it."

She smiled at him then, a new confidence filling her heart. Lordy, he was so stern! But perhaps he could smile once in a while. Maybe she could make him. Right now she felt as though she could do anything.

"Oh, yes. That's definitely not an omission or exaggeration. I've been a stay-at-home mom since Sam was born. I promise you, Mr. Evans, I can clean, cook and do laundry with my eyes closed." She could sew, too, and make origami animals out of plain paper and construct Halloween costumes out of some cardboard, newspaper and string. The latter skills probably weren't a high priority on a ranch.

"Just remember this is a working ranch, not a summer camp. There is a lot of work to be done and a lot of machinery around. Make sure the boy doesn't cause any trouble, or go where he shouldn't be going."

"His name is Sam, and you have my word." She'd watch Sam with eyes in the back of her head if she had to. She had a job. And one where she could still be there for Sam—so important right now as he went through the stress of a family breakup.

"Then bring your things inside. I'll show you around quickly. Bear in mind I was unprepared for you, so none of the rooms are ready. You'll have to do that yourself while I fix the baler."

He was letting them stay. She knew she should just accept it and be grateful, but she also knew it was not what he'd wanted or planned, and she felt compelled to give him one more chance to be sure. "Are you certain? I don't want to put you out, Mr. Evans. It's obvious this is a surprise for you. I don't want you to feel obligated. We can find other accommodation."

He paused. "You need this job, don't you?"

He gave her a pointed look and Emily shifted her gaze to her feet. She added a mental note: not only stern but keenly sharp, too. Yes, she did need the job. Until the money went through from the sale of the house, they were on a shoe-string and even then their circumstances would be drastically changed. It was why they'd had to sell in the first place. With no money coming in and Rob neglecting to pay child support, the savings account had dried up quickly and she couldn't afford to make the mortgage payments. She couldn't hide the frayed straps of her sandals and the older model, no-frills vehicle she drove instead of the luxury sedan she'd traded in six months ago. Everything was different. It wasn't the hardest thing about the divorce, but after a while a woman couldn't ignore practicalities.

He took her silence as assent. "And I need someone to look after the house. It doesn't make sense for you to pay to stay somewhere else, and days are long here. The deal was room and board, so that's what you'll get. How much trouble can one boy be, anyway?"

CHAPTER TWO

LUKE TRIED TO keep his body relaxed as he held open the screen door, but Emily Northcott was making it difficult. Whatever she had put on for perfume that morning teased his nostrils. It was light and pretty, just like her. Her short hair was the color of mink and curled haphazardly around her face, like the hair cover models had that was meant to look deliberately casual. And she had the biggest brown eyes he'd ever seen, fringed with thick dark lashes.

When he'd first advertised for a housekeeper, Emily was not what he'd had in mind. He'd figured on someone local, someone, well, *older* to answer his ad. A motherly figure with graying hair, definitely not someone who looked like Emily. Someone who lived nearby who could arrive in the morning and leave again at dinnertime. But when his local ads had gone unanswered week after week, he'd put Cait on the job. She'd been getting so clucky and meddling as her pregnancy progressed. He'd thought it would be a good project for her and would keep her out of his hair. It was only the promise of getting outside help that had ceased her constant baking and fussing over the house. Not that he didn't need the help. He did, desperately. But having Cait underfoot all the time had been driving him crazy.

Maid on Demand had seemed like the perfect solution, anonymous and impersonal. Except now he'd ended up worse off than ever—with a beautiful woman with a family of her own, 24/7.

He should have said no, flat-out.

He'd be a bald-faced liar if he said Emily Northcott wasn't the prettiest woman to pass through his door in months. Just the scent of her put him on alert. Not that he was in the market for a girlfriend. But he was human, after all.

But what could he say? No, you can't stay because you're too pretty? Because you're too young? She couldn't be more than thirty. And then there was her son. How could he turn her away for that reason either? He'd have to be cold-hearted to use that against her. So far the boy had hardly made a peep. And it was only for a few months, after all. Once things wound down later in the fall, he'd be better able to handle things on his own.

"Have a look around," he suggested, as the screen door slapped shut behind them. "I'm going to wash up. I've had my hands inside the baler for the better part of the afternoon. Then I'll give you the nickel tour."

He left her standing in the entry hall while he went to the kitchen and turned on the tap. The whole idea of hiring help was to make his summer easier, not add more responsibility to it. But that was exactly how it felt. If she stayed, it meant two extra bodies to provide for over the next few months. Twice as many mouths to feed than he'd expected. And having that sort of responsibility—whether real or implied—was something he never wanted to do again. He liked his life plain, simple and uncomplicated. Or at least as uncomplicated as it could be considering his family circumstances.

He scrubbed the grease from his hands with the pumice paste, taking a nail brush and relentlessly applying it to his nails. The plain truth was that not one soul had applied for the job—not even a teenager looking for summer work. Cait had put the listing with the agency nearly three weeks ago.

Things were in full swing now and he needed the help. Luke was already working sun-up to sundown. The housework was falling behind, and he was tired of eating a dry sandwich when he came in at the end of the day. He was barely keeping up with the laundry, putting a load in when he was falling-down tired at night.

They could stay as long as it meant they stayed out of his way. He didn't have time for babysitting along with everything else.

When he returned from the kitchen, Emily was in the living room on the right, her fingertips running over the top of an old radio and record player that had long ceased to work and that now held a selection of family photos on its wooden cover. His heart contracted briefly, seeing her gentle hands on the heirloom, but he pushed the feeling aside and cleared his throat. "You ready?"

"This is beautiful. And very old."

He nodded. "It was my grandparents'. They used to play records on it. Some of the LPs are still inside, but the player doesn't work anymore."

"And this is your family?"

Luke stepped forward and looked at the assortment of photos. There were three graduation pictures—him and his sisters when they'd each completed twelfth grade. Cait's and Liz's wedding pictures were there as well, and baby pictures of Liz's children. Soon Cait's new baby would be featured there, too. There was a picture of three children all together, taken one golden autumn several years earlier, and in the middle sat a picture of his parents, his dad sitting down and his mom's hand on his shoulder as they smiled for the camera. The last two pictures were difficult to look at. That had been the year that everything had changed. First his mom, and then his dad.

"My sister's doing. Our parents always had pictures on here and she keeps it stocked."

He saw a wrinkle form between her eyebrows and his jaw tightened. He wasn't all that fond of the gallery of reminders, but Cait had insisted. He'd never been able to deny her anything, and he knew to take the pictures down would mean hurting Cait, and Liz, too, and he couldn't do it.

"Your dad looks very handsome. You look like him. In the jaw and the shape of your mouth."

Luke swallowed. He could correct her, but he knew in reality the handsome bit no longer applied to his father. Time and illness had leached it from his body, bit by painful bit. Luke didn't want to be like him. Not that way. Not ever. The fact that he might not have a choice was something he dealt with every single day.

"I have work to do, Ms. Northcott. Do you think we can continue the tour now?"

She turned away from the family gallery and smiled at him. He'd done his best not to encourage friendliness, so why on earth was she beaming at him? It was like a ray of sunshine warming the room when she smiled at him like that. "I'd love to," she replied.

Luke didn't answer, just turned away from the radio with a coldness that he could see succeeded in wiping the smile from her face. "Let's get a move on, then," he said over his shoulder. "So I can get back to work."

Emily scowled at his departing back. She had her work cut out for her, then. To her mind, Luke Evans had lived alone too long. His interpersonal skills certainly needed some polishing. Granted, her life hadn't been all sunshine and flowers lately, but she at least could be pleasant. She refused to let his sour attitude ruin her day.

"Do you mind if I turn the TV on for Sam? That way we

can get through faster. I don't want to hold you up." After his comment about Sam being a distraction, Emily figured this was the easiest way. After Evans was gone to the barn, she'd enlist Sam's help and they'd work together. Make it fun.

As they started up the stairs, Luke turned around and paused, his hand on the banister. "I apologize for the sorry state of the house," he said. "My sister hasn't been by in a few weeks and with haying time and the new calves..."

"Isn't that why I'm here?"

"I don't want to scare you off," he said, starting up the stairs once more. Gruff or not, Emily got the feeling that he was relieved she was there. Or at least relieved *someone* was there to do the job he required.

She followed him up, unable to avoid the sight of his bottom in the faded jeans. Two identical wear spots lightened the pockets. As he took her through the house she realized he hadn't been exaggerating. The spare rooms had a fine film of dust on the furniture. The rugs were in desperate need of a vacuuming and he'd left his shaving gear and towel on the bathroom vanity this morning, along with whiskers dotting the white porcelain of the sink. The linen closet was a jumbled mess of pillows, blankets and sheets arranged in no particular order, and the laundry basket was filled to overflowing.

The tour continued and Emily tried to be positive through it all. "The floors are gorgeous," she tried, hoping to put them on more of an even footing. "They look like the original hardwood."

"They are. And they have the scratches to prove it."

She bit back a sigh and tried again. "Scratches just add character. And the doors are solid wood rather than those hollow imitations in stores these days. Such a great color of stain."

"They need refinishing."

Emily gave up for the time being; her attempts at anything

positive were completely ineffectual. She simply followed him down the hall. The smallest bedroom was painted a pale green and had one wall on a slant with a charming oval window looking over the fields. She fell in love with it immediately. A second room was painted pink and one wall had rosebud wallpaper. A third door remained closed—she presumed it was his room. But when he opened the door to the final room she caught her breath. It must have been his parents' room, all gleaming dark wood and an ivory chenille spread. It was like stepping back in time—hooked rugs on the floor and dainty Priscilla curtains at the windows.

"What a beautiful room." She looked up at Luke and saw a muscle tick in his jaw. It was almost as if seeing it caused him pain, but why?

"It belonged to my parents," he answered, and shut the door before she could say any more.

Back in the kitchen the clean dishes were piled in the drying rack, the teetering pile a masterpiece of domestic engineering. In the partner sink, dirty dishes formed a smaller, stickier pile. The kitchen cupboards were sturdy solid oak, and Emily knew a washing with oil soap would make them gleam again. The fridge needed a good wiping down. She paused a moment to glance at the magnetic notepad stuck to the fridge door. It was simply a list of phone numbers. She frowned as she read the names *Cait* and *Liz,* wondering why he didn't simply have his sister's numbers memorized. After his brusqueness, there was no way on earth she'd ask.

Overall, the house was a throwback to what felt like a happier, simpler time. "All it needs is some love and polish, Mr. Evans. You have a beautiful home."

The tour finished, Luke cleared his throat, his feet shifting from side to side. "I really need to get back to fixing the baler. This weather isn't going to hold and I have help coming tomorrow. The job is yours, Ms. Northcott."

She grinned at him, ready to tackle the dust and cobwebs and bring the house back to its former glory "You've got a deal."

"Shouldn't we talk salary?"

A shadow dimmed her excitement, but only for a moment. "I thought that was all taken care of through the agency. Unless you've made a change regarding…" She paused, glancing down at Sam.

"One boy won't eat much. The wage stands, if it's acceptable to you."

"Agreed."

"You'll be okay to get settled then?"

"Oh, we'll be fine. Does it matter which rooms we take?"

"One of the two smaller ones at the end of the hall would probably be best for your son," he replied. "My sister Liz's pink room probably wouldn't suit him. The other is still a bit girly, but at least it's not pink. You can take the one on the other side." The master bedroom, the one that had been his parents.

"Are you sure you don't want me to take the pink room? The other is…" she paused. She remembered the look on his face when he'd opened the door, but had no idea how to ask why it hurt him so much. "The other is so big," she said.

Luke tried not to think of Emily in his parents' room, covered with the ivory chenille spread that had been on the bed as long as he could remember. He had never been able to bring himself to change rooms, instead staying in the one he'd had since childhood. Nor did he want Sam there. But Emily…somehow she fit. She'd be caring and respectful.

"The room has been empty a long time. You may as well use it. The other is so small. It's just a room, Emily. No reason why you shouldn't sleep in it."

But it wasn't "just a room", and as he looked down into her

dark gaze, he got the idea she understood even without the details.

"Mr. Evans, I don't know how to thank you. This means a lot to me…to us."

Her eyes were so earnest, and he wondered what was behind them. Clearly she was a single mom and things had to be bad if she accepted a short-term position like his and was so obviously happy about it. She hadn't even attempted to negotiate salary.

"What brought you here? I mean…you're obviously a single mother." No husband to be found and insistent on the Ms. instead of Mrs. No wedding ring either, but he saw the slight indentation on her finger where one had lived. "Recently divorced?"

The pleasant smile he'd enjoyed suddenly disappeared from her mouth. "Does it matter if I'm divorced?"

He stepped back. "Not at all. I was just curious."

"You don't strike me as the curious type."

He hoped he didn't blush. She had him dead to rights and she knew it. He had always been the stay-out-of-others'-business-and-they'll-stay-out-of-yours type.

"Pardon me," he replied coolly.

But her lack of answers only served to make him wonder more what had truly brought her here. What circumstances had led Emily Northcott and her son to his doorstep?

"Yes," she relented, "I'm divorced. Sam's father is living in British Columbia. I'm just trying to make a living and raise my son, Mr. Evans."

She was a mom. She had baggage, if the white line around her finger and the set of her lips were any indication. It all screamed *off limits* to him. He should just nod and be on his way. Instead he found himself holding out his hand, scrubbed clean of the earlier grease, with only a telltale smidge remaining in his cuticles.

"Luke. Call me Luke."

The air in the room seemed to hold for a fraction of a second as she slid her hand out of her pocket and towards his. Then he folded the slim fingers within his, the connection hitting him square in the gut. Two dots of color appeared on Emily's cheeks, and it looked as though she bit the inside of her lip.

Not just him then. As if things weren't complicated enough.

"Luke," she echoed softly, and a warning curled through him at the sound of her voice. He had to keep his distance. This was probably a huge mistake. But where would they go if he denied her the job? What were they running from? He wanted to know everything but knew that asking would only mean getting closer. And getting close—to anyone—was not an option. Not for him.

He was already in over his head. The fields and barns were the place for him, and he would let Emily Northcott sort out her own family. She could just get on with doing her job.

He had enough to handle with his own.

CHAPTER THREE

THE REST OF the day passed in a blur. Emily began her cleaning upstairs in the rooms that she and Sam would occupy. Sam helped as best as a five-year-old boy could, helping change the sheets, dusting and Emily put him to work putting his clothes in the empty dresser while she moved on to her room. It was late afternoon when she was done and continued on to the kitchen, putting the dry dishes away before tackling the new dirty ones and searching the freezer for something to make for supper. The baked pork chops, rice and vegetables were ready for six o'clock; she held the meal until six-thirty and finally ate with Sam while Luke remained conspicuously absent. It wasn't until she and Sam were picking at the blueberry cobbler she'd baked for dessert that Luke returned.

He took one look at the dirty supper dishes and his face hardened.

Emily clenched her teeth. What did he expect? They couldn't wait all night, and she'd held it as long as was prudent. As it was, the vegetables had been a little mushy and the cream of mushroom sauce on the chops had baked down too far.

"We didn't know how long you'd be," she said quietly, getting up to move the dirty dishes and to fix Luke a plate. "We decided to go ahead."

"You didn't need to wait for me at all." He went to the sink to wash his hands.

Emily bit the inside of her lip. Granted, dinnertime with the surly Luke Evans wasn't all that appealing, but it seemed rude to discount having a civil meal together at all. Still she was new here and the last thing she wanted was to get off on the wrong foot. She picked up a clean plate, filled it with food and popped it into the microwave. In her peripheral vision she could see Sam picking at his cobbler, staring into his bowl. He could sense the tension, and it made Emily even more annoyed. He'd had enough of that when things had got bad between her and Rob. The last thing she wanted was to have him in a less-than-friendly situation again.

"Eating together is a civil thing to do," she replied as the microwave beeped. "Plus the food is best when it's fresh and hot."

"You don't need to go to any bother," he replied, taking the plate and sitting down at the table. Sam's gaze darted up and then down again. Was he not even going to acknowledge her son?

Perhaps what Luke Evans needed was a refresher course in manners and common courtesy.

She resumed her seat, picked up her fork and calmly said, "I wasn't planning on running a short-order kitchen."

"I didn't realize I was nailed down to a specific dinner time. I am running a farm here, you know."

Sam's eyes were wide and he held his spoon with a purple puddle of blueberries halfway between the bowl and his mouth. Emily spared him a glance and let out a slow breath.

"Of course you are, and I did hold the meal for over half an hour. Maybe we should have simply communicated it better. Set a basic time and if you're going to be later, you can let me know."

"I'm not used to a schedule."

Emily looked at Sam and smiled. "You're excused, Sam. Why don't you go upstairs and put on your pajamas?"

Obediently Sam pushed out his chair and headed for the stairs.

Luke paused in his eating. "He listens to you well."

Now that Sam was gone Emily wasn't feeling so generous. "He has been taught some manners," she replied, the earlier softness gone from her voice. "Eating together is the civilized thing to do. Respecting that I may have gone to the trouble to cook a nice meal would go a long way. And acknowledging my son when you sit at the table would be polite, rather than acting as though he doesn't exist."

Luke's fork hit his plate. "I hired you to be a housekeeper, not Miss Manners."

"I'm big on courtesy and respect, Mr. Evans. No matter who or what the age. If you don't want to eat with us, say so now. I'll plan for Sam and I to eat by ourselves and you can reheat your meal whenever it suits you. But I'd prefer if we settled it now so we don't have any more confusion."

For several seconds the dining room was quiet, and then Luke replied, "As long as you understand there may be times when I'm in the middle of something, I will make every attempt to observe a regular dinner hour."

"I appreciate it."

"And I didn't mean to ignore your son."

"He has feelings, too, Mr. Evans. And since his father left, it is easy for him to feel slighted."

Luke picked at the mound of rice on his plate. "I didn't think of that."

"You don't know us yet," Emily responded, feeling her annoyance drain away. Luke looked suitably chastised, and she couldn't help the smile that she tried to hide. She'd seen that look on Sam's face on occasion, and it melted her anger.

"Look, I put in an effort for our first dinner here. I might have gotten a bit annoyed that you weren't here to eat it."

Luke lifted his head and met her eyes. Her heart did a weird thump, twisting and then settling down to a slightly faster rhythm, it seemed.

"I have lived alone a long time," he admitted. "I'm sorry I didn't think of it. You might need to be patient with me."

"Maybe we all need to be patient," she replied, and he smiled at her. A genuine smile, not the tense tight one from this afternoon. The twist in her heart went for another leap again and she swallowed.

"There's cobbler," she said, a peace offering.

"Thank you, Emily," he answered.

She went to the kitchen to get it, hearing the way he said her name echoing around in her brain. She'd fought her battle and won. So why did she feel as if she was in a lot of trouble?

After the supper mess was cleaned up, Luke went out to the barns and Emily put Sam to bed, following him in short order. She was exhausted. She vaguely heard the phone ringing once, but Luke answered it and the sound of the peepers and the breeze through the window lulled her back to sleep.

But the early night meant early to rise, and Emily heard Luke get up as the first pale streaks of sunlight filtered through the curtains. The floorboards creaked by the stairs and she checked her watch…did people really get up this early? She crept out of bed and tiptoed down the hall, looking in on Sam.

He looked so much younger—more innocent, if that were possible—in slumber. He wasn't a baby any longer, but it didn't change the tender feeling that rushed through her looking at his dark eyelashes and curls. He was so good, so loving. So trusting. She didn't want what had happened with his father to change that about him. It was up to her to make sure he had a good life. A happy life. She was determined. He would never doubt how much she loved him. He would always know that she would be there for him.

Back in her room, she slid into a pair of jeans and a T-shirt, moving as quietly as possible. She wanted to get an early start. Make a decent breakfast and get a load of laundry going so she could hang it out on the clothesline. The very idea was exciting, and she laughed a little at herself. Who knew something as simple as fresh-smelling clothes off the line would give her such pleasure? Despite Luke's reticence, despite getting off on the wrong foot last night at dinner, she was more convinced than ever that she'd done the right thing. She'd taken him on and he hadn't given her the boot. She'd be the best housekeeper Luke Evans ever had. And when she got her feet beneath her, it would be time to start thinking about the future.

She was beating pancake batter in a bowl when Luke returned from the barn, leaving his boots on the mat and coming into the kitchen in his stocking feet. Emily had found a cast-iron pan and it was already heating on the burner. He stopped and stared at her for a moment, long enough that she began to feel uncomfortable and her spoon moved even faster through the milky batter.

"I didn't think you'd be up yet."

"I heard you leave a while ago. I wanted to get an early start." She dropped a little butter in the pan and ladled a perfectly round pancake in the middle of it. "You're just in time for the first pancakes." She was glad he was here. Now he'd get them fresh and hot from the pan, better proof of her cooking abilities than the reheated dinner of last evening. She wasn't opposed to hard work, and it felt good having a purpose, something to do. It was just a taste of how it would feel when she got a permanent job and could provide for herself and for Sam.

"Lately I've been grabbing a bowl of cereal. Pancakes are a treat. Thank you, Emily."

His polite words nearly made her blush as she remembered how she'd taken him to task for his manners at their last meal. She focused on turning the pancake, the top perfectly golden brown. "I'm glad you get to enjoy them fresh, rather than warmed up, like last night's supper." She flipped the pancake onto a plate and began frying another. "Besides, when you sleep in you miss the best part of the day, I think."

She wanted to ask him if this was his regular breakfast time but held back, not wanting to harp on a dead topic. Still, she felt as if she should already know, which was ridiculous. How could she possibly know his routine, his preferences?

Everything about Luke Evans was throwing her off balance and she was having to think and double-think every time she wanted to ask him something, measure her words, trying hard to say the right thing and not the first thing that came to her mind.

"What time do you want lunch?"

"I'm used to just grabbing a sandwich when I come in."

She put down the spatula. "A sandwich? But a working man can't live on a sandwich for lunch!"

He laughed then, a real laugh aimed at her open-mouthed look of dismay, she realized. She picked up the spatula again, trying to ignore the light that kindled in his eyes as he laughed. When Luke was grumpy, she wished he were nicer. But when he was nice, something inside her responded and she wished for his sterner side again. She didn't want to have those sorts of reactions. She wasn't interested in romance or flirting. She didn't know how, not after so many years with one man. She was never going to put herself in a position to be hurt like that again either. She deserved more. So did Sam.

"You're making fun of me."

"You sound like my sisters. They both fuss and flutter. I haven't starved yet, though."

The awkwardness had seemed to fade away between them, but what arose in its place was a different kind of tension. It made her want to hold her breath or glance over and see if he was watching her. She couldn't help it—she did, and he was. His blue gaze was penetrating, and she had the simultaneous thoughts that his eyes were too beautiful for a man and that she wished he still wore his hat so they would be at least a bit shadowed.

She handed him the plate of pancakes, taking care to make sure their fingers never touched. "Fresh from the pan."

"They smell delicious. And about lunch... I try to come in around noon, when the boys take their break. Sometimes when I'm haying I take my lunch with me though. I'll be sure to let you know."

Emily bit her lip and turned back to her pancakes, feeling a warmth spread through her. His tone at the end had held a little hint of teasing, no malice in it at all. She could nearly hear the echo of Rob's angry voice in her head, telling her to stop nagging. She had told herself his leaving had been out of the blue, but things hadn't been right for a while before he left. He had complained about her always trying to tie him down to a schedule. She hadn't. But she'd taken pride in her "job". She loved it when they all sat down together. It had been a bone of contention between them that they didn't eat dinner as a family. Since he'd left she'd made it a point to sit with Sam over dinner and talk about their favorite parts of the day.

But Luke wasn't her family, he was her boss. "It's your house," she said quietly. "I overstepped last night. Whenever you want your meals, I'll make sure they're on the table. That *is* what you pay me for, right?"

"Are you okay?"

"Fine. Why?"

"You got all…meek all of a sudden. If you want something, Emily, just ask. If I don't like it, I'll tell you."

She swallowed. Had she become so used to tiptoeing around Rob that she'd forgotten how good honesty and straight-talking felt? She took a breath. "Okay. It would be helpful if I knew what time you'd like your meals so I can plan around them."

His chair scraped against the floor as he rose, came forward and reached around her for the maple syrup. His body was close—too close. When she sucked in a breath, she smelled the clean scent of his soap mixed with a hint of leather and horses. Oh, my. Heat crept into her cheeks.

"Was that so hard?" he asked.

Her brain scrambled to remember what they'd been talking about. Oh, yes. The timing of meals. "Um…no?"

He retrieved the syrup and moved away while Emily wilted against the counter.

"I'll try to let you know when I plan to be in," he said, pouring syrup over his pancakes. "You were right, so don't apologize. It's just business courtesy, that's all." Luke dismissed it with a wave and picked up his fork.

Just business. He was right, and Emily felt chagrined at her earlier behavior. She was far too aware of him and he was her boss. Why shouldn't she simply ask questions? She would of any other employer.

"I have to run into town this morning to pick up a part for the baler. I'll make a stop at the hospital, too, I guess. Cait and Joe had a baby girl last night. Anyway, if there's anything you need, I can get it while I'm there."

A baby! He said it as blandly as he might have said *Rain is forecast for today,* and it left Emily confused. What was she missing? She remembered the first moments of holding Sam in her arms after his birth, and despite Luke's tepid response she knew his sister and brother-in-law had to be over the moon. As brother and uncle, he should be, too. "A girl! Lovely! They must be so happy."

Luke went to the coffeepot and poured himself a cup, then took down another and held it out, asking her if she wanted some. She nodded, wondering why he wasn't excited about the baby. After his reaction to Sam yesterday, she was beginning to think her assessment that he didn't like children was dead-on. "Is everyone healthy?" she asked, hoping there were no complications.

"Oh, yes." He gave a shrug. "Another girl. That's four nieces."

"Do you have something against girls?"

The cup halted halfway to his mouth. "What? Oh, of course not. We just keep hoping for a boy. To keep the Evans and Son going, you know?"

Emily watched him as he got out juice glasses—three of them—pouring orange juice in two and leaving the third one empty but waiting. He had remembered Sam, then. At times last night and this morning it had seemed as though Luke forgot Sam was even there.

"This is the twenty-first century, Luke." She smiled at him, poured another pancake. "A girl could take over the farm as well as a boy, you know. Evans and Niece might not have the same ring to it, but I didn't have you pegged for one worrying about an heir to the empire. Besides, you might still have some big, strapping prairie boys of your own." She added the pancake to the stack on the warmer with a smile. But her teasing had backfired. He stared at her now with an expression that seemed partly hurt and partly angry.

"I don't plan on having a family," he replied, then dropped his gaze, focusing on cutting his pancakes, his knife scraping along the porcelain. Emily stared at him for a second, absolutely nonplussed, and then remembered she still had a pancake cooking and it needed to be turned if she didn't want it to burn.

He finished the meal in silence as she cooked more pancakes, stacking them until the warmer was full. The quiet stretched out uncomfortably; Emily wanted to break it somehow but after his last words she had no idea what to say that would be a good start to a conversation. He'd clearly ended the last attempt.

He finished what was on his plate and came over to the stove, standing at her elbow. She wished she could ignore him and relax, but he was six foot something of muscled man. She couldn't pretend he didn't exist. Not when all of her senses were clamoring like the bells of a five-alarm fire. She gripped the spatula tightly.

"Are there any more of those, Emily?"

She let her breath out slowly, not wanting him to sense her relief. Extra pancakes—was that all he wanted? "Take as many as you like," she replied. "I can make more for Sam when he gets up."

He lifted four from the warming tray and Emily swallowed against the lump that had formed in her throat. My, he did have a good appetite. Was there nothing about the man that wasn't big and virile? On the back of the thought came the unwanted but automatic comparison to Rob. Rob in his suits and Italian loafers and his fancy car. Rob going out the door with a travel mug and a briefcase in the morning. When those things had disappeared so abruptly from her life it had broken her heart. She'd built her whole life around their little family, loving every moment of caring for their house and watching Sam grow. She'd lost the life she'd always dreamed of and it still hurt.

But it was time to start dreaming about something new. Emily lifted her head and caught a glimpse of the wide fields out the kitchen window. The golden fields were Luke's office.

His jeans and boots and, oh, yes, the T-shirts that displayed his muscled arms were his work clothes. The prairie wind was his air conditioning and the sun his office lighting.

She smiled, knowing that the wide-open space was something she'd been missing for a long time. The memories would always be there, but they hurt less now. As she looked out over the sunny fields, she knew that leaving the city had been the right thing to do. She was moving forward with her life, and it felt good.

"What are you smiling at?" Luke asked the question from the table, but he'd put down his fork and was giving her his full attention. And the pancake batter was gone, leaving her with nothing to do to keep her hands busy. Six pancakes remained; certainly enough for her breakfast with Sam. She put down the bowl and brushed her hands on the apron she'd found in the drawer.

"I was just thinking how nice it must be to go to work in the outdoors," she replied, picking up her cooling coffee. Anything to let her hide just a little bit from Luke's penetrating gaze.

"Not so nice on rainy days, but yeah…I think I'd go crazy locked up inside all day. You strike me as the inside kind."

"What makes you say that?"

He looked down at his tanned arms and then at her pale, white limbs. Then up at her face while a small smile played with his lips.

"Okay, you're right. Sam and I made it to the park but our backyard…" She sighed. "It was very small. Sam had a little slide there, a kid-sized picnic table. That was about it."

"Boys need room to run around."

She poured herself more coffee. "Yes, I know. Suburbia wasn't always part of the plan. I did grow up with more than a postage stamp for a yard, you know. In Regina."

"You're from Regina?"

"Just outside, yes. My mom was a stay-at-home mom and my dad sold cars." Telling Luke took her back to her college days when she'd been slightly ashamed of her modest home and she realized now that Rob had never quite fit in there. Perhaps this split had always been coming, and was not as random as she thought. She'd been trying to be someone she wasn't. Maybe he had, too. Now, despite the fact that she knew there would be a certain bit of "I told you so", home didn't seem so bad. She'd been afraid of being judged, but she knew that wasn't really why she didn't want to go back. She didn't want to go back a failure. She wanted to go back when she could look her parents in the eye and say that she'd fixed it. The way they'd always seemed to fix things. If money was tight or jobs were lost, they still always seemed to manage. And they'd stayed together. Not because they had to, but because they loved each other. Emily found it so hard to live up to that kind of example.

However, she could say none of this to Luke. What would he think of her if he knew? The last thing she wanted was to lay out a list of her faults and failings.

"And what took you to Calgary?"

She simply lifted an eyebrow.

"Ah," he chuckled, understanding. "Sam's father?"

She nodded, finally taking a seat at the table and curling her hands around the mug. The sun was up over the knoll now and gleaming brightly in the kitchen. This was where the questions would end. She had no desire to tell Luke the sordid details of the split. There would be no more breakfasts for two. She was here to work. It was glorious just to be able to make her own decisions now. She just kept telling herself that. Her parents didn't know she'd had to give up her house or that she hadn't received any child support. She'd been too proud to tell them. She'd been certain she'd turn things around before they got to this point. And she would. She just needed a little more time and a solid plan.

"And you?" To keep him from prying further into her personal life, she turned the tables. "You've been here your whole life, I suppose."

"Of course."

"The girls didn't care to be farmers?"

He looked at her over the rim of his mug, his blue gaze measuring. Luke Evans was no pushover, Emily realized. He saw right through her intentions. It should have put her off, but it didn't. Everything about Luke was intelligent, decisive. It was crazily sexy.

"The 'girls', as you say, got married and started their own families. Joe manages a farm-equipment dealership—he's the proud daddy this morning. Liz's husband is a schoolteacher. They both know their way around a barn, but that's not their life now."

"So you handle this alone?" She put the mug down on the table.

"I have some hired help." His lips made a thin line and his gaze slid from hers. Subject closed.

But she pressed on. "Then what about the Evans and Son on the sign? What about your dad and mom? How long have they been gone?"

He pushed out his chair and put his mug on top of his plate, taking the stack to the cupboard next to the sink. "I've got to get going. I have to get the boys started on their own this morning so I can run into town."

Emily knew she had gone too far. Something about his parents pushed a button. She had sensed it when she'd seen their picture, when he'd looked into their empty bedroom and again just now when she'd asked about them.

"About town…you really are short of groceries. Could we

go with you? We won't take extra time. We can shop while you run your errands."

He reached for his hat and plunked it on his head. To Emily, it seemed like armor to hide behind. And it added inches to his height.

Maybe some people didn't appreciate a closet full of fresh-smelling clothes, shining floors and a good meal, but she'd bet Luke would. She'd bet anything that he'd grown up exactly that way. His sisters had moved on, apparently to fulfilling, happy lives. Why hadn't Luke? Not that the farm wasn't successful. But it felt like a piece of the puzzle was missing.

"I can't expect you to cook without food, I suppose," he replied. "Be ready about nine, then. I need to get back as soon as I can."

"Yes, boss," she replied, putting his dishes in the sink to wash up.

It was all back to the status quo until he reached the screen door and then she heard his voice call quietly.

"Emily?"

She went to the doorway. "Yes?"

He smiled. "Good pancakes."

The screen door shut behind him, but Emily stared at it a good ten seconds before making her feet move.

Yes, indeed. She could wow Luke Evans in the kitchen. And she knew exactly what would be on the menu tonight.

CHAPTER FOUR

LUKE GAVE THE ratchet another turn and adjusted the trouble light. When had it gotten so dark? He stood back, staring at the rusted parts that made up the baler. It needed love. It needed replacing. But this repair would hold him through this season. And if things went well, he'd talk Joe into a discount and buy a new one next year.

He made a few final adjustments and straightened, rubbing the small of his back. Between the trip to town, Cait and the baler, he'd spent all of half an hour in the fields today. He frowned. It wasn't how he liked to run things. He wasn't a boss who gave orders and disappeared. Here everyone worked together and shared the load. But what could he do? He'd left the repairs until after dinner as it was, working in the dim light.

"Hi."

He spun at the sound of the small voice and saw Sam standing before him in his bare feet and a pair of cotton pajamas. The boy was cute as a bug's ear, Luke acknowledged, with his brown curls and wide chocolate eyes like his mother's. Eyes that seemed to see everything. Luke wiped his hands on a rag and tucked the end into his back pocket. "Shouldn't you be up at the house? In bed?"

A light blush darkened Sam's cheeks as his gaze skittered away for a moment. "I couldn't sleep. It's too hot."

"Your mom would open the window."

"She said she didn't want to hear a peep out of me," Sam admitted, and Luke hid a smile. Not hear a peep, so sneaking out of the house was okay?

"Then you'd better hightail it back in there, don't you think? You don't want your mom to be mad."

Sam swallowed and nodded and turned away, only to turn back again. "Why don't you like my mama?"

Luke's hands dropped to his sides as Sam asked the point-blank question. "What makes you think I don't like her?" he asked.

"Because you never said anything to her at supper. And she made veal. I helped. She only does that when it's special."

The veal had been good, as had the pasta and salad. Certainly much fancier than he was used to making for himself. "I suppose I had my head full of everything I need to do. I don't usually have company at the dinner table. I guess I'm not one for conversation."

Why on earth was he explaining this to a five-year-old boy? Besides, he knew it was a feeble excuse. He hadn't known what to say to her. He'd walked in to a house smelling of furniture polish and the fragrant lilacs she'd cut and put in one of his mother's vases she'd unearthed from somewhere. He'd instantly been transported to a time when the house had been filled with family. His mother's warm smiles. His dad's teasing. All of it had been taken from him in what felt like an instant, and he knew the chances of history repeating itself were too good to fool around with. But today he'd been taken back to a happier time.

He'd looked at Emily and felt the noose tightening. All through the meal he thought of her as she'd looked that morning as they ate alone in the quiet kitchen, with her pretty smiles and soft voice. It had felt domestic. Alarm bells had gone off like crazy in his head. He knew the signs. Watchfulness.

Blushes. He was as guilty of it as she was, and he had kept his distance ever since very deliberately. He'd had no idea what to say to her.

"I think you hurt her feelings," Sam persisted. His tone turned defensive and his brown eyes snapped. "My mama's a nice lady," he announced, lifting his chin as if daring Luke to dispute it, an action so like his mother Luke found it hard not to smile. "She cooks good and reads me stories and does all the best voices with my dinosaur puppets."

This was Luke's problem. He was too soft. He already felt sorry for the pair of them, and he didn't even really know the extent of their situation. Nor did he want to. He knew he shouldn't get involved. They were not his responsibility, and he didn't want them to be. He'd had enough responsibility to last a lifetime, and even though his sisters were on their own there was still the issue of his father's ongoing care. Emily was the housekeeper. Full stop.

Even Cait, in the first bloom of motherhood, had sensed something was up today. He'd said nothing, not wanting to mention Emily or her kid, instead dutifully admiring baby Janna. His sister was happy, but a family was not for him. So why did seeing her with Joe and her baby make him feel so empty? It was like that every time he saw Liz's girls, too. They thought he didn't particularly care for children. But the sorry truth was he knew he would never have any of his own and keeping his distance was just easier.

"I like your mom just fine, and you're right, supper was good. But my job is to fix this baler so we can roll up the hay out there and have feed for the winter."

Sam scowled. "Mama told me if we didn't stay here we had to go to Grandma and Grampa's. I don't even know what they look like."

Luke leaned against the bumper, watching Sam with keen eyes. When had she said such a thing? Before arriving or after he'd given her the job? He found the answer mattered to him. And how could Sam not know his grandparents? Regina wasn't so far from Calgary as to prevent visits.

"Oh, you must remember them."

But Sam shook his head. "My mama says they would be excited to see me because they haven't since I was a baby."

Three years. Maybe four, if what he said was true. Luke frowned. Even though he'd only known her a few days, he pictured Emily as the type to be surrounded by family. What had kept them apart?

"You should go on up to the house," he said, more firmly this time. "You don't want to get in trouble with your mom, Sam. Go on now."

Sam's lips twisted a little. "You don't like me either," he announced.

"What does it matter if I like you or not?" Luke was feeling annoyed now, having his character called out by a boy. Besides, it wasn't a matter of liking or not. It went so much deeper. Self-preservation, if it came to that. There was too much at stake for him to get all gushy over babies and such. "You get on up to bed."

Sam's little lip quivered but his eyes blazed. "That's all right. My dad doesn't like me either and my mama and I do just fine."

He spun on his toes and ran back to the house.

Luke sighed, watching him depart. He'd been sharp when he hadn't meant to be. It wasn't Sam's fault—or Emily's for that matter—that the years of stress and responsibility had worn him down. The boy had been through enough with his parents splitting up—Emily had as much as said so last night. He felt a moment of guilt, knowing Sam was feeling the loss of his father keenly. Did Sam never see him, then?

He rubbed a hand over his face, blew out a breath. Emily's domestic situation was none of his concern. Why he continually had to remind himself of that was a bit of a mystery. He turned out the trouble light and felt for a moment the satisfaction of another day done.

Followed by the heavy realization of all that remained to do tomorrow. And the day after that.

He squared his shoulders. "Suck it up, Evans," he mumbled to himself, shaking his head. Darn the two of them anyway. They'd had him thinking more over the last two days than he had in months, and not just about himself. About her, and the series of events that had landed her on his doorstep just at the moment he needed her most.

Emily was wiping up the last of the dishes and Sam was already sound asleep in bed when Luke returned to the house in the twilight. Sam had worked alongside her most of the afternoon, helping her dust the rooms and fetching things as she needed them. The bathroom fixtures shone and the floors gleamed again, and she sighed, not only from exhaustion but also from satisfaction. Sam had sometimes been more of a hindrance than a help, but it had been worth it to see the smile on his face and the pride he took in helping. It hadn't been until he'd nearly nodded off over his dinner that she'd realized he'd missed his afternoon nap.

Now he was tucked away in the small room, his dark head peaceful on the pillow. Meanwhile Emily had dishes to finish and the last of the dry sheets to put back on the spare beds before she could call it a night.

She heard Luke come in through the screen door and her heart did a little leap. It seemed so personal, having the run of his house, making herself at home. She heard the thump of his boots as he put them on the mat by the door and pictured him behind her. Now her pulse picked up as she heard his stockinged feet come closer. To her surprise he picked up the frying pan and moved to put it in the cupboard.

"Mr. Evans…you don't have to do that." She avoided his eyes as she picked up the last plate to dry.

"It's no biggie. I'm done for the day and you're not."

His shoulder was next to hers as he reached for another pot, the close contact setting off the same sparks as she'd felt at dinner. His jeans had been dirty with a smear of grease on one thigh, and his T-shirt had borne marks of his afternoon of work, but he'd gone into the downstairs bath and come to the table with clean hands and face and a few droplets of water clinging to his short hair.

It had been the wet hair that had done it. The tips were dark and glistening, and paired with the stubble on his chin it was unbelievably attractive. The economical way that he moved and how he said exactly what he meant, without any wasted words. He'd spoken to Sam only briefly during dinner, making little conversation before heading outside again. He hadn't even commented on the food, even though she'd pulled out all the stops and fussed with her favorite veal-and-pasta recipe. Emily tried not to be offended. Perhaps it was just his way. Perhaps he'd lived alone so long he wasn't used to making mealtime conversation. And that was quite sad when she thought about it.

"But our agreement…"

He put his hand on her arm and she stilled, plate in hand. She couldn't look at him. If she did, the color would seep into her cheeks. He was touching her. *Touching her,* and her skin seemed to shiver with pleasure beneath his fingers.

"Please," she said quietly. "This is my job. Let me do it."

"Pride, Emily?"

He used her first name and the sound of it, coming from his lips in the privacy of the kitchen, caused her cheeks to heat anyway. His hand slid off her arm and she realized she was holding the plate and doing nothing with it. She made a show of wiping the cloth over its surface. "Just stating the obvious."

"Who do you suppose cleans up when I'm here alone? I didn't realize putting a few things away would be a problem."

Oh, lordy. What right did she have to be territorial? "That's not what I meant," she replied hastily, putting the plate on the counter and reaching into the sink to pick up the last handful of cutlery. "Of course it's your kitchen…"

"Emily."

"You have more right to it than I do…"

She was babbling now, growing more nervous by the second as she felt his steady gaze on her. She bit down on her lip. She wouldn't say any more and make a bigger fool of herself. What did it matter if he put a dish away? She was the one caught up in a knot, determined to do everything perfectly. And why? She already knew that trying to be perfect didn't mean squat when it came down to it. She let out a slow breath, trying to relax.

"Why won't you look at me?"

She did then. She looked up into his eyes and saw that the blue irises were worried, making it impossible to maintain the distance she desired.

"You're paying me to do a job, so I should be the one to do it. If that's pride, then so be it."

"You're a stubborn woman, aren't you?"

Her lips dropped open and then she clamped them shut again, trying to think of a good reply. "I prefer determined."

"I just bet you do."

"Did you get the baler fixed?" She was desperate to change the subject, to turn the focus off herself and her failings. "I expect you'll be glad to be back in the fields tomorrow," she carried on, sorting the last of the cutlery into the drawer. The thought of the fields and waving alfalfa made her smile, gave her a sense of well-being. It had to be the peace and quiet, that was all. It had nothing to do with Luke Evans, or picturing him on top of a gigantic tractor in a dusty hat and even dustier boots.

"I can't expect the boys to handle things alone. I'll be glad to be back out with them again. I may be late for dinner tomorrow. Just so you know."

Oh, goodness, they were back to that again. She brushed her hands on her pants and inhaled, trying to appear poised. How could she explain that she'd actually enjoyed cleaning the homey farmhouse? That she'd felt more at home cooking a simple meal than she'd felt in a long time? Cooking anything elaborate for her and Sam seemed pointless, and she'd missed it.

"Thank you for letting me know. I'll plan something that keeps well, then. If you don't mind Sam and I going ahead."

"Of course not. Emily..." he paused and she gave in to temptation and looked up at him. He could look so serious, but something about his somber expression spoke to her. There was more to Luke than was on the surface. She was sure of it.

Their gazes clung for several seconds before he cleared his throat. "What I mean to say is, it is just great to have supper on the table when I come in and something better than a sandwich. It's a real nice thing to look forward to."

It was as heartfelt a comment as she'd guess Luke could come up with, and she took it to heart. She couldn't find the words to tell him that though, so she simply said, "Sam doesn't have such discerning taste. It was nice to have a reason to put together a real meal."

His gaze plumbed hers. "There was a reason I advertised for a housekeeper. The place looks great. And dinner was really good, Emily. I probably should have said so before."

She'd been slightly put out that he'd barely acknowledged

her efforts earlier, but the compliment still did its work, even though it was delayed. "I'm glad you liked it."

Why was he being nice to her now? She should be glad, relieved about all of it. But it threw her off balance. She furrowed her brow. Either she wanted his compliments and approval or she didn't. She wished she could make up her mind which.

"You're a very good cook."

"It was…"

She paused. So what if it was what she'd used to make for special occasions? She was tired of giving Rob any power. He had no business here. He had no business in her life anymore. He'd forfeited that privilege, and she'd done her share of crying about it. The only person keeping him front and center was her. "It is one of my favorites."

"So what's the story of Emily Northcott?" Luke folded up the dish towel and hung it over the door of the stove. "I mean, you must have a place in Calgary. Sam's father must be helping. Why pick a position that takes you away from home?"

Of course he'd ask right at the moment she'd decided not to mention Rob again. But the question struck a nerve. Somehow she wanted him to know. She wanted him to realize that she had tried everything she could to make things right. She already thought of him as stubborn rancher, a bit of a strong, silent type but she'd glimpsed moments of compassion, too. How would he remember her after she moved on? Not as a victim. Never that. She wanted him to see what she wanted to see in herself. Strength. Resourcefulness. Pride, but not vanity.

"I was a stay-at-home mom. Once I got pregnant and my ex started working, we agreed on a plan. I had my degree in science, and I put Rob through school by working for a laboratory. The idea was for him to start work and then he'd support me as I took my pharmacy degree. But then we had

Sam, and Rob said he would support us both. I was thrilled. Having Sam changed everything. Being his mom was the best job I'd ever had. I know it's not a job in the strict sense, but I really felt like I was doing something important, making a home for us, bringing him up. And I was thankful to have that choice. I know not everyone does."

Remembering those days stung. Rob had pretended the arrangement was perfect, but in the end it wasn't what he'd wanted. Emily had been too blind to see it until it was too late. "And then he left."

She cast a furtive look at the stairway, knowing Sam was asleep but still worried that if he woke up he'd hear her talking.

Luke followed her gaze. "You don't want him to hear us talking about it?"

Emily nodded, relieved he'd taken the hint so quickly. "He's been through enough. He's asleep, but any mention of his dad and he gets so upset."

"He thinks his dad doesn't like him."

Her head snapped around. "What?"

"He told me. He said I don't like him and his dad doesn't like him and that he does just fine." He pinned her with a steady look. "He's quite a kid, actually. But it made me wonder. Are you fine, Emily?"

She ignored the question, instead focusing on thoughts of Sam. Did he really believe that? That his father didn't like him? Sadness warred with anger at the situation. She hated that he didn't feel loved by both parents.

"I'm sorry he said that to you," she whispered, faltering for a moment, letting the despair in for just a second. Then she closed it away. There was nothing productive in feeling sorry for herself. "I'll have him apologize, Luke."

His gaze darkened and his jaw tightened. "No need. He

was just being honest. He's a good kid. You've done a good job with him. It's not easy being a single parent."

The compliment went to her heart. "Thank you. But I worry about what he's missing. If I'm enough, you know?"

"You just do the best you can."

She leaned back against the counter, looked up at Luke, wondering at the tight tone of his voice. What did he know of it? And yet she got the feeling he somehow understood. "I can't even put food on the table at the moment," she admitted.

His face flattened with alarm. "It's that bad?"

"Let's go outside," she suggested. Luke was standing too close again and she needed the fresh air and open space.

They left the porch light off to keep the Junebugs away, and Emily sat on the step, letting the first stars provide the light while they waited for last dregs of twilight to fade and the moon to rise. She had been at the ranch for two days, and the whole time Luke had felt like a boss, or like a complete stranger. But not tonight. Tonight he felt like an ally, despite the fact that they barely knew one another. It had been a long time since she'd had an ally. Since she'd had an unbiased ear to talk to.

Emily breathed in the fresh prairie air and the heavy scent of lilacs. "I love these," she said quietly. "Nothing smells better than lilacs."

Luke sat down beside her and the air warmed.

"My mother planted them," he said, putting his elbows on his knees and folding his hands. "I'm not much for flower gardens, I don't have time. But I've always tried to keep her lilacs. They smelled nice on the table tonight. Mom used to do that, too."

"What happened to her?"

"She died when I was nineteen. Brain aneurism."

Emily heard the grief in his voice even though it had to be ten years or more since her death. "I'm sorry, Luke."

He coughed. "It's all right. Right now we're talking about you. And why your ex was crazy enough to leave you and Sam and not even provide for both of you."

His words reached inside and illuminated a place that had been dark for a very long time.

"When he left, I had to start looking for work. No one wanted someone who hadn't been in the workplace for five years. Technology has changed. I had no references—the staff where I'd worked was all new. Rob hasn't paid a dime in child support." She twisted her fingers together as she looked over at Luke. "Not one."

"Surely a judge…"

Emily laughed bitterly. "Oh, yes. But it was an Alberta court and Rob moved to British Columbia. And I don't have the funds to fight him on it."

"I'm sorry. Of course you've had a difficult time of it."

She hadn't anticipated a helping hand and a caring tone. Not from a stranger. In a few stolen moments, Luke Evans had shown her more consideration than she'd had from any other quarter in several months. Then she reminded herself that she had promised to rely only on herself and she straightened her shoulders.

"It could have been worse," she admitted. "He didn't hurt us. Not physically. He just left. Said our life wasn't what he wanted and he was starting over."

"It doesn't always take punches to leave scars."

And, oh, she knew he was right. "Rob did lots of damage. They're just the kinds of scars that you can't see. I think they take longer to heal, too. The money is a practical difficulty, but the real kicker is how he has washed his hands of Sam. Sam is his son. I don't understand how a dad does that, Luke. I don't understand how I could have been so wrong. His abandonment made me question every single thing I thought I'd known about myself."

Luke was silent for a few moments. Then he said quietly, "You can't blame yourself for everything."

Emily wanted him to see she wasn't the kind of woman who let life happen to her. She was resourceful. But the kind way he was treating her was throwing her off balance. She'd wanted to create distance between them and instead she felt that he understood, perhaps even better than her friends in Calgary had. How was that possible?

The Junebugs thumped against the screen door, trying to get inside to the light that shone from the kitchen. Luke got up and brushed a hand down his jeans. "Let's walk," he suggested.

They strolled down the lane towards the road, past the mowed grass and to a cedar fence that was ornamental rather than functional. At the bottom Luke turned to her and she swallowed, feeling out of her league being alone with him like this. Unlike the fence, his appearance was for function rather than flash and just about the sexiest thing she'd ever seen, from the shorn hair to the faded jeans and dark T-shirt. The shirt clung in such a way that she could see the shape of his muscles, made strong by years of farm work. The sight of him with the moon behind him was something she knew she'd carry with her for a long time, burned on her mind as surely as the straightforward *E* of the Evans brand.

He was so completely opposite to the men she knew. It made her nervous and, at the same time, exhilarated. She told herself that after a year of being alone it was just a reaction. One that would go away as soon as she left the ranch.

"You didn't see it coming, did you?" Luke picked up the last thread of their conversation.

It hurt to talk about Rob. Not because she still loved him, but because she'd been so blind. While she wanted to blame him entirely, she couldn't help wondering if she might have done something differently. "He just announced one day that he was moving to start a new business. Said it was something he had to do for himself." She shook her head as though she still couldn't believe it. "I thought he meant he'd get started and we'd follow later. But he didn't. It wasn't just a job. He wanted his freedom and he took it."

She rubbed the toe of her sandal in the dusty dirt, making a swirly pattern that turned into a heart with a winding tail. "We had some savings that I protected once I realized what was going on. I needed to pay for housing, food. Clothing." She'd moved the savings money knowing that if Rob wanted to claim it, he'd end up creating more problems for himself. "We've been living on that while I tried to find a job to support us both."

Luke said a not-so-nice word that made Emily snort with surprised laughter.

"I called him that several times, too, over the last year. And I'll admit, I waited, thinking he'd come to his senses, that it was just a sort of crisis he'd get out of his system and we could put it all back together. But when he didn't, and the bills were piling up and the bank account dwindling, I filed for divorce and support."

"Sometimes life throws you one hell of a monkey wrench and all you can do is deal. Put one foot in front of the other," Luke replied.

Emily looked over at him, but his face was shadowed in the dark. Was that the voice of experience? His mother had passed away years ago. That must have been difficult. There was so much she didn't know about Luke Evans. On one hand she wanted to know more, to find some sort of solidarity with someone. On the other she knew she'd be better off to leave well enough alone, so she kept the questions on her tongue unsaid.

They turned and started walking back towards the house.

An owl called from a nearby line of trees and Emily jumped at the sound, chafing her arms with her hands.

"You're cold."

"No, it's good," she replied. "I needed this. I needed to get away. So did Sam. That's the real reason we left Calgary. Everything there was a reminder to Sam of our old life. He couldn't move past just wanting it back—how could he? He's not quite five. He doesn't understand. *I* don't understand. Sam just wanted Daddy to come home. He wanted family vacations and a huge pile of presents under the Christmas tree. I couldn't provide all of that on my own. Lord knows I did my best."

Emily shoved her hands into her pockets. "I'm not lazy, Luke. I applied for jobs for months. Anything I found was minimum wage or shift work or both. On minimum wage I can't afford babysitting. And shift work is horrible for finding good child care." She pursed her lips. "But this job is the best of both worlds. I get to do something I'm good at *and* be with my son. I've sold the Calgary house and I'm going to start over." She smiled, but it didn't chase away the cold. "I hope. I suppose if it doesn't work, there's always my parents. But no one wants to move back in with Mom and Dad, do they?"

Luke halted in the middle of the driveway. He looked up at the house, then up at the sky, and finally blew out a breath. She watched his Adam's apple bob as he swallowed. "It might not be so bad," he said quietly as the owl hooted. He turned to her and she felt her chest constrict beneath his gaze.

"But I don't think you'll need to worry. You strike me as the kind that always lands on her feet, Emily."

Luke studied her face as she smiled up at him. There was no denying that Emily was beautiful. But there was more. There was a quiet resolve to her that was equally attractive. She was a hard worker—he could tell that in the sheer volume of tasks she'd accomplished today. Even as her world spun out of control, she seemed in charge of it. Grounded. Calm in the middle of a storm. Sam thought the sun rose and set in her, because she put him first. He remembered the way she'd smoothed Sam's hair today, or had firmly made him mind his manners during dinner. Her kid was damned lucky.

"I hope you're not saying that just to be nice. I don't want pity, you know."

"Would I say anything for the sole purpose of being nice?" He raised an eyebrow.

"Good point." Her eyes sparkled up at him and he felt an unusual knot in his gut as her tongue wet her lips.

It was only a partial lie. He did feel sorry for her. Sorry that she'd been hurt and sorry she was having to deal with things alone. He knew all too well how that felt. To know that everything rests on your shoulders. To know that any decision you make affects others forever. He'd wished for a helping hand so many times when he was younger, first when his mom had died and then when his dad fell sick with Alzheimer's. He knew what it was to bear the weight of a family on his shoulders. In the past two days he'd questioned his sanity in letting Emily and Sam stay, but now that he knew a little more about their situation, he was glad.

And he was smart enough to know that if he told her such a thing she'd be furious. He was on good terms with their friend, Pride.

Meanwhile his body was tense just from being near her. He only wanted to help. Why then did just the soft scent of her, the sound of her voice, make his body tighten?

"If we keep on as we've started, I think we'll get along just fine," he said, thinking it sounded incredibly hokey, but he had to say something. She was a mother, for God's sake. A mother with a ton of baggage she was carrying around. The fleeting impulse to kiss her was beyond crazy. That was definitely a complication he didn't need.

"I think so, too," she agreed.

They drew nearer the house, the walk coming to an end and with it their confidences in the dark. "Thank you for telling me about your situation," he said. He looked up and thought he saw movement at the curtain of Sam's room, but in the dark he couldn't be sure. Was the boy watching them? Now that he knew more about it, he could understand Sam being mixed up and protective of his mother. Not that it excused bad behavior. There'd be no more sneaking out after bedtime.

"It was only fair. I'm a stranger, right? You agreed to this arrangement without knowing anything about me. You don't need me to bring trouble to your door. No fear of that, anyway," she said softly. "Rob doesn't care enough to come after us."

She tried to make it sound as though she didn't care, but he knew she did. He wondered what kind of man didn't love his kid enough to keep in touch, to know where they were? Luke didn't want the added responsibility of children, but if he had them, he'd do a damn sight better job of parenting than that.

He wasn't sure how a man could let his wife go either. Especially one like Emily.

"I'm sorry," he offered, and meant it.

"Me, too." She sighed in the moonlight. "One of these days you'll have to tell me your story," she suggested.

"Not likely," he replied quickly. "Not much to tell."

She laughed, and it seemed to lighten the evening. "Now why don't I believe that? You're pretty close-mouthed when it comes to your own saga." She grinned, looking impish in the moonlight. "But you have been kind and generous, letting us both stay."

"No one's ever accused me of being either," he replied, their steps slowing, scuffing along in the dirt of the driveway.

"Most would say I'm practical." He'd had to be, getting the girls the rest of the way to adulthood and making sure the farm could support them all. There hadn't been time for what most twenty-year-olds had been doing—working hard, but playing harder. It made him think of the old Bible verses from Sunday school, about leaving childish things behind.

"Do you ever wish you'd finished your degree, Emily?"

She looked up at him, putting one hand on the wood railing of the steps. "When the money was dwindling, I confess I did. But sometimes you exchange old dreams for new ones. After five years, this is what I do best. I love being home with Sam. I loved looking after my house and cooking and doing all the special things I couldn't do if I'd been working all day. I was very fortunate, you know?"

"And do you ever think of going back?"

She paused, her expression thoughtful. "Maybe. But not pharmacy. Something else. Something that uses my strengths. I guess I just don't know what that is yet."

For several seconds they stood there staring at each other. Luke's gaze dropped to her lips and then back up to her eyes. Maybe it was the moonlight, or the way her hair curled around her collar, or the soft sound of her voice that reached inside of him and made him want. And what he wanted was to kiss her—for the second time in ten minutes.

Which was absolutely plumb crazy. There were a dozen solid reasons why he shouldn't.

And he wouldn't.

But he couldn't help thinking about it just the same.

"Well, Mr. Evans, I believe we both have early starts in the morning." She turned to go up the steps. "There is a lot more to be done around here. I think tomorrow I'll examine your vegetable garden."

Lord, she had a lot of pride. But Luke understood that. It made him want to lend his assistance. "I haven't tended to the weeds in a while. The potatoes are sure to need hoeing."

He took a step forward, and his gaze dropped to her full, lush lips. He was standing in the moonlight with a beautiful woman and all he could do was talk about gardens and chores. Had it been that long since he'd dated that he had lost all concept of conversation? The moment stretched out and he leaned forward, just a bit until the floral scent he now recognized as hers filled his nostrils.

He reached out and took her fingers in his hand and felt them tremble.

This was ridiculous. She'd just got through telling him about her disintegrated marriage and he was contemplating coming on to her? He straightened, took a step back.

"It's been a long day," she whispered, pulling her fingers away and tucking them into her pockets. He heard the nervous quaver in her voice and knew she understood exactly what direction his thoughts had taken.

"I'll see you in the morning."

She went inside, closing the door quietly behind her, but for several minutes Luke sat on the porch, thinking.

How could a man just walk out on his family that way? Leave his responsibilities behind? A real man did what needed to be done. His dad had instilled that in him from the time he was younger than Sam. But just because Northcott had left his wife and kid didn't mean they were suddenly Luke's responsibility. For the last decade, he'd had the ranch to worry about, and his sisters until they'd made their way on their own. Now it was the ranch and his father's failing health. It was more than enough. He didn't need to take on any wounded strays.

He just had to remember to shut down any more thoughts

of kissing her. Uncomplicated. That was exactly how this was going to stay. And after she was gone, he'd manage on his own once more.

Just like he always did.

CHAPTER FIVE

EMILY CALLED HER parents first thing after breakfast, once Luke was out of the house and she'd sent Sam upstairs to get dressed. She kept the call brief, merely letting them know of the change of situation and a number where they could contact her.

Then she hung up, feeling like a big fat coward. Her parents had no idea how tight things had become financially, and she didn't want them to either. She knew her dad would insist on helping, something they could not afford now that he was retired. Maybe Luke was right. Maybe she did have too much pride. But there was satisfaction in knowing she was doing it herself. And refusing help also meant she was one-hundred-percent free to make her own choices. She liked that.

She liked being at the Evans ranch, too. She had a purpose, something that had seemed to be missing for too long. She hung out a load of laundry, smelling the lilacs on the air as she pinned the clothes on the line. Sam handed her the clothespins, his dark hair shining in the morning sunlight. "I like it here," she said easily, taking another of Luke's T-shirts and hanging it by the hem. "What about you, Sam?"

Sam shrugged. "It's quiet. And I haven't been able to see much."

"Maybe this afternoon we can take a walk. Search out some wildflowers and birds' nests." Emily felt a catch in her heart, wishing for a moment that he had a brother or sister to keep him company. "I can ask around about some day camps, too, if you like."

"I like the horses," Sam replied, handing her another clothespin. "Do you think I'll be able to ride one?"

Emily frowned. Sam was five and a full-grown horse was so…huge. "I don't know," she answered honestly. "Luke has quarter horses, and he's very busy."

Sam looked disappointed. "Don't worry," she added, ruffling his hair. "Once we get settled it'll all come around all right. Promise."

Sam went off to color in an activity book while Emily fussed around the kitchen, taking a tray of chicken breasts out to thaw for supper. Their conversation had made her think. Keeping Sam busy might be harder than she'd thought. She'd have to think of ways to keep him entertained. She looked at the chicken and then around at the kitchen. Luke had thanked her for the meal last night but it was clear to her that he appreciated plain cooking. Why not keep Sam occupied today by baking? He loved helping her at home. An apple cake, perhaps. And cookies. Sam loved rolling cookies.

With the house tidied and the laundry under control, Emily liked the thought of spending the day in the kitchen, mixing ingredients. She hummed a little as she got out a mixing bowl and began setting out what she'd need. She imagined Luke coming in to rich spicy smells and the smile that would turn his lips up just a bit at the edges.

Her hand stilled on a bag of sugar. Why should it matter if he smiled at her or not? Her stomach did a flutter as she remembered the way his hands had squeezed her fingers last night. He was being nice, that was all. Maybe that was it. He didn't come across as a typically nice person, so last night's chat in the dark had thrown her off balance.

She knew the recipes by heart and when Sam came back

downstairs, they began mixing, rolling and baking. The apple cake, with its topping of brown sugar and cinnamon was cooling on the stovetop and Sam took a fork and pressed on the peanut butter cookies in a crisscross pattern. She'd just sat Sam up to the table with a few warm cookies and a glass of milk when the screen door slammed. Emily pressed a hand to her belly, brushing the flour off the white-and-blue apron she'd found in a drawer. Luke was back already? And the kitchen was still a mess, with dirty dishes and flour dusting the counter surfaces!

"Luke, you here?"

The voice was male but it definitely wasn't Luke's. Emily bit down on her lip as Sam paused mid drink and looked at her.

"Wait here," she instructed Sam, and took a breath. Whoever was there was comfortable enough to come into the house without knocking.

"Hello?" She stepped through the swinging door of the kitchen and moved towards the foyer, where she could hear footsteps. "Can I help you?"

A tower of a man came around the corner. He topped Luke by a good three inches, and Luke had to be close to six feet. Instead of Luke's uniform of jeans and T-shirts, this man wore dress trousers and a shirt and tie, and he carried a box cradled under one arm. Short-cropped walnut-brown hair and warm brown eyes assessed her. "You must be the new housekeeper," he said, but he smiled, making the to-the-point introduction friendly rather than brusque. "I'm Joe. Luke's brother-in-law."

This was Cait's husband, Emily remembered. The one who worked at the equipment dealership. "The new dad," she replied, holding out her hand. "Congratulations. I'm Emily Northcott."

His dark eyes were warm and friendly as he took her hand.

"My wife is very glad you're here at last. She was worried about her big brother managing everything." He inclined his chin for a moment. "It smells good in here."

She withdrew her hand from his, feeling unease center in her belly. When she'd met Luke and shaken his hand, there'd been a queer fluttering and the heat of his skin against hers. With Joe there was none of that. It shouldn't have been different. Luke wasn't any different. He was just a guy.

If that were true, why had she felt the curl of anticipation when the screen door had slammed?

Now his brother-in-law was here and she was feeling that she should play host. "There's coffee and warm cookies, if you'd like some," she invited.

"I wouldn't say no." He put the box on the floor by the door. "Cait in the hospital means cooking for myself right now. If you think Luke's bad in the kitchen…I think I can burn water. Cait got her mother's cooking skills, thank God."

Joe followed her into the kitchen and stopped at the sight of Sam at the table. "Your son?" he asked.

"Yes, this is Sam. Sam, this is Mr. Evans's brother-in-law, Joe."

"You're not a cowboy like Luke," Sam stated, taking the last half of his cookie and dunking it in his milk. Crumbs floated on the top of the creamy surface.

Joe looked down at himself and back up. "No, I guess you're right! I work at the tractor dealership in town."

"I could tell by your clothes."

Joe laughed while Emily resisted the compulsion to curb Sam's matter-of-fact observations.

"Believe it or not, Sam, I've done a fair share of farm jobs. Not like Luke, of course." Joe looked at Emily and winked. It was clear that Luke had already made a solid impression on her son. "But I've been known to lend a hand now and again."

"Luke has a four-wheeler and a tractor and horses. I haven't seen them yet, though. Not up close."

Sam's dark eyes were wide with honest disappointment. Emily hadn't realized that Sam had noticed all those things in addition to the horses. She wondered if she could convince Luke to take him for a ride on the quad or tractor one of these days.

She handed Joe a mug of coffee and put the cream and sugar in front of him as he sat at the table. "Is your wife coming home from the hospital soon?" She offered him a cookie.

"Maybe this afternoon."

"You must be excited."

His eyes gleamed. "We are. We've been waiting a long time for Janna to arrive. Cait has been worried about Luke, though. The ad for the housekeeper didn't get results and Cait is a mother hen. It's one less thing for her to worry about. And then I won't have to worry about *her*."

It was clear to Emily by the way Joe spoke, from the gleam in his eyes, that he loved his wife very much. It was beautiful but caused a sad pang inside her. She'd thought she had that once. Had Rob ever looked at her that way? She'd thought so. Now she wondered if her radar had been flawed all along. She wasn't sure she could ever trust her judgment again.

"Look what the cat dragged in."

Luke stood in the doorway of the kitchen, his hat in his hands and a smile of pure pleasure on his face. "How's the new father?"

"Anxious to get my family home."

"Mom and baby?" Luke stepped inside the kitchen and Emily felt the disconcerting swoop again, the one that felt like riding the roller coaster at Calaway Park. Trouble.

"Home this afternoon, I hope. I brought your parts out that

you asked for. Have a cookie, Luke. They're mighty good. I get the feeling you lucked out with your housekeeper."

"I could have come in and picked them up." Luke angled Joe a telling look. "Unless Cait sent you out here to do a little recon."

Joe didn't even look away, just smiled crookedly at Luke. "I'm not in a position to say no to that woman at the moment," he replied. "And even if I tried, she'd remind me about the twelve hours of labor she just had to endure."

Luke took a cookie from the plate and met Emily's eyes across the kitchen. It was as if an electric wire sizzled between them, and she held her breath. Last night he'd come close to kissing her. At the time she'd put it down to her own fanciful thinking in the moonlight, but she was sure of it now. With his blue gaze flashing at her, she knew she'd been right.

He bit into the cookie and a few crumbs fluttered to the floor. She watched, fascinated, as his lips closed around the sweet and his tongue snuck out to lick away the bits that clung to his bottom lip.

Oh, dear.

She suddenly realized that Joe was watching them with one eyebrow raised and she forced a smile, grabbing a dishcloth and starting to run some water into the sink. "I'm afraid the kitchen is quite a mess," she said, knowing it was inane conversation but desperately needing to fill the gap of silence. "I'd better get started on these dishes."

"And I'd better get back to town." Joe stood up, brought his cup to the sink. "Nice to meet you, Emily."

"You, too. Congratulations again." She squeezed soap into the running water. She didn't dare look at him. She'd blush, she just knew it. She'd been horribly transparent when she'd met Luke's gaze.

"Thanks for bringing the parts out," Luke said, grabbing

another cookie. "I'm heading back out, but now I can get a start on them tonight."

A start? Emily's head swiveled around to look at him. Did he work from dawn until dusk every day?

"Oh, and I brought out some rhubarb," Joe added. "Liz sent it. She said if you couldn't use it now to freeze it. I'm betting Emily could work her magic on it though."

"I can try," she said softly, watching the two of them leave the kitchen and head to the front door.

It was all so normal. A family who cared and looked after each other. Even the idea that Joe had been sent to scope her out for the family didn't really bother her. It was what families did, she supposed. When Luke needed a tractor part, his brother-in-law brought it. Cait worried about him and his other sister sent rhubarb. It was their way of showing they cared. The kind of big family she'd always wanted and had never had.

Sam hopped down from his chair and asked if he could go play in the yard. She let him go, not wanting him to see the telltale moisture gathering in her eyes. She was a good mother. She knew that. She loved Sam and had never regretted staying home with him. But who was there for her?

She scrubbed at the mixing bowl that had held the cake batter and sniffed. Suddenly she wished for an older sister or brother. Someone she might have called when her life was falling apart to reminisce with about childhood. Someone to share her hurt with—and someone to make her laugh again.

Someone like Luke, last night. He'd listened. He'd even made her laugh a little. But Luke was different. There was nothing brotherly about the way she reacted when she was near him. That frankly scared her to death.

"I thought I'd bring you the rhubarb before I headed out."

For once she hadn't heard him come back in and his deep

voice shimmered along all her nerve endings. She swallowed, hating that he'd caught her in a moment of self-pity. "Thank you, Luke. I'll make sure I do something with it right away."

"Em?"

He shortened her name and the intimate feeling of being alone with him multiplied.

"Are you okay?"

She gave a little laugh. "Oh, it's foolishness. You caught me being a little sorry for myself, that's all."

"Why?"

He took a step closer.

She could hardly breathe. "I don't know your family, but I get the sense that you all look after each other. It's nice, that's all. I don't have any brothers or sisters."

"You've handled your situation all alone, haven't you?"

"Pretty much. Friends can only take so much of hearing your troubles, you know? I'm not very much fun these days. So many of them are couples, and I was suddenly the odd man out. They were Rob's friends, too, and it is awkward if you're suddenly picking sides. It was just…"

"Easier to stay away?"

She looked up, surprised yet again that he seemed to understand so easily. "Yes, I guess so. Sometimes I miss the easygoing, fun Emily I used to be."

"Taking the responsibility of the world on your shoulders tends to have that effect," he replied, coming to her and putting his wide hands on her arms. "You are doing the best you can, right?"

She swallowed, tried to ignore the heat from his hands soaking through the cotton of her shirt. "Taking care of Sam is everything to me." She blinked, feeling herself unravel at the kind way he was looking at her. "Not being able to support us makes me feel like such a failure."

He lifted one hand and gently traced his thumb beneath her eye, lifting the moisture away from the skin. "You are not a failure, Emily. You only fail if you stop trying. And I might not know you well, but I can see you're no quitter."

It was a lifeline to cling to and she shuddered in a breath. But when she looked up into his eyes, everything seemed to drop out of her, making her feel weightless, feel that the clock on the wall had suddenly stopped ticking.

His fingers tightened on her shoulder as he drew her closer. For a few precious seconds his lips hovered only an inch from hers. Her heart hammered, wanting desperately for him to kiss her and terrified that he actually might.

Then his breath came out in a rush and he moved back, wiping a hand over his face. "What am I doing?" he asked, more to himself than to her, she realized. Her face flamed with embarrassment. He'd stepped back, but she would have kissed him. If he'd stayed there a moment longer, she would have leaned in and touched his lips with her own.

"I'm sorry." He put his hands in his pockets and the blue heat she'd seen in his eyes was cool and controlled now. "That isn't why you're here. I overstepped, Emily. It won't happen again."

Why on earth was she feeling such profound disappointment? Kissing him would complicate everything! And there was Sam to consider. What if he saw them? He still hadn't quite grasped the unalterable fact that his father wasn't coming back.

"It would be confusing to Sam if he were to see," she said quietly. "And I am not in the market for a relationship. You must know that."

"I do. Of course I do." He had the grace to look chastened. "I don't play games, Emily. I'm not interested in romance either, and I won't toy with you. What happened just now was…an aberration."

He paused, and Emily knew he was measuring his words. What was he protecting? Luke seemed fine when he was dealing with others, but when it came to himself he was irritatingly closed off. He had been open and laughing with Joe, but with her he put the walls back up. She wondered why.

"I don't understand you at all, Luke. You can be very distant, and then last night it was almost as if you were right there in my shoes. Why is that?"

He stared out the window and she wondered if he was avoiding looking at her on purpose.

"I know what it's like to have so much responsibility on your shoulders, that's all. I was only twenty when I took over this farm, and I'm the oldest. Cait and Liz were still in their teens. It's not easy being thrust into the role of primary caregiver and provider. I understand that, Emily. After last night… let's just say I want to help you get your feet beneath you again."

Emily felt her pride take a hit. Had she really seemed that desperate? "Rescuing women and puppies, is that it?"

He frowned. "It's not like that. There was no rescuing involved. I did need help. It was such a relief to come inside last night and know that the house wasn't in shambles. To have a meal hot and waiting rather than throwing something together at the last minute. Why is it so hard for you to accept that this is important? I'm not a particularly charitable man, Emily. I'm not one for pretty words."

She pondered it for a moment, not liking the answer that came to her mind.

"Don't you think what you've done has value?"

He did know how to get in a direct shot, didn't he? Emily dropped her eyes and reached for a dish towel.

"Economics, Emily. The value of something goes up when it's in short supply. Believe me, I've had to keep up with the ranch and the house and…everything else on my own. I appreciate what you've done more than you know."

She wondered what he'd really been going to say in the pause. What everything? "You're just saying that."

"Why would I?"

He came close again. Emily could feel him next to her shoulder and wanted so badly to turn into his arms. She clenched her jaw. How needy could she be, anyway? So desperate that she'd let herself be swayed by a husky voice and a pair of extraordinary blue eyes? She'd gone months without so much as a hug. Wanting to lose herself in his embrace made her weak, and she couldn't give in. Her control was barely hanging on by a thread. She was afraid of what might happen if she let herself go. At the very least, she'd make a fool of herself, especially after their protests that neither of them were interested in romance. She didn't want to look like a fool ever again.

"Did *he* tell you it wasn't important?"

Emily didn't have to ask who *he* was. She'd told Luke enough last night for him to paint a fairly accurate picture. "Staying home with Sam was a mutual decision," she whispered. "But it didn't stop him from getting in the little digs that the financial burden of the family rested on his shoulders. And he never quite saw that while I didn't carry the finances, I looked after everything else, and gladly." She swallowed. "We decided together. I did have to remind him of that on occasion."

She twisted her hands in the dish towel, knowing if she turned her head the slightest bit she'd be staring into his eyes again. The temptation was there. To see if the flare in his eyes was real. Rob hadn't appreciated her. She knew that now. He'd shouldered the financial responsibility of their family and then he'd had enough. She didn't realize how much she needed the validation until she heard it from Luke's lips—a relative stranger who seemed to appreciate her more in two short days than anyone had in years.

"There are some things you can't put a price tag on," Luke said. "He was a fool."

Emily's pulse leapt. Yes, he had been a fool. She had put everything into their family only to be discarded. She turned to Luke then, dropping the dish towel to the countertop. It was a seductive thing, to feel that she was being seen. Really seen.

"I know," she whispered. "I know it in my head. It's harder to convince my heart."

A muscle ticked in Luke's jaw as silence dropped. Emily couldn't have dragged her gaze away if she'd tried. Their gazes meshed, pulling them together even as they both held back.

"Dammit," Luke uttered, then curled his hand around the nape of her neck and moved in to kiss her.

She was vaguely aware of lifting her hands and placing them on his arms. The skin below the hem of his T-shirt sleeve was warm, covering solid muscle from his long days of manual labor. Every square inch of Luke Evans was solid, a formidable, unbreachable wall. Except his mouth. Oh, his mouth. It was incredibly mobile, slanted over hers and making her weak in the knees. He tasted like peanut butter cookies and coffee and the way he was kissing her made her feel like a strawberry, sweet and ripening on the vine in the summer sun.

His muscles relaxed against hers, but with the easing off came a new and wonderful complication: he settled into the kiss now, pulling her body flush against his, making her feel that it could go on forever and nearly wishing it would. She melted into him, resting against the solid wall of his chest, surrendering.

His cell phone rang, the holster vibrating against her hip-bone. The ring tone sounded abnormally loud in the quiet kitchen and Emily staggered backwards, holding on to the counter for support. For one sublime second Luke's gaze collided with hers, hot and perhaps a little confused. Blindly he reached for the phone and then the moment disintegrated into dust as he turned his attention to the display.

Emily grabbed at the discarded dish towel and began drying dishes, wiping each one with brisk efficiency before putting it on a clean portion of countertop. What had they done? Got completely carried away, that's what, and right after they'd said they wouldn't. Heat rushed to her cheeks and flooded through her body. It had been perfectly, wonderfully glorious.

But so wrong. If he'd set out to prove a point, he'd done it. She was vulnerable. Hungry for affection. She put down a mixing bowl and dropped her forehead to her palm. She'd been weak, when only minutes before she'd determined this wouldn't happen. How could she keep the promises she'd made to herself and to Sam if she indulged in such a lack of self-control?

"I've got to get going," Luke's voice came from behind her and she straightened, stiffening her spine.

"Of course. You have work to do."

"Emily…"

That one word—her name—seemed full of unasked questions. Was he feeling as uncertain as she was?

"Luke." She said it firmly, shutting down any doubts. This couldn't happen again. Thinking about whatever chemistry was zinging between them was bad enough. Acting on it was just wrong. She had a plan. It wasn't a perfect plan, but it would be good for her son. A mother did what she had to do. That included taking this job until she could find a more permanent situation.

"I…uh…"

Her throat constricted. She couldn't bear to hear him apologize or say what a mistake it had been.

"You'd better attend to whatever that was," she said, nodding at his phone.

"We'll talk later?"

One more complicated look and he spun on his heel, heading out the door again without waiting for her to answer.

Talk? Emily put her fingers to her lips. They were still humming from the contact with his. They wouldn't talk about this at all—not if she could help it.

CHAPTER SIX

LUKE MADE THE last turn around the field, leaving a swath of sweet-smelling grass behind him and a sense of relief in its wake. The sun shone benevolently down on him right now, but by tomorrow night that would change. The forecast was for rain and thunderstorms. As long as the fine weather held out for another day the first cut would be done and baled and, most importantly, dry. If everything went on schedule. And if the repairs he'd made to the baler held. A lot of ifs.

He checked his watch. Nearly lunch. The Orrick brothers had been raking the east field and would eat their meal in their truck. Luke could have brought his lunch with him, but he looked forward to going back to the house and seeing what Emily had cooked up. Usually he appreciated the thought of peace and quiet and solitude at mealtime. But lately he'd found himself looking forward to Emily's quiet greetings and Sam's chatter.

As he turned the tractor south towards home, he frowned. This wasn't something he should let himself get used to. Cooking or not, being around Emily wasn't the best idea. Not after yesterday. What had he been thinking, kissing her like that? He'd got carried away. She'd turned those liquid brown eyes on him, so hurt and insecure. She'd hate his pity, but he was sorry that she had to carry the weight of her family on her own, knowing there was no way out from beneath the weight of responsibility. Sorry that she'd been married to a man who didn't appreciate all she did. Her lip had quivered and he'd wanted to make it up to her somehow.

Oh, who was he fooling? He touched the throttle, speeding up as he hit the straight dirt lane. He had wanted to kiss her, plain and simple. Still did, if it came to that, even though he knew it was a huge mistake. He could justify it six ways from Sunday, but the truth was she was the prettiest thing he'd laid eyes on in forever. She was out here in the middle of nowhere, but she didn't turn up her nose like so many of the girls did these days—like ranching was some sort of second-class occupation. She breathed deeply of the air, enjoying the space and freedom. And the way she touched Sam, ruffling his hair and showering him with hugs. It was the sort of affectionate touch that was second nature to a mother. The kind he'd grown up with. His mother had been firm but loving. His father, too.

Until his mother had died and everything changed.

The house was in sight, and he spied Emily and Sam in the vegetable garden. For a moment it felt so incredibly right. But then the feeling grew heavy in his chest. It couldn't be *right*. Emily was far too hurt from her divorce, no matter what she said. And Luke liked Sam but he didn't want kids. He didn't want to be married, either. The last thing he wanted was the burden of caring for a family, risking putting them through what he'd been through. Each time he visited his father he was reminded of what the future could hold for him. Seeing his dad suffer quelled any ideas Luke had about a family of his own. No, he'd run the farm and leave the marriage and kids thing to his sisters.

And no matter what Emily said, she was the marrying kind. She wasn't the kind of woman a man trifled with. She certainly wasn't the type for an eyes-open-no-strings fling. So that left them right back at boss and employee.

He pulled up to the barn and wasn't surprised to see

Sam bounding along to greet him. He was a good kid. He minded his mother and was polite and didn't get into things he shouldn't get into. "Hey, Sam."

"Luke! We're weeding your garden and I only pulled up one bean." His face fell a little. "I hope that's okay."

"One little bean plant isn't going to make any difference, don't worry," Luke assured him. The boy had clearly forgiven him for any slights made earlier as he aimed a wide smile at Luke. He noticed Sam had lost his first tooth and couldn't help but smile back at the lopsided grin. "Tooth fairy give you anything for that?"

"A dollar," Sam announced proudly.

Luke cleared his head, pushing away the earlier thoughts of kissing Emily. Sitting on a tractor for hours always gave him way too much time to think. What was he so worried about? It wasn't like he was falling in love with her or anything. It had just been a kiss. Nothing to lose sleep over.

Except he had. It had been ten past midnight when he'd checked the alarm clock last night. Replaying the taste of her, the feel of her in his arms. He walked towards the garden with Sam, watching Emily bent over the tiny green plants. His gaze dropped to the curve of her bottom and his mouth went dry. She straightened, standing up in the row of peas and put her hands on her lower back, stretching.

Little pieces of her hair curled up around the edges of one of his baseball caps, the curved brim shading her eyes from the sun. She wore cutoff denim shorts and a T-shirt the same color as the lilacs by the front verandah, the cotton hugging her ribs, emphasizing her spare figure. His gaze caught on the long length of her leg and he swallowed. It was impossible to stop thinking about yesterday when he'd held her in his arms.

"We might actually get this first cut done before the weather changes," he remarked as he approached the rows of vegetables. Now he was reduced to talking about the weather? It wasn't a good sign when he felt the need to keep things to nice, safe topics. He looked over the garden. Half of it was neatly weeded and tended, the tiny shoots healthy and green. The other half was slightly scraggly. "Thank you for doing the garden. It was on my to-do list."

"It was no trouble. The inside of the house is under control now and it was too beautiful a day to waste. I like being outside, and so does Sam. Don't you Sam?"

Sam nodded, his bangs flopping. "Yup. Mom showed me what a pea plant looks like, and a bean and the carrots, too!" He held up a small pail. "And I took the weeds to the compost pile, too."

"You're a good help," Luke said, unable to resist the boy's excitement. How often had he done this very thing? All the kids had. Working in the garden had been part of their summer chores. "I like working in the outdoors, too."

"Mom said you're too busy to take me on the tractor or anything."

Luke angled his head and looked at Sam, assessing. Sam was what, almost five? At that age, Luke had already been helping in the barns and riding on the tractor with his dad. The memories were good ones, and Sam hadn't experienced anything like that.

"I'm going to be raking hay this afternoon. You can come with me if you like."

Maybe it was a bad idea. He was trying to keep his distance and he wasn't sure Emily would appreciate him encouraging her son. But neither could he stand the thought of the boy feeling alone, left out. Luke knew that helping his dad had made him feel a part of something. The sound of the machinery, the time out of doors, the sense of accomplishment. What could it hurt, just this once?

Sam's eyes lit up and he practically bounced on his toes. "Mom? Can I?"

Emily's dark eyes were centered on him again and he felt the same tightening as he had yesterday when he'd held her body against his. Lord, she'd been sweet and soft and when he'd kissed her every single thought in his brain had gone on vacation.

"You don't have to do that, Luke. You're busy. Sam can wait for another time."

Sam's shoulders slumped in disappointment and he scuffed a toe in the dirt, the action reminiscent of his mother. Clearly Sam had wanted to go, and it was no big deal having him on the tractor with him. Hadn't the boy suffered enough disappointments lately? Luke looked at Emily, knowing she was acutely unhappy with the path her life had taken. He knew she was trying to do her best, but that cloud of unhappiness affected Sam, too. She couldn't keep him tied to her apron strings forever.

"It's just a tractor ride," he answered. "I'm going to be sitting there anyway, raking what we cut yesterday. The boys will be coming along behind, doing the baling. No reason why he shouldn't come along. It'll be a chance for him to learn something new. And give you a little time to yourself."

"Please, Mom?"

She paused.

"He'll be safe with me, Emily. I promise. You have to let go some time."

Her gaze snapped to his and her lips thinned but he held his ground. Sam was a boy. He needed freedom to play and see and do things. Luke understood Emily being protective, but an afternoon in the sun would be good for him. Luke was not her ex. If he made a promise he'd keep it. "It's only a tractor ride," he repeated.

* * *

Emily paused, taken aback by Luke's words. Was she over-protective? She didn't think so. She was only focused on Sam feeling loved and secure. His expressive eyes had looked so hurt, so broken since his father left and she'd do anything to keep that from happening again. She didn't want Sam to get any hopes up.

But perhaps Luke was right. It was just a tractor ride, after all. Didn't Sam deserve some fun? "I'll think about it over lunch." She put off a firm decision, needing him to see that she wasn't going to accept being nudged or coerced. He should have done the courtesy of asking her in private. Heavens, he'd barely said two words to Sam the first few days and now here they were, seemingly thick as thieves.

"Lunch is ready, by the way. I made chicken salad this morning and a cobbler out of that rhubarb your sister sent."

He sent her a cheeky smile from beneath his hat. "You might have to stop treating me so well. I'll get round and fat." He stuck out his stomach and Sam giggled.

Emily pressed her lips together. The man was exasperating! It was almost as if he and Sam were in cahoots together. Which was probably preferable to his taciturn moodiness the first few days, but she didn't want Sam to get too attached. He could get a good case of hero worship without much trouble. And this job wasn't permanent.

Sam bounded on ahead to wash up and Emily took off her cap and shook out her hair. She looked straight ahead as she asked, "You might have asked me first, rather than putting me on the spot."

"What? Oh, I didn't think you'd mind. He did mention something about the tractor the other day, didn't he?"

"That's not the point."

His steps halted, churning up a puff of dust. "Look, I know you're worried about him and it's something he might find fun. I don't get your problem."

She angled him a look that said *Get real.* "My problem is, he's had too many promises made to him that have been broken. Have you seen how he looks at you? Like you hung the moon and the stars. He's been missing a father figure and suddenly here you are."

Luke laughed. "I doubt it. He snuck out of bed the other night and told me off for not complimenting you on your veal."

Emily's mouth dropped open. "He what?"

"Came to the shop and told me you were a nice lady and that his dad doesn't like him and he doesn't care whether I do either. Now, normally a five-year-old boy's opinion wouldn't bother me, but it occurred to me that perhaps I hadn't been as welcoming as I might have been. Don't read too much into it. Like I said, it's just a tractor ride."

Emily folded her hands together. "I guess I can't blame him for being protective. His trust has been shaken."

"Just his?" he asked quietly, walking along beside her again. "Are you really planning never to trust anyone again?"

How could he blame her for being a little gun-shy? "Let's just say trust is a valuable commodity and it has to be earned."

"Yes, and your ex is a prime example of earning it and then abusing it. There's more to building trust than time."

His words cut her deeply. She had trusted Rob and he'd ground her faith in him beneath his heel when he left. She'd made a lot of progress since then. She'd stopped blaming herself for everything. She'd stopped feeling so desperate. She'd started focusing on the good—as much as that was possible. But trust…that was something she wasn't sure she'd ever quite accomplish again.

"If you're so smart, what else is there?" She didn't bother to keep the annoyance out of her voice. Sometimes Luke was far too sure of himself. Like he had her all figured out.

"Actions. Hell, instincts, if it comes to that."

His observations made her uncomfortable, because her instincts had told her from the beginning that Luke was a man she could trust. And he'd kept his word about everything since her arrival.

"Right now I don't put a lot of credence in my instincts."

He stopped, his boots halting in the dusty drive and she kept on a few steps until she realized he wasn't with her anymore. She looked over her shoulder at him. His eyes flashed at her. "And I've done something to...not earn your trust? Is that it?"

He had her there. And yesterday's kiss...she couldn't blame him for that either. She'd wanted it as much as he had. Not that they'd talk about it. No way.

"I'm cautious, then," she responded, as they reached the steps. "Very, very cautious."

"So can Sam come with me or not?"

She left him in the doorway taking off his boots. "I'm still thinking," she said. She'd already made up her mind that Sam could go, but she wasn't going to let Luke think he'd won so easily.

Just as they were finishing the meal, a cloud of dust announced an approaching car. They both looked out the window and Emily heard Luke's heavy sigh. "Who is it?"

"My sister, Liz."

"The rhubarb sister."

He smiled at her summary. "Yes, that's the one." Emily watched as he checked his watch and tapped his foot. "Dammit, she's got perfect timing," he muttered.

Liz parked the car in the shade of a tree and Emily felt the strange, nervous feeling she'd had yesterday meeting Joe. As though she was an imposter, a tag-along.

"I'm sorry, Emily. I think the family is curious about you, and you've been put under the microscope."

"Why would they do that?"

Luke plopped his hat on his head. "Because you're not the matronly housekeeper they expected. Because you're staying here. Because you're young and pretty." He sighed. "Because people who are married think that everyone else in the world should be married, and they feel free to stick their noses in."

Emily opened her mouth and then closed it again, unsure of how she was supposed to react to that little tidbit. It wasn't the meddling that shook her—she half expected that. It was the *young and pretty* part. She was only twenty-eight but there were days she felt ancient. And pretty…she'd been living in T-shirts and yoga pants for so long that she forgot what it was like to feel pretty.

She wouldn't dream of admitting such a thing to Luke, though. Surely his family wasn't putting the cart this much before the horse. "Married?" The thought was preposterous, and she laughed. Even if she did want to get married—which she didn't—she'd only known Luke for a few days.

He raised his right eyebrow until it nearly disappeared beneath his hat. "Ridiculous, isn't it? But I'll bet my boots Liz is here to check you out. She'll have some good excuse. But don't worry, she means well. This should be the end of it. You can thank the Lord that I don't have more sisters to interfere."

With that he went outside to greet Liz.

Liz came towards the house, carrying a blond-headed baby on her hip and with two more youngsters trailing behind. Emily bit down on her lip. She was an object of curiosity now. Yesterday's longing for siblings and a close-knit family dissipated as she realized that intimacy also meant interference. The last thing she wanted was to be scrutinized. Judged. And to come up short.

"What brings you out, Liz?" Emily heard him call out and

closed her eyes. She could do this. Liz would never know how Luke's voice gave her goose bumps or how they'd kissed until they were both out of breath. Emily fluffed her hair, smoothed her fingertips over her cheeks, and let out a calming breath.

Luke met his sister in the yard. The twin girls took off running across the lawn, burning off some stuck-in-the-car energy.

"Strawberries," Emily heard the woman say. "I brought out a flat of strawberries."

"I'm in the middle of haying. When would I have time for strawberries?"

They'd reached the porch and Emily stood just inside the screen door of the house, wanting to scuttle away but knowing how that would look—as though she was running from something. Hiding. She had nothing to hide.

"Joe told us you've finally got some help. It's about time, Luke. Joe said she's very pretty, too. You've been holding out on us, brother."

"No big surprise, Nosy Nellie. Cait put the request in at the agency, after all. You can't fool me."

Emily's cheeks flamed as Liz looked up and suddenly realized Emily was standing behind the screen door. For a second, Liz got a goofy look on her face as she realized she'd been caught. Then she replaced the look with a wide smile.

"Joe was right. You are pretty. I'm Liz, Luke's sister."

Good heavens, was everyone in Luke's family so forthright?

"Berries are in the trunk, Luke. Be a good brother."

Luke's jaw tightened as Liz smiled and adjusted the weight of the baby on her hip. Emily looked to him for guidance, but he gave none. Emily couldn't stand to be impolite, so she opened the door. "Come on in. We were just having lunch. Come have some cobbler."

Liz swept in and Emily heard Luke's boots tromp off down

the steps. First Joe and now Liz. The family obviously thought there was more to the arrangement than a simple trading of services. Which there wasn't. Much. Emily wondered how fast the telephone wires would burn up if Liz knew that they'd kissed yesterday.

"Don't mind Luke," Liz admonished, nosing around the kitchen. "He's always a bear in haying season. No time to call his own, you know? Not the biggest conversationalist either."

Emily was tempted to set Liz straight on that. Last night and just a few moments ago Luke had managed to hold his own quite well in the conversation department. She wondered how he managed that. He seemed to say a lot, but none of it really told her anything. Except that he'd been left in charge of the family at a young age.

But she did not want to open that can of worms with Luke's sister. She wasn't a busybody and knew exactly how awful it was to have people pry into her situation. She would keep the conversation impersonal. "Rain's coming, Luke said."

Great job, Em, she thought. First words she spoke and she was parroting the forecast? Perhaps she could have come up with something slightly more inspired.

Liz nodded. "He'll work until dark tonight, I expect. Good to get the first cut in though. What do you think of the house?"

Emily busied herself fixing a bowl of cobbler and ice cream for Liz. "It's charming. Much nicer than the cookie cutter houses in the city."

Liz nodded. She sat at the table and perched the baby on her knee, bouncing her a little and making the little girl giggle. "I think so, too. Luke's done some work to it since taking it over, but for the most part it looks just like it did when we were growing up. Of course, I'm living in town now. And I've got the little ones to keep me busy."

Luke came back in, carrying a wooden flat filled with boxes of crimson strawberries. "I think the twins have made a new friend," he said dryly.

Emily and Liz went to the window. Sam and Liz's blond girls were racing through the yard, playing what appeared to be a rousing game of tag.

"It's good for Sam. He hasn't spent much time with friends since…"

She stopped. Since the divorce. Since there was no longer any money for playgroups and preschool.

"He'll have to come play with the twins while you're here. It'll get them out of my hair," Liz offered freely.

Another tie to break later? Emily wasn't sure it was a good idea. But then she balanced it against Sam being alone here in an unfamiliar place and no children to play with. "That might be nice."

"Call anytime." Liz replied, putting the baby down on the floor. The little girl rocked back and forth for a minute before setting off at a steady crawl. "You and Luke could come over for dinner."

"Liz," Luke warned, and Emily had to look away. It was such an overt bit of matchmaking that she squirmed in her chair.

"What? Look, both Cait and I are thrilled you have some help at last. That's all. And Emily doesn't know a soul besides you. And we all know what great company you are."

He raised an eyebrow at her.

"I'm heading back out. The boys are going to wonder where I am. Emily, tell Sam I'll take him out with me another time. He should enjoy the girls while they're here." He put his plate in the dishwasher and cut himself a massive slice of apple cake. "For the road," he said, flashing a quick grin.

She nodded and walked with him to the door.

"Are you sure you're okay with my sister?" he asked quietly, pausing and resting his palm against the frame.

Emily forced a small laugh. "You have work to do. I'll be fine."

"She's meddling. Thinking that this is more than it is."

That should have relieved her but didn't. Would it be so awful for them to think that he liked her, for heaven's sake? Not that she wanted him to, but was it incomprehensible that he might? "Don't worry about it. And it's good for Sam to have playmates for an hour or so. He's been lonely." She paused. "Are you really going to work until dark?"

His gaze plumbed hers for a long moment. It was a simple question but brought with it a picture of how the evening would unfold...Sam in bed, darkness falling, Luke coming to the house in the twilight. All of it played out in her mind as she gazed up into his eyes. How did he feel about coming home to her at night? Was she an intrusion? A complication? Or welcome company, as he was to her, despite his sometimes prickly ways?

"Probably close to it," he finally answered. "We'll go until it starts to cool off, then there are chores here to see to. You and Sam should eat without me. Just fix me a plate."

There wasn't any reason for her to feel disappointed, but she did. After only a few days she'd gotten used to seeing him during meals. Company, whereas before mealtime had meant an empty space at the head of the table.

"I'd like to make a run into town for sugar and pectin. Anything you need?"

He shook his head. "Not that I can think of. Thanks for asking, though." He started off but turned around again. "Don't let Liz needle you into anything," he warned. "Cait's the bossy sister, but Liz has a way of getting what she wants without you even knowing how."

CHAPTER SEVEN

As EMILY WENT back inside, three sweaty heads ran past her into the house.

"Whoa, slow down!" Liz called from the kitchen, laughing as the children scrambled in demanding a snack. The baby was heading for the stairs, and, without a second thought Emily picked her up, breathing in the scent of baby powder and milk. She closed her eyes for a moment, enjoying the feel of the weight on her arm, the smell that was distinctly baby. Sam had left those baby days behind him long ago. Emily had always hoped the time would be right to have another, but it had never worked out. Now she was a little glad it hadn't. She couldn't imagine being responsible for two precious lives in her current circumstances. Knowing she would probably never have any more caused a bittersweet pang in her heart. Being a single mom was tough. She knew she wouldn't deliberately grow her family without being in a secure relationship. And after the crumbling of her marriage, she never intended to go down that road again. Still, it was hard to say goodbye to those dreams.

As she opened her eyes, blue eyes reminiscent of Luke's stared up at her and she smiled. "Let's find your mama," she murmured, and settling the baby on her hip, she entered the kitchen to find Liz mixing up lemonade and three expectant faces watching.

Liz looked so comfortable that it reminded Emily that this was Liz's childhood home. Emily was the trespasser here and she felt it acutely as she watched Liz add sugar to the lemonade then open the correct drawer for a wooden spoon. Emily envied the other woman her level of comfort with, well, everything. And yet she had to admit she was drawn to Liz's breezy ways.

"Out on the porch with you three," Liz admonished, filling three plastic cups with the drink. "One cookie each. No sneaking."

When the kids were settled on the verandah she came back to the kitchen. "Thanks for grabbing Alyssa," she said, taking the bundle from Emily's arms. "The stairs, right? It's always the stairs."

Emily couldn't help but laugh. Liz might be a bulldozer but she was a pleasant one, and it had been a long time since Emily'd had a mom-to-mom visit with anyone. She'd been too busy coping to realize she was lonely.

Compared to Luke's reticence, Liz was bubbly and open. "How is it you are so different from your brother?"

"What do you mean?" Liz asked, grabbing her purse and taking out a biscuit for the baby to gnaw on.

"Luke's so…"

Emily struggled for the right word, thinking of how Luke looked at her and seemed to get to the heart of any matter with a few simple words. Liz's keen gaze was on her now.

Instantly Emily recalled the kiss and the way he'd cupped her neck confidently in his palm. "Intense."

"Luke's too serious, but I can't blame him. It's a wonder he didn't disown the two of us." She flashed a smile that hinted at devilry. "Oh, Cait and I gave him awful trouble."

"Surely your parents…"

"Oh, this was after Mom died and Dad had to be put in the

care home. Luke was different before that happened. Always running with his guy friends, you know?"

Care home?

Luke had said so little about his upbringing. Now the bits and pieces were starting to come together. Luke had said he'd been responsible for his sisters and the farm at an early age. She tried to imagine one parent dying and the other incapacitated. What an ordeal they must have gone through. "How old were you?"

"Luke was twenty. Cait was almost seventeen and I was fifteen. Old enough to know better, really. But at that age—when you're a teenager it's 'all about me', you know? We were still in high school."

Emily did know. But she also knew that Luke would have put himself last, making sure everyone was looked after ahead of himself. She imagined him waiting up for them at night, perhaps pacing the floor with lines of worry marring his forehead. Had those days put the shadows she saw in his eyes? "And Luke?"

Liz frowned. "He didn't tell you any of this?"

"Not much. Why would he? I've only been here a few days, Liz. We haven't had heart-to-hearts."

She smiled, but once the words were out she knew they weren't exactly true. Maybe not baring of souls, but she'd told him more about her marriage than she'd told anyone. They'd had moments of closeness—up to and including the kiss that had nearly melted her socks. Not that she'd admit that to his sister.

Liz dipped into her cobbler, holding the spoon in the air. "Well, Luke should be the one to tell you, not me."

"Luke isn't exactly big on social chitchat," Emily replied, but Liz just laughed.

"He does tend to be on the serious side. You ask him,

Emily. Maybe he'll talk to you. He never talks to either of us."

Maybe Luke was just a private person, Emily thought, but didn't say. Liz was his sister. She had to know him better than most. And she did feel a little odd, talking about him when he wasn't here. As curious as she was, Liz was right. This was something Luke should tell her himself. If he ever did.

"Joe said there's something going on between you."

Emily's back straightened, pulled out of her thoughts by Liz's insinuation. The camaraderie she'd begun to feel trickled away as she remembered Luke's warning. Liz was here to check her out, and the last thing she wanted was to be judged. "You are direct, aren't you?"

Liz raised her eyebrows. "Luke's our brother. We love him. We want him to be happy."

"And that's not with me." Of course not. Emily was not a brilliant prospect in anyone's book. She was damaged goods. She didn't even have a long-term plan.

Emily went to a cupboard and found a large mixing bowl and began stemming the first box of berries. She didn't like that she'd been the topic of conversation around the family water cooler.

"I didn't say that, you did."

The berries flew from one hand to the other and pinged into the stainless-steel bowl as Emily removed the stems. "I'm a single mother with a very small income."

"Money isn't what Luke needs." Liz's voice held a tinge of condemnation. "After what Joe said, I thought maybe you realized that. I guess I was wrong."

Emily's hands fell still. She had always considered that the outside world saw only the surface. That people looked at her and automatically categorized her in little columns of pluses and minuses. Lately she was pretty sure there were more minuses than pluses. Now she wondered if that was simply her own insecurity talking. "What does Luke need?" she asked quietly, picking up another berry but plucking off the stem at a more relaxed pace.

Liz brought another box to the side of the sink. "A companion."

Emily dropped the berry in the bowl. Luke was barely thirty. He didn't need a companion. He needed a wife and partner, and she wasn't up for applying for either position. "Then he should get a dog."

Liz laughed at her dry tone. "Fine, then. He needs a helping hand. Someone willing to share the load. He's been carrying it by himself for a long time. Not that he's ever complained. Someone should shake him up a bit. Why not you?"

A helpmate. Emily knew that was what Luke's sister was getting at and it made her pause. That's what she'd tried to be for Rob and it had blown up in her face. "I'm not interested in that," she informed Liz. "Nothing against your brother. He's very nice. But I'm not looking for a boyfriend or husband. I rely on myself now, not someone else."

Liz looked at her speculatively. "No one said you didn't."

But Emily knew that's what it would mean. She had built her whole existence around someone else. Rearranging her life around Rob's schooling and then his job. Staying home with Sam. Looking after everyone's needs and sacrificing her own. It had little to do with the type of work, she realized, but with the principle behind it. How long had she been Rob's wife, Sam's mother? How long had it been since she'd been plain Emily Northcott, woman?

"Liz, I appreciate that you want your brother to be happy. But surely you can see how ridiculous it is to be discussing this. There are no romantic notions. I work for him."

"If you say so," Liz replied, but Emily knew by her deliberately casual tone that she wasn't convinced. And why should she be? It wasn't exactly true. Emily thought about Luke far too often throughout the day and then there was the kiss. She ran her tongue over her lips, remembering the taste of him there. Knowing it wasn't what she wanted and yet dying to know if he would do it again.

"Either way, can we be friends?" Liz's sandy-colored ponytail bobbed as she reached beneath the cupboard for a colander to wash the berries, completely oblivious to Emily's quandary.

Friends? The request came as a surprise after being grilled about Luke. But an offer of friendship was hard to resist. She'd felt so disconnected in recent months. All of her friends were 'before divorce' friends. There'd been no money or time for cultivating new relationships since. Liz was only looking out for her family. Emily could hardly fault her for that. If she didn't feel so uncomfortable, she might have admired her for it.

Liz reached for the teakettle and filled it with water. "Come on, Emily," she invited. "Let's have a cup of tea and a gab. The kids are playing and Luke's going to be gone for hours. With the little ones underfoot I don't get out much either. What's the harm?"

What was the harm, indeed? Emily couldn't hold out against the temptation of a social afternoon. She got out the teabags and put them on the counter. "He told me you'd bull-doze me, you know." But she smiled when she said it, holding no malice against Luke's vivacious sister. She would have done the same thing for her brother or sister, if she'd had one.

"Of course he did."

Emily lifted a finger in warning. "But leave off the match-making, okay? Luke's no more interested in me than…"

She had been going to say than I am in him, but she couldn't say the words because she *was* interested in him, more than she would ever admit.

"Matchmaking? Perish the thought." Liz affected an

innocent look so perfectly that Emily found herself grinning back. "Listen," Liz continued, getting out spoons. "Luke has always said he will never get married anyway. So nothing to worry about, right?"

"I'd like to make some jam out of these berries," Emily said to Liz, offering an olive branch as the kettle began to whistle, trying to ignore Liz's latest bombshell. Never get married? She forced her mind back to the present. "Where's the best place to shop for jars and pectin?"

For the next hour the baby napped, the kids played in the sunshine and Liz and Emily stemmed the remaining berries, chatting easily about lighter topics. But the whole time Emily thought of Luke and his past. She couldn't help wondering why he was determined to be alone. Had he had his heart broken? Was it any of her business to ask? If she did, would he answer? She couldn't help the sneaky suspicion that Liz's throwaway comment had been intended to do just that—make her wonder.

The farmyard was dark except for the light Emily saw coming from the machine shed. It was past ten o'clock and still Luke hadn't come in. He hadn't had any supper, either. She'd waited for him long after Sam had gone to bed, finishing up the last batch of jam and leaving it to set on the kitchen counter. She couldn't forget all that Liz had told her during their chat—and what she hadn't.

She carried a warm plate in her hands as she crossed the gravel drive. The man had to eat something. If he wouldn't come in, she'd take it to him.

She balanced the plate on one hand and opened the door to the shed. All that was visible of Luke as she entered was his legs. The rest of him was underneath her car. A long yellow cord disappeared along with the upper half of his body—a trouble light illuminating the dirty job of changing her oil.

Clanking sounds echoed on the concrete floor as he put down the filter wrench and oil began draining into the catch pan.

"Luke?"

At the sound of her voice he slid out from beneath her car, the sound of the creeper wheels grating loudly in the stillness. The rest of his legs appeared, then came his flat stomach, his broad chest and muscled arms and then his head—now devoid of hat, his hair dark with sweat in the oppressive heat of the shop. Her gaze fixed on his arms as he pushed himself up to sitting.

Emily felt a bead of perspiration form on her temple in the close atmosphere of the shop. Throughout the afternoon the heat had increased until the kids had dropped, sapped of their energy. It hadn't let up after sundown. Even the peepers were quiet tonight, and when the creeper came to a halt, the silence in the shop was deafening.

"What are you doing with my car?"

"Changing your oil. It looked like it'd been a while."

It had, but that wasn't exactly the point. "I...you..." She didn't quite know what to say that didn't sound grouchy and angry. Especially since she was both of those things. Part of it was the heat. But a bigger part was that he'd taken it upon himself to do this without even consulting her.

"You might have asked me first."

Luke shrugged. "It's just an oil change, Emily."

Pride kicked in. "And the cost of the filter, and the cost of the oil."

"If it means that much to you, I'll deduct it from your pay."

Her hand shook beneath the warm dinner plate. She didn't want to lose any of her precious paycheck right now. And if she were to lose any of it, she should be the one to say where it went.

"That really wasn't on my list of things to do with my first check, Luke." She was trying—and failing—to keep a quiver out of her voice. "It's been a long time since I had my own pay. I'd like to be the one to decide what happens to it. And besides, it's after ten o'clock. You've already spent the day outside while I was inside with Liz...."

Suddenly the lightbulb came on. "That's it, isn't it? You're avoiding me because you think Liz put a bug in my ear."

He couldn't meet her eyes. "What's on the plate?"

"I'm right!" Victorious, she let out a breath. "You can't stay out here all night, you know. And you can't avoid me forever. For what it's worth, Liz barely told me anything. You could have saved yourself the trouble."

Luke put on his most nonchalant expression. "Your oil needed changing and I wanted to do it for you. Now, are you going to share that plate or did you just bring it out here to torture me?"

He got to his feet, looking sexier than a man had a right to in dusty jeans, work boots and a grease-stained T-shirt, and she had the thought that he could change her oil or tune up her car any time.

She held out the plate. "You should have come in for supper—you've got to be exhausted. The car could have waited. I know you want to get the hay in." She tried a smile. "You have to make hay while the sun shines, I've heard."

"That's true," he said. "With this heat—we need to get it baled before the rain comes tomorrow. I'm guessing thunderstorms. And there is always the chance of hail."

"Then take a rest."

He reached for a rag and wiped his hands before taking the plate. His fingers were long and rough, with a half-healed scratch running the length of one. He made a living with his hands and hard work. There was something earthy about that and she found it incredibly attractive.

"Lasagna. And garlic bread." He stared at the contents of

the plate with undisguised pleasure. "My God, that smells awesome. Do you know how long it's been since I had lasagna?"

"That's a good thing, then?"

He went to a wheeled stool and sat down. "Oh, yeah, it's a good thing." The shop began to fill with the scent of spicy tomatoes and beef. "Pull up a pew, Emily."

There was little space to sit, so she perched on the edge of a homemade sawhorse. Luke cut into his lasagna with the side of his fork, took a bite, and closed his eyes. Emily smiled, pleased she'd made the extra effort. Luke was turning out to be a pleasure to cook for. "It was better, fresh," she apologized.

"You say that, but I doubt it," he remarked, biting into the garlic bread, flakes off the crust fluttering down to the plate. "It's perfect just the way it is. I didn't realize how hungry I was. You didn't bring any water, did you?"

"Oh! How could I have forgotten?" She reached into the pocket of her light sweater and produced a bottle of beer, so cold it was already sweating with condensation. "I thought you'd appreciate a cold one."

He stared at her as if she were a gift from the gods. "What?" she asked, smiling. "You're not difficult to read, Luke."

Well, not about food, she amended mentally. In other ways he was a definite puzzle. Emily considered for a moment that perhaps Liz's perspective on what happened and Luke's could be very different. Not that Liz had it easy. Losing a parent had to be devastating. But having to step into that role as Luke had...

Luke popped the top and took a long drink. "That is exactly what I needed." He sighed, swiping the final slice of bread along the plate to get the last of the tomato sauce. "Thanks for bringing it out. You didn't need to do that."

"It was kind of quiet in the house."

He nodded. "Yeah, it gets that way."

Emily looked down, studying her toes. Had Luke been lonely? Up until now she really hadn't thought about him living in the house all alone, but now she wondered how it must be to come home to it every day, with no one there to talk to or share the silence with. At least she had Sam.

She picked a wrench up off the tool bench and toyed with it, putting it down and picking up another. When she looked up at Luke she could tell he was gritting his teeth. He came forward and took the wrenches, placing them back on the pegboard. The whole bench was precisely arranged and Emily wondered where he inherited his penchant for neatness from. "Sorry," she murmured.

"It's all right." His voice sounded oddly strained. "I try to keep things organized so…so I can always find the size I need."

"Tools on pegboard and everything on lists." She had noticed Luke had a list for everything at the house. Phone numbers. Groceries. To-do tasks. She often did the same thing, but she thought it an unusual trait in a man. "You really are quite neat and tidy, Luke. For a guy." She attempted to lighten the strange tension that had come over the room.

"I'm a one-man show. Keeping organized saves me a lot of time," he explained. He finished putting the tools away reached for his beer, toying now with the bottle as he sipped. "You survived Liz's visit?"

"We had tea and stemmed strawberries."

"And talked about me."

Emily felt a flush creep into her cheeks. "My, don't we have an inflated opinion of ourselves."

He laughed, the sound filling the quiet shed and sending a tingle right through to her toes. Laughter had been another one of those things that had been missing for a long time. Something that slipped away so innocuously that she hadn't realized she'd missed it until hearing it again.

"Liz was sticking her nose in. If Cait didn't have a newborn at home, she would have been here, too. Be thankful they didn't tag-team you. You wouldn't have stood a chance."

Emily stared at him. He was smiling as though it was a big joke. "So it's funny that I was put under the microscope today?"

He lowered the bottle slowly. "I forgot. You don't have brothers and sisters. It's what they do. We're born to aggravate each other. I guess I'm just used to it."

"Well she wasn't aggravating *you* today, was she?" Emily's back straightened. Granted, she'd had a nice visit with his sister, but Luke didn't know that. For all he knew he'd thrown Emily to the wolves and he was relaxed as could be, smiling like a fool.

His smile slid from his lips though when she fired that question at him. "What exactly did Liz say to you, Emily?"

"Worried?" She asked it in an offhand manner, but the smile from earlier was gone. "She didn't say much. She mentioned you looking after her and Cait and how they'd been holy terrors. But really, that was all."

Luke seemed to relax, turning the bottle in his fingers. "And she said I should ask you about the rest."

The bottle stopped turning.

"Why don't you tell me about your dad, Luke?"

"There's nothing to tell." His voice was hard and his knuckles went white on the bottle.

"He's in a special-care home, right?"

His head snapped up and his blue gaze flashed at her. "Liz has a big mouth."

"Then make me understand what makes you so different from your sister. Because I'm guessing it had to do with the fact that you had to leave your childhood behind in a hurry to take over this farm."

Emily went to him and put a hand on his arm. "Please,

Luke. I shared bits of my story with you. Can't you do the same? Maybe talking about it will help."

"All the talking in the world won't change things," he bit out.

"But it might make you feel less alone," she reasoned. "I know I felt better after talking to you. What happened to your father?"

It was quiet for several seconds and Emily didn't think he was going to answer. But then his voice came, low and raspy, as if the words were struggling to get out.

"Dad had been acting weird for a while. We'd all noticed it, but after Mom died…it was clear there was more to it than simple stress forgetfulness. It wasn't until he nearly burned down the house making eggs in the middle of the night that we couldn't ignore it any more."

"What happened? What was wrong with your father?"

"Early-onset Alzheimer's. Dad's been in a care home since. Over the years it's got progressively worse. Not so much at first. Sometimes the fog would clear and we had good visits, you know? We could talk about the farm, the girls, my mom. But those times got fewer and farther between and lately… he's really gone downhill. I don't expect he's got much time left."

Emily remembered the pictures on the old radio in the living room. The first day, she'd seen Luke's face turn sad as he looked at the picture of his parents. The bedroom upstairs, with its faded doilies and chenille spread, looking lost and abandoned…she'd bet now that no one had slept there since his father had been put in care. And he had given it to her. She felt a little weird about that, but honored, too. What a heart-breaking decision to have to make about your one remaining parent.

"Liz mentioned you having power of attorney. That means the decision fell to you, didn't it?"

He lifted tortured eyes to hers. "Yes. As well as the day-to-day running of the farm, and looking after the girls."

"But surely they were grown enough to look after themselves…"

Luke laughed, but it was laced with pain. "Cooking, laundry, cleaning, yes. But at fifteen and nearly seventeen, they needed guidance. I was twenty. My prized possession was my truck. I wasn't ready to be a parent to two hormonal teenage girls. I wasn't that much older than they were and I was trying to keep them from making mistakes. Trying to make sure they finished school, had opportunities, you know?"

"And so you sacrificed yourself."

"What else could I have done? And look at them. They graduated, got jobs, met fine men and started families. You can imagine what a relief that is. Think if it were Sam."

He'd been taking on responsibility all his adult life. And she'd been whining about her problems yesterday. Luke had been so understanding. More than understanding—caring.

She had been in danger of caring right back, and this new knowledge touched her, making her respect him even more. Making her grieve a little bit for the young man who had had to grow up so quickly. "And all this while you grieved for your parents."

His eyes shone for a few moments until he blinked.

"What did you give up, Luke? You put the girls first, so what dreams did you put aside for later?"

Luke put the bottle beside the empty plate and placed his hands on his knees. "It doesn't matter now."

"I think it does. You were twenty, carefree and with your life ahead of you. That must have been cut short…"

"I worked on the farm for a year, but I'd planned on going to college. I wanted to study genetics so I could play with our breeding program. The idea of going away for a while was exciting. Even after Mom died, I only planned to stay a year to help and then I'd be off. But as things progressed with Dad, I knew I couldn't leave. My responsibility was to the family, and to abandon them would have been the height of selfishness."

He gave her a knowing look. "You know as well as I do that you put family first. You'd do it for Sam. You're doing it for him now by making a life for him. But Emily, don't give up on your dreams either. You give up on them and you'll end up old and bitter like me."

Luke got up from his stool, worry lines marring his tanned brow. He reached out for her arm, but seemed to remember the state of his hands and pulled back. Emily felt the connection just the same as if he'd touched her.

She met his gaze. The connection seemed to hum between them every time their eyes met, but she would not shy away from eye contact. She was stronger than that. "You are not old and bitter," she whispered.

"Em…"

She swallowed. Luke was standing in front of her car now, his thumbs hooked in the front pockets of his jeans. For a moment she remembered what it had been like when he'd stepped forward and kissed her, so commanding and yet gentle. There could be no more repeats of that. He was right. She couldn't give up on her dreams, even if right now that meant doing the right thing for Sam.

"Why don't you go back and get your pharmacy degree?"

She pondered the idea for a moment. "It's not what I want anymore. I have Sam now and want to be close to him. Going to school and trying to support us…he'd be in daycare more than out of it."

"What about online learning?"

The idea was interesting. "Maybe. But not pharmacy. Not now." She smiled at him. "Priorities change."

He smiled back. "Don't I know it?"

Her heart took up a strange hammering, a persistent tap like a Junebug hitting a screen door time and time again.

"Thank you for telling me, Luke. I know it couldn't have been easy."

"It wasn't. But you were right. I do feel better, I think. Liz and Cait have different memories than I do. In some ways that is good. But it's hard talking to them about it. I don't want them to feel responsible for anything, and I think they will if I let on how hard it was."

"Would you do it again?"

It was a loaded question, and one Emily had asked herself often since the disintegration of her marriage. Would she marry Rob again, knowing what she knew now? But then she thought of the good times, and about Sam, asleep in his room with the June breeze fluttering the curtain and the moon shining through the window. Nothing could take away the love she had for her boy. She knew her answer. What was Luke's?

CHAPTER EIGHT

LUKE LEANED BACK against her bumper. What in the world had possessed him to talk to Emily this way? He never opened up to anyone, not even his sisters who had been with him all the way. He kept to himself, and that was how he liked it. And then Emily had blown into his life and turned everything upside down.

She had him talking. That was more of a surprise than his reaction to her. If he wasn't careful, she'd have him wishing for all kinds of things he'd stopped wishing for years ago.

But her question stayed with him, and he looked at her, perched on the sawhorse, her cheeks flushed from the heat and her hair mussed from running her hand through it too many times. Would he do it again the same way? Sacrificing what he'd wanted to look after his sisters?

"Of course I would. They'd lost both their parents. They needed guidance and support. Who else would have stepped in?"

"What about support for you, Luke?"

Damn her eyes that seemed to see everything.

"I could say the same for you, Emily. Who is supporting you now?" She opened her mouth, but he cut her off. "Don't bother, I know the answer. No one. You're going it alone, too. What about your parents? Any other family?"

"I want to do this on my own. I need to. I know they are there if I need them."

"And then there's Sam."

Her eyes blazed and her back straightened. "Everything I do is for Sam!"

Luke smiled indulgently. "Calm down, I know that. Just as you get why I did what I had to for the girls. Choosing myself first would have been self-centered, especially when they needed me so badly."

"You're a good big brother," she murmured. "Do the girls realize how much you gave up for them?"

He shrugged. "Does it matter? They are healthy and happy and I am happy for them." He fought against the sinking feeling in his chest. He was happy for them with their strong marriages and beautiful children. He was thrilled they both had clean bills of health. He also knew that all three of them couldn't be so lucky. Not that he would wish their father's affliction on either of them. Of course not. But it stung just the same, seeing them with their picture-perfect lives and knowing the same wasn't in the cards for himself.

It was a good thing Emily's job only lasted until September. He would manage again after that. He'd put up with Cait coming and going and fussing. Getting closer to Emily wasn't an option, not when he'd just have to push her away again.

"That's all I want for Sam, too," Emily said softly. "He's essentially lost his father and his home and any place he's belonged. Kids do better in consistent environments. Yanking him from place to place isn't good for him. This is kind of like summer vacation for him. I know I've got to figure some things out and find us a more permanent situation."

"You're a good mother, Emily. Did you see his face today at the garden? He's having the time of his life. He's enjoying the outdoors, the freedom. And for all Liz's meddling, the twins are good girls. He could do worse for playmates. You're doing the right thing."

"I don't want him to get in your way, though. I know you have a farm to run. This thing about the tractor…don't feel obligated."

Luke blinked in surprise. What was it about the tractor? Was she worried he'd get hurt? Or did she just not trust him with her son? "Did I give you the idea I didn't like children, Emily?"

"Well, yes, kind of." A mosquito buzzed in front of Emily's face and she brushed it away. He couldn't tell if she were blushing or not because the heat kept her cheeks flushed, but he saw her shift her weight on the sawhorse and wondered.

"You weren't excited about the baby. In fact, you lamented the fact that the newest member of the family was another girl, and came right out and said you didn't want a family. Liz's kids were here today and you barely gave them a glance. You can't honestly say you want him underfoot," she challenged. "He would get in your way."

Luke stilled, feeling as if he'd been struck. Was it that obvious? Did Cait and Liz feel the same way? That he didn't care about their kids? He had kept his distance because it was a constant reminder of how different his life was. But he hadn't considered that they might feel slighted. Unloved. Regret sliced through him.

And he would die before explaining why to Emily. It was bad enough he'd said as much as he had.

"I never meant to give that impression. Of course there are times he needs to be at the house, but there's also no reason why he can't come with me now and again. He can play with Liz's kids. The Canada Day celebrations are soon. There'll be lots of activities for the kids. Has he ever ridden a horse?"

She shook her head.

"I'm not very good at showing my feelings, Emily. That's all. Don't take it personally."

"It is lovely here. The house is a joy and I'm loving the fresh air and freedom of it. I think Sam is, too. If he gets in the way, just tell me, Luke. He's my son, not yours. My responsibility. You don't need to feel like you have to...whatever."

Her words shouldn't have stung but they did. Yes, Sam was her son, and a reminder that Luke would never have one of his own. He would never burden a family the way he'd been burdened.

"Just enjoy the summer, Emily. Think about what you want to do when it's over. Just because I had to give up my dreams doesn't mean you have to give up yours."

The fluorescent lights hummed in the silence.

"I should go in, it's getting late."

Luke cleared his throat. "Your oil is definitely drained. I'll put on the new filter and be behind you in a few minutes." He boosted himself away from the hood of the car and reached for a plastic-wrapped cylinder on the workbench.

"Luke?"

"Yeah?"

"Could you show me how to do that sometime? How to change my oil and stuff? I'd like to be able to do it for myself."

After all they'd talked about tonight, the simple request was the thing that touched him most. She was so intent on being independent. And she trusted him. For some weird reason, she trusted him and it opened something up inside him that had been closed for a very long time.

"Next time we get a rainy day, I promise," he said. "Now get on up to the house. It's after eleven. And morning comes early."

"Yes, boss," she replied, but the tension from her face

had evaporated and she smiled as she picked up his plate and empty bottle. She paused by the door. "Luke?"

He looked up from his position on the creeper. "Em?"

"Thanks for the talk. I'll see you in the morning."

She scuttled out the door, but Luke leaned his head back, resting it on the grill of the car and closing his eyes.

Emily had snuck past almost all of his defenses tonight. And if he wasn't careful, she'd get through them all. And then where would they be?

Curses. Emily put one foot after the other going back to the house in the dark, the echo of a wrench sounding behind her in the stillness. His last word to her had been the shortened version of her name and it had sent a curl of awareness through her. She entered the dark house, left the dishes in the kitchen and felt her way up the steps, using the banister for guidance. In her room she paused, thinking about what had been said and what hadn't. Luke had held back at times, and she wondered why. Now she was more aware than ever that the two bedrooms were only short steps away from each other. She'd be beneath her sheet tonight, listening to the breeze in the trees, and he'd be just on the other side of the wall, doing the same thing.

Damn.

She could do this. She refused to fall for Luke Evans. Maybe they'd reached a new understanding of each other tonight, but that was all. She had to put Sam first, and that didn't include fooling around with the boss. What she needed to do was appreciate what was good about the situation. All the great things about living on a farm could be theirs for the next few months.

Then there was sitting across from Luke at the table, seeing his face morning, noon and night, washing his clothes, smelling the scent of his soap as she hung up his damp towel in the morning. She swallowed. That was the problem. She didn't want to be attracted to him, but she was. She couldn't not be. He was one-hundred-percent strong, virile male, hardworking and honest.

But attraction and acting on it were two very different things. As she lay in the dark, listening for him to return to the house, she thought about what he'd said about school. There was merit there. Perhaps she could talk to her parents after all. It would do Sam good to have family around him more as she got back on her feet. And with her summer's earnings she could buy a laptop and take a few courses.

She was still waiting and planning when she finally drifted off to sleep.

Luke squinted up at the sky, watching the broad roll of clouds balling up in the west. They were still a long way away, but as he wiped the sweat trickling off his brow, he knew they were thunderheads. The forecast had been right for once, though he wished it hadn't. He turned the wheel of the tractor, making one last pass with the rake, watching the Orrick boys work the baler. Hail would wreck what was cut, making it good for nothing. They'd finish, by God, before the rain came. They'd finish if it killed him.

It was a race against time and no one stopped for a lunch break as they worked, dirt mixing with sweat on their brows in the sweltering waves of heat. The thunderheads piled on top of each other, reaching to massive heights and creeping their way eastward to Brooks, Duchess and everywhere in between. He thought of Emily and Sam back at the house. He should have brought his cell. He had no doubt Em could handle a thunderstorm, but he would have liked to hear her voice, to make sure she wasn't out somewhere when the storm hit. To ask her if she'd brought in the hanging baskets. If Sam was okay.

He shook his head. When had he started to care so much? How was it that she snuck into his thoughts no matter where he was or what he was doing?

The thunder was just starting to grumble when the last bale was rolled. James and John Orrick took off their caps and wiped their foreheads, looking up at the sky. The sun still beat down relentlessly but it was coming. There was no sense denying it. "Just in time," James commented, putting his cap back on his head.

Luke scanned the field. The surface of the huge round bales would protect the hay on the inside. Nothing would be lost today. As long as it was just a thundershower. Tornadoes weren't common, but they happened now and again. And if he'd learned anything over the last nine years, it was that you simply had to accept the weather and roll with the punches. He thought of Emily and Sam again. They would be safe in the house. But he wanted to be home with them. To know they were there—warm and dry and safe. No matter how much he hadn't wanted the responsibility of them, he felt it anyway. It would have been easier if it felt like a burden, but it didn't. It felt right, and that was what had kept him up at night.

"Might as well head in, boys. Go home and shut your windows."

Everyone laughed, but it was a tight sound. The air had changed, bringing a shushing sound with it. It was a restless sound, like the wind holding its breath.

They made their way back to the farmyard. The hanging baskets were off the hooks and tucked under the porch roof, their leaves limp in the midday heat. So Emily was aware of the impending storm. Luke's stomach growled since he'd missed lunch, but at the same time a whicker sounded from the corral; Bunny and Fred and Caribou were still outside, nervous just like anyone else at the change in the air. Luke thought about letting them out into the pasture, but then scanned the clouds. If there was hail, he wanted them to be indoors. He forgot about lunch and went to put them in the barn, secured them in their stalls and soothed them with pats and fresh water. Back at the house, all was quiet. Sam was sitting at the table with a coloring book, scribbling busily at a picture of one of the latest superheroes.

Emily appeared at the dining-room door, smiling but he could see she was nervous underneath the cheerful exterior. "You're back. Did you finish?"

"Just." He turned his head towards the door. "You took down the baskets."

"Hard to miss that change in the air. I hope it's not bad. I'd hate for hail to take out the garden. Everything's just starting to come along. Not to mention crops. Do you think it'll be bad, Luke?"

He shrugged. "I hope not, but it's out of my hands. The hay's baled and the horses are in. That's about all I can do. Maybe it'll miss us altogether."

The tension left her face at his reassurances. "I wasn't sure when you'd be in. I made you a sandwich and put it in the fridge."

Luke knew Emily had never been a farm wife, so how was it she seemed to know exactly what he needed and when? He washed his hands and sank into a chair as exhaustion finally crept in now that he'd stopped. He'd been going flat-out for days now and not sleeping well at night. He hadn't visited his father in two weeks and felt guilty about it. He thought of Emily far too often and felt guilty about that as well. There was nothing to do right at this moment, though, and it all seemed to catch up with him. He drank a full glass of cool, reviving water before biting into the thick sandwich of sliced ham and cheese. As he swallowed the last bite, she quietly put a slice of rhubarb pie at his elbow.

"Thank you, Emily."

"You're welcome."

There was a low rumble of thunder in the distance, and the leaves of the poplars twisted in the breeze. He took his dirty dishes to the sink. The hot breeze from the open window hit him in the face. He closed his eyes.

"Hey, Em? I'm going to lie down for a few minutes."

She came to the door, holding a red crayon in her hand. "Are you feeling all right?"

He smiled. "Just tired. It's this heat. It just saps you."

"Okay."

He went to the living room and sank on to the plush cushions of the sofa, hanging his stocking feet over the arm. He closed his eyes. He'd get up in a few minutes, a short break was all he needed. His breaths deepened as he thought of all the little things Emily did, lifting his burdens and doing it with a smile. She had made the house like a home again, with voices and laughter and delicious smells.

It was just like it used to be, he thought as he drifted off to sleep. Like when Dad came in from a tough day and Mom met him with a kiss and a cup of coffee…

Emily heard the deep breaths coming from the living room and her hand paused, the crayon a few inches from the paper. Luke was plain worn out. She'd seen it in the dark circles beneath his eyes and the tired way he'd sunk into his chair in the kitchen. She watched Sam color a comic-book character in his coloring book and exhaled, wishing the sultry air would clear. It was close, suffocating. The leaves on the trees tossed and turned now, restless in the wind coming before the storm. The weather was as unsettled as she was. Calm on the surface but churning inside.

Emily paced a few minutes, coming to stop at the door to the living room. She looked down at Luke's face, relaxed in sleep. The scowl he wore so often was gone and his lips were open just the tiniest bit. He had long eyelashes for a man. She hadn't realized it before, but watching him sleep gave her the chance to really examine his face. He snuffled and turned his head, revealing a tiny scar just behind his left ear.

How could she make it through two more months of this if she already felt the tugs of attraction after a handful of days? There had been no repeats of the kissing scene. Not even a glance or small touch. And still he was on her mind constantly. When she lay in bed listening to the frogs or when she was mixing up batter or taking clothes off the line. She replayed the kiss over and over in her head, remembering what it was like to feel desirable. To feel her own longings, emotions she'd thought quite dead and buried. She was starting to trust Luke. The world was not full of Robs. Deep down she'd always known it, but it was easier to think that than to face the truth.

Emily swallowed. A cold puff of air came through the windows, the chill surprising her. It didn't take a genius to figure it out. She hadn't been enough to make Rob happy, and she wasn't sure she could survive failing again. She was tired of apologizing for it. He had been selfish leaving when they might have worked it out. He hadn't appreciated what he had…and now she looked down at Luke. Luke, who was so handsome he took her breath away. Luke, who had kissed her in the kitchen with his wide, strong hands framing her face and who said thank you for everything.

She turned away from Luke's sleeping form. It was impossible she was even *thinking* such a thing. She shook her head. Didn't she need to get Sam settled and her life in order first? Of course she did. She couldn't lose sight of the goal. Self-reliance came first. She'd made a promise to herself and she meant to keep it. And a promise to Sam. To even think of indulging herself in what—an affair? Luke wasn't interested in a relationship. In kids. He'd made it clear when he'd talked to her about what she was going to do when she left the ranch. Even entertaining the idea was selfish—thinking of herself rather than of what was best for Sam in the long run.

Emily had been so caught up in her thoughts that she hadn't noticed the room growing dark. What had been distant rumbling was now persistent, grumbling rolls of thunder. A flash went through the room, like a distant camera flash, and seconds later the thunder followed. She hurried to check on Sam, who had put down his crayons and stared at her with wide eyes.

"Boomers comin'?"

"I think so, honey."

Sam's dark eyes clouded with uncertainty. Her boy tried to be brave and strong, but she knew he hated thunderstorms. "Don't worry, okay? We're snug as a bug here."

Sam slid from his chair as another flash of lightning speared the sky. "I need to close the windows, Sam. It's starting to rain and I don't want things to get wet. You can come with me if you want."

But he shook his head, his hair flopping. "I'll stay here. I don't wanna go upstairs. Hurry back, Mommy."

Emily darted from room to room, shutting windows against the angry raindrops beginning to fall. Upstairs in Luke's room, the window stuck. She pushed down on the slider, making progress, but only in half-inch increments. The wind blew back the curtains, twisting them in her face as she struggled with the swollen window frame.

Just as it slid into the groove a fork of lightning jutted out of the sky, lighting up the whole house—followed by an astounding, foundation-shaking blast of thunder. The burst was so violent her heart seemed to leap and shudder before settling again into a quick, shocked rhythm.

She heard Sam scream and raced out of Luke's room to the stairs. She skidded into the dining room—no Sam. Emily pushed a hand through her hair, forcing her breath to calm. The bang had frightened her, too. "Sam?" she called, as another lightning strike and clap of thunder reverberated through the house.

"In here."

Luke's gravelly voice answered her from the living room.

She found them huddled together in a great walnut rocking chair. Luke's feet were planted square on the floor, and a terrified Sam was cradled in his arms, his bare feet resting on Luke's thigh as he curled up in Luke's lap. The strong arms she couldn't forget being around her now circled her son securely and the chair rocked ever so slightly.

The sight did something to her heart. It confirmed what she'd sensed at the beginning—Luke was a good, caring man hidden by a crusty exterior. He wasn't telling Sam that being afraid was silly or making him buck up, that it was only a little storm. He was simply holding him, comforting him. Rain started coming down in torrents now, hammering on the roof and windows so loudly it made a vibrating hum. Luke's gaze met hers, calm and accepting. Whether or not it made sense, Emily knew in that moment that this was where they were meant to be. This was where they would both put themselves back together before moving on.

"Sam," she said gently, "Mommy's here now. It's okay."

The storm raged around them, echoing through the house. Sam shook his head and only burrowed deeper into Luke's shirt.

"It's okay, Emily. He's fine where he is."

Had she really accused Luke of not liking children? The way he held Sam was strong and caring and sent a slice through her heart as sharp as a fork of lightning. Had Sam been missing the presence of a man in his life? At first she had thought it was just Rob he missed. But she could tell he missed having a man to look up to.

She knew after a year of struggling that she could do this on her own. But there was something about having Luke in her life right now that somehow divided the burden.

A terrific crash sounded, not thunder but sharper and harder, and Emily sank into a nearby chair, her hands shaking. Lightning had hit something and she didn't have the courage to peer out the window and see what. She heard Luke murmur something reassuring to Sam as his toe kept the chair in motion, rocking and soothing. Her son whom she loved more than life itself. And the man who was proving that the shell she'd built around her heart wasn't as tough as she thought.

At the same time, the house went strangely quiet as the power went out. The fridge stopped its constant hum and the clock on the DVD player went dark.

"Looks like we'll be grilling tonight," Luke said easily.

After several minutes the storm made its way east. Emily looked over at Sam. His head had drooped and Luke smiled. "He fell asleep about five minutes ago," Luke said.

"I can move him…"

"Leave him. He's comfortable."

He had to stop being so nice. It only made things more impossible. "Luke…surely you can see the problem. He already trusts you…"

"If he does, why can't you?"

"It's not that simple." She kept her voice a low murmur, needing Sam to stay asleep. "What happens in August when we have to leave, Luke? When he has to say goodbye to you? And this ranch? If he gets too attached, how can I pull him away? How can I do that to him again?"

"He's a smart kid. He knows this is temporary…"

"He's only five." She dug her fingers into the arm of the chair.

"He already loves being here," Luke argued. "So whether

you go now or in a few months, you may have that to deal with anyway." He gave her a knowing look. "Or are we not talking about Sam here? I think it's you. You don't want to get attached to this place. Because you like it here."

"Of course I do…"

"And saying goodbye will be…"

She imagined driving away and watching Luke get smaller in her rearview mirror. After only a few days, she knew she'd miss him.

"I'm a big girl. I know how the world works."

"You sure do."

Sam let out a delicate snore. Luke's lips curved and then he lifted his head, sharing the smile with Emily.

Something clicked inside her. Suddenly it wasn't about protecting her heart from Luke anymore. He'd already breached the walls. She was in perilous danger of caring for him, truly and deeply caring.

She sat for a few moments, wanting to snatch Sam away from the security of Luke's arms, knowing it was foolish and petty. She should have foreseen she'd get in too deep.

But this job could give her the start she needed. She only had to keep the goal firm in her mind—a temporary retreat to regroup and then move forward. If she did that, it would all be fine.

She would enjoy every blessed minute she could, she decided. She'd be here when the beans ripened and the pea pods popped in the sunshine. Sam could maybe go for that horseback ride—maybe they both would. She could spend an hour on the porch with a paperback while Sam played.

When she looked back at Luke, his lips had dropped open as he dozed off, too. Seeing them sleeping together made her feel as though she was losing Sam, even as her head told her it was a ridiculous thought.

She had spent months worrying about the lack of a male

influence in Sam's life. Now that he had it, she wasn't sure she could resist the man—the real live cowboy, as Sam put it—who was putting stars in both their eyes.

CHAPTER NINE

FOR THE NEXT week Emily, Sam and Luke settled into a routine. Luke spent his days working the fields and Emily did the hottest work in the mornings. In the afternoon she ran errands or took time out to play with Sam, roaming the extensive yard looking for wildflowers and animal tracks. Luke made an effort to arrive for dinner and they all ate together. And as the sun sank below the prairie, Emily listened to the peepers and the breeze through the open windows of her bedroom. Luke was right next door and often she lay awake at night knowing the head of his bed was only a wall away. What was he thinking as his head lay on the pillow? There was a sense of comfort that came from knowing he was so close, but she wondered what to do with the attraction that kept simmering between them.

Because it *was* simmering. He hadn't touched her again. There hadn't been any more kisses. But the memory of the first kiss always seemed to hover between them, and every time she looked at him she felt the same jolt running from her heart down to the soles of her feet. It stood between them like an unanswered question. The only thing Emily could do was focus on her job. Feelings, attraction…it was all secondary right now. She had to keep her eye on the prize—self-reliance. She would need Luke's recommendation when she went job-hunting at the end of the summer, and she wouldn't do anything foolish to jeopardize it.

One mild evening Luke took Sam for a walk around the corral on Bunny's back, getting him used to the feel of the horse before letting Sam take the reins himself. After that, Sam was permanently smitten with both Luke and with the mare. It was all he talked about as he helped in the garden or dried the dishes, standing on a stepstool. He visited with Liz's twins one afternoon while Emily shopped for groceries. Emily had a look at the old record player and thought she might have a go at fixing it up. The cabinet was filled with old LPs. What would it be like to hear the scratchy albums again?

They all slipped into the routine so easily that it felt, to Emily at least, a little too real.

Then Luke came home with Homer.

At first Emily just heard the barking and she wrinkled her brow. Had a neighbor's dog strayed into the yard? Her heart set up a pattering, as she knew Sam would be paralyzed with fear. He'd never quite gotten over his fear of dogs since he'd nearly been attacked. She dried her hands on a tea towel and headed for the door.

Sam was making a beeline for the porch, his normally flushed cheeks pale. Emily scooped him up as Luke approached, holding a leash in his hand attached to a brown-and-white dog that limped behind.

Luke paused several feet away from the steps. Sam was clearly afraid of the new pup. It showed in the pallor of his face and how he clung to his mother.

"Sam, this is Homer."

No response. Luke's heart sank. He'd seen the dog weeks ago and had fallen in love. Oh, he knew that sounded ludicrous, but he had a soft spot for dogs and especially one like Homer, who needed a home so badly. But Homer had been in no shape to be adopted and in the hectic pace of haying season, it had gone to the back of Luke's mind. Until the veterinarian had called a few days ago. Luke had thought of Sam, too. He'd thought Homer could be a playmate. He hadn't thought about the boy being afraid.

"You don't have anything to fear from Homer," Luke said easily. He put his hand on Homer's back and the dog sat, his tongue hanging out happily. "He's the gentlest dog you'll ever meet."

Sam shook his head and clung to Emily even tighter. Luke noticed the shine of tears in her eyes and resisted the urge to sigh. He had to help the boy. Had to show him he didn't need to be afraid. He wasn't sure why, but he knew that it was important to help Sam overcome this hurdle. Maybe because he saw in Sam's eyes what he'd seen too often in his own—knowledge and understanding. Even at such a young age, Sam had been hurt and had grown—painfully—because of it. Luke couldn't fix that. But maybe he could make this better.

"We had an incident in the park last year," Emily said quietly. "Someone had their dog off leash and it started to go at Sam. I reached out and grabbed its collar." She looked down at Luke with liquid chocolate eyes. "He's been terrified ever since."

Homer whined and Luke heard distressed sounds coming from Sam's throat.

"Homer, hush."

Luke gave the firm order and the dog immediately quieted. He squatted down and put his hand on the brown-and-white fur. "Stay." He dropped the leash. Then he stood, went to Emily, reached out and touched Sam's back.

"Look at him now, Sam. Harmless as a flea." He spoke softly to the boy, knowing a gentle and steady touch was required. Sam obediently turned his head and looked at the mutt, whose tongue was hanging out in happy bliss as he panted.

Luke couldn't accomplish putting Sam at ease while he

had a death grip on his mother. "Come here, buddy," he said, and he lifted Sam right out of her arms and settled him on his hip. He half expected Sam to cry and reach for Emily, but he didn't. Knowing Sam trusted him did something to Luke's insides, something warm and expansive. Luke pointed at the dog. "Do you know what's special about Homer?"

Sam shook his head.

Luke looked over at Emily and smiled, hoping to thaw the icy wall that had suddenly formed around her. "Homer had an accident a while back. He's been at the vet's, because he was a stray and no one claimed him. A few weeks ago he was still wrapped up in bandages. You never saw a sorrier sight than that dog. He didn't even bark. He just looked up at me with his big, sad eyes."

He shifted his gaze to Sam, pleased that he had the boy's full attention. Sam's eyes were wide, listening to Luke retell the story. "Now he's healed up, but because he was hurt so badly, no one has given him a home." Luke paused, wondering if he should explain what fate would have befallen Homer had he not brought him home. "He isn't perfect, you see. But I think it doesn't matter if someone isn't perfect, don't you?"

Sam nodded. "Mama says everyone makes mistakes."

Luke swallowed. This was what he'd tried to avoid for so long, why he kept his nieces at arm's length. He was afraid of caring, and he'd been right. Holding Sam this way, hearing his sweet voice talk about his mama only reminded Luke of his vow to not have children of his own. How could he be so selfish, knowing he could pass his genes on to another generation? How could he have a family, knowing they might have to go through what he'd already suffered?

But the longing was there. It was there when he held Sam, and it was there when he looked at Emily, and if he wasn't careful it could have the power to break him.

He cleared his throat. "Dogs aren't that different from

people, you know. Give them a full belly and a little love and they're pretty contented."

Sam's shoulders relaxed and his gaze focused on Luke's face. Luke's gaze, however, fell on Emily. The ice in her gaze had melted and she was looking at him in a way that made his heart lift and thump oddly against his ribs. Lord, she was beautiful. Those big eyes that seemed to reach right in and grab a man by the pride. He realized he'd been holding his breath and staring a little too long, so he looked away and shifted Sam's weight on his hip.

"Homer won't hurt you. I promise. The biggest danger to you is that he might lick you to death." With an unprotesting Sam on his arm, he knelt before the dog. He stroked the fur reassuringly and Homer stretched a little, loving the attention. Still, Luke didn't force the issue, just let Sam watch his fingers in the dog's fur.

Sam's eyes were wide as he touched the soft coat. Soaking in the attention, Homer rolled over on to his back and presented his belly to be scratched.

That was when Sam noticed, and it all came together.

"He only has three legs!"

"Yep." Luke gave Homer's belly a scratch and the dog twisted with pleasure. "Doesn't slow him down much, though, does it? The vet told me he fetches tennis balls and who knows, maybe he can help me round up cattle if I can train him right. If you squat down like me, and hold out your hand, he can smell you. That's how you say hello."

Luke made Homer sit again and was beyond pleased when Sam followed his calm instructions. He balanced on his toes and held out his fingers, but when Homer moved to sniff he pulled them back.

Luke reassured him, wanting him to try again. They'd come this far. To stop now would mean two steps back. And Sam could do it. Luke knew he was just timid and that the worst of the fear was gone. Sam and Homer would be friends. He couldn't give the kid back what he'd lost, but he could give him this companion.

"Watch." He held out his hand and Homer gave a sniff and a lick. "Want to try again?"

He held out his fingers and Homer sniffed, licked and gave a thump of his tail.

"Give him this," Luke suggested, standing and reaching into his pocket. He took out a small dog biscuit and handed it to Sam. "Put it flat in your hand, and tell him to be gentle."

"H-Homer, gentle," Sam said, holding out his hand. Luke could see it trembled a bit, but Homer daintily took the treat and munched.

"See?"

"I did it!" Sam turned to his mother and beamed. "I did it, Mom!"

Emily smiled. "You sure did, baby," she replied. Homer barked and Sam jumped, his eyes wide again, but Luke chuckled. "That's just his way of saying thank-you," he said. He reached into his denim jacket and took out a rubber ball. "Homer, fetch," he commanded, tossing the ball, and the dog was up and off in a flash.

"Why don't you play fetch with him for a bit, Sam? Then I can talk to your mother."

Sam moved off with the dog and Luke looked up at Emily.

"I didn't know he was afraid."

"I wish you had asked, Luke. When I heard the barking, and saw Sam's face..."

"I'm sorry, Emily. Homer's been at the vet's for weeks and I couldn't stand to see him put down. Not when I could give him a good home. And I thought Sam would love him. Especially after all he's had to give up."

Was that a sheen of tears he detected in her eyes? His heart took up the odd thumping again.

"What you just did...that was great. Sam's been timid around dogs for months. Every time we meet a new dog, it's the same thing..."

Luke exhaled and smiled, until he heard the word *but*.

"But what happens when we leave, Luke? Homer is one more thing he will have to leave behind. Did you think of that?"

He hadn't, but he realized now he should have. "Take him with you."

But that was the wrong thing to say. "Take him with us? I don't know if he'd be welcome at my parents', and if Sam and I get an apartment...not everyone will accept pets. Then what happens when I'm gone to work and Sam is at school?"

Luke knew she was right. He climbed the steps and went to stand before her, needing her to understand. "Obviously I didn't think it through as well as I should have."

"I don't know how much more I can take away from him," she whispered, and he heard the catch in her voice.

He put his hand on her arm, feeling her warm skin beneath his rough fingers. "You are not taking anything away, Em. You give to him constantly. You give him love and acceptance and security. He is lucky to have you as a mother."

"You're just trying to get around me." She sniffled a little and looked away from him, but he put a finger under her chin and made her look back.

"Maybe." He felt the beginnings of a smile as he confessed. "If you'd seen Homer there, Em. He was skin and bones and bandages. Look what some love and attention accomplished. How could I just leave him there? I couldn't. I'm sorry for causing you problems, though."

"First me and Sam, now Homer. You do have a way of picking up strays, don't you?"

"Hey, you found me."

The sound of Sam's laughter drifted up over the porch and everything seemed to move in slow motion. Emily looked up into his eyes and he was helpless. "I guess I did," she murmured, and it was all he could do to keep from kissing her the way he'd been wanting to for days.

But what would it accomplish? Nothing had changed. And he wouldn't play games. It was bad enough his heart was getting involved. Acting on it was another matter entirely. It would get messy. People would get hurt. And he was kidding himself if he thought it was only Sam and Emily who'd pay the price.

Because ever since their arrival, *he*'d felt like the stray who'd been taken in. And he didn't like that feeling. He didn't like it at all.

They went to the Canada Day celebrations on the first of July and Emily finally met Luke's sister Cait and baby Janna. Unlike Liz and her bubbly nosiness, Cait was more reserved, with a warm, new-mother contented smile. Liz and her husband Paul were there with the girls, who tugged Sam along to the various games. They all ate cotton candy and hot dogs dripping with ketchup and mustard and as darkness finally fell, the three of them joined Cait, Joe, Liz, Paul and the kids on some spread-out blankets to watch the fireworks. It was impossible not to feel like a family. Like someone who belonged here. She knew it wasn't so, but it didn't stop the wishing. It would be foolish to imagine things were more than they seemed, but Emily wondered if some day she might find this somewhere, with someone.

The trouble was, she couldn't envision it at all. It was only Luke she saw in her mind and that fact bothered her more than she wanted to admit.

Emily sat cross-legged on the rough blanket, looking down

at Sam and watching his sleepy eyes droop while he valiantly struggled to keep them open. It was well past his bedtime, but he had wanted to stay and she didn't have the heart to say no. His head was cradled in her lap and she smoothed his hair away from his forehead as twilight deepened and the crowd gathered, waiting for the pyrotechnics show.

"He's tired."

Luke kept his voice low and spoke close to her ear, so close she felt the heat rise in her cheeks as the rest of her body broke out in goose bumps.

"He wouldn't miss this for the world."

"Neither would I."

Emily turned her head the slightest bit, surprised by how close Luke was when her temple nearly grazed his jaw. She knew he could be talking about the fireworks or visiting with neighbors or simply being there with his sisters and family. But Emily wanted to believe he meant being there with her and with Sam. How many times over the last week had they all been together and she'd felt the tug? A sense of déjà vu, knowing this had never happened before?

"Luke, I..." She didn't know how to tell him what was in her heart. There were times when she even felt guilty for taking a wage for the work she was doing. Not because what she did wasn't of value, but because she knew very well she was getting more than financial gain out of it. Sam was happy, she was happy, and she hadn't expected to be, not for a very long time.

There was a bang and the first jet of sparks flew upwards. Emily turned her head to the fireworks display as Sam sat bolt upright and exclaimed at the blue and purple cascade flowering in the sky. Emily heard Sam's name called and nudged him as Liz's twins gestured wildly for him to join them on their blanket just ahead. "Go on," she smiled. "You can watch with the girls. I'm right here."

Sam scooted up to the next blanket, leaving Emily alone with Luke.

Darkness formed a curtain and everyone's eyes were fixed on the dazzling display in the sky while Emily's heart thundered. Luke shifted on the blanket, moving behind her so that she could lean back against his strong shoulder to watch. She could smell the aftershave on his neck, feel the slight stubble of his chin as it rested lightly against her temple. One after another the explosions crested and expanded, a rainbow of colors, but all Emily could think about was Luke and how close he was. If he turned his head the slightest bit...if she turned hers...

His fingertips touched her cheek, and she turned her face towards the contact. Her heart stuttered when she discovered him watching her, unsmiling, his blue eyes fathomless in the dark of the evening, reflecting the bursts of fireworks but focused solely on her. Her mouth went dry, afraid he was going to kiss her and wanting him to so badly she thought she might die from it.

"Em."

In the din of the explosions she didn't hear him say her name but she saw it on his lips. Locking her gaze with his, she let herself lean more into his shoulder, the only invitation she dared permit herself. It was all he needed. His gaze burned into her for one last second before dropping to her mouth. His fingers slid slowly over her chin to cup her jaw, cradling the curve in the palm of his hand. And finally, when she thought she would surely burst into flames, he kissed her.

His lips were warm and mobile, skilled and devastating. As Emily clung to his arm with her hand, she realized that there was never anything tentative with Luke. He was always strong, always sure of himself, and it took her breath away. He was always in control, and she wondered, quite dazzled, what it would take to make him lose that control? To lose it with her?

The finale began with rapid bursts of color crashing into the air. Emily's fingers dug into the skin of his arm, and she felt the vibrations of a moan in his throat as the kiss intensified, making everything in her taut with excitement and desire.

A final bang and gasp and then there was nothing but applause from the crowd.

Luke gentled the kiss, tugging at her bottom lip with his teeth before moving away, making her whole body ache with longing. His gaze was still on her, but there was something different in it now. Heat. And, Emily thought, confusion.

She looked past him to the crowd and was mortified to see Liz, Cait and their husbands watching. Liz's mouth had dropped open and Cait's soft eyes were dark with concern. Joe and Paul simply had goofy smiles on their faces. Emily looked past them, afraid that Sam had seen the sparks going off behind him rather than above, but he and the girls were still chattering excitedly about which bursts had been their favorites and the horrendous noise.

She scrambled to her feet and straightened her blouse. Luke took his time, getting to his feet and gathering the corner of the blanket to fold it. Emily grabbed the other side to help. She had to keep her hands busy. Avoid the assessing looks from Luke's family. Why had she let herself be carried away?

But she'd created another problem. Holding her side of the blanket meant folding it into the middle, which meant meeting Luke face-to-face. There was the silent question as which of them would take the woolen fabric to fold again. Emily dropped it, letting Luke fold it into a square.

Cait and Joe took the stroller and said goodbye, but Liz—bless her—acted as if nothing had happened and stopped to ask if Sam was going to day camp in the morning. Emily, Luke and Sam followed along back to the parking lot. Sam's feet started to drag, so Luke lifted him effortlessly on his shoulders and carried him to the truck.

Sam fell asleep on the drive home.

Emily couldn't bring herself to say anything to Luke. She didn't want to ask why. She didn't want to analyze it. She was terrified to ask what it meant or if it would happen again. The radio played a quiet country-and-Western tune and she stared out the window at the inky sky and the long, flat fields shadowed by the moon. When they reached the house, Emily was first to hop out and she took Sam in her arms.

"I need to get him into bed," she whispered, unable to meet Luke's gaze. He didn't protest or stop her. They both knew she was running away from what had happened. Her arms ached under Sam's weight—when had he grown so much?—and she was out of breath by the time she got to the top of the stairs. When she finally had him tucked between the sheets, she paused. The light was on in the kitchen. Luke was waiting for her, she knew it. She hesitated, her hand on the smooth banister. If she went down, they'd have to talk, and she was afraid to talk. She was afraid of spoiling the balance they'd achieved so effortlessly during the past week. She was afraid they'd stop talking, that he'd kiss her again. And she was afraid it would go further. Much further. She imagined him carrying her to his room, imagined feeling his skin against hers….

No, it was too much. So much more than she was prepared to give. To accept.

So she went into her own room and shut the door, biting her lip as she changed into her nightgown and slid between the soft cotton sheets.

Several minutes later she heard him turn off the light as he stopped waiting. His slow steps echoed on the stairs, creaking on the tread third from the top. The steps paused beside her door as her heart pounded with fear and, Lord help her, anticipation.

Then the steps went away and she heard him go into his room. Muffled sounds as he shed his clothing—she swallowed—and the sound of the mattress settling as he got in bed, his head only inches from hers, and yet so far away.

She lay awake for a long time, replaying the kiss, listening for his footsteps, and wondering what it was she wanted—if she even knew anymore.

The morning sun was high when Luke stopped to survey the herd below. Caribou's chestnut hide gleamed in the summer sun and the gelding tossed his head, anxious to get going again. Luke had taken the morning to check fence lines of the north pasture now that he and the hands had moved the herd east to graze on fresh grass. He could have done it on the quad, but he was a horse man at heart. Spending a morning in the saddle had sounded perfect at 7:00 a.m. when the dew was still heavy on the grass.

It had given him ample time to think.

Caribou shifted restlessly and Luke let him go, moving into a trot to the dirt lane that ran between sections. What the horse needed was a good run, a chance to burn off some energy. Luke could use it, too. He was wound tighter than a spring, and it was all due to Emily. Emily with her shiny mink hair and big eyes. Emily with her soft smiles and even softer skin. His fingers tightened on the reins. He'd been a damned fool last night, kissing her at the fireworks. It was bad enough it was in public, but with his family there? It was as good as putting a stamp on her as far as they were concerned.

And that wasn't his intention. Not at all. His sisters would pester him to death wondering what was going on. If Emily was "the one". It didn't matter that he'd made it clear there would never be a Mrs. Luke Evans. It was just better that way. He never wanted to saddle a wife with an invalid.

A yellow-headed blackbird bobbed in the bushes as he passed. What had been his intention, then? Why hadn't he just left Emily alone and kept his lips to himself? He'd asked himself that question all morning and had yet to come up with an answer. What did he want from Emily? Things had not changed. It would be pointless to start anything up knowing it could go nowhere.

He was right back to where he'd started—a fool. A fool to get so wrapped up in her that he'd given in to his wants and kissed her without thinking of the repercussions. Now she wasn't even talking to him. She'd scooted up to bed last night and had avoided him this morning with the excuse of getting Sam ready for day camp. All-business Emily. She'd made her feelings perfectly clear. It was better this way, but it made him snarly just the same.

The gate was up ahead. He slowed Caribou to a walk and squinted. Emily was coming through the gap, all long, tanned legs in beige shorts and a red T-shirt. His body gave a little kick seeing her waiting for him. Her hair glinted with surprising red tints but he couldn't see her eyes behind her sunglasses. He didn't need to. He could see by the tense set of her shoulders and the line of her lips that something was wrong.

He gave the horse a nudge and cantered to the gate where she was waiting, pulling up in a cloud of dust. It had to be important if she'd come all the way out here to find him.

"What is it? What's happened?"

She looked up at him and took off her glasses.

His stomach did a slow turn. The chocolate depths of her eyes were more worried than he'd seen them. "Is it Sam?"

His question seemed to break through and she shook her head. "No, no it's not Sam. He's still at day camp with the twins." She peered up at him, hesitated, then said gently, "It's your father, Luke."

His father. All his energy seemed to sink to his feet, making them heavy but the rest of him oddly numb. "Is he gone?" His voice sounded flat and he had the strange thought that for just a few moments the birds had stopped singing in the underbrush.

"No. But Liz called and they want you to come."

Relief struck, automatically followed by dread. He had known something like this was coming and had buried himself in work to avoid thinking about it. Dad was getting frailer by the day, and it had been nearly ten years since he had gone into the home—a long time for someone with his disease. Luke knew the facts. But it didn't make it any easier.

"Okay."

"Luke?"

He stared down at her. She was biting her lip and he watched as the plump pink flesh changed shape as her teeth worried the surface.

"You don't look so good, Luke."

He didn't feel so great either.

"What can I do to help you?"

He realized that she'd walked all the way out from the house in the July heat to find him. He held out a hand. "Get on. We'll double up going back to the house."

"But I…I can't get up there."

"Sure you can. I'll take my foot out of the stirrup. Give me your hand and swing up."

A brief look of consternation overtook her face and he felt his annoyance grow. Was she so turned off by his presence that she couldn't stand to touch him now? He held out his hand. "Come on, Emily. It's the fastest way back to the house. I need to get to town."

She put her foot in the stirrup and clasped his forearm,

taking a bounce and swinging her leg over the saddle so that she was shoehorned in behind him. The stirrups were too long for her now and Luke slid the toes of his boots back through as he slid an inch forward, giving her more room. Even so, they were spooned together and he felt every shift of her body torturing him as Caribou started off at a walk.

He swallowed tightly. It had to be bad if Liz had phoned in the middle of the day.

"Where's Sam?" It didn't escape his notice that Sam was absent.

"Day camp, remember?"

He hadn't remembered, and he felt a spark of panic before telling himself to exhale and relax. It had only been a momentary thing and he was distracted. He swiveled in the saddle, half turning to meet her gaze. "Right. You would never have left him alone. I know that."

He faced front again, frowning. Emily might know about his father but she hadn't put the other pieces together. The lists, the precise order. It was all there for a reason. Just because he'd forgotten about day camp didn't mean anything except he had other things on his mind.

And yet there was always that little bit of doubt.

Her hand rested lightly on his ribs, an additional point of connection. What would it feel like for her to put her arms around him and hold him close? He wished he could know, but it was better if he didn't. He knew she still didn't understand what it all meant—to his father, to this ranch, to him. And he didn't want to explain. Right now he just needed to get to the nursing home. To see his father, the shell of a man he remembered. To hope that it was not too late.

And maybe, just maybe…there was always the forlorn hope that his dad might even recognize him one more time.

"Hang on," he said. And when her arms snaked around his middle, holding on, he felt his heart surge as he spurred the gelding into a canter and hastened their way home.

CHAPTER TEN

EMILY WRAPPED HER arms around Luke's waist, feeling the steel waves of pain and resentment binding him up in one unreachable package. His strong thighs formed a frame for hers as they headed for the farmyard and barns. She wished she could be out riding with him under different circumstances. A pleasure ride, stopping beneath the shade of a poplar or walking along the irrigation canal. She wanted the Luke of last night back, even as much as that man frightened her with the force of her feelings. The man she clung to now was in pain. She knew how that felt, and she wished she could take it away, make it better for him somehow.

He slowed the horse to a walk when the barn was in view, letting Caribou cool down. Emily said nothing as she dismounted and then he hopped down beside her. Silently they worked, removing bridle and saddle and Emily slid the blanket from the gelding's back and draped it over a rail in the tack room. He turned Caribou out into the corral and locked the gate, still saying absolutely nothing. Emily was beginning to worry. She didn't want him going to town alone. When he was about to head for the truck, she stopped him with a hand on his arm.

"Wait. We'll take my car."

"I don't want you to go."

The clipped words were not unexpected, but they stung just

the same. He had not let her in since she'd arrived at the gate so now was no different. She knew that. She also knew he needed help. Whether he realized it or not, he'd been there for her when she needed it most. She would return the favor.

"Liz is there and someone will have to pick up the kids at day camp. And you're in no shape to drive. So shut up and this once let someone do something for you."

She stood her ground, staring him down and watched him struggle. Didn't he think she could see how he always took care of everyone else? She wasn't blind. Married or not, his sisters still turned to him when they needed him. And he was there. Seeing his face when she'd told him about his dad had been all she needed. Someone had to be there for Luke.

"We're only wasting time," she said, quieter now, but no less sure of herself.

"We'll take your car but I'm driving." He gave in with a terse nod.

She could agree to that, so long as he wasn't alone. "Give me two seconds to grab my purse and keys," she replied, already dashing to the house. Liz had sounded tearful on the phone. Emily didn't want to think the worst, but she was sure that that was what Luke was thinking and getting him there as soon as possible would be best for everyone.

Liz and Cait were waiting outside the nursing home, sitting on a bench surrounded by petunias and geraniums. Baby Janna was asleep, bundled in a carrier and Liz's youngest was in a stroller, playing with a bar of brightly colored toys hooked along the top. When Luke strode up the walk, Liz rose and went to him, wrapping her arms around his neck. Cait was slower getting to her feet but when she went to Luke, he opened an arm and she slid in beneath it.

Emily blinked back tears for the trio who bonded amid so much pain. In the absence of parents, Luke had been their father figure even if he'd only been a few years older. Seeing them through to adulthood must have been so difficult, but he had done what needed to be done. Emily hung back, watching Luke give his sisters a squeeze and then asking the difficult question: "How bad?"

Liz was sniffling and Cait had to answer. "He fell last night. Nothing is broken, but the doctor says…"

Luke waited.

"He says it's time for palliative care, Luke."

Pain slashed across Luke's face, but he stood strong. "We knew this day would come, Cait."

"It doesn't make it easier."

"I know it. I want to talk to the doctor."

Emily felt so very in the way. Luke didn't need her. He had his sisters. This was a family problem and she wasn't family. Still, there had to be something she could do to help. They all needed to be with their father. She stepped up and searched Luke's eyes, then Liz's.

"I'm so sorry about your father. Is there anything I can do?"

Luke shook his head. "Thank you for asking, Emily." He seemed to think for a minute, and then leaned over and dropped a kiss on her cheek. "You've already helped so much."

Emily's cheek burned where his lips had touched it, even if it had been an impersonal peck. She had a sudden idea and turned to Liz. "Why don't you let me pick up the twins? Then you can stay as long as you need."

Liz's face relaxed and Emily felt Luke's hand at her back, a gentle contact that told her she'd said the right thing.

"If you do, take them back to my house. Paul's gone to Medicine Hat but he'll be back later to take over. It would be a godsend, Emily."

"You need to be with your father, Liz. You all do. I can

take Alyssa, too. It's no trouble. You just do what needs to be done."

Liz gave her the house key and got the car seat out of her car while Luke wrote directions to Liz's house on a slip of paper. When the baby was installed in the seat and buckled safely in, Luke stayed behind.

"Em, I don't know how to thank you." He braced a hand along the window of the open door of her car.

"It's not necessary, Luke. I'm happy to do it. Otherwise I'd just feel helpless."

"Helpless?"

How could she explain that Luke—and his family—had come to mean so much to her? That seeing him hurting caused her to have pain as well? They'd known each other such a short time. Her mother had always said she had a heart as big as all outdoors. It kept getting her into trouble. She felt things too deeply.

"You know, sitting around, waiting for news. At least this way I feel useful." She looked up, discovered he was watching her with a curious expression and dropped her lashes again before she gave away too much. "You should go. See your dad and talk to the doctor. I'll catch up with you later."

"You're right," he replied, shutting the car door as she buckled her seatbelt.

She drove away, only looking in the rearview mirror once and saw Luke going through the doors with his sisters. She was glad she could help, but she would rather be with him, sitting by his side.

But he didn't want that or else he would have asked. He hadn't even wanted her to come along. As she turned down a quiet street, she blinked a few extra times to clear the stinging. She was glad now that she hadn't gone downstairs last night.

She was falling in love with Luke Evans, and hearing him say he'd made a mistake would be more than she could take.

Paul and Liz returned just after seven-thirty. Emily had fed the kids and the twins were curled up with Sam on the sofa watching a movie—the girls in pink pajamas and Sam in the spare sweats and T-shirt that he'd carried in his backpack to camp. Alyssa was sweet-smelling from her bath and Emily nuzzled the baby's neck lightly, inhaling the scent of baby lotion as she prepared an evening bottle. Caring for four had been busy, but fun. The laughter, the pandemonium—they were things that had been missing from Emily's house, having had an only child. She had reconciled herself to knowing that the large family she'd wanted would never happen. Now she wondered if she might find a second chance someday. She had to get her life in order first, but she realized her heart was not as closed to the idea as it had once been. After her divorce, she'd been so determined never to go down that road again. Never to put Sam in the position of getting hurt. And yet here she was. And for a moment she wondered if rekindling those dreams meant she was putting her own wants ahead of the needs of her son. How did that make her any different from Rob, who had chosen his own dream ahead of his wife and son?

As she sat in a rocker and fed Alyssa, she banished the uncomfortable idea and turned her thoughts back to Luke. She couldn't stop wondering about his father and what the doctor said. How was Luke holding up? She lifted the baby to her shoulder and began rubbing her back just as Liz and Paul drove into the yard. Em's heart did a little rollover as they came in the back door. Liz looked so weary, even as she greeted Emily and smiled.

"Thank you, Emily, for watching the kids. It means so much that I could stay with Cait and Luke and Dad today."

Emily's lips curved wistfully when Alyssa put her chubby arms out for her mother and Paul went into the living room to check on the older kids. She missed the feeling of the baby's weight on her arm, and her heart warmed when Alyssa tucked her head against her mother's neck, utterly contented as she stuck two fingers in her mouth.

"It was no trouble. The kids had fun, I think. I just made spaghetti for supper. There are leftovers in the fridge for you and Paul if you're hungry. I wasn't sure if you'd have a chance to eat."

Liz's eyes filled with tears as her fingers stroked the baby's hair. "Oh, Emily, you really are wonderful. I hope you don't mind me saying… Cait and I both hope you're here to stay more permanently."

Emily's heart ached. Staying meant staying with Luke and despite last night's kiss she knew it was impossible. "My plans are still the same, Liz. But I'll be here until the end of the summer. Hopefully things will have normalized with your father by then."

"That's not what I meant," Liz said, settling Alyssa on her arm. "After last night…"

"Don't read too much into it," Emily replied lightly, though butterflies went through her stomach as the memory danced through her mind. "It was just a kiss." A kiss that hadn't been mentioned again. It was almost as if it had never happened. As if neither of the kisses had happened now that Emily thought of it. And yet, at the time they had been heart-stoppingly intimate… The way Luke looked at her, as though she was the only woman on earth. The way his fingers touched her face. She hadn't imagined the connection between them. But they had just been caught in the moment. They had to be, for him to become so distant afterwards.

"I don't think it was just a kiss."

Emily needed to change the subject and while Liz and her

husband were back home—together—Emily wondered about Luke. "Is Luke still at the home?" she asked, busying herself with putting the children's dirty glasses in the dishwasher.

"Yes, he wanted to stay with Dad."

Alone. Emily felt annoyance niggle at her. Didn't his sisters realize that Luke needed support, too? Someone should be with him. Liz and Cait didn't have to go through this alone— why should Luke?

He needed her. She wished she were stronger. She wished she could stay emotionally uninvolved. That was her problem—she let herself feel too deeply. Her heart twisted as she realized he'd supported her at a time she needed it most. She couldn't turn her back on him. But there was Sam to think of, too. She wasn't sure the care home was the place for him, not at such a time. "I'll go pick him up," Emily said, reaching for her purse. "Can I come back and pick up Sam later?"

The sound of laughter at a song in the movie echoed from the living room. Liz's keen eyes watched her closely, but for once Emily didn't care what she thought. "Why don't you let him stay here? He can have a sleepover with the girls. We've got an air mattress and sleeping bag and it'll be fun. After what you did for me today—it's the least we can do. He can go to camp with the girls in the morning and you can pick him up after."

It was a perfect solution. "If you're sure…"

"Of course I'm sure. Don't be silly."

Emily settled everything with Sam, who was overjoyed and not the least bit apprehensive about spending the night away from her.

The evening had mellowed, losing the July glare and settling into a hazy, rosy sunset as Emily drove back to the nursing home. Inside, all was quiet. Her shoes made soft sounds on the polished floor. Dialogue from a television turned low murmured from a common room and the hushed voices of staff kept the place from feeling totally empty. She got the room number from an attendant and walked down a quiet hall. When she got to the correct room on the right she peeked around the doorway.

Luke was sitting in a chair beside the hospital bed, leaning forward with his elbows on his knees, the very picture of defeat. The blinds were closed and the only light came from a tiny lamp in the corner. There was no movement from the man beneath the white-and-blue sheets, but Emily could see that Luke had his father's hand folded within his own. There were tears on Luke's face; silent ones, leaving a broken, shining trail down his tanned cheeks, and he lifted his father's hand to his lips and kissed it.

Emily backed out of the room and leaned back against the wall, pulling in a shaking breath as she struggled to hold on to her composure. Luke was the strong one. Luke didn't show emotion. The man who handled everything without complaint was *crying*.

She closed her eyes. Everything slid into place, but it wasn't a comfortable feeling. She had fallen in love. It was unexpected and unwanted, but it was undeniable. She had been attracted to him from the beginning—to his strength, to his kindness, to his generosity. But it was this human side of him, the part that crumbled apart with his father's hand in his, that toppled her over the edge. Perhaps it was the sense that he had so much love to give but spent his life alone. Or perhaps it was sensing that he needed love so desperately. That he was hungry for it and would rather starve than ask for it.

Where it would lead she had no idea, nor was tonight the time to worry about it. Tonight, other things were more important. Like the fact that Luke was alone in there. His sisters had gone home to their husbands and families, but Luke had stayed. Who was there for him? To whom could he unburden himself at the end of the day? She'd told Liz the plan was the same—that she would be leaving at the end of the summer. It was still true. Luke did not return her feelings. She wouldn't delude herself into pretending he did, or wish for what wouldn't be. A few kisses meant little in the bigger scheme of things.

She hadn't meant to fall for him, and no one could be more surprised, but she'd spent enough time lying to herself in the past few years that she knew she had to be brutally honest. The timing was horrible—her whole situation was in flux and she was coming out of a devastating divorce. But she loved him. She would not be leaving the ranch with her heart intact. There was nothing she could do about it. It was too late.

Now she had two choices. She could back away, protect herself. Leave, if it came to that. Or she could take what precious time she had to help him through this.

There really was no contest. She was tired of running away from her failures and away from memories. This time she would stand.

"You always were a sucker for punishment," she murmured to herself. She let out her breath and stepped back around the corner.

Luke held his father's hand in his. It felt small now, and he thought of being a child and putting his hand within his father's wide palm, innocent and trusting. He'd worshipped his father, wanted to do everything just like him. He'd followed him through the barns and fields, learned to ride, learned to herd cattle and work the land. As he'd grown, they'd had their differences. New things had become important.

Luke had felt the need to stretch his legs, explore new places and people as he'd become a young man. They'd argued. There'd been resentment on both sides, but none of it mattered now. The tables were perfectly turned. Luke was the parent. His father was the one with the small hand, the one relying on Luke to be strong and do the right thing for everyone.

Only there was nothing he could do. There never had been, and knowing he was helpless was almost more than he could bear. Luke pressed the frail hand to his lips and felt the tears sting behind his eyes. He let them come, sitting in the semi-darkness, away from the forlorn gazes of his sisters and the sympathetic pats from the nurses. He let grief and exhaustion have its way for once. There was no one to see. No one to witness the coming apart that had been building since that horrible night when the fire department had come and he couldn't ignore the signs any longer. No one should have to go through this…this awful watching and waiting. He would never put anyone through such an ordeal. Never.

He'd made the promise long ago, but it had come with a price. Tonight he paid that price as he sat alone, wondering why the hell it had all gone wrong and wishing, with a sinking sense of guilt, that he could turn back the clock and do things differently.

He squeezed the hand and there was no squeeze back. Luke laid his head on the edge of the bed and wept.

The fingers on his shoulder were firm and strong and he knew in an instant it was Emily. Damn her for coming and seeing him like this. He swallowed against the giant lump in his throat, choking on the futility and pain as he struggled to regain control. He swiped his hand over his face, wiping away the moisture he'd allowed himself to indulge in. But she'd seen him this way. Broken. He hated that she could see his weakness, but it came as a relief, too. It felt good to stop pretending. He didn't have to be strong for her the way he'd always had to be for Cait and Liz. With Emily he could just be Luke.

Emily stood behind him and looped her arms around his neck, pressing her lips to the top of his head in a gentle kiss.

They stayed that way for a few minutes until he regained his composure, and then he reached for her hand, tugging her to his side and pulling an empty chair over alongside his.

"You came." His voice came out rough, and he cleared this throat quietly.

"Of course I did."

"I couldn't bring myself to leave him here alone. Not yet."

Emily held his hand in hers and her thumb moved over the top of his hand, warm and reassuring. "It's okay, Luke. It's all okay."

"I've never lost it like that before."

"Then it's about time. Would you rather be alone?"

She felt as if she was holding her breath as she waited for him to answer. He could send her away right now and that would be the end of it. It would break this damnable connection that seemed to run between them. It would solve his problems where she was concerned. He was going to have to send her away some time—they had no future together. Now was probably a good time. Before things went any further.

But he gripped her fingers, needing her. Wanting her to stay with him. "No. Stay, please."

She squeezed his fingers back, saying nothing. She just sat with him. Beside him, somehow knowing exactly what he needed. Just as she'd done all day. She'd come with him to the nursing home and she'd stepped in to help instinctively, making it easier on all of them. Helping him by helping his family. Emily was weaving herself into his life without even trying. God, even now he couldn't imagine going back to the empty house without her. He'd told himself that anything more was simple physical attraction. But he'd been wrong. He was falling for her. He cared about her. And he needed her. Perhaps that was the most disturbing of all. He didn't want to need anyone.

He knew in his heart he shouldn't be letting her get this close, but tonight he didn't have the strength to push her away. He looked down at his father's still features and felt his insides quiver.

Tonight he realized that people did not have to die for you to grieve for them.

Emily had no words to make things better, so she simply sat and held his hand. After nearly an hour, and when the shadows grew long, he finally sighed and lifted his head. "I think it's time to go." He looked around suddenly. "I never even thought—Emily, where is Sam?"

Emily smiled. It was the second time today he'd asked about her son—what a change from his attitude when she'd first arrived. "It's okay. He's staying at Liz's for the night. He was very pleased to be having a sleepover. When I left them, the kids were watching a Disney movie and eating popcorn."

"You left him with my sister?"

"Shouldn't I have?" She wondered why Luke was frowning at her.

"It's just…you don't let him out of your sight. You're the mama bear."

He was right. She was protective of Sam. "You were the one who said I had to stop holding on so tight. And tonight you needed me more."

His gaze clung to hers as the softly spoken words hovered in the room. She knew he would never admit needing her, but it was true. Sam was fine. Emily knew Luke had been right all along. She'd focused solely on Sam because he was all she had. That wasn't true any longer, but would Luke let her in?

"He's such a good boy, Emily."

She picked up her purse, her throat thickening as she recalled hearing Sam's laughter mingled with Luke's as he'd ridden around the corral. "I know."

"And you're a good parent. You always put him first."

Emily looked up at him as they shut off the light. She wasn't sure he was so right about that part. Lately she'd been putting herself and her own wants ahead of those of her son. She'd bought into Luke's logic that Sam was already going to miss the farm so why not let him enjoy it? But it was really her. She didn't want to leave yet. And as much as she wanted to be there for Luke tonight, that fact niggled at her.

"So are you, Luke. You looked after your sisters. You still do. It was so clear when you saw them today. They lean on you. You are their guidepost."

He shut the door quietly behind them and held her hand as they walked down the hall. "Not many understand that. But you do."

"I hope the girls realize it, too," Emily remarked. "I think they are so used to you being their rock that they forget you're human, too."

He stopped, staring at her with surprise. "What are you saying, Emily?"

She lifted her chin and looked right in his eyes, still red-rimmed from his visit with his father. "I mean they are so used to you looking out for them that they might forget you need support, too. It goes both ways."

"They were younger than me. They didn't see things the same way I did."

Emily nodded. "Undoubtedly. Is that why you've never married? You were too busy bringing up your sisters? Too busy living up to your responsibilities to have a relationship?" She squeezed his fingers. "How much have you really sacrificed, Luke?"

His jaw tightened. "I suppose I've never met the right one."

He tried to brush off her questions, but the tense tone of his voice made the attempt fall flat. What wasn't he saying?

She might take offense if the situation were different, but they both knew she was not a girlfriend. She wasn't sure what she was to him anymore. Not yet a lover, not just an employee, more than a friend.

They exited into the warm night, into fresh air and the scent of the roses that flanked the walkway. "It's more than that, isn't it?"

He let go of her hand. "What do you mean?"

Emily paused, letting Luke carry on for a few steps until he turned as if he was wondering why she wasn't keeping up with him anymore.

"I mean, you keep people at arm's length. Oh, now and again something comes through—like seeing you with your sisters, or when you held Sam during the storm, or tonight, with your father. But the rest of the time…" She paused, searching for the right words. "You're a fortress. And you're the gatekeeper, too. You decide who is allowed in, and you only show bits of yourself when you want."

He stared at her as if she'd slapped him.

"You don't know anything about it."

"Because you haven't told me."

He scoffed, turning away. "Like you've told me everything?"

What more was there to tell? She shrugged her shoulders. "I told you that Rob left us. I told you why and what's happened since. What more do you want? Because if I tell you that his leaving destroyed my confidence, made me question every single thing about myself, whether I was a good wife or mother, what are you going to do, Luke?" His face paled and he took a step backwards. She kept her voice calm, rational. "That's it exactly. You're going to close yourself off and run away. Because you don't let anyone get close. Even when they really, really want to be."

She wanted to reach him desperately. He was right, she hadn't told him everything, but she also hadn't felt she needed to. He seemed to understand anyway, and now she'd gotten defensive and attacked him on a night when he was already dealing with so much. "Please," she whispered, and heard her voice catch. "I don't want to argue. I want to help. Please let me in."

"I can't," he murmured, turning away.

"Is it really that bad?"

"Please, Emily." He begged her now. "Can we not do this right now?" His voice cracked on the last word. "That small, frail man in there is the last parental connection I have. He doesn't even recognize me. Do you know what I could give for one more moment of clarity, one more real conversation? To have him look at me and say my name? His organs are shutting down. My father is going to die. Maybe not tonight. Or tomorrow, or next week. But soon."

He put his hand on the car-door handle and sent her a look so full of pain that it hit her like a slap. He opened the door and shot out a parting stab: "What does it say about me that I'm relieved?"

Emily had broken through. Luke had opened up. But now she only felt despair, knowing she'd only ended up causing him more pain.

CHAPTER ELEVEN

THE CAR RIDE home was interminable. Luke kept his hands on the wheel and his mouth shut. What had possessed him to say such a thing in the first place? As they turned on to the service road leading to the ranch, he sighed and thought back over the years to all the visits. All the times that his father had been lucid; Luke and the girls had been hungry for those moments when they had their father again.

Then the more frequent times when his father had been forgetful, repeating himself, focused on one tiny detail about something that happened before Luke had ever been born. Or the times Dad got so frustrated that he lashed out, mostly with hurtful words but sometimes with hands. When that happened, Luke knew that his father would never be the same. He was an angry, hostile stranger. Yet, each time Luke visited there was a tiny bit of hope that it would be a good day. The death of those hopes took their toll on a man. All the things he'd said to Em he'd never breathed to another soul. It was her. She got to him with her gentle ways and yes, even with her strength. She had no idea how strong she was.

And she had no idea how much he loved her for it. Nor would she, ever.

Luke parked the car and got out. He got as far as the steps and stopped. He couldn't go in there. Not tonight.

"Are you hungry? Did you even eat since breakfast?"

Emily's voice was quiet at his shoulder but he shook his head. He wasn't hungry. He was just…numb. He wanted to grab on to her and hold on and knew he couldn't. Not just for him, but for her. The way she turned those liquid eyes up at him damn near tore him apart. She'd kissed him back, making him want things he had decided he could never have. She made herself invaluable in a thousand different ways and each one scored his heart.

He shook his head but still couldn't make himself climb the steps.

"Luke?" The quaver in her voice registered and he turned to look at her. Her big eyes were luminous with tears…for him? The weight of carrying everyone's emotions suddenly got heavier.

"You're scaring me," she whispered.

He had to snap out of it.

"I'm sorry, Em. I just…can't go inside. I don't know why." But he did know. The memories were there. And the fears lived there, too. They lived in the clues he left himself as an early-warning system, in the shadowed corners where he told himself he could never let anyone get too close.

It had worked up until now. Until Emily.

"Then let's walk. It's a beautiful night and I don't need to stay close to the house for Sam. Let's just walk a while, okay?"

Relieved, he nodded. Walking was good. He pointed north, knowing exactly where he needed to be. Emily took his hand and he let her hold it. The link made him feel stronger. Grounded him in a world spinning out of control.

The evening was as mellow as he'd ever seen it this early in July. The wide-open sky swirled together in shades of pink, peach and lilac as the sun began to dip over the prairie. Even the green leaves on the shrubs and poplar trees seemed less brash in the evening light. The air was perfumed with fresh grass and timothy and the faintest hint of clover. Why had he ever considered leaving, as though this place wasn't enough? The ranch was in his blood. Something tightened inside him. So many things were in his blood and that was the whole problem.

He led Emily over the fields to the top of a knoll. He stopped and took a deep breath. From here they could see for miles. Evans's land went on for a huge portion of the view. This was his. His responsibility. His heritage.

His privilege.

"Oh, wow," Emily breathed, and he looked over at her. Lord, she was beautiful. He'd thought so from the first. Her hair had grown a little longer in the days she'd been here, the flirty tips of her short cut now softer around her face. She had held him together today, as much as he didn't want to admit it.

"I'm scared, Em."

Sympathy softened her face even more. "Oh, Luke. I'm sure that is hard to say."

He nodded. "It is. I don't have the luxury of being scared. I've known for a long time that this family is my responsibility, but there was always this little bit of 'not yet' as long as Dad was alive. It was easier to deny, I suppose. I'm starting to have to face the truth. It's all on me now. And I don't want to face it. I want to go back to being twenty and full of myself and with my life ahead of me. Not predetermined."

He shook his head. "I'm a selfish bastard. I've got everything I could ever want and I'm ungrateful."

"No you're not." She turned her back on the view and gripped his wrists. "I can only imagine how hard this is for you. He is your father."

"I never asked for this. We were still reeling from Mom's death and I think Dad must have had an idea that things weren't right. He and I went to the lawyer's one day and he changed his will and gave me power of attorney. He told me it was because one day the farm would be mine. I had no idea how soon...I think he knew what was coming and was preparing. He knew I would have to make the decisions when he couldn't. But putting your own father in a home..." His voice cracked. "It was hell on earth making that decision."

Remembering how ungrateful he'd been back then left a bitter taste in his mouth. "I wanted to finish school. To get away from Evans and Son like it was a foregone conclusion." He stared past Emily's shoulder at the blocks of color below: the dull green of the freshly hayed fields, the lush emerald of pasture, the golden fields of grain crops. "We had words about it."

"And he was already sick?"

"Yes." He turned his attention back to Emily, expecting to see revulsion on her face. Hell, he hated himself for ever having felt it and now saying it out loud was like admitting he was a self-absorbed kid. But her eyes were soft with understanding, and she took a step forward and wrapped her arms around his waist, resting her head on his chest.

He let his arms go around her, drawing strength from her.

"We thought he was just grieving for Mom and having difficulties. We made all sorts of excuses. It wasn't until the smoke alarms went off that we realized. The kitchen had some fire and smoke damage. That was all. But it could have been worse. He was a danger to all of us. The hardest thing I ever did was put my father in a home. Especially after the words I'd said to him. And the girls...they were dealing with teenage angst and emotions and missing our mother. I was barely more than a kid myself."

He paused, wondered how much of the truth to tell her and settled for half. "I never want to have that responsibility again. I've been son, brother, parent, breadwinner and sole operator of this ranch and that's enough for me. I raised my family and it was one hell of a painful experience. I don't want to raise another one."

She pulled away from his chest. Perhaps he hadn't shocked her before but he had now. Her face had gone white as she stared up at him. What would she say if he told her the rest?

But he couldn't bring himself to say it out loud. And what good would it do for her to know he wanted things that he could never have? It would only hurt them both further, because it was as plain as the nose on his face that she was developing feelings. That was his fault, and up to him to fix.

"I see."

He swallowed, hating the dull pain in her voice. "I thought you should know so you didn't get…" Oh, God, this was tearing him apart on top of everything else. He didn't want to hurt her. "So you didn't get your hopes up. About us."

"You mean after the kisses." She dropped her hands from his ribs as though his skin was suddenly burning her fingertips. It was what he wanted. He needed to push her away, so why did it have to hurt so much?

"I shouldn't have kissed you. Either time. I certainly didn't plan it. You're a desirable woman, Emily. Don't let that fool of an ex-husband let you think otherwise. But I'm not in the market for a wife and you should know that from the start."

She turned her back on him, staring over the naked fields now with her shoulders pulled up. He *had* hurt her. He'd only hurt her more if he kept on. The sky was a dusky shade of purple and he knew they had to be going back. Off to the east, the first howl of a coyote echoed, lonely and fierce.

Emily turned back to face him and he expected to have tears to contend with. But there were none. Her face was impassive, showing neither hurt nor pleasure. She merely lifted her eyebrows the slightest bit and replied, "Then it is a good thing that I'm not looking for a husband, either."

* * *

Emily held herself together all during the long, silent walk back to the house, all the while she called Liz to check up on Sam, and even up until she brushed her teeth and climbed under the covers of her bed. But once she put her head on the pillow, the tears came. She would not sob; she refused to let Luke know that she was crying over him. Hadn't it only been short weeks ago she'd claimed she'd hardened her heart to love? How wrong—how arrogant—she'd been. She'd had chinks in her armor and Luke had got past each one. She hadn't even recognized the feeling inside her as hope, but it had been there. She had envisioned getting on with her life. The possibility of more children, the big family she'd always longed for. Who was she kidding? She had pictured it happening with Luke. Maybe not right away. But somewhere in the back of her mind he'd emerged as her ideal.

She sniffled into her pillow, her heart hurting. Hadn't she just done the same thing as before? She had given of herself. Anyone could cook and clean, but it had been more than that. She'd done so with care, trying to make things better for Luke. It had been personal from the start. She'd been looking for his approval, she realized. Not approval of the job but approval of her. She'd set herself up for this. It wasn't all Luke's fault.

She was conscious of him lying in the next bedroom, and struggled to keep her breathing quiet. She couldn't stay here. She couldn't face him day after day, feeling the way she did, and knowing it would never go anywhere. Oh, she couldn't just pack up and leave in the morning. She would give it a few days. Let things resume some sort of normalcy, give Luke a chance to get his father settled. But it was time to go back to the old emergency plan. At least now she had an idea of what she could do. She was good at taking care of people and she loved children. She would go to her parents' place, find work as a housekeeper and look into some night courses. She could take early childhood education or perhaps even a teaching assistant course—both positions that would mean she could support Sam in all the ways that mattered.

She fluffed her pillow and let resolve flood into her. Thinking ahead felt so much better than the hurt. The idea took hold and she closed her eyes, desperate to look forward, willing sleep to come.

She had simply been lonely, thinking of herself, swept away by fancy. But she couldn't afford to think only of herself. She had Sam, and he came first. In time she'd stop caring about Luke Evans and simply thank him for showing her the way to her independence.

Sleep snuck in, merciful but bittersweet. If that were true, then why did she still feel this aching hole inside her?

CHAPTER TWELVE

JOHN EVANS WENT into the palliative care unit the following afternoon. Emily scrubbed bathrooms, brought clothes in off the line and picked Sam up from camp as Luke and his sisters spoke to the doctor and care worker. She did not offer to go with Luke and he didn't ask her. After his revelations of the night before, it seemed like an unspoken conclusion that he would handle things on his own. It felt as though they'd said all that could be said, and yet so much seemed left unspoken.

For three days Luke worked the farm, Emily fulfilled her housekeeping duties and Sam finished camp and played with Homer in the hot July evenings.

Each day tore into Emily's heart a little more. She saw Luke struggling with emotions, the wear and tear showing in the lines on his face and the weary set to his shoulders, though he never complained. He never talked to her about it either, not after that last night when he'd been so open and honest and sharing. It was, she realized, all she was going to get from him. Whatever had been between them—for his part—had run its course. It wasn't the same for her. Each bit of distance between them cut a little deeper. She was surer than ever that she had to go. It hurt too much to stay.

She waited until Sam was in bed one night before giving Luke her notice.

"Luke?"

He looked up from the magazine he was reading. A summer shower was falling and he'd turned on the lamp behind him, casting the room in a warm glow. It was so cozy here. So... right. But Luke didn't love her, and she couldn't survive staying without it. She wanted more. She needed more, deserved more...and so did Sam. If nothing else, Luke's turning her away had made her realize that she was the marrying kind. Even after the disaster of her first marriage, she still believed in it. Still believed in two people making that commitment to each other. She knew now that her words to the contrary had only been a way to cover up the pain of failing the first time.

And she was not the one who had given up. She wasn't the one who had walked away. No, it was all or nothing with her, even now. And she was asking more than Luke could give. No, it was time to cut her losses. Moving forward would be best for her and best for Sam.

"This isn't going to work. I know I should give you more notice, but..." she swallowed and gathered her strength, forcing out the next words. "Sam and I are going to leave tomorrow. We're going to my mom and dad's in Regina."

Luke's face showed nothing, until she looked into his eyes. Steely blue, they met her gaze, and there was surprise and perhaps regret. But whatever his feelings, he shuttered them away again as he folded the cover back over the magazine and put it down. "I was afraid you were going to say that."

For the briefest of moments, her heart surged, but the flare quickly died. He'd expected this. And there was nothing in either his words or his expression to tell her he was going to ask her to change her mind.

"Thank you for all you've done for us." Oh, how awful that sounded. She pushed forward. "Working for you made me see that I'm good at this. I was looking for an office job and overlooked the job I've been doing for years. What you said about school...I'm going to look into childhood education. I love children and I think I'd be good at it."

And if that meant surrounding herself with the children of others rather than her own, that was okay. She'd do the best she could and she would provide a good life for her son.

"You'll be wonderful at it, Emily." He offered her an encouraging smile. "You're a wonderful mother. Kind and patient and firm."

The words were the right ones, but the polite, friendly tone cut into her.

"Thank you." She lifted her chin. "I realized I was overlooking my skills rather than capitalizing on them."

His gaze settled on her warmly. "You've made such a difference here. Not just with what you do, but with your kindness and generosity."

Her breath seemed stuck in her chest. Really, this polite veneer was killing her. She wanted to demand that he fight for her. That he tell her he hadn't meant to slam the door on them so completely. Something to let her know that he cared, that they had a chance. But he said nothing. He was as determined as ever to keep her out.

"I need to finish packing. Excuse me, Luke."

"I'll write you a check for your wages."

How could she take money? It seemed to cheapen what they'd had. And yet what did they have, really? Some feelings and a few kisses. She had to take the money. Not just because she needed it, but because if she refused he would know. He'd know that this had gone way beyond a business arrangement and into deeply personal territory, and she'd been hurt and humiliated enough.

"Thank you, Luke."

He picked up his magazine again and Emily felt her tenuously held control shatter. Without saying another word, she left the room and went upstairs to pack her suitcase.

* * *

When her footsteps sounded on the stairs, Luke dropped the magazine and ran a rough hand over his face. Keeping up the pretense just now had damn near killed him. The last few days had been hell. Not just putting Dad in the palliative care unit, but wanting, needing Emily beside him and knowing he'd been the one to turn her away. What had he expected she'd do after his cold words? He'd thanked her and then flat-out told her they had no future. She'd answered him back in kind but he'd seen the hurt behind her eyes. He never should have hired her. Never should have kissed her. Definitely never should have fallen in love with her. She made him want things he couldn't have—the home and wife and marriage that seemed to make everything complete.

She didn't understand why he was turning her away, or that he was doing it for her own good. And she sure as hell didn't know what it was doing to him to let her go.

Marriage was enough of a risk, and Emily had already lost once. He couldn't ask her to take a gamble on him when she didn't even know the odds. And the odds had been all too clear as he watched his father slide further and further away. He could end up just like his father. Then where would Emily be? And Sam? Looking after an invalid? Making heart-breaking decisions they way he'd had to?

She didn't know what it was like. Couldn't know unless she'd been through it.

He'd heard her crying in her room. Quietly, but crying just the same, and it had taken every ounce of restraint not to go to her and tell her he didn't mean it. Her leaving came as no surprise, and he had tried his best to make it easier on her. He pushed out of the chair and went to the office, digging out the checkbook and taking a pen from the holder. His hand shook as he filled out her name and the date and the pen hovered over the amount.

How could he put a price on all she'd given to him?

In the end he figured out her wage and doubled it, then ripped it out of the book and put it in an envelope, licking and sealing the flap.

He'd check her car's oil and fluids before she left, too. He realized that he'd never made good on his promise to teach her how to do those things for herself. But he'd do them this time. Just to be sure she got to Regina okay.

And maybe one day she'd realize that letting her go was the kindest thing he could have done.

It was still raining the next morning when Emily put Sam's suitcase in the trunk. Sam wore a sullen look. "I don't want to leave the fun kids. I don't even know Grandma and Grandpa. They're old and I won't have anyone to play with. And I was teaching Homer to roll over!"

"Sam!" Emily felt her patience thin. "Your grandparents love you. And you will make new friends."

Sam got into the car without another word and Emily sighed, regretting the sharp tone. Inside her purse was the envelope Luke had given her with her pay inside. She couldn't bear to open it and see the last glorious weeks reduced to a number sign. Luke stood nearby, straight and uncompromising. But when Emily slammed the trunk shut Sam opened his door and scrambled out again, running to Luke and throwing his arms around Luke's legs.

Luke lifted him as if he weighed nothing and closed his eyes as Sam put his arms around his neck.

Emily couldn't watch. She wasn't the only one who had come to care for Luke. Sam idolized him, and would have followed him around as faithfully as Homer if Emily had allowed it. Luke had patiently taught Sam how to sit on a horse and the difference between garden plants, the taste of hay ready for cutting and how the cattle could tell a man when bad weather was imminent. He had so much to give and refused to give it.

"Bye, squirt. Be good for your mom, okay?"

"Okay, Luke. Bye."

Emily vowed not to cry, but it was a struggle. She finally met Luke's gaze and nearly crumpled at the pain in the blue depths. All he had to do was say the word and she'd stay. One word. The moment hung between them until she was sure she would break.

"Goodbye, Emily."

She hadn't truly realized what the term *stiff upper lip* meant until she forced herself to keep her own from trembling. She swallowed twice before she trusted herself to say the words, "Goodbye, Luke."

She turned to go to the driver's-side door but he spoke again. "I checked your oil and everything last night. You should be fine now."

Stop talking, she wanted to say. Didn't he know each word was like the lash of a whip? "Thank you," she murmured, her hand on the door handle.

"Emily…"

His hand closed over hers on the handle. She slowly turned and his arms cinched around her.

The light rain soaked into the cotton of his shirt, releasing the scent of his morning shower and fabric softener as he cradled her against his wide chest. She clung to him, her arms looping around his ribs, holding him close. Did this mean he'd changed his mind?

All too soon he let her go and opened her door. She stepped back, her lip quivering despite her determinations. She had to face the truth. Luke's resolve that he'd raised his family—that he didn't want the responsibility—was stronger than any feelings he had for her. Numbly she got into the car and dropped her purse on the passenger seat while Sam sat, silent, in the back.

"Be happy," Luke said, and shut her door.

She turned the key and the engine roared to life. She put it in gear and started down the driveway.

At the bottom she glanced in the rearview mirror. He was still standing in the same spot, his jeans and flannel shirt a contrast to the gray, dismal day. She snapped her gaze to the front and to the wipers that rhythmically swiped the rain from the windshield.

She had to stop looking back. From now on it was straight ahead.

Luke went back into the house once her car had disappeared from sight. He closed the door and the sound echoed through the hall. His footsteps seemed inordinately loud in the empty kitchen. He should go to the barn and tackle a few of the tasks he'd been saving for a rainy day. Instead he found himself wandering aimlessly from room to room, ending in the living room. A white square caught his eye and he went to the old stereo, picked up the piece of paper and stared at her elegant handwriting.

If he'd ever wondered if she could do everything, here was his answer. After all these years of the record player not working, she'd fixed it.

He carefully moved the picture frames from the top, stacking them to one side as he lifted the hinged cover. Memories hit him from all sides: being at his grandparents' house and hearing the old albums, then his mom and dad bringing it home and putting on the Beatles and Elvis. Those LPs were still there, but Luke flipped the switch and sent the turntable spinning, placing the needle on the album already in place.

The mellow voice of Jim Reeves singing "I Love You Because" filled the room. Oh, how he'd complained as a boy when his parents had put on the old-fashioned tunes. Now he was hit with a wave of nostalgia so strong it almost stole his breath.

And as he listened to the lyrics, he wished he could take back the words that had sent her away.

What was done was done. He'd stayed strong despite it all, loving her too much to sentence her to a life of pain and indecision. But damn, it hurt.

It hurt more than he'd ever imagined possible.

Sam held a bouquet of black-eyed Susans, daisies and cornflowers in his hand as Emily cut more stems for the bouquet. Her mother's wildflower garden was a rainbow of blooms right now, and Emily snipped a few pinky-purple cosmos blossoms to add to the mix. Sam waited patiently, but as Emily handed over the last flowers, she knew. He wasn't happy. And she knew why. Nothing had been the same since they'd left Luke's.

"What's the matter, sweetheart?" She forced a cheerful smile. "Aren't the flowers pretty for Grandma?"

"I guess," he muttered, looking at his feet rather than the profusion of flowers in his hand. Emily sighed. One of them pouting was enough.

"Grandma made cookies today. Why don't we have some once these are in water?"

He shrugged. "They're not as good as yours."

Emily knelt beside him. "I know there have been a lot of changes lately. And I know it's been tough, Sam. But Grandma and Grandpa are very nice to let us stay with them."

More than nice. They'd welcomed Emily and Sam with open arms and without the criticism Emily had expected. She'd come to realize their lack of contact over the years had been partly her fault. She'd always seemed too busy to visit and hadn't been as welcoming as she should have been. It was good to mend those fences, but it wasn't enough. Sam wasn't the only one discontented. Emily compared everything to Luke's house. Not as modern or updated as her parents' home but with far more character and redolent with decades of happy memories. The garden here was pretty, but she found herself wondering if the peas and beans were ready and if Luke was finding time to pick them. The wheat was ripening in the fields and she pictured Luke with the Orrick boys, high on a tractor amid the waving golden heads. August was waning and Labor Day approaching, and she wondered if he'd celebrate with Liz and Cait and the children. Remembering Canada Day caused such a chasm of loneliness that she caught her breath.

She thought about his father, and if he was still hanging on or if the family was grieving.

She had thought it would take time to forget about him, but forgetting had proved an impossible endeavor.

"Mom?" Sam's voice interrupted her thoughts and she forced a smile.

"What, pumpkin?"

He scowled. "You aren't supposed to call me pumpkin anymore."

"What should I call you?" She smiled. Sam was her one bright spot. She'd begun working part-time for a local agency and he met her at the door every single time she came home. He brought her books every night, first learning to read his own and then settling in for a bedtime story. He would start school soon and she was determined to sign up for her courses and find them their own place. But there were some days, like today, when she missed when he'd been a toddler, and names like pumpkin had been okay. What would she do when he was older and didn't need her anymore?

"I don't know. No baby names."

"I'll try. No promises." She grinned and ruffled his hair.

"I miss Luke. And Homer. And the horses. And the kids."

Oh, honey. She missed all those things, too, and more. Mostly Luke. She wanted to promise Sam everything would be better soon, but it seemed unfair. He was entitled to his feelings. He shouldn't be made to feel as if they were insignificant.

"Me, too, sweet…Sam," she amended, gratified when he smiled. "But we knew all along that it was temporary, remember?"

"I thought…maybe…"

"Maybe what?"

"That Luke was going to be my new dad. When he kissed you and stuff."

She felt her cheeks color. "How do you know about that?"

He shrugged again—a new favorite five-year-old gesture since his birthday. "I saw you. At the fireworks. Everyone did."

Emily stood up and took his hand, starting towards the house. "Luke and I liked each other for a while," she said, not sure what to tell him that would explain things without getting complicated. "But it wasn't like that," she finished awkwardly.

"I wish it was. I liked it there. Even better than Calgary."

They'd reached the back steps when her cell phone vibrated in her pocket. "Go inside and give these to Grandma. Bet she'll give you an extra cookie." Emily took the phone out of her pocket and her heart took a leap as she saw Luke's name on the call display.

It vibrated in her palm, and before she could reconsider she flipped it open and answered it.

"Hello?"

"Emily?"

Oh, his voice sounded just as rough and sexy over the

phone. Her spine straightened and her fingers toyed with the hem of her top. He could still cause that nest of nerves simply from saying her name.

"Luke. Is everything okay?" She knew he'd never call unless something was wrong. He'd said all that he'd needed to say.

"Dad's gone, Emily."

His voice cracked at the end. There was a long pause while Emily wondered if he was going to continue. Her throat tightened painfully. "Are you okay, Luke?"

He cleared his throat. "I think so. I need to ask you a favor."

Anything. She almost said it, hating herself for being so easy even if it was only on the inside. Her fingers gripped the phone so tightly her knuckles cramped. "What is it?"

"Can you come?"

Her knees wobbled and she sat down on the back steps, the cool cement pricking into her bare legs. "You want me to come for the funeral?"

"Yes. And to talk."

Her breath caught in her chest. She hadn't thought she'd ever hear his voice again, let alone see him. But she couldn't get her hopes up. "Talk about what?"

"There were things I should have said but didn't."

"You seemed to say enough." He had been the one to turn her away, and now he expected her to come when he crooked his finger? She knew it was a difficult time for him and she wanted to help, but she refused to put herself in the position of being hurt again.

"I know, and I need to explain."

"I don't know..." She wanted to be there for him, but the wounds were still too fresh. She was still too close to be objective.

"The service is the day after tomorrow. If you can't get away, I'll come to you afterwards. Give me your address."

Come here? Impossible. As kind as her parents had been, Emily had glossed over her pain at leaving Alberta. She'd let them believe she was so down because of her divorce—they had no idea she'd been foolish enough to have her heart broken all over again. Luke showing up here would create all sorts of problems. Especially considering what Sam had just said.

"No, I'll come," she decided. If it was that crucial, she'd take a day and go.

"Thank you, Emily. It means a lot."

What was she doing? Setting herself up for another round of hurt? Getting over him was taking too long. Maybe they would be better this way. Despite what had happened, it felt as if they'd left loose ends. Maybe they needed to tie those off. Cauterize the wound so she could finally heal.

"I'm sorry about your dad," she said quietly, pressing the phone to her ear, not wanting the conversation to end so soon. Lord, she *had* missed him. The line went quiet again and she thought she heard him take a shaking breath. Her heart quaked. She had so many things she wanted to say, and her one regret over all these weeks was that she'd never told him exactly how she felt. Would it have made a difference if he'd known she was in love with him?

"We'll talk about it when you get here," he replied.

After the phone went dead, Emily sat on the steps a long time. She was going back. The memory of his face swam through her mind, scowling, smiling, and that intense, heart-stopping gaze he gave her just before he kissed her. She would see him the day after tomorrow.

If nothing else, she would tell him how she felt. How his dismissal of her had cut her to the bone. And then she would let him go once and for all.

CHAPTER THIRTEEN

EMILY TURNED UP THE drive at half past twelve. The midday sun scorched down and Emily noticed the petunias in the baskets were drooping, in need of a good deadheading and watering. Luke's truck sat in the drive, and the field equipment was lined up in a mournful row next to the barn. The farm work had ceased for today, a sad and respectful silence for the man who had started it all and passed it on to his son.

His son. Luke stepped through the screen door and on to the porch as she parked. He rested one hand on the railing post while Emily tried to calm both the excitement of seeing him again and the sadness of knowing the reason why he'd traded in his jeans and T-shirts for a suit. Black trousers fitted his long legs and the white shirt emphasized the leanness of his hips and the breadth of his shoulders. The gray tie was off-center and her lips curved up the tiniest bit. Luke was the kind of man who would hate being bundled up in a tie.

She stepped out of the car. Her shoes made little grinding noises on the gravel as she walked to the house. Luke waited as she put her shaking hand on the railing and climbed the steps to the porch.

God, how she'd missed him. She faced him, drinking in every detail of his features. Regular Luke was irresistible. But this dressed-up Luke felt different and exciting. He'd had a haircut recently—a razor-thin white line marked the path of his new hairline. His mouth, the crisply etched lips that remained unsmiling, and his eyes. She stopped at his eyes. She had expected pain and sadness. But what she saw there gave her heart a still-familiar kick. Heat. And desire.

"You look beautiful," he said quietly. He reached out and took a few strands of her hair in his fingers. "You let your hair grow."

She reached up and touched the dark strands without thinking. When she realized what she was doing she dropped her hand to her side again. "I felt like a change." She meant to speak clearly but it came out as a ragged whisper. If she reacted like this now, how would they make it through a whole afternoon?

"Emily…"

She waited. As the seconds passed, she wondered how long before they would have to leave for the church. He'd said he wanted to talk to her, but they wouldn't have much time. Surely he had to be there early. To be with his sisters. To say goodbye. With every second that slid past she felt Luke sliding away as well.

Luke drew in his eyebrows and pushed away from the post. Emily took a step forward and put her hand on his forearm. Her fingers clenched the fine white fabric and she got a little thrill as the muscle hardened beneath her touch.

"Why is it so hard to say what I need to say?" he wondered aloud, putting his hand over hers. "I've said it a million times in my head, Em. Over and over again since you left."

Emily looked up. In her heels she was only a few inches shorter than he was and impulsively she tipped up her face, touching her lips to his. "Then just tell me," she whispered, meeting his gaze evenly. "I came all this way…"

"Yes, you did." He smiled a little then. "You were always there when I needed you, Em. Right from the start. Until I sent you away. I kept looking for your car to drive up the lane because somehow you always seemed to know what I needed. But you didn't come."

"You made it all too clear in those last hours that I wasn't needed at all."

"It's completely my fault." He cupped her jaw with a wide hand. "I'm the one who forced you to leave."

"You didn't force me anywhere. I left because you made it clear you were not interested in pursuing anything further. And because my own feelings were already involved."

She could give him that much. She did want to tell him how she felt, but he was the one who had asked her here. He was the one who'd said he had something to tell her. Whatever it was, she wanted him to get it off his chest.

His gaze warmed as he looked down at her. "I know they were," he said quietly. "It was why I needed to stop what was happening between us before it went too far. I needed to push you away so I didn't have to face things. I didn't tell you everything, Em, that night on the hill. I held back the real reason why I promised never to let myself get too close to anyone. And I hurt you because I was too afraid to say it out loud. If I didn't say it, there was still part of me that could deny it."

"Then tell me now," she replied, gripping his hand, drawing it down to her side. "I'm here. I'm listening."

"It's more than I deserve."

"It's not. You gave me—us—so much while we were here." Emily took a deep breath, gathering her courage. "I fell in love with you, Luke."

The blue depths of his eyes got suddenly bright. "Don't say that, Em…"

"And as often as you looked for me to come back, I waited for the phone to ring. Hoping it would be you. I promised myself if I got another chance, I'd tell you how I felt. Because you need to understand. I vowed I would never love anyone again after what I'd been through. I swore I would never put

Sam through anything like that ever again. And I fell for you so hard, so fast, it was terrifying."

He pulled her close, his hands encircling her back and she closed her eyes. For weeks she'd despaired of ever feeling his arms around her again. Now she hung on as if she would never let go.

All too soon he pushed her away. "I can't," he said, running a hand over his closely cropped hair. "I can't do this. Please Em...let's sit."

She sat on the plush cushion of the porch swing, the springs creaking as he sat beside her and put his elbows on his knees. It had taken all she had to say the words and she was glad she had. For a brief, beautiful moment she had thought it was all going to be okay. But he kept pushing her away because of this...something that he still kept hidden inside. "I think you'd better just come out with it," she suggested. "Whatever it is, I can take it, Luke."

"Did you know there's a hereditary component to Dad's disease?"

Light began to glimmer as she realized what he was saying, and what he wasn't. Why hadn't she considered he'd be afraid he'd get it, too? "No. No, I didn't know that. It must be a worry for you."

Luke twisted his fingers around and around. "Sometimes early onset is completely random. But sometimes it's not. My father was fifty-three, Emily. At a time when my friends' fathers were going to graduations and giving away brides, my dad was forgetting who his children were, getting lost on roads he'd travelled most of his life. He should never have been around machinery or livestock—looking back, it's amazing something didn't go drastically wrong sooner. He could have killed us all that night if the smoke detectors hadn't been working. And I bore the brunt of it, don't you see? I resented it and felt guilty about it. Now he's gone, and it's a relief. Not because I wanted him to die, but because…"

His voice broke. "Because he was already gone and we simply spent the last years hoping for crumbs. That might be me down the road, and I won't do that to a family. I won't put them through what I went through. The pain and guilt and awful duty of caring for someone like that."

"Luke…"

"No, let me finish. I didn't turn you away because I didn't care about you. It's because I care too much to see you destroyed by having to go through what I went through."

She swallowed against the lump in her throat. He wasn't saying he didn't love her. He was putting her first, trying to keep her safe, and it made her want to weep. "Shouldn't that be my choice, Luke?"

"You don't know what you're asking." His voice was suddenly sharp and his eyes glittered at her. "Emily…" He put his head in his hands for a moment, taking a deep breath, collecting himself.

"How can you say no to something when you aren't even sure?" She felt him slipping away and fought to keep him there, in the moment with her. "There are no guarantees in this life, Luke. Are you willing to sacrifice your happiness for something that might or might not happen?" She paused. Put her hand on his knee and squeezed. "Are you willing to sacrifice *my* happiness, and Sam's? Because we both love you. We love you and we love this farm."

"Don't make it any harder than it has to be."

"Too late." She surprised herself with the strength of her voice. "It's already done. Look at me."

His gaze struck hers and she forged ahead. "You cannot keep me from loving you, Luke. I already do. Turning me away now won't prevent me from being hurt."

"I'm doing this for you!" Luke sprang off the seat and

went to the verandah railing, gripping it with his fingers. "I'm thirty years old. I might only have a few years left before symptoms…before…"

He turned his head away, unable to voice the possibilities.

He was terrified. Emily understood that now. He'd been through hell and he was making decisions based on that fear. She could understand that so well. Heck, she'd been there just a few months ago. So afraid of being hurt again that she was prepared to spend the rest of her life alone. But Luke had changed that for her. She went to him and touched his arm, pressing her cheek against his shoulder blade.

"You're afraid. I know you think that by sacrificing yourself you're keeping others from being hurt. I know what it is to be scared. When I left Calgary, I swore I would never fall in love again. That I would never make myself that vulnerable. The sudden loss of my marriage did a number on me. I blamed myself. I thought I wasn't good enough. And then I met you. You don't think I'm still scared?" She gave a little laugh. "You talked to me about dreams, but it isn't easy to follow dreams, especially when you have a five-year-old boy depending on you to keep his world safe and happy. I felt like every time I hoped for something more I was being self-indulgent. Not putting Sam first." She turned him around so he was facing her. "I was so scared to love you that I packed up and left. But I'm not leaving now, Luke. I'm sticking around. Nothing changed in my heart when I left except that you were here and I was there. I refuse to let you sacrifice your life for me."

"You don't know what it means," he repeated. "Dad was early onset. We were told long ago that there is a fifty-fifty chance that we kids have the genetic mutation."

Fifty-fifty. For a moment Emily quailed. It was difficult odds.

"And have you been tested?"

He shook his head, staring out over the lawn that was starting to brown in the late summer heat. "The girls did. Their risk is low. They married and had the children…"

A muscle ticked in his jaw. "How could I marry, knowing I might pass this on to my own children? To give them a life sentence like that?"

"Then why not be tested?"

He shook his head. "And what? What if I have the gene? I'd spend every day wondering how old I'd be when I started showing symptoms. I'd question every time I forgot the smallest detail, wondering if this was the beginning. I can't live that way, waiting for the other shoe to drop."

Tears gathered in Emily's eyes. Suddenly everything made sense. The absolute precision of the tools in the workshop, each piece hung on exactly the right peg. The list he kept on the fridge with the pay and work schedule. It had seemed obsessively organized at the time, but now she understood. It was his safeguard. An early-warning system, a way to keep him on track just in case.

He said knowing would make him question. But not knowing was doing the exact same thing.

"You already are," she whispered. "All the things in the house, just so. Numbers and to-do lists and having everything in a specific place…"

"I knew that if something was out of place, and I couldn't remember putting it there…"

Silence dropped like an anvil.

"You are already living the disease, Luke." The look of utter shock that blanked his face made her smile. She grabbed his hands and squeezed them. "Don't you understand? You are so afraid of dying that you stopped living. You're already second-guessing everything and missing out on what might be the happiest time of your life. Love, Luke. A wife and children. Laughter and happiness. You have given your family all of yourself. What is left for you?"

"I don't know."

"If there wasn't this disease hanging over your head, what would you do?"

"But there is…"

"Forget it for a minute. If you were free of it…"

Luke looked down into her glowing face and felt something he hadn't felt in over a decade—hope. He had been so afraid. Hell, he still was. But her question penetrated the wall he'd built around himself. If there was no chance of being ill? It was an easy answer.

"I'd ask you to marry me."

She hadn't expected that response, he realized, as her face paled and she dropped her hands from his arms.

He glanced at his watch, knowing he didn't have much time. Liz and Cait expected him to be there soon and this might be his only chance to say what he needed to say. He'd wanted to make her understand that his reasons went far deeper than not wanting responsibility. Her ex-husband had destroyed so much of her confidence. If he could only give her one thing, it was that he wanted her to know that this was about him. That she had so much to offer someone.

But she was making him want things he'd convinced himself he'd never have. More than want. It was so close he could see it all within his reach.

"It occurs to me that in less than an hour from now I'm going to bury my father. And if I continue the way I'm going, I'm going to bury myself right with him, aren't I?"

She nodded ever so slightly.

"You are the strongest woman I have ever met, Emily Northcott. No woman in her right mind would choose this. You should be running right now."

"But I'm not."

"No, you're not." His heart contracted as he realized the gift she'd truly given him. "You were strong for me when I wasn't strong enough for myself. And I love you. But it doesn't change the facts."

"Then take the test."

"As long as I don't, there's still hope…"

And as long as he didn't, it would hang like a noose around his neck, slowly tightening. They both knew it.

"If I took the test…if it came back positive…would you promise to leave me?"

When he looked down at her face there were tracks of tears marring her makeup. "No," she whispered. "I would not make such a promise. I would stay with you. No matter what the test says."

"I don't want this for you…"

"When you love someone you love all of them. Even the bits that aren't perfect." She smiled, though her lower lip quivered. "You know that, Luke. You knew it when you took in Homer. When you took in two lost strays like Sam and me."

"You should have more children," he continued, quite desperate now. "I know you want them. You said so when you talked about going back to school. I can't put this on another generation, Emily."

"Then you'd better have the test. Because you deserve to be a father, Luke. If not to your own…" she smiled up at him wistfully. "Sam adores you."

"You're asking me to make this permanent?"

"Yes. Yes I am. Either way. Unless you didn't mean it when you said you loved me…"

Luke gripped her shoulders. "I love you more than I thought I could ever love anyone!"

She smiled at him so sweetly he gathered her up in his arms and held on. "Damn, what did I ever do to deserve you?" His voice was ragged. Was it really possible? Could he possibly have a normal life? A wife and the son he'd always wanted? Sam was a gift. The son of his heart if not genetics. Over the last weeks, Luke had found himself listening for Sam's laugh and missing it terribly. It had seemed that he should be there, playing with Homer, asking questions at the dinner table, tagging at Luke's heels in the barn.

"Even considering this feels so selfish," he admitted, pressing his lips to her hair.

"I know. Don't you think I've felt it, too? But you deserve a chance at happiness, Luke. We both do. And I'll be beside you every step of the way. If you'll let me."

"You aren't afraid?"

"Of course I'm afraid. But you healed me, Luke. You made me see I still believed in love. In marriage. I want to grow old with you. And if that isn't possible…I'll take whatever time God gives us."

She was right. He knew if he'd asked his parents, they would have said the same thing even had they known how their lives would be cut short. They had loved each other with a steadfastness that had been beautiful. Cait had found Joe and Liz had found Paul. Their relationships hadn't always been easy. And neither was his with Emily. But he loved her. He wanted to spend his life with her. And if he were ever going to be selfish in his life, he figured he might as well make it count.

"What about school? Your job? I know your independence is important to you. I would never want to take that away from you, Em. Don't get me wrong. I want to love you and provide for you and protect you. But I also want you to be your own person. To be happy. Whatever you want to do, the choice is ultimately yours."

He knelt on one knee on the porch, clasping her hand in

his. "So will you marry me, Emily? Marry me and let me be a father to Sam and bring a family home to this ranch?"

Her bottom lip wobbled and he squeezed her fingers. "Everything else we'll figure out as we go along. I will spend every moment making sure you don't regret it. No one will love you harder than me, Em."

"Oh, Lord, I know that!" She knelt in front of him, pressing her palm to his.

"Do you mean it? Really mean it?"

He nodded. "Every word. Marry me, Emily." He smiled. The weight that he'd carried for nearly as long as he could remember lifted. He pulled her close and kissed her, tasting lipstick and tears.

She nodded as he drew back and touched her lips with his thumb.

The phone rang and Luke knew they were running late. But for once his family would have to wait. He let it ring, waiting for Emily's answer.

"Yes, I'll marry you," she whispered, and then her smile blossomed. "As soon as it can be arranged."

EPILOGUE

THE DRIZZLY AUTUMN day couldn't dampen the celebratory mood as the Evans extended family exited the church. First Liz and her brood, dressed all in pink. Then Joe, holding a squirming Janna in his arms and Cait with a hand over her slightly rounded belly. Emily's parents, beaming with pride and squiring a handsome Sam in a new suit between them. And finally, Luke and Emily, grinning from ear to ear. Baby Elina was nestled in Emily's arm, the heirloom Evans christening gown draped over Emily's wrist.

Back at the farm Emily, Liz and Cait laid out food buffet style. Once the kids had filled their plates, the adults followed while Elina was changed into a frilly pink dress and passed between grandparents, aunts and uncles.

Emily and Luke stole a private moment in the kitchen while Liz and Cait flipped through the family albums, the music from the old stereo creating a joyful noise throughout the house.

"Happy anniversary," Emily whispered.

"I first kissed you in this very spot. Do you remember?" Luke pressed his forehead to hers and Emily closed her eyes, wondering how on earth she'd ended up so blissfully happy.

"You cursed before you did it, you know. You were reluctant about everything…"

"Then I am a very lucky man that you persevered."

"I knew a good thing when I saw it."

"I love you, Emily. And our children."

Today the minister had performed two baptisms. Not just baby Elina in her silk-and-lace gown, but also Sam, who hadn't been baptized as a baby. Today Luke had claimed both children, even though the adoption of Sam had gone through months earlier.

"I love you, too. Are you ever going to kiss me though? We're sure to be interrupted at any moment."

He was laughing as he pressed his lips to hers, holding her close. She gave back equally, twining her arms around his neck and standing on tiptoe.

"Hey, Dad, can I change out of this suit and show the girls the new kittens?"

Sam's voice announced his arrival in the kitchen and Luke muttered a light curse as Emily laughed and loosened her arms.

"Oh. Yuck," Sam said.

"Yes, go change," Luke said. "And be smart. We'll both get in trouble if the twins get their dresses dirty."

"Yes, sir."

The swinging door flapped shut as Sam ran out.

"He called me Dad." There was a note of wonder in Luke's voice and Emily smiled.

"Em…when I think of all you've given me…I never would have had the courage to take the test if it hadn't been for you. Suddenly I had more to gain than I had to lose."

"And was it worth it?"

"You'd better believe it," he replied confidently. "I never thought I'd have this. Never thought I'd have love, and a family of my own. I know there are no guarantees, even if it did come back negative. I'm going to grab every last drop of happiness I can."

Emily's heart was so full she couldn't hold it all in any

longer. "Hey, Luke, you know how we talked about the big family I always wanted?"

He raised his eyebrows as a slow smile curved up his cheek. "You thinking of trying again?"

She grinned back. "I think it's too late for that," she answered.

He reached out and took her hand. "Oh, Emily."

"Do you suppose we'll break the girl streak this time?" she asked.

"Who cares?" He raised their joined hands and kissed her thumb. "Every day with our family is a gift, and perfect—just the way it is."

SOLDIER ON HER DOORSTEP

BY
SORAYA LANE

All the characters in this book have no existence outside the imagination of
the author, and have no relation whatsoever to anyone bearing the same name
or names. They are not even distantly inspired by any individual known or
unknown to the author, and all the incidents are pure invention.

First published in Great Britain 2011
by Mills & Boon, an imprint of Harlequin (UK) Limited,
Eton House, 18-24 Paradise Road, Richmond, Surrey TW9 1SR

© Soraya Lane 2011

ISBN: 978 0 263 88887 4

23-0611

Harlequin (UK) policy is to use papers that are natural, renewable and
recyclable products and made from wood grown in sustainable forests. The
logging and manufacturing processes conform to the legal environmental
regulations of the country of origin.

Printed and bound in Spain
by Blackprint CPI, Barcelona

Dear Reader,

Soldier on Her Doorstep is truly the book of my heart. From the moment I put pen to paper Alex and Lisa captured my emotions, and their romance was all I could think about—a tortured soldier and a grieving young widow, along with a little girl who needs to find her voice again. I truly believe in the power of love—a man and a woman overcoming their past to embark upon a new future together. But this story is also about the healing power of an animal. Lilly may have lost her father, but she finds ongoing comfort from her faithful dog. When all seems lost, there is nothing more special than the love an animal can offer you.

Because this is my debut novel, I want to thank some very important people in my life. My own hero, my wonderful parents, the best writing friend a girl could wish for, a great agent, and incredibly talented editors who helped to make this story what it is today.

I hope you enjoy reading *Soldier on Her Doorstep* as much as I enjoyed writing it.

Soraya

For my mother, Maureen.

Writing romance for Mills & Boon is truly a dream come true for **Soraya Lane.** An avid book reader and writer since her childhood, Soraya describes becoming a published author as 'the best job in the world', and hopes to be writing heart-warming, emotional romances for many years to come.

Soraya lives with her own real-life hero on a small farm in New Zealand, surrounded by animals and with an office overlooking a field where their horses graze.

Visit Soraya at www.sorayalane.com

CHAPTER ONE

ALEX DANE didn't need a doctor to tell him his pulse-rate was dangerously high. He pressed two fingers to his wrist and counted, trying to slow his breathing and take hold of the situation.

His heart thudded like a jackhammer hitting Tarmac.

If he didn't have such a strong sense of duty he'd just put the car in gear again.

But he couldn't.

He checked the address on the crumpled scrap of paper before screwing it into a ball again. He knew it by heart, had committed it to memory the day it was passed to him by a dying friend, but still he carried it with him. After all these months it was time to get rid of the paper and fulfill his promise.

Alex dropped his feet out onto the gravel and reached back into the car for the package. His fingers connected with the soft brown paper bag and curled to grasp it. He felt his heart-rate rise again and cursed ever having promised to come here.

It was everything he had expected and yet it wasn't.

The smell of fresh air—of trees, grass and all things country—hit him full force. Smells he had craved when he'd been traipsing across remote deserts in war zones. From where he stood he could only just make out the house, tucked slightly away from the drive, cream weatherboards peeking out from an umbrella of trees that waved above it. It was exactly as William Kennedy had described it.

Alex started to walk. Forced himself to mimic the soldier's beat he knew so well. He swallowed down a gulp of guilt—the same guilt that had plagued him on a daily basis ever since he'd set foot on American soil again—and clenched his hand around the package.

All he had to do was introduce himself, hand over the items, smile, then leave. He just needed to keep that sequence in his head and stick to the plan. No going in for a cup of coffee. No feeling sorry for her. And no looking at the kid.

He found himself at the foot of the porch. Paint peeled off each step, not in a derelict type of way but in a well-loved, haven't quite gotten around to it yet way. A litter of outdoor toys was scattered across the porch, along with a roughed-up rug that he guessed was for a dog.

Alex looked at the door, then down at the bag. If he held it any tighter it might rip. He counted to four, sucked in as much air as his lungs could accommodate, then banged his knuckles in fast succession against the wooden plane of the door.

A scuttle of noise inside told him someone was home. The drum of footsteps fast approaching told him it was time to put the rehearsal into practice. And his mind told him to dump the bag and run like he'd never run before. A damp line of sweat traced along his forehead as he fought to keep his feet rooted to the spot.

He never should have come.

Lisa Kennedy unlocked the door and reached for the handle. She smoothed her other hand over her hair to check her ponytail and pulled the ties on her apron before swinging it open.

A man was standing at the foot of the porch, his back turned as if she'd just caught him walking away. It didn't take a genius to figure out he was a soldier. Not with the short US Army buzz-cut, and that straight, uniformed way he stood, even when he thought no one was watching.

"Can I help you?"

Was he a friend of her late husband's? She had received

plenty of cards and phone calls from men who had been close to him. Was this another, come to pay his respects after all these months?

The man turned. A slow swivel on the spot before facing her front-on. Lisa played with the string of her apron, her interest piqued. The blond buzz-cut belonged to a man with the deepest brown eyes she'd ever seen, shoulders the breadth of a football player's, and the saddest smile a man could own. The woman in her wanted to hold him, to ask this soldier what he'd seen that had made him so sad. But the other part of her, the part that knew what it was to be a soldier's wife, knew that war was something he might not want to recall. Not with a face that haunted. Not when sadness was raining from his skin.

"Lisa Kennedy?"

She almost dropped the apron then. Hearing her name from his lips made her feel out of breath—winded, almost.

"I'm sorry, do I know you?"

He closed the gap between them, slowly walking up the two steps until he was standing only a few feet away.

"I was a friend of your husband's." His voice was strained.

She smiled. So that was why he'd been walking away. She knew how hard it was for soldiers to confront what another man had lost. She guessed this guy had been serving in the same unit as William and must have just been shipped home.

"It's kind of you to come by."

Lisa reached out to touch his arm, her fingers only just skimming his skin before he pulled away. He jumped like she'd touched him with a lick of fire. Recoiled like he'd never felt a woman's touch before.

She slowly took back her hand and folded her arms instead. He was hurting, and clearly not used to contact. Lisa decided to approach him as the stranger he was. A wave of uncertainty tickled her shoulders, but she shrugged it away. The man was nervous, but if he'd served with William she had to trust him.

Now that she'd had longer to study him, she realized how

handsome he'd be if only he knew how to smile, to laugh. Unlike her husband—who had had deep laugh lines etched into his skin, and a face so open that every thought he'd had was there for all to see—this man was a blank canvas. Strong cheekbones, thick cropped hair, and skin the color of a drizzle of gold, tanned from hours out in the open.

She put his quietness down to being shy—nervous, perhaps.

"Would you like to come in? I could do with an iced tea," she offered.

She watched as he searched to find the right words. It was sad. A man so handsome, so strong, and yet so clearly struggling to make a start again as a civilian.

"I... Ah..." he cleared his throat and shifted on the spot.

Lisa felt a tug at the leg of her jeans and instinctively reached for her daughter. Lilly hadn't spoken a word to anyone but Lisa since she'd been told that Daddy wouldn't be coming home, and clung on to her mother at times like she never wanted to let go.

The look on the man's face was transformed into something resembling fear, and Lisa had a feeling he wasn't used to children. Seeing Lilly had certainly unnerved him. Made him look even sadder, more tortured than before, if that were possible.

"Lilly, you go find Boston," she said, fluffing her daughter's long hair. "There's a bone in the fridge he might like. You can reach it."

Lisa looked over at the man again, who had clearly lost his tongue, and decided that if he was used to orders then that was what she'd give him. A firm instruction and a knowing look.

"Soldier, you sit there," she instructed, pointing toward the big old swinging chair on the porch. "I'm going to fix us something to drink and you can tell me exactly what you're doing here in Brownswood, Alaska."

Something flashed across his face, something she thought might be guilt, but she ignored it. He moved to the seat.

Lisa stifled a smile. When was it that you became your own mother? She was sounding more like hers every day.

This man meant her no harm, she was sure. He was probably suffering something like shell-shock, and nervous about turning up on her doorstep, but she could handle it.

Besides, it wasn't every day a handsome man turned up looking for her. Even if it was only sharing a glass of tea with a guy who didn't have a lot to say, she wouldn't mind the company.

And he'd obviously come with a purpose. Why else would she have found him on her doorstep?

Alex summoned every descriptive word for an idiot he could and internally yelled them. He had stood there like a fool, gaping at the poor woman, while she'd looked back and probably wondered what loony hospital he'd come from.

What had happened to the sequence? To the plan? He looked down at the paper bag on the seat beside him and cursed it. Just like he'd done when he'd first held it in his hands.

William had said a lot about his wife. About the type of person she was, about how he loved her, and about what a great mom she was. But he had sure never said how attractive she was.

He didn't know why, but it made the guilt crawl further, all over his skin. He'd had a certain profile of her in his mind. And it wasn't anything like the reality.

Maybe it was the long hair. The thick chestnut mane that curled gently into a ponytail. The deep hazel eyes framed by decadent black lashes. Or the way her jeans hugged her frame and the tank top showed more female skin than he'd seen in a long time. A very long time.

Then again, the fact that she was minus the pregnant belly he'd been expecting might have altered his mindset too. Would he have even noticed her figure if he hadn't been searching for the baby? Alex knew the answer to that question. Any man would. Lisa was beautiful, in a fresh-faced, innocent kind of way, and he'd have to be cold-blooded not to notice.

So had she lied to her husband about the baby she was expecting? Or had Alex lost track of time and the baby was already born?

Alex went through the plan in his mind and cursed ever coming here. He hadn't introduced himself. He hadn't smiled. And he hadn't passed her the bag or refused to stay.

His assessment? He was a complete dunce. And if the kid had any instincts whatsoever she'd probably be scared of him too. He'd looked at her as if she was an exotic animal destined to kill him.

When he'd been deployed it had been all about the plan. He had never strayed from it. Ever.

Here, one pretty woman and a cute kid had rendered him incapable of even uttering a single word.

Or perhaps it was glimpsing family life that had tied him in knots. The kind of life he'd done his best to avoid.

Alex looked up as he heard a soft thump of footfalls on the porch. He took a deep breath and made himself smile. It was something he was going to have to learn to do again. To just smile for the hell of it. Sounded easy, but for some reason he found it incredibly hard these days.

But he needn't have bothered. The only being watching him was of the four-legged variety, and he beat Alex in the smile stakes hands down. He found himself staring into the face of a waggy-tailed golden retriever, with a smile so big he could see every tooth the canine owned. He guessed this was Boston.

"Hey, bud," he said.

As he spoke he realized how stupid he must sound. He had been tongue-tied around Lisa, yet here he was talking to her dog.

Boston seemed to appreciate the conversation. He extended one paw and waved it, flapping it around in midair. Did he want Alex to shake it?

"Well, I'm pleased to meet you too, I guess."

A noise behind him made Alex stop, his hand less than an inch from taking Boston's paw. Lisa was walking out with a tray. He pretended not to notice the flicker of a smile she tried to hide. At least he was providing her with some afternoon entertainment.

She placed the pitcher of iced tea and a plate of cookies on the table in front of him.

If he'd felt like an idiot before, now he felt like the class clown.

"I see you've met Boston," she commented.

Alex nodded, a slow movement of his head. How long had she been standing there?

"He's well trained," he finally said.

Lisa laughed. It caught Alex by surprise. It seemed like forever since he'd heard the soft tinkle of a woman's happiness.

"Lilly likes to teach him tricks. You could say he's a very fast learner." She tossed the dog a broken piece of cookie. "Especially when there's food involved."

They sat there for a moment in silence. Alex fought for the words he wanted to say. The bag seemed to be staring at him. Pulsating as if it had a heart. He knew he could only make small talk for so long until he had to tell her. It had been eating away at him for months now. He had to get it out.

She pulled over a beaten-up-looking chair and sat down in it. He watched as she poured them each a glass of tea.

"I'm guessing you served with my husband?"

He had been expecting the question but still it hit him. Gave him an ache in his shoulders that was hard to shrug.

Alex allowed himself a moment to catch his words. Talking had never really been his thing.

"Lisa." He waited until she was sitting back in her chair, nursing the tea. "When your husband returned from leave, we were assigned to work together again."

He fought to keep his eyes on hers, but found it was easier to flit between the pitcher and her face. She was so beautiful, so heartbreakingly beautiful, in a soft, unassuming way, and it made it harder to tell her. He didn't want to see the kind features of her face crumple as he described the end. Didn't know if he could bear seeing this woman cry. Seeing those cracked hazelnut eyes fill with tears.

"We became very close during that tour, and he told me a lot about you. About Lilly too."

"Go on," she said, leaning forward.

"Lisa, I was there with him when he died." He said those words fast, racing to get them out. "He passed away very quickly, and I was there with him until the end." He eliminated the part about how the bullet should have been for him. How William had been so intent on warning Alex, on getting him out of harm's way, that he had been shot in the process. *Always putting his men first*. That was what the army had said about him. And it was a statement Alex knew first-hand to be true.

He looked back at Lisa. He had expected tears—uncontrollable sobbing, even—but she looked calm. Her smile was now sad, but the anguish he had worried about wasn't there.

Her quiet helped him to catch his breath and conjure the words he'd practiced for so long.

"Before he died, he scrawled down your address. Told me that I had to come here and see you, to check on you, and to tell you that…"

Lisa moved from her seat to the swinging chair, her body landing close to his. He could feel her weight on the cushion, feel the heat of her so close to him. This time when she reached for him he didn't pull away. Couldn't.

He turned to face her.

"He told me to tell you that he loved you and Lilly. That you were the woman he always dreamed of."

Now she did have tears in her eyes. A flood of wetness threatening to spill, overflowing against her lashes. She gave him a small, tremulous smile.

"He said that he wanted you to be happy," Alex finished.

Alex felt a weight lift as he said the words—words that had echoed in his head from the moment he had been told them— as if he had been scared that he might forget them. Words that had haunted him.

"Typical," she said, tucking one foot beneath her as she dabbed at her eyes with the back of one finger. Her other hand left his arm. He could feel the heat of where it had been. "He goes and leaves me, then tells me he wants me to be happy."

Alex looked away. He didn't know what comfort he could offer.

Then his fingers touched the bag.

"I have some things of his," he said. "Here." He passed it to her and another feeling of relief hit him. It felt so good to finally pass it on to her. The guilt would have eaten him alive had he not gone through with this. And he didn't need any more guilt to live with. He was carrying enough already.

He felt her sit up straighter.

"What's in here?"

"Some letters, a photo of Lilly, and his old tags."

"He asked you to give these to me?" she pressed.

Alex nodded.

"Have you read them?" she asked, her fingers already clasped around the cluster of papers inside.

"No, ma'am."

She slipped them back into the bag and leaned forward to place it on the table.

"My husband trusted you to come here, to visit me, and I don't even know your name," she said lightly.

Alex stood.

"Alex Dane," he said, arms hanging awkwardly at his sides.

"Alex," she repeated.

The smile she gave him made him want to run. Even more so than earlier, when she'd opened the door. This woman was supposed to be grieving—unhappy, miserable, even. Not kind and smiling. Not ponytail-swishingly beautiful.

He had been prepared for sadness and she'd thrown him.

"Thank you for the tea, but I'd better get on my way," he announced abruptly.

"Oh, no, you don't," she said.

He grimaced as she grabbed a hold of his wrist, but didn't let himself resist.

"You're staying for dinner and I won't take no for an answer."

He let himself be frog-marched toward the front door and fought not to pull away from her.

He should never have come.

A set of blue eyes peeking out from beneath a blonde fringe watched him from the end of the hallway. The smell of baking filled his nostrils. A framed photo of William smiled down at him from the wall.

He was in another man's house. With another man's wife and another man's child. He had stepped into someone else's life and it wasn't right.

But, even though he knew it was wrong, he felt strangely like he'd arrived home.

Not that he should know what a home felt like.

Lisa filled the kettle and set it to boil. Despite his odd behavior, she felt at ease with Alex in her home. It wasn't like she had a lack of visitors—ever since she'd heard the news of William's passing she'd had family and friends constantly dropping by. Not to mention her sister, acting as if she was a child needing tender care. It seemed she always had an excuse to drop past.

And she'd had plenty of soldiers visit. Just not for a while now.

She glanced over at Alex. He was sitting only a few feet from her, yet he could have been on the other side of the State. There was a closed expression on his face, and she was certain he was unaware of it. From what she'd read about returned soldiers there were many who never recovered from what they'd seen at war. Others just needed time, though, and she hoped this was the case with Alex. She could feel that he needed help.

Part of her was just plain curious about him. The other more demanding side of her wanted to interrogate him about William's death, and about what it was that troubled him. She guessed she had some time to ask questions, but how much could she ask him over one afternoon and dinner?

"Do you take sugar?"

She watched as he looked up at her, his gaze still uncertain.

"One sugar. Thank you."

She spooned coffee granules into each cup, added sugar, then poured the now boiled water. Lisa could feel him watching her, but she didn't mind. There was something oddly comforting about knowing that he'd been with William at the end.

She cleared her throat before turning around and passing him his coffee. She noticed that his eyes danced over her body, but she had the feeling he wasn't checking her out. It was more as if he was making an assessment of her, looking for something.

"I don't have a handgun on me, if that's what you're worried about." She laughed at herself, but he didn't even crack a smile. Instead his face turned a burnished red. She felt an unfamiliar flutter herself. Maybe she'd been out of the game for so long she didn't even know when a man *was* checking her out! It felt weird. Not uncomfortable, but not exactly something she was ready for. Although now she'd obviously made *him* uncomfortable. "I'm sorry, Alex. I was joking."

He looked away. "I'm just confused, that's all."

She raised an eyebrow in question.

Alex sighed and clasped the hot mug.

"William mentioned you were expecting another baby."

Uh-huh. The penny dropped. She almost felt disappointed that Alex *hadn't* been sizing her up, but then she guessed it wasn't really appropriate for a widow to get excited about another man anyway. It was just that she hadn't seen her husband for such a long time, and it had been months since his passing, and she…wanted to feel like a woman again. Not just a widow, or a mother, or a wife. Like a woman.

It didn't mean she didn't love her husband. She did. She had. So much. She blinked the confusion away and smiled reassuringly at Alex, knowing how uncomfortable he must be, saying something like that. It wasn't like she owed him an explanation, but the guy had traveled from heaven only knew where to visit her, to fulfill some dying wish of William's, and she didn't mind sharing. Not if it gave him some peace of mind before he left and went back to his own family.

"I fell pregnant when William was home on leave. I had an inkling and took an early test the day before he left."

Alex was still blushing. She guessed he wasn't used to talking pregnancy and babies with another man's wife. But he'd asked.

"I lost the baby during my first trimester, but I couldn't quite figure out how to tell William. He was so excited that we were finally having a second child, and he was unsure about being away again. I didn't want to let him down. But then he died, so he never knew." Lisa paused. "If I hadn't lost the baby it would have been born a couple of months ago."

She took a sip of coffee and then gazed into the liquid black depths of it. It was still hard talking about William, knowing he wasn't ever going to be coming back, but she was dealing with it. She felt like the deepest grieving was over, but sometimes it was still hard. Sometimes the sadness was...trying.

"Sorry. Time kind of gets away from you when you're away," he said.

Lisa nodded.

"Were you right in not telling him what had happened to the baby?" he asked.

Alex's question surprised her. He wasn't accusing her. Nor offering an opinion. It seemed he was just asking it the way he saw it.

"Yeah, I think so." Her voice sounded weak even to her own ears. "I'm glad he died thinking that I was going to have a baby to love. That Lilly would have a brother or sister."

She hadn't talked about her miscarriage to anyone, really. Not even her mother. It felt good to get it out, especially to someone who wouldn't make a fuss or make the pain of it come back to her.

Alex didn't respond. He'd wanted to know but she guessed he hadn't banked on hearing that.

"I'm sorry. I mean, I'm just…"

"Not sure what to say?" she finished for him, trying to put him at ease.

"Yeah."

She nodded. Her usual response would be to touch, to reach for the person she was talking to. But she stopped herself. Alex wasn't her usual company, and she needed to give him space.

"Would you like something to eat?"

He shook his head. "No, don't go to any trouble."

Lisa rolled her eyes at him, getting used to his short answers and lack of expression. "I write cookbooks for a living. Believe me when I say that fixing you something to eat is not going to put me in a tailspin."

She placed her hands on the bench and caught a smile on Alex's face. Not a big smile, just a gentle curling of his lips at each corner and a dance of something she hadn't seen in his eyes earlier. A lightness that had been missing before.

"You'll have to battle it out with Lilly, though. That girl eats like a horse," she said wryly.

Alex chuckled. A deep, sexy baritone kind of a chuckle that finally made Lisa feel like they were having an adult, woman-to-man kind of conversation.

"I'm hungry, but I don't think she'll be much competition."

They grinned at one another and Lisa hollered for her daughter.

"Lilly! Time for a snack."

A cacophony of feet on timber echoed down the hallway. She watched as first Lilly appeared, then Boston, his tongue hanging out the side of his mouth. They were inseparable, those two. Best friends.

She placed a glass of milk on the counter to keep her daughter busy while she dished out the goodies.

"Would you like to say hello to our guest?"

Lisa knew it was highly unlikely, but the therapist had said to act like everything was normal. To ignore her not talking and just behave as usual—as if she was still speaking to people besides her mother and the dog.

Lilly shook her head, but she wasn't as shy as she'd been. She climbed up onto the third stool, leaving the one in the middle empty, her eyes wide and fixed on Alex.

"This is Alex," Lisa told her. "He was a friend of Daddy's."

That made Lilly look harder at him. Her big eyes searched his face intently.

Lilly smiled and gave him a little wave.

"Hi," he said.

Lisa was more shocked at hearing Alex talk, albeit monosyllabically, than if Lilly had spoken! "Alex is a soldier," she explained.

Lisa glanced at Alex and saw how uncomfortable he looked at being so thoroughly inspected by a child. Back straight, pupils dilated, body tense. She guessed if you weren't used to the curiosity of a child it might come as a surprise. Did he not have a family?

She left them both looking at one another and opened up the pantry. Lilly would guzzle that milk in no time and start wriggling for something to eat. Everything was neatly stacked before her—jars and containers filled with all sorts of goodies. She made Lilly eat plenty of fruit and vegetables at other times, but a mid-afternoon snack was their one daily indulgence and she loved it. Lisa reached for her homemade brownies and iced lemon cake, putting the containers within reach and placing an array of each on a big square white plate.

"I hope you have a sweet tooth, Alex. This will have to do for the meantime."

He still looked like a nocturnal animal caught within the web of a bright light, but she ignored it.

"Are you planning on staying in the area?" She pushed a plate of baking toward him.

"Ah…depends on what the fishing is like. I hear it's pretty good," he said awkwardly.

"You're a fisherman, then?"

She watched as he finished his mouthful, Adam's apple bobbing up and down.

"I just like to look out at a lake and fish. You know—take time out. It's more about the sitting and thinking than serious fishing," he acknowledged.

Oh, she knew. It was exactly why they'd bought this house in the first place. Was he camping out alone? After being away on tour she'd have expected he'd want to be with his family. With friends.

Lisa moved away to locate some napkins and stopped for a heartbeat to look out the big kitchen window. The water seemed to lull her, made her feel like anything was possible as she briefly stared into its depths. She'd never really liked fishing, but she loved to think, to just sit and stare at the water. When she'd heard the dreadful news that her husband had died, that was exactly what she'd done. For hours every day.

Lilly tugged at her arm. She hadn't even seen her slip off the stool. Lisa bent down so Lilly could cup her hand around her ear.

"Tell him we have lots of fish to catch."

She smiled and nodded at her daughter.

"Tell him," Lilly insisted.

The little girl hopped back on her stool and smiled at Alex. He looked confused.

"Lilly wants me to tell you we have lots of fish here."

"Fish?"

Lilly nodded while licking at her fingers, devouring what was left of the brownie. Then she reached, slowly, for Alex's hand. She gave it a tap and jumped down.

Alex looked from Lilly to her.

"I…ah…think she wants you to go with her. To the lake."

Lisa held her breath as Lilly stood, looking expectantly up at Alex. If she didn't know better, she'd have thought his hands were shaking. He didn't move, his eyes flitting between her and her daughter, but then slowly he shifted his feet and drew himself up to his full height. He towered above Lilly. Like a bear beside a bird.

"Okay," he said uncertainly.

Lilly reached for his hand and tugged him along, and all Alex could do was obey. He looked like a placid cattle beast being led off to slaughter, but Lisa wasn't going to step in and save him.

It was the first time Lilly had interacted with a stranger in a long while. Lisa didn't care how uncomfortable their guest was. This was a major turning point. Lilly hadn't spoken to him, but she'd definitely wanted to communicate.

There was no way she was going to intervene. She couldn't.

Lisa nodded at Boston to go with them, then held her breath. Alex was either going to bolt at the first chance or respond to Lilly, and for both their sakes she hoped it was the latter.

He was a stranger, so she knew how odd it was, but deep down she hoped he *would* stay for dinner. So they could talk about William. About the war. She felt a bond with him, knowing that he'd probably spent more time with William than she had in the past couple of years. It was an opportunity she didn't want to miss.

Besides, although she'd never admitted it to her family, she was kind of lonely. At nights, mainly. She always had been, but at least she'd known one day it would be a house she would share full-time with William. That one day in the future she would have him home every night for dinner.

Lisa put down her coffee with a shaky hand and decided to change her mind and follow them after all. It wasn't that she didn't trust this Alex with her daughter, she just wanted to make sure it wasn't too much for Lilly. Or for Alex.

Right now she was Lilly's chief interpreter. And besides, she was curious to see how this unlikely pair were going to get along down by the lake.

CHAPTER TWO

"HAS Lilly always been quiet?"

Alex glanced at Lisa as they turned back toward the house. They'd been walking along the river, back and forth, Alex throwing a stick out into the water, Lilly clapping her hands and wrestling it back from Boston the moment he retrieved it.

It wasn't like he'd asked Lilly much when they were alone—he didn't even know what to say to a child—but she seemed very quiet for a little girl.

"She's been virtually mute with everyone but me since William died."

Alex nodded thoughtfully. "How old is she?"

"Six."

He'd wanted to know whether the little girl was able to speak or not, but he didn't want to talk about it. He knew what it was like to have a rough time as a kid, and it wasn't a place he wanted to go back to, even in talking about someone else. When he'd joined the army he'd tried to leave all those memories, those thoughts from his past behind.

"She's having a good day today, though. I thought she'd be too shy to be around you but she's not at all," Lisa said.

Alex liked that the girl wasn't afraid of him, but he didn't want to get involved. Didn't want to bond with anyone. Not even the dog.

"Boston seems pretty protective of her," he commented.

That made Lisa laugh. He wanted to jump back, to walk away from her. It all seemed too real, too normal, to just be talking like this after so long thinking, wondering how he was going to cope seeing her, and now to hear her laugh like that...

"That dog is her best friend. I don't know what we would have done without him. Worth his weight in gold," she told him.

They kept walking. Alex didn't know what to say. Part of him wanted to get in the car and drive—anywhere, fast, just to get away—but the other part of him, the part he didn't want to give in to, wanted to stay. To be part of this little family for a few hours, to see what William had lost, to know what his friend had sacrificed to let *him* live.

"Come on, Lil, let's go back inside."

She came running when her mother called, but Alex knew deep down that her being so quiet wasn't right. He hadn't exactly had much experience with children, but he knew that she should be squealing when the dog shook water on her, yelling back to her mother when she called. Instead she smiled quietly, not obviously sad or grieving, but obviously mourning her father in her own silent way.

He wished he didn't know what she was going through, but he did.

The army had been his only family for years. It had been the source of all his friendships, the place where he had a home, his support.

So he knew exactly how alone a person could feel.

Lisa rummaged in the fridge to find the ingredients she needed. It was going to be an early dinner. The only way she had been able to relieve Alex from being Lilly's sidekick was to order them both inside because it was almost dinnertime. Now she had to rustle something up. Fast.

She thought about the times William had returned from duty. He'd always been ravenous for a home-cooked meal. Hadn't often minded what it was, so long as it resembled comfort food. The type they missed out on over there in the desert.

"How long were you on tour this time, Alex?" she queried.

He was back sitting on the bar stool, casually flicking through one of her older cookbooks. He looked up. She could see a steely glint in his eye. Got the feeling it was a back-off-and-don't-talk-about-the-war kind of look emerging.

"Months. I kind of lost count," he finally admitted.

She didn't believe it for a second. Her husband had always known exactly how many days he'd spent away each time. Had probably been able to work out the hours he'd been away from home after each tour if he'd had a mind to.

"You been back awhile, or fresh off the plane?"

There he went with that look again. "About a week."

It was like a wall had closed, been built over his eyes, over his face, as soon as she'd started talking about the army. She could take a hint. There was no reason to pry.

"Well, I'll bet you're hankering for a nice home-cooked meal, then."

He nodded. Politely. She was desperate to ask him more. Why he wasn't sitting right now with his own family having a meal. What had made him come here to visit her so soon after he'd arrived home.

She wondered at how he and William had gotten on. They were so different. Alex was quiet and guarded—or maybe that was just a reaction to her questions. Her husband had been open and talkative. Forward.

But she knew from all the stories he'd told her that it was different at war. That men you might never have made friends with, men you ended up serving with, became as close to you as a brother. She hoped it had been that way with Alex and him.

She began peeling. Potatoes first, then carrots.

"I think what you need is Shepherd's Chicken Pie."

He smiled. A half-smile, but more open than before.

"Want to give me a hand?"

He nodded. "Sure."

"Would you mind slicing those potatoes for me? Knife's just in the drawer there. And then put them in the pot to boil."

Alex slipped down off the chair and moved to join her. She should have suggested it all along. Even if he wasn't sure what to do, keeping him busy and not interrogating him was probably the best way to help him relax and eventually open up a little about William.

She was desperate to hear some stories. If only the task didn't feel quite so similar to drawing blood from a stone!

"When you're finished there you can take over the dicing here, and I'll pop out back to pick some herbs," she instructed.

His arm moved slowly back and forth, his other hand holding the vegetables in place as he cut them. She'd never thought about it before, but the way a person cooked, prepared food, showed a lot. Her, she made a mess and enjoyed herself, when it came to family cooking especially, but Alex was meticulous. He sliced each ingredient with military precision. If she stepped closer, she'd bet she'd see that every piece of carrot was diced to exactly the same dimensions.

He was a soldier. The way he moved, held himself and carried out tasks, marked him as army. It comforted her.

William had been similar in many ways. Not exactly like Alex, but the soldier aspects still made her think of him.

"You all right there for a moment?" she asked him.

He stopped slicing and looked at her. She could see a softness in his gaze now, a change that showed her she'd been right to just give him a task and leave him be.

"Sure."

Lisa served the pie. The potato top was slightly browned, the gravy running out over the spoon as she manhandled it into three bowls.

"Lilly, why don't you take yours into the TV room? You can watch a DVD."

Her daughter nodded eagerly. Lisa hardly ever let her eat away from the table, but tonight she wanted the luxury of chatting openly to their guest.

Lisa passed her a smaller bowlful, and then set the other two on the table.

"I really can't thank you enough, Alex. For coming here to see me."

He quickly forked some pie into his mouth—so he didn't have to answer her, she guessed wryly.

"I've had plenty of soldiers drop by, but none for a few months. Still the odd call sometimes—to check up on me, I guess—but not many house calls." She paused, but he didn't respond. She tried again. "William didn't often tell me the names of his soldier friends. Well, he called them by their last names, so I kind of got lost."

"Yeah, that's army for you," he muttered.

She took a mouthful of dinner herself, and gave him time to finish some more of his.

"The time you spent together—did you…ah…get along well?" she pressed cautiously.

His lips formed a tight line. His face was serious, eyebrows drawn together. His entire body rigid. She'd pushed him too far, too soon.

"Ma'am, I…" He stopped and took a breath. "I'm not really one for talking about what happened over there."

She felt embarrassed. She should have known better. It was just that she felt like they only had a few hours together and she wanted to hear everything. Was curious to find out more.

"I'm sorry, Alex. Listen to me—interrogating you when you've come here out of kindness," she apologized.

He put down his fork. "I don't mean to be rude, I just…"

"I understand. My husband was a talker—he liked getting everything off his chest," she explained.

They both went back to eating. The silence that was suspended between them felt knife-edged.

* * *

He knew she wanted him to open up, but he couldn't. It just wasn't him. And what could he say? *Yeah, William and I got on real well while we knew each other. Before he took a bullet intended for me. Before he died trying to save me.*

The food was great. He did appreciate it. But she was treating him like the good guy here. What would she think if she could actually see what had happened over there? Could watch it like a movie before her eyes and see William dive into the line of fire to cover *him*?

He forced more food down. Anything to put the memories back on hold.

"Where's home, Alex? Where do your family live?" she asked.

Alex felt a shudder trawl his backbone. He fought the tic in his cheek as he clamped his jaw tightly. He didn't want to talk about his family. Or lack of. He didn't want to talk about why he didn't have a home. "I don't have a place at the moment," he bit out tersely.

"But what about your family? They must be excited to have you back?"

He shook his head.

Lisa watched him, her eyes questioning, but to his relief she didn't ask again. He didn't want to be rude, but there were some things he just didn't want to talk about.

She didn't need to know he was an orphan. He didn't need any sympathy, pity. Lisa was best not knowing.

"Well, I'm glad we were able to have you for dinner," she said after a long pause.

"I promised William I'd find you." He looked up, braved her gaze. "I set out as soon as I was debriefed."

She nodded. "Well, I certainly appreciate you coming here."

"Great food, by the way. Really good," he said stiltedly.

It didn't come easy to him. Just chatting. Making small talk. But he didn't want to get on the topic of family again, and she was making a real effort for him. It wasn't that he didn't appreciate it, he just wanted to keep certain doors firmly closed.

"I'm going to check on Lilly. Help yourself to more," she offered.

Lisa pulled the door to Lilly's room almost shut, leaving it so a trickle of light still traced into the room, and wiggled her fingers at her. She'd read her a story, kissed her good-night, then turned the light out.

She heard Alex down in the kitchen. He might have been in the army for years and be as quiet as a mouse, but he was well trained. He'd cleared the table and started the dishes all before she'd scooted Lilly upstairs to bed.

"You don't need to do that." She swallowed her words as soon as she saw the kitchen. The counter had been wiped down, the dishwasher light was on, and the sink was empty. He'd even fed the dog the leftovers.

He shrugged. "It's the least I can do."

She didn't know about that. He'd traipsed from goodness-only-knew-where to get here, brought things to her that meant the world, and started to cheer up a six-year-old who was undergoing serious counseling for trauma. Lilly had been happy and bubbling when Lisa had marched her up to bed.

"Alex—stay the night. Please. It's too late for you to find somewhere in town," she said.

He looked uncomfortable. She wished he didn't. A frown shadowed his face. Whatever it was that was troubling him was firmly locked away. She'd seen it written on his face tonight at the table.

"I really appreciate the offer, but you've already cooked me dinner and…"

"Don't be silly."

The man seemed to have no family. Or none that he wanted to talk about. No place to go nearby anyway. She wasn't exactly going to turf him out. Not after what he'd done for her. Not when he'd been the man to give William comfort as he died.

"Lisa, I didn't come here expecting accommodation," he said abruptly.

She put her hands on her hips. "No, you came from miles away to do something nice for a stranger. It's me who feels like I owe you."

He had that awkward look again. On his face, in the angles of his arms as they hung by his sides. He looked up at the clock on the wall. It was getting late. "Are you sure? I can pitch my tent out back."

Lisa laughed. "Oh, no, you won't. Come on—I'll show you the guestroom."

Alex hesitated. "I've got my camping gear…"

"Don't be silly. The bed is made. You can get a good night's sleep. Come on," she said firmly.

He didn't look entirely comfortable about the situation, but he didn't argue. She smiled.

Resigned acceptance traced across his face. "I'll…ah…just grab my things from the car."

Lisa went to flick the switch on the kettle. She reached for an oversize mug and stirred in some of her homemade chocolate.

By the time he reappeared, duffle bag slung over his shoulder, she had a steaming mug of hot chocolate waiting for him.

"This is for you," she said, passing the cup to him before walking off.

She led the way up the stairs. She didn't turn, but she could hear him following. The treads creaked and groaned under his weight, as they had done under hers. She led him to the third bedroom and stepped aside so he could enter.

His big frame seemed to fill the entire room. The spare bed looked too small for him. She stifled a laugh. He looked like a grown-up in a playhouse.

"Just call if you need anything. Bathroom's the last room down the hall."

He nodded.

"Well, good night then," she said.

"Night," he replied.

Lisa pulled the door shut behind him. And walked away.

The image of him standing forlorn, bag over one shoulder and hot chocolate in hand, stayed with her, though.

She went back down the stairs, careful to avoid the noisy steps, and flicked off the lights. She reached to switch on a lamp instead.

The paper bag Alex had given her rested on the side table. Her fingers took ownership of it. Lisa found herself wondering whether the bag had come with Alex from war or if it was something he had put the items in after he'd arrived home.

She tipped out the contents. A crinkled photo of Lilly fell on to her lap. Lisa retrieved it and held it up to the light. Lilly was maybe four years old in the shot. Her blonde hair was caught into a tiny ponytail, and she was sitting on the grass.

Lisa remembered the day well. William had been between postings. They'd had an entire summer together—probably the best summer of her life. Lilly had been entertaining them right up until that moment, when she'd gotten a bee sting.

It had been William she'd run to for comfort. It always had been when he'd been home. Like she wanted to spend as much time with her daddy before he left as possible.

Lisa put the photo back on the table. She reached for William's tags this time, and slung them around her neck. The cool hit of metal chilled her chest, but she didn't remove them. Instead she let her left hand hover over them. Feeling him. Remembering him. Loving him.

Then she took the letters out. There were three of them in total. She guessed he had been waiting for an opportunity to send them.

Her heart skipped when she unfolded the first one. Saw his neat, precise writing as it filled the page.

To my darling wife.

He'd always started his letters the same way. He hadn't been one of those soldier husbands who'd been macho and brave with his family. He'd always told her he loved her on the phone, whenever he'd been able to call, regardless of how many men surrounded him. They'd always been close.

Lisa bit the inside of her lip as a wave of tears threatened. Her bottom lip started to quiver and she pushed her teeth in harder. But every word she read, every sentence that pulled her into his letter, made more tears form, until they rained a steady beat on her cheeks.

She could taste them as the salty wetness fell, trickling into her mouth.

William had died months ago, and in the year before that she'd only seen him once—the six weeks he'd spent at home on leave.

But when she read the words he had so lovingly penned for her it made her feel as if they'd never spent any time apart at all. As if he was in the room, his warm body tucked behind her on the sofa, whispering the words in her ear.

They'd been best friends, her and William. Friends before they'd become lovers.

They were friends first—that was what they'd always said to one another. Friends because they would do anything for one another, comfort one another and support one another through anything. Friends because they didn't want to hold one another back or stop the other from doing what they wanted.

And as his friend she had a strange feeling that he wouldn't be nearly as upset about the tiny flare of attraction she had briefly—very briefly—felt for the man staying upstairs as most deceased husbands would. He was so different from William, but Alex reminded her in so many ways of him. Made her pine for her husband all over again.

William had always said to her, every time he'd left to go back offshore, that if anything ever happened to him she was to move on and be happy. That she wasn't to grieve and stay in a black hole of sadness.

It wasn't that she wanted to move on. Not yet. Not at all. She just didn't want to feel guilty for being mildly attracted to another man. A flicker of attraction, nothing more, but still something she had wanted to chastise herself for at the time.

With Alex upstairs, she didn't want to feel unfaithful to William. Because she *had* felt a stirring within herself. She couldn't lie. There was no denying it. He had made a tiny beat pound inside her chest.

He was a troubled soldier. She was a widow.

But it didn't mean she couldn't appreciate that he was an attractive man.

Was it right that she'd asked him to stay the night? She hoped so. From his lack of response earlier, it was obvious he didn't have anywhere else to go.

And she'd never turn a friend of William's away.

CHAPTER THREE

Lisa watched through the window as Lilly tripped along the lakefront, looking over her shoulder every few steps to check that Alex was following. The child had dragged him outside as soon as they'd finished breakfast, and he'd been forced to accompany her. She wasn't talking to him, but her expressions said a million words. Boston trotted along behind, his nose tipped to sniff the air.

Lisa moved away to put her coffee mug in the sink, and stopped for a heartbeat to look out the other, larger kitchen window. The water twinkled at her, comforted her. Then a tree, waving, caught her eye. Made her glance at the little cottage only just visible.

She tried not to smile.

That was it!

She had always believed in destiny, and as the cottage peeked back at her an idea hit her.

It was the perfect solution.

It would give Alex time to fish, and she could get to know the man who had seen her husband gulp his last breath and try to help him.

She looked at the cottage again. When they'd first moved here they'd talked about doing all sorts of things to it. Turning it into guest accommodation…making it into a studio for her to write in. But in the end having strangers to stay for a bit of extra money had worried her more than anything, and the last thing she'd want would be to work on her recipe books away from the kitchen.

The last time William was home they'd had a poke around out there. Dumped some old boxes and wiped some cobwebs away. Then they'd decided it would be for Lilly—as a playhouse while she was young, and as a teenage retreat for when she was older.

They had called it a cottage, but it wasn't really worthy of the name. Maybe a cabin was more fitting? There was one large room that doubled as the living and sleeping quarters, plus an old bathroom and a measly kitchenette.

Alex caught her eye. He glanced into the house at her. She raised a hand in a wave. He didn't smile back, but she saw recognition in his eyes. Like he was reaching out to her.

He was afraid.

She decided to go out and rescue him.

She was no therapist, but she could tell when people needed healing, and Alex Dane needed a lot of rest and recovery.

So did Lilly.

Lisa just had to convince him to stay.

Alex felt lost. It wasn't that he didn't like it here—the place was magical. A silent lake bordered the property, and it felt as if it belonged exclusively to this parcel of land. But he could see it was huge in size. The neighboring properties would border it too. And on the other side a huge state forest or something equally large loomed.

But even though the place felt magical he still felt uncomfortable. It had been so long since he'd been around people who weren't soldiers. So long since he'd been able to just relax, act like a normal human being.

He looked back to the house again and saw that Lisa was outside now, walking toward him. She was hard not to watch. There was an openness, a kindness about her face that seemed to draw him in. But these days that kind of face was more terrifying to him than armed insurgents. It made him more nervous, more unsure, than any wartime scenario.

"You like it out here?" she asked as she approached him.

He looked back at the water. "It's pretty special."

She moved to stand right next to him. He didn't look at her.

"I've lived in Alaska all my life, and when I saw this place I knew I'd live here forever," she said wistfully.

He envied her that—having a place to call home all your life. He'd moved from town to town into different foster homes before he'd been old enough to escape that life. Having a house, a place, anything that remained the same, was something he'd always wished for.

"You mentioned you wanted to do some fishing?" she prompted.

Alex nodded. He hooked his thumb over his shoulder to point. "I've got my rod, a sleeping bag and some camping equipment in the car. Thought I'd just see where the wind took me for a while."

He could feel her eyes roving over him. It made him feel uncertain.

"But you were planning on staying in Alaska?"

He shrugged. Perhaps.

Lisa turned away and started walking. He didn't want to watch her but he couldn't help it. She had tight jeans on that hugged her legs, ballet flats covering her feet, and a T-shirt that skimmed her curves. He swallowed a lump of...what? It had been so long since he'd felt attracted to a woman that he didn't know what to think.

He ground his teeth. What he had to think of was that she had belonged to someone else—to the very man who had taken a bullet for him. And she was also someone's mommy.

He determinedly averted his gaze.

"Alex, there's something I want to show you."

His head snapped up. Maybe if he'd been better at sticking to the plan he wouldn't be torturing himself like this.

Still, it would be rude not to follow her.

He started to walk. Then stopped when he saw her standing at the foot of a hodge-podge-looking cabin perched behind a cluster of low trees. He hadn't even noticed it before. Although if you weren't looking it wasn't exactly visible for all to see.

Lisa pushed at the door, and he watched as it slowly fell open. She stood back and gestured to him with one hand. "Come have a look."

He obeyed. He had no idea what he was looking for, but he had a scout around with his eyes. The interior was dim. Light filtered in through grubby windowpanes, it smelt a touch musty, and there was an old bed lying forlorn in the corner.

He looked at her for an answer.

She smiled. "If you're looking for a place to bunk down for a while, we'd love to have you."

Alex looked from Lisa, where she stood on the grass outside still, back into the cabin. Stay? Here?

She must have seen the scared rabbit look on his face.

"I mean, just until you figure out where you want to go. A couple of weeks, perhaps?" she offered gently.

He kept staring at her incredulously. He couldn't help it.

"It's not that I wouldn't want you to stay in the house. I just thought you'd prefer some space," she went on.

He shook his head. A slow movement at first that built up to something faster. "Lisa, I…"

"No, don't refuse." She ignored his frantic head-shaking and started to walk back toward the water. It was only meters from the cabin—so close you could practically swing through the trees and land in it.

She swung back around to face him. "I need to fix the cottage up, and it's not like I'm ever going to be able to do it myself. Please. You can stay, fish, help me out, then move on once it's done."

He didn't know what to say. It wasn't that he didn't like the idea of staying here. The place was great. But how could he take up this kind of hospitality knowing that her husband wasn't coming home because he'd chosen to save Alex's life? How could he look at that little girl every day and know that he was the reason she wasn't going to see her daddy ever again?

"I can't stay." His voice was gruff but resolute.

"Alex." She moved closer to him. He saw her hand hover, as though she was about to touch him, and then she crossed her arms. Perhaps she'd already sensed he was damaged goods. "Please. It would mean a lot to me."

Until he braved telling her the truth.

He ignored the familiar trickle of guilt. It had followed him his whole life, was something he was used to living with. But he still recognized it.

"I don't…" He clenched his fists in frustration at not knowing the right thing to say.

She waited patiently.

"You don't want me here," he finally gritted out.

She looked surprised. This time she did reach for him.

He tried to ignore the flicker within him at her touch. There was something too intimate, too close, about seeing her fingers over his forearm. He didn't want to be touched by her.

"I *do* want you here," she insisted. "To be honest, I'd appreciate the company. And fixing this place up was meant to be William's task once he came home."

He fought not to grind his teeth. There was the guilt again. If William hadn't sacrificed his own life for Alex's he'd be here, home, attending to the cabin himself.

"Think on it. If you do decide to stay you'll be helping me out, and you'd have somewhere to fish," she wheedled with a smile.

Her grin was infectious. He didn't know when he'd last wanted to laugh, but she was having some sort of effect on him.

"I don't know," he muttered, but he saw a flicker of something cross her face. She knew he was cracking.

"Just say you'll think about it," she insisted.

He nodded. Just a hint of a nod, but she didn't miss it.

"You think it'll take just two or three weeks to fix this place up?" he asked warily.

She nodded, a gleam of obvious triumph in her eyes.

Alex sighed. It wasn't like he had anywhere else to go. And he owed it to her to help out. "Okay, I'll stay for a while," he said.

"Great!"

He still wasn't completely sure about it, but at least he could do something for her. He had no plans. No direction. He'd just wanted to give her William's things and then spend some time alone. Find himself. Think.

He looked around. The water twinkled at him. The trees seemed to wave. The cabin looked sturdy, albeit rundown.

There were plenty of worse places he could have ended up.

Besides, it was just a few weeks.

"It feels like the right thing, you know, having you here for a while. Makes me feel like part of William is here with you," she said softly.

"Thanks, ma'am. I really appreciate it." He did. Even if he found it hard to show. Foster care did that to you. Stripped you of emotion. Besides guilt and anger, that was. The army hadn't helped much either.

She just smiled.

"I'll make sure to stay out of your way," he added.

Lisa shook her head. "You don't need to stay out of my way. But you might want to stay in the house again tonight, until we've had a bit of a tidy up in here."

He nodded his agreement.

"Come on—I'll show you around," she offered.

Alex fell into step beside her. "You been here a long time?"

Lisa slowed so their steps matched. "We moved here before we were married. It's the kind of place you find and never want to leave."

He liked that. The idea of having a place that you knew would make you happy for life.

"You have a place that you want to settle now that you're a civilian?" she asked.

He shook his head politely, but it was hard to unclamp his jaw to find words.

She glanced at him. Made eye contact briefly. He read her face, knew that she hadn't meant to make him uncomfortable.

"I grew up here. Alaska born and bred," she continued.

Much better. He could listen to her talk all day so long as he could keep his own mouth shut about his past. Some things were better left forgotten.

Like where he was from. Family. And why he had no one in his life besides the army. Army life *was* family life for him. It was virtually all he'd ever known.

Lisa didn't know quite what to feel. Had she pushed Alex too hard? The last few hours had passed pleasantly, but she was worried about forcing him if he wasn't ready.

Maybe she had been a touch insistent. But that was beside the point. He needed a place to stay—somewhere to just be himself and work through the issues he'd brought home with him.

She could do with the company, and Lilly could do with whatever it was that Alex did to her. Her face hadn't lost the shine it had enjoyed all morning. Not a word had been said, but her actions had been more than obvious. The girl was happy and, lately, that was rare.

Alex was a mystery, though. Why did he have nowhere to go? No family? At least none that he wanted to talk about?

She hoped he'd tell her. Eventually. But she only had a few weeks to coax it out of him—unless he decided to stay on longer. But the flighty look in his eyes told her that staying put was not part of his plan.

Alex hacked at the over-hanging branches as if they'd done him some serious harm in the past. He had acquired a good pile already. A body of leaves, branches and debris littered the ground beside him.

It felt good to work up a sweat.

The morning air was coolish, but nice against his hot skin. His stomach was growling for breakfast but he ignored it. Even when it hissed and spat like a cougar.

Yesterday he'd had mixed feelings about staying. Issues about hanging around. But this morning everything seemed different. Maybe it was the good night's sleep—his first in a while—or maybe the fresh air was doing something to him, but he just felt different. And it was good to be doing something positive.

It was still unnerving. Being around William's family. Staying in another man's house. But William was gone now, and Alex had made him a promise. He might have fulfilled that promise, passing William's widow the items and telling her the words, but what kind of man would he be to come all this way and not help a woman in need? He owed it to the man. Owed him his life, in fact.

Even without this drawing them together, making him feel closer to William even though he had passed away, he and William had shared a bond. They had been in the same small unit more than once, and being posted to the places they had been sent meant they'd shared a kind of trust that was hard to explain. It was what made being here even harder—because he knew how much William had cherished what he'd left behind to serve his country.

Alex might have lost his family young, but honor and integrity were high on his list of morals. Of values. He knew how different his own life might have turned out if he'd had his family, if he hadn't lost everything as a child. Even the memories he'd clung to all these years didn't make up for what he'd lost. So he knew how important this little family was.

Lisa and Lilly only had each other now, and if she wanted the cabin fixed up he was happy to be of assistance. It was *his duty* to be there for them, to serve them.

Part of him hoped that staying, doing what he could, would help him put some demons to rest. But even if it only gave him peace of mind for a short time it would be a welcome reprieve from the guilt he had lived with of late.

He looked up at the cabin. It was shabby, there was no denying it, but it was habitable. Plus the view was incredible. Deciding to stay here might be the best decision he'd made in a long time.

He was officially discharged from the army, and he had no idea what he wanted to do. There was enough money in his savings account to keep him going for a while—a very long while—and he didn't want to start anything until his head was clear.

He just wanted to work with his hands. Fish. Chill.

And preferably not get too attached to his host family if he could help it.

"Morning."

He looked up. Lisa was watching him. She was dressed, but she still had that early morning glow. Her hair was wet, hanging down over her shoulders, leaving a damp mark on her T-shirt that he could see from here. She was nursing a cup of something hot.

"Morning," he replied. He reached for his own T-shirt, tucked into the back of his jeans, and tugged it on.

"You've been busy," she remarked.

He stepped back and looked at the mess he'd made. "Too much?"

She laughed. "I don't think any amount of work in or around that cabin could be called too much."

He wasn't used to casual chat with a woman anymore, but he was starting to warm to her. She was so easy, so relaxed. As if she expected nothing from him. Yet he knew she'd expect more. An answer. An explanation.

He swallowed the worry.

"You ready for some breakfast?"

His stomach doubled over in response. "I didn't want to go poking around in the cupboards."

She motioned with her hand for him to follow. "You're welcome to anything we've got here. Make yourself at home."

If only she knew how promising that sounded to him. Only he didn't really know how to make himself at home anywhere. Except in an army camp, perhaps.

"I hope you're hungry." She threw a glance over his shoulder.

"Yes, ma'am."

Lisa stopped and gave him one of those heart-warming smiles. "Good—because I've got eggs, bacon and sausages in the pan for you."

He'd never thought breakfast could sound so good.

"Oh, and Alex?"

He walked two beats faster to catch up with her step.

"Please don't call me ma'am again. It makes me feel like an old lady."

He sucked a lungful of air and fell back a pace or two behind her. And wished he hadn't. He had to fight not to look at the sway of her hips.

The term *old lady* hadn't crossed his mind when he'd looked at her. Ever.

Lisa patted the bacon down with a paper towel to absorb the grease and then placed it on a large plate. She saved a rasher for herself, and slipped the spatula beneath the eggs to turn them. She hoped he liked them easy-over.

"Do I take all your work out there this morning as notice that you're definitely staying?" She didn't look over her shoulder, just continued getting breakfast ready. She thought he'd feel less pressured without her watching his face.

"Ah...I guess you could say that," he answered warily.

She pursed her lips to stop from smiling. "Excellent." She spun around and just about tossed the plate and its entire contents over Alex. "Oh!"

He moved quickly, grabbing the plate and steadying her with the other hand.

"Sorry. I was just…"

She felt a sense of cool as his hand left her upper arm.

"…going to help you with the plate," he finished.

Lisa felt bad that his tanned cheeks had a hue of crimson adorning them.

"Aren't you having any?" he asked in concern, looking at how much she'd given him.

That made her smile. She couldn't cook breakfast and not partake. "Just a small version for me."

She sat down at the table with him, her own plate modestly loaded. His hands hovered over the utensils.

"Please start," she told him, wanting to put him at ease. "Eat while it's hot."

He did.

She watched as he firmly yet politely pierced meat and cut at his toast, practically inhaling the breakfast. She wondered if she'd served him enough.

"I've got work to do today, so I'm not going to be any help to you out there," she said.

Alex placed his knife and fork on the edge of the plate and reached for his coffee. She forced herself not to watch his every move. Strong fingers curled around the cup and he wiped at the corner of his mouth with the other hand.

"Where do you work?" he asked.

She was pleased he'd asked. Maybe food *was* the way to communicate with a man after all.

"I work from home," she explained, rising to collect the toast she'd left cooling in a rack on the counter. She brought it back to the table. "As I mentioned before, I write cookbooks, so I'm usually trying out new recipes, baking things."

He swallowed another mouthful of coffee. "Right."

"And today I'm under pressure, because my editor wants recipes emailed to her by the end of next week."

He looked thoughtful. She opened a jar of homemade jam and nudged it toward him. Alex dipped a knife in and spread some on a piece of toast.

"Do you have to take Lilly to school soon?"

She shook her head. "Spring break." She sighed. "But she hasn't gone back to school since William died, so I've had to start home-schooling her."

Alex looked like he was calculating how long that was.

"I do my best, but I need to get her back there." She sighed.

"Have you tried therapy?" he asked.

She blew out a deep breath. "Yup."

She couldn't tell if he approved or not. For some reason his opinion mattered to her.

"I'd better get back out there," he said.

She rose as he did, and collected the plates.

"Thanks for breakfast," he added.

He looked awkward but she ignored it. "No problem. I owe you for taking on the jungle out there."

The look he gave her made her think otherwise. That he thought *he* owed *her*. The way his eyes flickered, briefly catching hers, almost questioning.

"You need a hand with those?" he offered.

Lisa turned back to him. To those sad eyes trained her way. "I'm fine here. I'll have lunch ready for later, but help yourself to anything you need. The door's open."

She watched as Alex walked out. His shoulders were so broad, yet they looked like they were frowning. He looked so strong, yet sad—tough, yet soft. As if he could crush an enemy with his bare hands, yet provide comfort to one of his own all in the same breath.

She wished there was more she could do for him. But something told her that whatever she was doing was enough for now.

Lisa looked out the window as he appeared nearby. He

reached for the ax and dragged it upward in the air before slicing through a tree stump. She felt naughty watching him. Indulging in seeing his muscles flex and work, seeing the tension on his face drain away as he started to gather momentum.

She would be forever grateful that he'd come all this way to give her William's things. It had given her some sort of closure. Made his passing more final, somehow.

The tags Alex had given her had been William's older ones— the more current ones had come home with his body—but she had taken comfort in wearing them.

This morning she had tucked them in her jewellery box, along with the folded letters and the photo of Lilly.

She had made a decision too.

To stop grieving. To be brave and take a big step forward.

William was gone. It had taken her a long while to admit that.

He'd been a great husband and an even better father. But he'd also been a soldier. And that meant she'd always known that this day, being alone, could come, and she had to face it.

The reality of being a soldier's wife was that you had to risk losing him. That you couldn't hold him back.

Well, she'd loved William with all her heart, but she'd also accepted that his being a soldier, facing live combat, could mean he could be taken from her.

And he had.

This was the first day of her new life as a woman dealing with life, accepting what had happened to her, and being the best mother she could be. Not a widow. The word was so full of grief, so depressing, and if she stopped thinking of herself that way it might make it easier to move forward.

She had loved her husband. In her heart she knew no one could ever attempt or threaten to replace William. He had been too special, too important to her.

But she did want to keep a smile on her face and try to be happy. If Alex's company helped her do that, then she wasn't going to feel bad about it.

CHAPTER FOUR

THERE was something nice about having a man in the house again. Although Alex wasn't technically *in* the house, having him in the cabin was equally as good.

She'd never felt nervous, exactly—not out here—but there had always been a certain element of unease that she'd never been able to shake. A longing to have a man at home every night. Someone to protect the fort. Someone in the window if you came home after dark.

It was stupid, but it was true. She was a woman and she liked to feel protected and nurtured.

The phone rang. She saw the caller identification as it flashed across the little screen.

Great.

Lisa had been avoiding her sister since Alex had arrived, but Anna wasn't someone who took to being avoided very well. Her mother? Well, she wasn't so bad, but her sister could be downright painful sometimes.

"Hey, Anna." She put on her best sing-song voice as she answered the phone. If Lisa didn't talk to her now, Anna would be likely to turn up here before dark to check on her.

"Hello, stranger."

Lisa could tell her sister was worried. She had that slightly high-pitched note to her voice. "Sorry, hon, I've just been flat out trying to get these recipes in order."

"You still need a life, though, right?" Anna said.

Lisa glanced out the window and spied Alex working on a cabin window. He was trying to force it open. Did having him here constitute having a life?

"Hmm, I know. I just want this book to be good."

"They're always good," her sister replied instantly.

The vote of confidence helped.

"How about you and some of the girls come by on Saturday afternoon for a tasting?" Lisa suggested.

"Love to. Want me to organize it?"

"Sounds good," Lisa agreed.

"Just the usual gang?" Anna asked.

Five women were plenty, Lisa thought. "Yup—and Mom."

She heard Anna flicking through what she presumed was her calendar. That girl knew what everyone was up to!

"Nope. Mom has that charity fundraiser meeting going on. I'll tell her you asked, though," Anna said.

Lisa tucked the phone beneath her ear and rinsed her hands in the sink. Her eyes were still firmly locked on Alex.

"You sure you're okay?"

Lisa nodded.

"I can't hear you if you're nodding," her sister said dryly.

Damn it! It was like Anna had secret cameras installed in the house!

"I'm fine. I just need to get all this sorted," Lisa told her.

"Need me to come by?" Anna asked.

"*No!*" she yelled. "I mean, no. I'm fine." The silence on the other end told her she hadn't convinced her sister. "Come by with the girls on Saturday afternoon. I just need some time and we'll catch up then, okay?"

As Lisa said her goodbyes and hung up the phone she felt guilty. She usually shared everything with her sister. Everything. And yet she had a very big something hanging around out back, staying with her for the next few weeks, and she had omitted even to mention it.

Lilly was marching back and forth outside, Boston at her

heels. She had a huge stick in her hand—one that Alex had no doubt cut down before she'd claimed it.

Lisa went about fiddling with quantities and ingredients, dragging her eyes from the window.

She couldn't deny that she liked what she saw. But then what woman wouldn't?

Alex walked inside with Lilly on his hip. He'd thought the dog was going to attack when he'd first picked her up, but after a few gentle words and a futile attempt to stop the kid crying he had hoisted her up and into the house.

But his feet had stopped before they'd found her mom.

Lilly's cries had become diluted to gentle hiccups. It was awkward, holding her so close, but he'd had little choice. It had been a very long time since he'd held another human being like that.

Lisa was swaying in time to the beat of the music playing loudly in the kitchen. Her hair was caught back off her face with a spotted kerchief, and she had a splodge or two of flour on her cheek. The pink apron added to his discomfort. It had pulled her top down with it, and she was displaying more cleavage than he guessed she would usually show.

And she still hadn't noticed them above the hum of the music.

"Huh-hmm." He cleared his throat. Then again—louder.

She looked up, lips moving to the lyrics. Her mouth stopped, wide open, before she clamped it shut.

Lilly burst into much louder tears as soon as her mother noticed her, and all Alex could do was hold her out at a peculiar angle until Lisa swept her into her own arms.

"Baby, what happened?"

The lips that had been singing and smiling only moments earlier fell in a series of tiny kisses to her daughter's head. Lisa nursed her as she moved to turn off the speaker that was belting out the tunes.

"Shh, now. It's all right—you just got a fright," Lisa crooned.

She hugged her daughter tight. Alex couldn't take his eyes off them. It tugged something inside him, pushed at something that he hadn't felt in a long while.

"How about Alex tells me what happened while you catch your breath?" she murmured.

He cringed. Taking care of kids wasn't his thing. This one might have taken a shine to him, but he had no experience. No idea at all. "I'm sorry, she just…ah…she fell from a tree. I should have been watching her. I…"

Lisa drew her eyebrows together and waved at him with her free hand. "She's a child, Alex. And she's *my* child. If anyone should feel bad for not watching her it's me."

A touch of weight left his shoulders. But not all of it.

"I was…"

"Enough." She put Lilly down and crouched beside her. "If you wrap children in cotton wool they can't have any fun. Tumbles and bruises are all part of being a child."

He swallowed. Hard. She was inspecting Lilly, checking her, but she wasn't angry.

"You're fine, honey. How about you go play in your room for a while? Take it easy, okay?"

Lilly was still doing the odd snuffle, but Lisa simply gave her a pat on the head and blew her a kiss.

"I'm sorry," he muttered.

"Alex! For the last time, it was *not* your fault. Do I look angry?" she asked.

He ran his eyes over her face. He had seen her look worried before, concerned, but, no, not angry.

She obviously wasn't like most moms.

"You're just in time to try a few things," she said, changing the subject.

That sounded scary. He followed her, then sat down at the counter. Same spot he'd ended up when he'd arrived.

"I want your opinion on this slice. And this pastry."

That didn't sound too hard, he thought.

She straightened her apron and wiped at her cheek. He was almost disappointed when the smudge disappeared.

"What's your book called?" he asked curiously.

She turned around, turning her wide smile on him. "I'm thinking *Lisa's Treats*, but my editor will probably have other ideas."

Huh? "Doesn't that bother you?"

She fiddled with a tray, then scooped a tiny pastry something onto her fingers.

"What?"

"Not being able to choose the title yourself?" he explained.

She raised an eyebrow before lifting the pastry to his mouth. He opened it. How could he not? She was holding something that smelt delicious in front of it.

"They know how to sell books. I just know how to write what's inside. Good?"

He swallowed. *Very good*. "Good," he agreed.

"Just good?" she probed.

That made him nervous. Hadn't she just asked for good? "Great?" he tried.

"Hmm, I'd prefer excellent." She whisked away, and then twirled back to him. "Try this."

Once again she thrust something into his mouth.

Oh. Yes. "Incredible."

"Good." She had a triumphant look on her face.

He was still confused, but he tried to stay focused on the food. If he didn't look at the food he'd have to look at her. And the niggle in his chest was telling him that could be dangerous. Very dangerous.

"And this?"

This time when she twirled around she had a spoon covered in a gooey mixture. It looked decadent. Delicious. Just like her.

"Last up—my new chocolate icing."

She leaned across the counter toward him. Too close. He

fought the urge to lean back, to literally fall off the stool to get away from her. Lisa's eyes danced over his. The connection between them scared him rigid.

He sucked air through his nostrils and tried to stop his hands from becoming clammy.

Lisa held the spoon in the air, waiting for him to taste from it. He gathered courage and obeyed, his face ending up way too close to hers.

"Good?"

He could almost feel her breath on his skin. Or was he imagining it? He raised his eyes an inch. She didn't pull away. There was a beat where he wondered if she ever would.

"Excellent." He was learning how to play this game. Praise at least one word higher than what she'd asked for.

"Okay—that's me done for the day, then," she announced briskly.

She walked away from him fast. Like she'd been burnt. The flush over his own skin was making him feel the same. He glanced around the kitchen. At the trays littered across the bench, the dishes piled in the sink and the ingredients scattered. Maybe it would be polite to help, but he needed to get out of here. Put some distance between them.

Yet still he lingered. Good manners overrode emotion.

"Want a hand with all this?" he asked tentatively.

She gave him a cheeky grin. "Want a hand outside?"

Alex shrugged his acquiescence. Inside, his lungs screamed.

"Great, then I'll leave this till later," she told him happily.

Two hours later Alex was still working outside while she tinkered inside the cabin. She flicked a duster around all the surfaces, before giving the bed a good thump and making it with the linen she'd brought out.

She liked having him here. Every hour that passed she couldn't help but think she'd done the right thing asking him to stay. It wasn't just the effect he had on Lilly, he affected her too.

All went quiet outside, and he appeared in the doorway. His body filled the entire frame.

"How you getting on out there?" she asked. She could see a line of sweat starting to make a trickle across his forehead. It made her gulp. He was…well, very manly. And it was doing something to her, if the caged bird beating its wings with fury inside her stomach was any sort of gauge.

"Getting there."

She used her head to indicate where the water was. He followed.

"Thinking it will take longer to get this place habitable?" she asked.

He shook his head.

If she'd just spent years at war, and years before that in army bunkers, she'd probably think the cabin wasn't half bad either. Lisa fiddled with the duster and then stopped. She pinned her eyes on him. "Alex, I was thinking—did you actually see…you know…how William died?"

His shoulders hunched. He stopped guzzling water like he'd just emerged from the desert and stayed still. Deathly still.

So he *did* know.

It didn't matter if he didn't want to tell her. She already knew William had died from multiple bullet wounds. She'd just always wondered *how. Why?* What had actually happened over there? Who had fired? For what reason?

He dropped to an armchair in the corner. Dust thumped out of it but he seemed oblivious to it. Lisa knew she'd been wrong in asking so soon, but she couldn't take it back. Not yet. Not now.

The question hung between them.

"We were…" He took a long pause before continuing. "I mean, we came under fire."

She sat down too. On the bed. Despite just having made it.

"They think there was one, maybe two guys waiting for us. Snipers."

She could see the torment on his face. The emotion of pulling memories to the surface again. But she wanted to know.

"I'm sorry. I can't talk about it." Alex jumped to his feet and walked out the door. Fast.

Lisa sighed. She should never have pushed him. It was too early to be asking him things like that. Things that didn't really matter anymore. Not when nothing could be done about it.

"Alex, wait." She rushed out after him.

Emotion seeped from him. She could see it. Feel it. Smell it. He practically radiated hurt and confusion as she walked slowly up behind him. He had one hand braced against a tree. The other hung at his side. She stopped inches away from him, her body close to his. She didn't touch him.

"I'm sorry, Alex. I had no right to ask you that."

In a way she was lying. She *did* have the right to know. But not yet. Not until he was ready to tell.

She stood there for a moment. Watching him. Waiting. "We need some ground rules. If you want to talk about what happened, you can—anytime." She paused. "But I won't ask you about it again."

She sensed relief from him. He swiveled—just slightly, but their eyes met. She understood. She still struggled with telling people that William was gone sometimes. Felt all alone and lost.

"When you're ready to talk, tell me," she reiterated.

He just stared at her. His eyes acknowledged her words with a faint flicker.

"Sound okay to you?" she pressed.

"Yeah." His voice lacked punch.

Lisa turned and went back into the cabin. He needed some tender loving care. There was obviously no one to give it to him. But she wasn't going to ask him about that either.

This had to be a safe place for him. A place where there was no pressure and where nobody asked him questions they had no right to ask. At least not yet. Not before he trusted her. Not until she had made him feel comfortable enough to talk. Not until he'd had time.

And she wanted him to hang around, so the last thing she was going to do was push him away. He made her feel close to William, somehow. Comforted her.

Alex lay on the bed. It was almost too short for him, but if he kept his legs slightly bent he fit fine. Besides, it wasn't the bed that was stopping him from falling asleep.

It was Lisa.

Every time he closed his eyes he saw her. Sometimes Lilly was there as well. But he saw Lisa every time.

When they were open he saw her too.

It was a no-win situation.

Today had been tough. The hard labor had done him good, fired him up and taken the edge off his turbulent emotions. But being in such close proximity to a woman he found so darn attractive had put even more strain on him.

He was guilty. Guilty as a man who'd just committed a crime. Guilty as a bird who'd just stolen a piece of bread. And he hated it.

When he'd agreed to come here, to visit William's widow, he'd formed a picture in his mind of what it would be like. She would be plain, pleasant, standing in the doorway with a child beside her and one hand on an extended pregnant stomach. She would fall to her knees crying as he said the words he'd rehearsed. He'd pass her the things, put one hand on her shoulder as comfort, then turn and walk away.

Turning back had never been part of the plan. Neither had getting caught up in the emotion of her pain.

But then he'd also banked on the guilt falling away once he'd fulfilled his promise. Rather than wishing the woman before him was his own wife and that he'd just arrived back home. Or that he could just die, then and there, and give her her husband back.

He felt the excruciating guilt again now, like a knife through his chest. Saw everything flash beneath his eyelids as if it was happening all over again.

He turned as William called his name. So fast, so quick. He looked up, tripped as William launched himself at him and threw him to the ground.

A round of bullets echoed just before they hit the ground, then more. Punching through the air. Then the wet, warm splatter of blood hit him in the face.

He opened his eyes and found William staring at him, gasping.

The sniper was gone. Silence thrummed through the air like it was alive.

He moved William off him, gently. Placed him on the ground, on his back, propping his head up and listening hard to his rasping words. William ordered him to take the photo in his pocket, scrawled the name and address of his wife, then whispered words for her. He told him where to find the letters he had waiting for her at camp. To give them to her. To find her. Then he took his last breath.

Alex sat up, exhausted from his own thoughts. He dropped his head into his hands. How had this situation become so complicated? He could get up right now. Get up and leave. Start driving and never look back. But could he? Really? Could he just turn his back on Lisa and Lilly now?

He knew the answer to that. He'd only known them such a short time, and yet he felt something between them. He and Lilly understood one another, even though they didn't talk. He didn't get what to do around kids a lot of the time, but he knew about loss, about heartache. Especially about losing a parent. Or in his case both.

A shudder ran down his back—the same shudder that always came when he thought about his parents. About the other time he'd been splattered with blood that wasn't his own.

It was as if he'd cheated death twice. As if the grim reaper had come for him and somehow he'd managed to avoid him.

Twice. His parents had been taken, his friend had been taken, and yet he was still standing. Why?

The image in his mind turned back to Lisa, and the feeling of sadness that had just ruptured inside him was replaced by harrowing guilt once again.

If he'd ever fantasized about the kind of woman he could settle down with, he knew the picture would have looked a lot like her. Beautiful, so beautiful, and yet so much more. She had a way about her—a way of looking at a person or situation with complete understanding. He'd been so impressed with how she'd handled Lilly's fall today. Careful, methodical in checking her, yet not allowing the child to make a fuss.

And she was dealing with her daughter's inability to communicate with others well too. She must feel worried, but she stayed calm. Treated Lilly as if nothing had changed.

Alex knew first-hand what being in Lilly's shoes was like, and he wished he had the courage to tell Lisa how well she was doing. That she was doing the right thing.

Lisa. Her name consumed his mind.

He was attracted to her. More than attracted to her, he realized. But he wouldn't act on it.

Couldn't.

If it wasn't for him her husband would be coming home after his term serving overseas. If it wasn't for him her daughter wouldn't be traumatized. Grieving.

But he wasn't going to run out on them.

He lay back down and squeezed his eyes shut.

If he wasn't entertaining such intimate thoughts about another man's wife, maybe sleep would have found him by now.

CHAPTER FIVE

LISA resisted the urge to swipe her finger through the lemon icing as she arranged the cakes on a tray. It was stupid, but she was nervous.

Before she ever sent a book away to her editor she always hosted an afternoon get-together, so it wasn't like she had first-time jitters. Besides, they were her friends coming over—not a bunch of strangers. But there was something about living in a small town that jangled your nerves when it came to gossip.

When you knew it was you who was about to become the center of it.

She shrugged off the worry and rolled her shoulders. The knot at the base of her neck didn't disappear, but she felt a touch more relaxed.

Her kitchen looked ready for some sort of fairy birthday party. Pink macaroons, swirls of lemon zest atop white icing, and just about everything chocolate a girl could want. She hoped it was enough to distract her sister from the man living in her cabin.

She reached for a mini-cake and took a huge bite. The sugar rush made her feel mildly better, but she still felt as if she was doing something illicit.

A tap at the door made Lisa swallow fast, lick the icing from her teeth and throw the rest of the cake in the trash. She heard footsteps echo down the hall.

It was her sister. The other girls would wait to be let in.

"Hi!"

Yes, definitely Anna.

I am a grown woman, she chanted silently. I have nothing to be ashamed of. I still love my husband. Alex is only staying because he has nowhere else to go. Because he can help me out.

"There you are." Anna passed her a bunch of flowers and kissed her cheek.

"You're early," Lisa said.

"Hardly." Anna ran her eyes over the food. "Looks delicious."

Lisa walked the flowers into the kitchen and dropped them on the counter. She reached for a vase and filled it with water.

"So, little sis, what's been happening?"

"Nothing." Lisa took a breath and turned the water off. "I mean…you know—just working on recipes, baking up a storm, that kind of thing."

"Huh."

She didn't like that noise. It was the noise Anna always made when she knew something was up. When she didn't believe her but was happy to let it lie. Temporarily.

Lisa glanced at the cabin and prayed that Alex wouldn't emerge. Or be anywhere within sight of the kitchen or lounge for the next hour.

"Lisa, I…"

A rumble of heels on timber followed by a knock saved her.

"Anna, be a gem and get the door, would you?"

Her sister paused, gave her a look, and walked out.

Lisa leaned against the counter and tried to calm down. This was awful. She'd never been good at secrets—especially not ones like this.

She forced herself to fiddle with the flowers, set the vase on the center island and took a final look at the goodies.

This was going to be a long, long afternoon.

* * *

"Lisa, this is amazing!"

"Mmm."

She grinned as her friends licked at their lips and reached for more.

"You know you *are* allowed to say when you don't like something," she said.

"Honey, you're the best. You know you are, or people would stop buying your books," Anna defended her loyally.

She leaned into her sister and laughed. "You're family—you have to say that."

Lisa looked up as she heard a noise. Please, don't let it be Alex. Surely he wouldn't have just changed his mind and walked in? She'd told him the girls were coming over, and his joining them had seemed to be less likely than him pouring out his heart to her.

"Mom!" She jumped to her feet. What was her mother doing here?

"Hello, darling."

Lisa looked at Anna. Her sister just shrugged.

"I thought you had a meeting today?" Lisa said.

"Turns out I managed to sneak away," her mother replied with a smile.

She smelled a rat. They had a group attack planned. She could feel it.

"Where's my granddaughter?"

Lisa watched as her mother folded her sweater over a chair and placed her handbag on top of it.

"Yes, where *is* Lilly?" Now Anna was looking around.

"She's just out playing with Boston. Looking for bugs, climbing trees." Lisa took a deep lungful of air and determined to slow her voice.

Nothing got past those two, though. While her friends kept nattering and sipping coffee, her mother and sister were watching her as if she was up to something.

"Oh—my—word."

Lisa's head swiveled to lock eyes on her friend Sandra. A crawl of dread trickled sideways through her stomach.

"Who is *that*?"

Lisa squeezed her eyes shut for a moment, then looked out the window. Every woman in the room had her eyes trained on the exact same spot.

At least he had his shirt on. The other day, when she'd caught a glimpse of his bare chest, she'd realized the sight was enough to send any woman crazy.

Alex was standing next to Lilly. The pair of them were side by side as he demonstrated how to throw the fishing line into the water. Lilly had her tongue caught between her teeth, was trying hard to mimic him, but the rod was almost as big as she was.

Lisa saw him as her friends would. Big, strong man, with shoulders almost as wide as Lilly was long. Muscled forearms tensing as he cast the line back and forward.

He bent over to correct Lilly's grip and almost ended up wearing a piece of bait in his eye. She started laughing. It took a moment, but Alex started too. They both stood there, this giant and his fairy, giggling.

Lisa had never seen anything like it.

Had Lilly even laughed like that once since she'd been silent? It looked so natural. Seeing Lilly respond like that to Alex was special. Very special.

"Huh-hmm."

Lisa realized where she was again.

"Yes, Lisa. Who *is* that man cavorting with your daughter?" her sister asked pointedly.

She decided not to turn to face Anna. "I wouldn't say he was *cavorting*, exactly."

She grimaced and waited for it. Sandra spoke before her sister had a chance to reply.

"I don't care what he's doing, but I wish he was doing something to me!"

That set the whole room off laughing.

"Enough, ladies, enough." Lisa pulled herself away from the window and faced the room. "He's just an old friend of William's come to visit. The last thing he needs is us ogling him. Besides, you're all married."

The women kept their eyes on the view.

"I'll get some more coffee," she muttered.

"And I'll help," snapped Anna.

Her sister grabbed her elbow and marched her to the kitchen.

She guessed that talking about the handsome man outside the window was non-negotiable.

Lisa chanced a glance at her sister's face.

Definitely non-negotiable.

But she didn't have to tell them that he was living in the cabin.

No way.

Lisa felt as if she'd been a very naughty girl. Hell, she was thirty years old, not thirteen, and yet somehow she was still cast as the little sister. Was that something she was stuck with for life?

"Start talking," Anna ordered.

She straightened her shoulders, evaded her sister's stare and filled the jug with water. "There's nothing to tell. I don't know why you're making such a fuss."

"Such a fuss!" Anna threw her hands in the air. "Lisa, you've been avoiding me for days, then I find out you've got a man here. Are you seeing him?"

She glared. "Don't you *dare* ask me that!" Lisa growled the words at her. How could Anna accuse her of seeing another man? Every beat of her heart reminded her she still loved William. She might be attracted to Alex, but she was not doing anything inappropriate.

Anna just shrugged.

Her mother walked in. "I've heard enough, girls."

They both kept their mouths shut. They knew better than to argue with her when she spoke in that tone of voice.

"Let Lisa explain."

Huh. So she wasn't exactly off the hook.

Lisa pulled out a seat at the counter and sat down. Her neck was aching, shoulders tense, and she was exhausted. Like she'd run a marathon twice over. "His name is Alex. He served with William and he needed a place to stay."

"Stay!" Her sister nearly exploded.

A sharp look from their mother silenced her.

"Yes, stay," Lisa repeated. "And don't go jumping to any conclusions."

Anna kept her mouth shut for once.

"It's nice he felt he could come here," their mother remarked calmly.

Lisa smiled at her mother. "He's got some…well, some traumas to work through, and it just seemed like the right thing to do."

Anna still didn't look impressed, but Lisa ignored her.

"I see Lilly's taken a shine to him?"

Lisa's face was hot and flushed. The last thing she wanted was for her mother to be hurt. Seeing her granddaughter laughing with a stranger, even if she wasn't saying any actual words to him, was tough. She saw plenty of her grandmother, had done all her life, but she'd been closed off to everyone but Lisa herself up until now.

Except for this stranger. Except for Alex.

"Come on—let's get the coffee out to everyone. They're probably still drooling out the window," Lisa said.

"You still should have told us."

They both turned to look at Anna.

"I mean, how long have you even *known* this guy?"

Lisa put a hand on her mother's arm and gave her sister a narrow smile. "He's not a psychopath, if that's what you're worried about." She put on her bravest face. "And I wasn't trying to hide him. I wouldn't have had you here today if I was worried about you seeing him."

"We might need iced drinks!" A shout from the living room made them all turn. "It's getting hot in here!"

Lisa prayed that Alex hadn't taken off his shirt. Heavens, she'd have the girls here all evening if he had!

Lisa shut the door with a satisfied bang and leaned against it. The timber felt cool against her back. She'd been naïve to think her friends seeing Alex would go down without some interest, but she had been surprised by her sister's reaction.

The fact that her sister was still in her kitchen wasn't helping either.

Her mother she wasn't so worried about. But Anna?

She had as good as idolized William. The two of them had always gotten on well, right from the beginning when Lisa and he had first started dating. Once they were both married they had double-dated, hung out together whenever William was home on leave.

Anna and her husband were Lilly's godparents. They were all best friends. But it didn't mean Anna had a right to judge her.

She was judging herself enough, without needing to worry about others doing it too. Every time she felt her eyes drawn to Alex. Every time she felt a dusting of attraction. It made her feel guilty. Unfaithful.

Where William had been chatty and bright, like an energetic ball of sunshine, Alex was brooding. Lost in thought. Closed.

But she couldn't help the way she felt. The way she wanted to help him. Nurture him. Be the one to bring him slowly from his shell. It didn't mean she wanted to move on. At least she didn't think so. Confusion danced a pattern through her mind.

"Almost done, dear."

She smiled as her mother crossed the hall. "Thanks."

"Are you feeling okay?"

Lisa nodded. Her mother walked a few steps closer. "You should have told us, Lisa, just for your own safety. But this is your home, and it's your life. William's been gone now for months."

"I'm not *seeing* Alex, Mom." She felt like she was going to cry. Felt unfaithful to her darling husband just having to defend herself.

"Maybe not. But it doesn't mean you shouldn't if you want to."

Lisa swallowed away her emotion and linked arms with her mother. She dropped her head on her shoulder as they walked. Why did it have to be so hard?

"Can you tell Anna that?"

"Does that mean you *are* dating him?" her mother asked.

She flicked her mother on the arm and they both laughed.

No, but it didn't mean she hadn't thought about it. No matter how much her stomach crawled with guilt and worry, she couldn't deny thinking about Alex like that.

"So, do we get to meet this man?" Anna asked waspishly.

Lisa tried her hardest not to roll her eyes. "His name is Alex." She put up a hand before Anna had a chance to speak again. "And, yes, you can meet him right now."

Her mother smiled. Encouragingly.

"I'm just going to pour them each a glass of homemade lemonade and…"

"I'll get some cake," her mother finished.

Lisa filled the tray.

"Come on, then," she said, beckoning with her head. "And go easy on him."

It wasn't that she was worried about how he'd react to them. She'd told him plenty about her family. But he didn't like being asked about his past. His family. Or about war zones. She had picked up on that pretty fast, and she had no intention of pushing him unless he was mentally ready for it.

"Do you think it's okay to leave Lilly with him?"

Lisa ignored Anna's question. Was it okay? The kid hadn't spoken or shown interest in anyone except her and Boston for months, and yet she had taken to this guy like a bear to honey.

And he was hardly likely to hurt her. The man was more fright-ened of Lilly than she could ever be of him!

Plus, Alex just gave off the right vibes. Sad? Yes. Emotional wreck? Check. But dangerous? Even if *she* had judged his char-acter wrong William wouldn't have. Not after serving with him. If he trusted him enough to send him here, knowing that she'd be alone, then that was all that mattered.

She heard Lilly laughing. If she'd been alone she would have stopped to listen. Wondered at what Alex had said, or done, that she found so funny.

"Lilly! Boston!" Lisa called out to alert them. She didn't want it to seem like she was sneaking up on them. "Anybody hungry?"

Boston appeared first, leaping from the trees and landing on the path in front of them. He sported his usual big smile, tail wagging ferociously.

"Hey, Boston."

Boston was sprinkled with water and his big feet were cov-ered in mud.

A shadow caught Lisa's attention. It was like an umbrella had been whisked across the path. She felt rather than heard Anna go silent. Lisa looked up. And locked eyes with her guest.

"Hey, Alex."

He smiled. Less reserved than the smile he'd given her the day he arrived, but still cautious.

"I wanted to introduce you to some of my family," she told him.

He looked wary. She didn't blame him. She couldn't see the look on her sister's face but she could guess at it. As if he was the enemy. As if somehow this man was to blame for William not coming home.

Lilly suddenly burst from the trees.

"Bost…"

The name died in her mouth as she saw the others.

Lisa gave her a big smile, put down the tray and opened her arms. Lilly didn't hesitate before running to her mother.

"Say hello to Grandma and Anna."

Lilly gave them a wave and a big grin, before turning her eyes back to Alex. If she were older, Lisa would have thought she had a crush on the man.

"Alex, this is my mother, Marj, and my sister Anna." She gestured with her free hand.

"It's lovely to meet you, Alex." Her mother came forward and reached for his hand.

Alex moved slowly. Lisa found herself holding her breath.

"Marj," he said, like he was trying her name out. "I've heard a lot about you."

Lisa practically felt the silent words of her sister hovering in the air. *Wish we'd heard a lot about you.*

"And, Anna," he said, before she could say anything first. "Nice to meet you too." He held out his hand to her.

Anna clasped it. Lisa tried to ignore the tightness of her sister's smile. The way her eyes seemed to question him.

"What brings you to Brownswood?" her sister asked.

Alex looked uncomfortable. There was no way Lisa was going to let him feel bad about being here. Not when he had obviously faced a big battle just turning up here to meet her. She interrupted. "Alex was kind enough to bring some of William's things to me," she explained. Lisa started to walk, giving Alex the opportunity of some breathing space. "He was with William...ah...before his passing."

She glared back at her sister. The news had done little to change the look on her face, but she could see her mother softening.

"That was very kind of you, Alex," Marj said.

He shrugged his shoulders. Lilly squirmed and wriggled in Lisa's arms to get down. She bent and released her.

Boston took up the game and raced after Lilly as she ran, blonde hair streaming out behind her.

Lisa stifled a gasp as she watched. Lilly had caught Alex's hand, just lightly, as she moved past him. Just a touch, just a glimpse of contact, but contact nonetheless.

He didn't react. Well, hardly. But she didn't miss the slight upturn of his fingers. He had made contact back. And she guessed her sister hadn't missed the closeness between man and child either.

"Alex, are you okay taking the tray?" Lisa asked.

He turned around. Embarrassment fell upon his face like a shadow over water. Only he had nothing to be embarrassed about. Lilly was reaching out to him. There was nothing wrong with that.

"Sorry, I…"

"Don't be sorry. I just thought you could take this to the lake while I see these guys off."

He nodded.

"Come on, ladies," Lisa urged.

Her mother didn't hesitate, but Anna gave her another pointed look before saying, "It was lovely to meet you, Alex. Hopefully we'll see you again soon."

They started to walk back to the house. Alex had obviously been a touch uncomfortable, but the meet hadn't gone down too badly.

"He's awfully quiet," said Anna.

Lisa didn't need a thesaurus to figure out the meaning there. Not like William, her sister meant. William who'd worn his heart on his sleeve and been able to natter with the best of women.

"He's just come back from war—isn't that right, Lisa?" Marj said gently.

She nodded at her mother.

"You'd best remember that, Anna, and give the man a break," Marj said.

Lisa sighed. Sometimes having your mom around was the best medicine. It didn't matter what her opinion, or her own view, she was always supporter number one.

"You don't need to see us out, dear." Her mother patted her on the shoulder as they reached the house. "Go enjoy your afternoon."

* * *

Alex sat beside Lilly. He was still struggling with the whole kid thing. Not that she wasn't great, but he just wasn't used to it. Not to the enthusiasm. Not to the unpredictability. Not to the inquisitiveness. And she managed all that without saying a word.

He watched as she bit into a pink cake. He had no idea what the little bite-size sugar rush things were called, but they tasted good.

He listened to footfalls as Lisa approached. He didn't turn. He felt like he was slowly becoming desensitized, but there were things he would never shake. The quietness of the lake, or a bang that could signal danger.

"Hey, there," she said casually.

He liked that about Lisa. It was as if she knew what he was going through—understood, almost.

Alex drew one leg up so he could turn to look at her.

"Good…ah…cake." He held up what was left of the pink item.

"Macaroon," she corrected, dropping to sit beside him. "It's a rosewater macaroon."

He couldn't help the grin that stretched his face. "Rosewater? What happened to plain old strawberry?"

She laughed and reached for a tiny iced treat herself. "Went out with the nineties."

He guessed she saw the confusion cross his face when she started hiccuping with laughter. "Kidding, kidding!" She put up her hand. "I'm just doing a trial on some different things. There's still plenty of room for good old-fashioned flavors."

Lilly stood up and wriggled between them. She glanced up from under her lashes at Alex before cupping Lisa's ear. Then she dropped her hand, like an afterthought, and sat back down.

"Alex is gonna help me catch a real fish tomorrow," the little girl announced clearly.

"Really?" Lisa asked, determinedly nonchalant, but catching Alex's eye meaningfully.

He could see she was trying to stay relaxed. Lilly had spoken out loud. Not to him directly. But definitely so he could hear. She had changed her mind on whispering privately to her mother and actually spoken aloud.

He watched. He couldn't not. There was something mesmerizing about observing the pair of them together. As if Lisa wasn't enough, the girl was enchanting. Especially when she spoke.

"I'm going to do what?" he asked, trying to encourage her to talk again.

Lilly gave him one of her crooked quirks of a smile and then ran, arms stretched out wide as if she might fly.

"Catch a fish!" she called out.

"Huh." He stared at the water, feeling the quiet lull as he stared into it. "If you don't catch *me* with the hook first."

He looked sideways at Lisa. It didn't seem to matter when he looked at her, what time of the day, there was always a trace of a smile turning the edges of her mouth upward. But today there was a big one.

Lilly skipped off.

"You were great with her today, Alex." She turned to him, suddenly serious.

"You saw us?"

She nodded. "It means a lot to me."

He didn't speak as she paused. He recognized it now—she was thinking about William, or the past, or worrying about Lilly.

"And did you notice her speaking just then?" Her voice was low, but it thrummed with feeling.

He grinned. "I know."

"She always understood why Daddy was away, but since the service, since I told her, she's just been…different."

"Like with the not talking?"

Lisa closed her eyes. He wanted to reach for her. To cover her hand. Brush his fingertips over the soft smoothness of her cheek.

But he didn't. It had been a long, long time since he'd touched someone like that. Known what it was like to do something like that so naturally. So long since he'd had someone to care about him. Or vice versa. The army might have been a great substitute family, but it was all about control and order. What he'd missed out on were the casual touches and gentle love of a real family.

So instead he just watched. Absorbed her sadness and stayed still, immobile, unable to comfort her.

"I get it," he said.

She opened her eyes and looked at him.

"It's hard to talk sometimes. Just give her time," he elaborated. He knew that first-hand. Years ago he'd been Lilly. Deep down, after all he'd lost and what he'd seen, he still was that quiet child inside.

Lisa reached for his hand. Gave him the comfort that she herself needed. He almost pulled away, but the gentleness of her skin on his stopped him. Forced him to halt.

"That's why she likes you. Because you understand one another. Somehow," she added wryly.

He looked back out at the water. He guessed she was right. He did recognize what Lilly was going through. Maybe she sensed that.

When he turned back, Lisa's eyes were still tracing his face. Openly watching him. As if she was trying to figure him out.

"Are you still taking her to the therapist?" he asked.

"Next week." Lisa bent her knees up and moved to stand.

She leaned close to him, because she had to rise, and he felt it. Felt the heat of her body, smelt the faint aroma of baking on her clothes.

He turned away.

"I'll see you inside," she said.

Alex gave her a smile but stayed still.

"Come on, Lilly!" she called. "Time to come in."

But even as she called, pulling away from him, he saw the look on her face. Her eyes flickered when they settled on him. Something passed between them that he didn't want to recognize.

He dragged his eyes away. He was on dangerous territory here and he knew it. There was no room in his life for complications. His entire past had been complicated enough to last a lifetime.

She was a widow. Confused. Still in love with her husband. Definitely not the type of woman he would ever take advantage of. Ever.

He'd built a wall around himself for a reason. And he needed to remember that the gate was destined to stay firmly shut. He didn't want to love or lose again. Ever.

CHAPTER SIX

His head was pounding. Alex was fighting feelings of wanting to run, and others of wanting to stay in this cabin his entire life. Being with Lisa yesterday had affected him. Being the recipient of her warm gaze, seeing the appreciation in her eyes, had just made him feel like a traitor. So guilty. Yet he couldn't bring himself to tell her.

Then Lilly had kept talking all afternoon, forgetting her silence, and that had made him feel worried all over again.

He could see her walking down the path to him now, skipping over like she hadn't a care in the world. He knew otherwise, but it was wonderful to see such a lightness within her.

"Hey, Alex! Wanna fish?"

Alex didn't want to go fishing, but she looked at him with the biggest, most innocent gaze imaginable, and he couldn't say no. Just hearing her speak directly to him had him tied in knots.

"Aren't you sick of fishing?" he asked.

Lilly shook her head fiercely before reaching for his hand. She gave it a couple of insistent tugs. "Come on, Alex. Let's go in the boat."

He should have just said yes to fishing. Now he had to get the boat out and spend the next hour or more with the kid. He usually wouldn't have minded, but today—well, he just wasn't in the mood. But he knew what a big deal it was, her coming out and talking to him like that.

"Okay, go ask your mother and then come back out," He instructed.

She skipped off. He wished he could be more like her. Truth was, he *had* been her—in a way. He'd been the kid with no voice, the kid who'd lost a parent. Only he had lost both. Had gone from having two parents to none in a matter of minutes. So he hadn't had a mom to coach and nurture him like Lilly had.

Alex looked up as a whine hit his eardrums. Boston was sitting maybe a few meters away, his head cocked on one side, watching him. Alex let his elbows rest on his knees, staying seated on the step.

Even the dog knew he was troubled.

"You don't have to hang around with me," he said softly to the dog.

Boston changed the angle of his head.

"Seriously, you don't want to know my troubles."

The dog came closer, sitting so near he almost touched Alex's feet. But he faced away from him now. Had his back turned to Alex, his head swinging around as if to check he was okay with it.

Alex let his hand fall to Boston's soft back. His fingers kneaded through his fur. The motion felt good.

He'd always wanted a dog. From when he was a kid to when he'd dreamed of the life he'd never had while away serving. Now he knew why. There was something soothing about having an intelligent animal nearby who wasn't going to judge you. A dog who knew the comfort his fur offered and turned to let you stroke it. An animal who knew when to stay with you and when to leave you alone.

"I don't know if it's harder being here, or harder thinking about leaving," Alex mused.

Boston just leaned on him. Alex liked this kind of conversation. The dog wasn't going to think badly of him. He was just going to listen. But it was true. He'd run from this kind of life, stayed away for this very reason for so long, yet here he was starting to think about what he'd sacrificed for being scared.

Lilly appeared. Her tiny frame a blur of pink clothing against the green of the surroundings. She raised her little hand in a half-wave as she ran back toward him.

Boston wagged his tail. It thumped Alex's foot.

"What did your mom say, kiddo?" he asked.

Lilly grinned. "She said to stop bothering our guest, but if he asked me I could go."

Alex laughed. She never failed to lift his mood, even if he didn't want her to. "I won't tell if you won't."

Lilly wriggled over to him and grabbed hold of his leg.

He was getting too attached to these two beings, not to mention the third one inside the house, and it scared him. But he felt happy. Actually happy. And it wasn't an emotion he felt often, so he wasn't going to turn his back on it. Not yet.

Lilly sat in the boat as Alex hauled it. She looked like a queen sitting in residence as he labored it over to the water.

"Faster, Alex!"

He gave her his most ferocious look, but she just laughed at him. It made him laugh back—a real laugh, the belly-ache kind of stuff. Until he tripped over as Boston launched himself in beside Lilly, landing square in the middle of the boat.

Lilly's peals of laughter forced him to push up to his feet. Fast. "That dog needs to learn some manners," Alex grumbled. He looked over his shoulder quickly, but to his relief he couldn't see Lisa anywhere. It made him feel better. Not quite as embarrassed to have been felled by a dog.

"Can Boston come fishing too?" Lilly pleaded.

Alex was going to glare a refusal at her, but he knew it would do no good. The child who had once looked at him warily, with big clouds of eyes, closed off from him to a large extent, was now completely immune to his reactions.

"Does he have to?" Alex groaned.

Lilly swung an arm around Boston and hugged the dog tight to her. The dog looked like he was laughing.

Alex could see the irony of it. He was a tough soldier, a man who had fought for years on foreign soil, but here in Alaska the dog was head of the pack.

"Fine," he acquiesced.

She resumed her queen position, with Boston as her king.

Alex guessed that made him the peasant.

Alex eyed Boston as he sat, tongue lolled out, focused on the water. He didn't trust the dog not to launch himself straight out into the water if he saw something of interest, causing the boat to capsize.

"Careful with that line." He placed his hand over the end of Lilly's rod. "Hold it like I've shown you, and carefully cast it over."

"Like this?"

A surge of pride hit him in the chest. She'd finally started to listen. "Good girl."

The smile she gave him nearly split her face in half.

He grinned back. He hadn't spent much time with children, but this little girl—she was something else. Teaching her, talking to her, was so rewarding when she listened or followed his instructions.

"Now we sit back and wait," he said.

She fidgeted. Waiting probably wasn't her favorite part. For him, waiting was what he lived for. The sitting back, feeling the weather surround you, thinking, losing track of time, it meant everything to him.

For kids? It was probably the worst part.

The water lapped softly at the edge of the rowboat; the wind whispered over the surface, causing a tiny rock. Boston lay asleep, and Lilly had tucked up close to Alex, leaning against him to stay upright.

"Lilly, I want to tell you a little story about what happened to me as a boy," he said.

It almost felt wrong to make the mood heavy—especially when she'd only just stopped yapping to him—but he wanted to help her. Alex hated talking about his past, and usually never did, but this time he had to. If it meant he could do something to help Lilly overcome her fears and find her voice with others he needed to tell her this.

She looked up at him, her eyes like saucers. "Like a story?"

He nodded.

Alex kept his eyes out on the water, one hand firm on the rod. He swapped hands, putting it into his left so he could swing his right arm around her. He didn't want to scare her, or make her feel upset. He wanted to comfort her. Wanted to help her like he wished someone had helped him as a kid.

"When I was a boy—a bit older than you—my mommy and daddy both died." He gave her a wee squeeze when she didn't say anything. She felt soft, not tense, so he continued. "I was just like you, with no brothers or sisters, so when they died I didn't have anyone. You've got a mommy, but I had no parents at all."

He'd had great parents. The type who would do anything for you. But his life had gone in one fell swoop from happy families to sadness. From light to dark. That was why being here shook him so much. Because he felt responsible for ruining this little family as his had been ruined.

"So who looked after you?" Lilly whispered.

Her eyes upturned to catch his held such questions, such worry, that he didn't know what to say. He certainly wasn't going to tell her the whole thing. This story was to help her, not to get the lot off his chest. "Someone kind looked after me, but it wasn't like having my parents."

He felt bad, not telling her the whole truth, but the reality of being in care had been ugly. He'd come across decent people in the end, but foster care was no way to live life as a grieving child. It had made him hard. Steeled him against his pain. Made him feel like it was his fault he was there. Alone.

"The thing was, I was very scared. And very sad," he said.

He watched her little head nodding. "Me too."

"And, just like you, I stopped talking," he admitted.

She dropped her rod then. He scrambled to grab it. "Just like me?"

He passed her back the rod and waited for her fingers to clasp it. "Yep, just like you."

They sat there in silence, bodies touching. She felt so tiny next to him. So vulnerable. Alex's chest ached. The pain of memories that he'd long since put to rest was bubbling in his mind, but he had to help Lilly if he could.

"It was different when I wouldn't talk, though. Do you know why?" he asked.

She shook her head.

"Because you have a mommy who you can still talk to. I had no one. So when I stopped talking I didn't say a word to anyone. I had no one to talk to. You are very lucky, because your mom loves you and you can talk to her," he said quietly.

She sighed and let her head rest against his arm. "But I don't want to talk to anyone else."

"You talk to me." He whispered the words, conscious that maybe she hadn't actually thought much about the fact that she spoke to him.

"Something's different about you," she whispered back.

Alex wished her therapist could hear all this. Maybe to a professional it would make more sense. "Why? What's different about me?"

"You make me think of Daddy."

A hand seemed to clasp around Alex's throat. Squeezed it so hard he couldn't breathe. But this was Lilly. This was the child he was trying to help. He couldn't stall on her now. She was waiting for him to say something.

"Is it...ah...okay that I make you think of him?" he asked.

She gave him a solemn nod. "It's nice."

Damn it! The kid had pulled out his heart and started shredding it into tiny pieces. "So, when do you think you'll start talking again? You know—to other people?"

She shrugged. "When did you start talking?"

He didn't let his mind drift back to where it wanted to go. Couldn't. He had been *forced* to talk again. Forced to deal with the fate life had handed him.

Being picked on and bullied had been bad enough. But being the kid who didn't talk? That had made life even worse in the first foster home he'd been put in. But he'd been tougher by the time it came to the second home. Harder. He'd had to find his tongue again in order to stand up for himself, although he'd kept his voice to himself most of the time. Tough kids talked with their fists, and he'd had to learn that type of communication too.

Alex had gone all his life wondering what it would have been like if someone had genuinely tried to help him. Had talked to him and wanted to help make it right. The army had been like family to him up until now, but those men he'd served with had all had someone to go home to. They had been there for one another, and he'd known true support and compassion and camaraderie, but it wasn't the same as having a real family.

He let his arm find Lilly again and drew her close. It didn't matter how hard this was for him—he had to do it for her. "No one can tell you when it's the right time to talk again, Lilly."

She snuggled in. Alex's heart started pounding loud in his ears. Beating a rhythm at the side of his neck.

"When you see someone like your grandma do you want to talk to her? You know? When she talks to you first?"

"Yes." It was tiny noise, one little word, but it was honest.

"How about next time one of your grandmas or your Aunt Anna talks to you, you take a big breath, give them a big smile like I know you can, and think about saying something back?" he suggested. He could almost hear her brain working. Ticking. Processing what he'd said. "If you can't say anything, that's okay, but if you think hard about what you want to say back, and try really hard to say it, it might work."

"Will you help me?" she asked softly.

He put his fishing line between his feet to hold it and hugged her, tight enough to show he meant it. "I'll be here for you, Lilly. You just be strong."

"Aaaaggghhhhh!" Her squeal pierced his eardrum.

If he hadn't been so focused on Lilly, so consumed by his own dark thoughts, he probably would have seen it coming. The dog had leaped out of the boat, which now rocked precariously and tipped before he could do anything about it. Alex kept hold of Lilly, more worried about her than the fact the boat was turning over. They hit the water hard, but he still had hold of her. Had Lilly pressed tight against his chest, her forehead against his chin.

Alex instinctively started treading water. He could do it for hours if he had to. "You okay?" he asked urgently.

His eyes met laughing ones. Lilly looked like they were on some sort of adventure, not as if she could have drowned!

"Boston saw a duck!" she spluttered.

He followed her gaze. Sure enough, Boston was paddling fast towards a few ducks that were lazily swimming in the other direction.

He could have killed the dog!

"Mommy told you he liked ducks," Lilly laughed.

Hmm, so Mommy had. Alex shook the water from his eyes and swapped Lilly into his left hand, so he could use his right for swimming. He hoped for Boston's sake he wasn't feeling quite this annoyed when the dog showed up on solid ground.

What on earth…? Lisa almost turned away just to look back again. Why were they both soaking wet? She ran to get dry towels and headed out the door.

"What happened?" she called as she ran. Her heart was pounding. Talk about giving a mother a fright!

She watched as Alex gave Boston a dirty look. The dog was soaking wet too. Standing on the riverbank.

"Oh, no. Did he…?"

"Leap out of the boat and capsize us?" Alex was at least smiling, if somewhat wryly. "Yup."

Lisa laughed. She couldn't help it. She held out her arms to Lilly. "Come here, my little drowned rat."

Lilly scuttled into her arms and Lisa wrapped her in a towel. Then she passed one to Alex.

"He saved me," her daughter said proudly. "Alex grabbed me and swam me in, and then he went back for the boat."

Lisa smiled at Alex and mouthed *thank you*. He just shrugged. She turned back to her daughter. "Lilly, if I'd known you were taking Boston in the boat I would have been able to warn Alex. You know he isn't usually allowed in without a lead."

"Lilly Kennedy, did you forget to tell me that?" Alex asked incredulously.

Lilly looked sheepish.

"Off with you!" He ruffled her hair to show he wasn't cross with her. "And take that filthy mongrel with you."

"He's *not* a filthy mongirl!"

Lilly's struggle with the word had Alex and Lisa both in hysterics.

"Well, he *is* filthy, so off with both of you," Lisa finally managed to say.

They watched her run off after the dog, still wrapped in the towel.

"I think there's a hot shower with your name on it," Lisa hinted.

Alex grinned. "Good idea." He started to walk off.

"Thank you, Alex."

He turned back to her. "What for?"

She wanted to stay like this, in this moment, forever. He was so different, happy. Open.

"For saving her, for taking the time to talk to her. It means a lot to me," she elaborated.

"She's not exactly a hard kid to be around."

Lisa knew that. When Lilly was happy and talking she'd draw anyone in with her smile and chatter. These last few months it had been like having a nervous, tiny shadow of her daughter—a sliver of the fun little girl Lilly used to be. Her father had been away for a lot of her young life, but she had loved every minute with him when he'd been home, and had lived and breathed the excitement of having him return home one day for good once his term was over.

Now this stranger, this soldier, had turned up, and it was like Lilly's inner dragon had started to breathe fire within her again. Lisa couldn't thank him enough for that.

She stood and watched as Alex made his way inside. He might not say a lot, but when he did his words counted.

CHAPTER SEVEN

"ALL I'm saying is that it's hard to meet someone who'll take on a woman and a child," Marj said calmly.

"Great—thanks, Mom." Lisa scowled at the phone. "So you're likening me to used goods?" She scribbled down the final ingredient in a recipe and dropped her pen. Having her mother on speakerphone was not helping.

"Honey, you know I don't mean that," Marj protested.

Did she?

"I'm just saying that he must be a good man."

"Mom! For the last time, there is nothing—*nothing*—going on between me and Alex," Lisa said through gritted teeth.

"Well, what I'm saying is maybe you should give the guy a chance," Marj said.

Would it be so bad, moving on from William? Lisa heard a shuffle of feet and hit the hand control. She didn't want anyone else hearing this conversation. And she didn't want to discuss moving on. She still loved William. Period. What she felt for Alex was just attraction. A natural reaction for a lonely woman with a handsome man nearby.

"Honey?"

"Mom, I appreciate the support—I do. But I just need a little more time." She sighed.

She could feel his presence. Sure enough, within a handful of seconds Alex appeared in the living room.

"I've got to go. I'll come by soon." She hung up the phone. "Hi," she greeted him a little nervously.

He raised a hand in a casual wave. "Hey."

She tried not to let him see she was rattled.

"I didn't mean to interrupt you," he said, when she didn't say anything more.

"Don't be silly. It was just my mother. And I told you—the door is always open," she said in a rush.

He nodded. "She keeps a close eye on you, huh?"

"More like she's nosy. Her *and* Anna," she muttered. But she sensed he didn't really want to talk about her family. Well, that was fine. Neither did she.

"I'm about to head into town to run some errands," she told him.

Something crossed Alex's face that she couldn't put her finger on. Then his expression changed.

She waited.

"Would you…ah…like me to drive you?" he asked tentatively.

Lisa smiled. She'd love the company. "Sure—that'd be great." She watched as his face softened, like he hadn't known how she was going to react to his offer. "Let me grab a few things and we'll go."

"Am I okay like this?"

He looked down at his attire. She followed his eyes. What about him wasn't okay? Long legs clad in faded jeans. Tanned feet poking out below. Bronzed forearms hanging loosely from a fitted black T-shirt. Her gaze reached his handsome face and went down his gorgeous body again before she finally managed to wrench it away.

It was just an attraction. A natural reaction to a good-looking, fit, healthy male. It would pass, she told herself fervently.

"You look good. Add a pair of shoes and you'll be good to go," she said.

He wriggled his toes. She saw it. Which meant she was still

watching him. Darn it if her eyes weren't like magnets drawn to him!

"Let me get Lilly and my handbag and I'll see you at the car." Lisa forced herself to move. To walk away from him. She could feel him. Sense his big masculine presence. It was like when William had been home on leave, or between postings. The house had felt different. A feeling in the air. Only William had been a comfortable change. Solid, dependable. With Alex it was electric.

Lilly made the house feel alive, kept Lisa from ever feeling truly alone, but she couldn't deny that there was a sense of security, of strength, in a house when there was a man in residence. She dug her nails into her own hand. It was *William's* residence. Alex was just a visitor. Passing through.

But, wrong as it may be, there was definitely something comforting about having a man in her home. Even if it wasn't the man she was supposed to be sharing it with.

She looked at Lilly's closed bedroom door. There was a little thump and lots of giggling. Then there was a woof. Lisa guessed what was going on. Boston would be lying on the bed, on his back, legs in the air. His head would be settled on the pillows. Lilly would either have a bonnet on his head, socks on his feet, glasses on his nose, a blanket tucked around him, or all of the above. She treated the dog as if he was a living doll.

"We're going into town soon, honey," Lisa told her through the door.

"Can we take Boston?" Her voice was slightly muffled.

"Yes, we can take Boston."

Lisa let her forehead rest on the door. She owed a lot to that dog. Without him, Lilly would have been even worse. Would have been even more lost over William's death.

She heard a bout of giggles again. Lilly was definitely getting back to her old self. It was nice to have a daughter who was slowly filling up with fuel for life again.

"Get a wriggle on, girl. Two minutes!" Lisa warned.

Lilly didn't answer.

Strange as it might be, it was almost like things *were* getting back to normal again. Or as normal as life had ever been being a soldier's wife. Having Alex here felt right. In some ways. But deep down she didn't want it to be right. If she could wish for anything in the world, it would be to have William back.

So where did that leave her feelings for Alex?

Alex looked out the window as they chugged along. He didn't look at Lisa. He couldn't. Even though he'd intended driving her in, she'd laughed, told him to enjoy the scenery and jumped in on the driver's side herself.

Seeing her behind the oversize wheel of the baby blue Chevy had been bad enough when she'd waved him over before they'd left. There was something about her that just got to him. The casual ponytail slung high on her head, the way she wore her T-shirt, even the way her fingers tapped on the wheel to music.

He wound down his window and let a blast of air fill the cab. Boston straddled him and let his tongue loll out the window, nose twitching. Lilly wriggled next to him on the bench seat.

"Tell me again why Boston couldn't ride in the back?" Alex wanted to know.

Lisa laughed. Loud.

Relief hit him. Hard. Like a shock to the chest. He'd wondered if they were ever going to get that easy feeling between them back again. He'd missed it.

"Lilly won't have him in the back," Lisa explained.

He looked at the kid. She shook her head. Vigorously.

Alex pushed Boston back and wound the window up. He liked dogs, but four of them squished up-front seemed a bit— well, ridiculous. He went back to scanning the landscape. He might be biased, given the years he'd spent seeing sand and little else when he was deployed, but Alaska was beautiful. Incredible.

He'd dreamed of wilderness and trees and water every night before coming back to the US. Now he was here. In a part of the world that seemed untouched. It was the postcard-perfect back-drop he would have sketched when he was away. The idyllic spot he'd hankered for. As a child, he'd always dreamt of what his life could have been like, the kind of place he could have lived in with his family if they'd been around, and if he could have chosen anywhere Alaska would have made the list.

Even without Lisa and Lilly this place was perfect. *Although they sure did add to the appeal*, a little voice inside him whispered insidiously.

They'd only been driving maybe five, seven minutes before a stretch of shops appeared. They had an old-school type of quality—a refreshingly quaint personality. He'd driven into Brownswood this way, but he'd been so focused on following directions, on finding the Kennedy residence, that he'd hardly even blinked when he'd passed the row of stores. There was every kind of store here a person could need.

Lisa gave a toot and waved to an older woman standing on the street. She turned down the radio a touch and rolled down her window. "Hey, Mrs. Robins."

A few other people turned to wave. Small-town feel, small-town reality. The thought suddenly worried him. Was his being with her going to affect her standing? Surely she wouldn't have agreed to him coming along if she'd had hesitations? But still... He knew firsthand how small-town gossip started. And spread. When his parents had died it had been as if everyone had been talking about it. Pitying him. Whispering. But no one had stepped up to help him or take him in. They'd just watched as Social Services had taken him away.

Alex started pushing the painful memories back into the dark corners of his mind, like he always did. Just because he'd been doing better these past few days it didn't mean he was ready for this. Didn't mean he wanted to be seen or have to interact with anyone.

He did enjoy Lisa's company, he had to admit. That didn't mean he was ready to brave the world again, though. It had taken him years to learn how to force unwanted feelings down.

To push them away and lock them down. But now that he'd left the army after ten years he was struggling. Because he didn't want to be alone.

Having company again was kind of nice.

Lisa wasn't going to hide just because she had Alex with her. She had to keep mentally coaching herself, reassuring herself that she wasn't doing anything wrong, but it was hard.

These people had known her since she was a little girl. Known William since he was in diapers. Not to mention known them both together as husband and wife for a good few years. And the worry, the guilt, was eating at her from the inside. She cared about what people in her community thought about her. Plus she cared about her husband. She didn't ever want to be disloyal to him, or to his memory.

For some reason, though, it felt like she was.

But Alex was a friend. *A friend.* There was nothing wrong with having a friend who was a man. Nothing wrong at all.

Besides, she had been forced to start a new chapter in her life the day William had passed away. Like it or not, the residents of Brownswood were just going to have to accept that. She loved being part of the community, but would they expect her to be a widow forever?

Lisa focused her attention back on Alex. At her friend and nothing more. Pity about the flicker of fire that raced through her body when she looked at him. "Is there anything you need? Anywhere you want to go?"

Alex dragged his eyes back toward her. She didn't know what he had been looking at—maybe everything—but he'd seemed another world away in his own thoughts.

"Sorry?"

He *had* been another world away. He hadn't even heard what she'd said. "Is there anywhere you particularly want to go?" she repeated.

He shook his head. "Maybe a fishing shop, if there is one, but it's not really necessary."

Lisa pulled into a spare parking bay. It wasn't like they were hard to come by here, but she hated to have to walk too far. "I just need to do the grocery shopping, grab a prescription from the pharmacy, and take Lilly to her therapist appointment."

"I'll come help carry the groceries," he suggested.

She appreciated that he liked to be a gentleman but she didn't want him to feel like he owed her. Didn't want to need his help.

"Why don't you take a look around and meet me outside the store?" She pointed with her finger at the grocers. "I'll be about twenty minutes in there, and then I'll take Lilly to her appointment."

"Okay."

She watched as he gave Lilly a hand out of the cab, her petite fingers clasped in his paw. The one with the real paw whined, but stayed put.

"Won't be long, Boston." Lilly waved to her dog.

"See you soon, then," Alex said.

Lilly waved to him too.

Alex felt like a fish out of water. He hated that everyone he walked by would know he was new in town. It didn't look much like a tourist spot, so they probably looked at newbies as fresh meat on the block.

He decided to avert his eyes from the few people milling around and check out the shops instead. A hardware store, a small fashion shop, then a bookstore. He let his step quicken as he noticed a place across the road. Bill's Bait & Bullets. He crossed the road.

A stuffed moose head filled the window, along with an assortment of feathered varieties. He wasn't into hunting, but he loved to fish, and if the sign on the door was anything to go by then he was in luck.

"Howdy."

Alex nodded his head at the man behind the counter who'd just greeted him. He sported a bushy mustache and was a wearing a blue and white plaid shirt. He guessed this was Bill.

"You after anything in particular?" Bill asked.

Alex did a quick survey around the shop and eyed the rods.

"Looking to do a spot of fishing," he said, walking in the right direction. "Wouldn't mind a new rod. Or two."

The man rounded the counter and came back into view. "You've come to the right place, then." He walked over to the rods. "That what brings you here? Fishing?"

Alex didn't see the point in lying. Not when everyone around would be gossiping later. But he wasn't about to start telling this Bill all his business.

"Here to see an old friend." He left it at that. "I need a rod for me, and one for a kid. About so high." He gestured with his hands at what he estimated Lilly's height was. "Six, I think."

"Girl or boy?" Bill enquired.

He gave the man a stern look. Asking politely was one thing, getting nosy was another. It wasn't like fishing rods came in pink or blue. Bill was just trying to guess which kid in town Alex was buying it for.

"I just need a rod for a child," he reiterated firmly.

The man shuffled away, and Alex moved to look around the shop. It was at times like this he thought of William, about what he might be doing now if he'd survived. They'd spent a lot of time talking about what they liked to do, and William had always talked about his family.

When they'd kicked a ball around in the sand, sat back when there was nothing else to do, or lain side by side waiting for their orders, there had been nothing else to do but talk. And while Alex hadn't opened up much about his past, other than to tell William he had no family, his friend had reminisced about his little girl and his wife. Told him how he wanted to teach his daughter to fish and follow tracks in the forest one day.

So Alex felt good being here buying a rod. Felt right about doing something he knew William would have done, had he lived. He wasn't trying to take his friend's place—part of him still wanted to run when Lilly so much as looked up at him—but this was something he could do. In William's memory. This was the way he could help William's family through their loss.

Lisa found Alex leaning against the hood of the car when they returned for the second time. He'd long since packed the groceries into the back, after she'd met him at the vehicle with the bags, and he was now leaning with one foot against the front wheel arch and the other out front.

Lilly bounded up to him, then decided to give Boston, who was still inside the car, her attention instead. She'd coped well with the therapist. Now she was open as a spring flower, and Alex and Boston were helping to keep her like it.

"I didn't know if he was allowed out or not," Alex said, gesturing to the cooped-up canine.

"No, he isn't!" Even Lilly laughed at her mother's appalled expression. "He has a track record of stealing sausages from the butcher, snatching sandwiches—all sorts of things," Lisa explained.

Alex cracked a grin. It stopped her in her tracks. She'd seen him smile more than once now, plenty of times, but they were often sad smiles. Often haunted. This one was powerful. It showed off straight white teeth and set his eyes to crinkling.

"That the real reason he travels shotgun?" he asked.

"You've got me there." She smiled.

Alex opened the door and Lilly scrambled in. "She get on okay?" he asked.

Lisa gave him a thumbs-up. "Big progress." She crossed around the side of the car to jump behind the wheel. When she got in, it wasn't as crowded as she'd expected.

Lilly had crawled into Alex's lap.

Lisa's hand shook as she tried to put the key in the ignition. She turned on the engine. Then looked at Alex. His eyes were pleading. Torn between terror and something she couldn't identify. She was about to tell Lilly to get in her seat. About to take action. When Lilly's head fell against Alex's chest.

It nearly broke her heart.

Lilly had always sat like that with William. Lisa had always found them in the car like that, waiting for her to emerge from a shop.

And now she was sitting like that with Alex.

It was the first time since he'd come into their lives that she'd seen him fill William's boots. The idea of replacing William made her feel physically sick. But the ever-present thrum of attraction, of being drawn to Alex, quickly pushed away the nausea.

She met his eyes again. He didn't blink. Didn't pull his eyes away. The brown of his irises seemed to soften as he looked back at her. She watched as one hand circled Lilly, keeping her tucked gently against him. Lisa could see the gentle rise and fall of his chest. He still hadn't looked away.

She swallowed. Tried to. But a lump of something wouldn't pass. Lilly's doctor's words echoed in her mind, but she swept them away.

Something had changed between them. In that moment the goalposts had moved. It had been building up, simmering below the surface. But right now something had definitely changed.

She knew it and he knew it.

Alex wasn't pulling away from her daughter—but then she hadn't ever seen him truly pull away from Lilly before. They were like kindred spirits. The way they connected was—well, like nothing she had imagined, believed, could happen.

But he'd always pulled away from *her*. Always kept himself at a distance. Kept himself tucked away.

Not now.

Now Lisa could finally see with clarity that he felt it too. She'd been caught in his gaze too long.

Lisa placed her hands on the wheel. Her palms were damp. She put the car in gear, looked over her shoulder, then pulled out onto the road.

And then she saw her.

William's mother stood on the footpath. Watching them.

She raised a hand to wave to her, and cringed as guilt crawled across her skin. Swept like insects tiptoeing across every inch of her body. Brought that nausea to the surface again. Made her wish she could just stamp on the attraction she felt for Alex and go back to pining for William.

His mother raised her hand too. But Lisa could see the look on her face. It was pained and confused and upset.

Lisa thumped her foot on the accelerator to get away. She couldn't face her. Not right now.

She'd done nothing wrong, so why did she feel so guilty?

And why did she feel like nothing was ever going to be the same ever again?

She glanced over at Alex, taking her eyes from the road for a nanosecond. Lilly was still tucked against him. Boston had his head resting against his leg.

Could she really ever be with another man? William had been her one and only lover. The only man in her life. Her high-school sweetheart and best friend. The only man she'd ever wanted.

Did thinking about Alex romantically make her a bad person? She hoped not. Because there was no chance she could ignore Alex.

Not a chance.

She knew that now. And she didn't have the strength to fight it much longer.

No matter how much it was tying her in knots.

CHAPTER EIGHT

LISA couldn't look at Alex. She got the feeling he felt the same.

As soon as they'd arrived home he'd carried the groceries in for her, placed them in the kitchen, then made for the door. He hadn't even spoken to Lilly.

Lilly had fallen asleep against him on the short drive home, waking only when Lisa had taken her from his arms and carried her inside. She was still napping now.

Lisa poured herself a cup of strong, sweet tea.

She hadn't lied to Alex earlier, Lilly's therapy session had gone great. Lilly had smiled, drawn happy pictures, and nodded in answer to the questions the therapist had asked. She hadn't spoken, but she'd communicated in the way the doctor had asked her to. Through creative expression.

But at the end the doctor had called Lisa aside. She'd told her that Lilly was making a sudden burst of progress, and asked about Alex. Lilly had drawn pictures of him—a large man standing beside them. A man with a smile. Which meant he was both important to her and a current source of happiness.

The doctor had pointed out that she'd drawn a family picture. With Alex cast as the dad.

It was fine. Lisa could deal with that image in theory. But the doctor had cautioned her that Alex leaving at any stage, for whatever reason, might cause Lilly to go back, to retreat further into a state of grieving.

Lisa didn't even know if Alex had been officially discharged from the army. For all she knew he might only be back for a few months or so before he was redeployed somewhere millions of miles from Alaska. And he was only staying here for another—what?—two weeks? Would they just try to go back to normal and forget he'd ever existed once he left?

The very thought of him going back to the place that had taken William from her made her sick to her gut. But soldiers were soldiers, and they went where they were needed. She'd been a patriot all her life, and just because William had been one of the casualties of war it did not mean she had any right to want Alex not to go back. Or even to think it.

But the thought of him leaving worried Lisa, regardless of where it was he might go. She could ask him to leave now, before they became too attached to each other, but that could do Lilly as much harm as losing him in a week or more. She could explain that because he was a friend of Daddy's he had to go back to his own house, but did she really need to burst that bubble now if Lilly honestly thought he was staying for longer? Did she even understand that he wasn't here for good? Lisa was struggling with the idea herself.

She rubbed at her neck. The base of it seemed to hold all her stress these days. It was worry. She knew that. Her neck had prickled ever since... Well, she was going to stop thinking about that. About Alex. Every time she did it reminded her that she was a widow, and she didn't need a fresh wave of guilt on her conscience. Thinking about him didn't mean she was cheating. Didn't make her disloyal. Surely?

Seeing William's mother had given her a good enough dose of that.

Lisa looked around the kitchen. She could bake. That always made her feel better. But she'd already finished creating her recipes and ideas for the book. What she needed was a break. Plus that reminded her that she actually had to send her work to her editor.

The house was silent. Birds cawed in the trees outside, their noise filtering in. The sun let its rays escape in through the window, hitting the glass and sending slivers of light into the room.

What was Alex doing? She couldn't hear him, so he obviously wasn't working on the cabin.

She got up. Her feet seemed to lead her on autopilot toward the door. There was something forbidden about what she was doing. But she didn't stop. Just seeking him out felt like she was prodding a sleeping tiger.

It wasn't like she'd never gone out looking for him before, but today was different. Today she was haunted by the look in his eyes earlier in the car. Today she was a woman thinking about a man. Today she was fighting the widow who loved her husband still. Today she just wanted to be a woman who happened to like a man.

Lisa stopped before stepping outside to check her hair. She ran her hands across it, making sure her ponytail was smooth. She pressed her hands down her jeans and fiddled with her top.

She had no idea what she was doing. Why she was looking for him. But she had to see him. Had to prove to herself that there had been something between them in the car today. Something she wasn't imagining. Something that was worth feeling guilty over.

She followed the beaten path through the short grass and let her eyes wander out over the water. He was nowhere to be seen, but the lake calmed her as it always did.

Maybe that was why Alex had chosen to stay? Because he'd taken one look at that water and known he wanted to see it every morning when he woke up. She didn't dare wish that she'd been a reason factored into his decision.

Lisa gulped. Hard.

The door was ajar. Was he in there?

Her feet started walking her forward again. They didn't stop until she was at the door of the cabin, and still they itched to move.

She didn't know why, but she didn't call to him. Didn't tell him she was there. She didn't know why she was even seeking him out. She nudged the door open and took the final step inside. Her eyes found his straight away.

It was her who wanted to flee this time.

She looked into his face. Tried to ignore the fact that he was shirtless. That his tanned stomach with its tickle of hair was staring straight at her.

He remained wordless.

They just stared at one another. There was nothing to say.

They *had* both felt it in the car. It wasn't just her imagining it. She could tell from the sudden ignition of fire in his eyes that he felt the same.

He stood up. It was like a lump of words was stuck in her throat and no amount of swallowing was going to dislodge it. Or force it out.

His body sported an all-over tan. Or what she could see of it at least. His arms were firm, large. In a strong, masculine way—like he'd worked hard outside for a lot of hours. She didn't dare look down any further.

She met his eyes and wished she hadn't. She'd never seen him like this. Never.

"You need to go."

His voice had the strength of a lion's growl. She felt told off. He had demanded she leave and yet she couldn't.

"Alex." His name came out strangled.

He stopped in front of her. So close that she could feel the heat from his body.

She was immobile. Glued to the spot. She raised her hand from her side, moved it palm-first toward him. She ached to feel his skin.

He caught her wrist in a vice-like grip before she made contact.

"No." His voice was still firm, gruff, but it was losing its power.

They stared at one another, glared. His breath grazed her skin.

She wasn't going to look away. Every inch of her wanted him. She'd never felt so alive, so desperate.

"Lisa, I can't—" His voice broke off.

She could see the torment in his eyes. He looked cracked open, yet so strong. Determined.

But he was as weak as her.

When she'd been with her husband it had been warm. Soft. Comfortable. It had *never* been like this. Attraction, intensity, punched the air between them.

His grip on her wrist slackened but she kept it still. He shuffled one step closer to her, their bodies now only inches apart. His lips parted and his mouth came toward hers.

She leaned forward until their lips touched. Just. He caught her bottom lip in the softest of caresses.

Lisa let her hand fall against him. Felt the softness of his skin, just like she'd imagined, beneath her palm.

He moaned. She could only just hear it. His lips still traced softly against hers. It was the deepest, most gentle, most spine-aching kiss she'd ever experienced. And still it went on.

So soft that she almost wondered if she was dreaming it.

She opened her eyes.

The six-feet-plus of bronzed, strong male before her convinced her that it was real. That *he* was real.

It was as if he'd felt her eyes pop.

He pulled back. Hard. Then jumped away from her as though she was some sort of danger to him. Pulled away like she was poison.

"No!" He belted out the word.

She was numb. Couldn't move.

"No." Quieter this time.

She let her face ask the question. *Why not?*

"Leave, Lisa. Please, just leave."

His voice belied the emotion tearing him apart. Guilt cascaded through her. She was the cause of it. Of his pain. Why had she done it? Come looking for him?

"Alex…" she whispered.

"You're another man's wife, damn it! Leave!" he barked.

She shook her head, tears forming in her eyes. Because she wasn't a wife. Not anymore. William was gone. *Gone!* She was no man's wife. The knowledge hit her like a blow to the gut. She was going to tell him that, but he looked torn. Grief-stricken. He wouldn't listen anyway. Besides, she didn't want to talk to him.

His back was turned. So she walked out. Kept her chin high as the tears started to trickle down her cheeks.

This wasn't fair. Life wasn't fair.

She still loved William. But she wanted Alex too.

Was it wrong to wish for both?

Alex watched her leave. He couldn't drag his eyes away from her if he tried. And he had tried.

It was like he was lost in her. Powerless to pull away from her. But she wasn't his. She could *never* be his.

Hadn't he already thought all this through?

His body had rebelled. She had felt so good against him. Lips softer than a feather pillow, hands lighter than a brush of silk.

He straightened and reached for his shirt.

Yes, he had already decided that she was forbidden. But that was before. Before Lilly had tucked up on his knee like a puppy. Before their afternoon out in the boat. Before Lisa had looked at him like that.

Before he'd let himself fall in too deep.

It was reminding him too much of what he'd lost. What it had been like to be a child with happy parents. And how much it hurt losing something like that. He'd long ago decided you were better not having it in the first place than risk losing it.

The last foster-family he'd been with had put a roof over his head and food in his belly, but he'd still felt like they'd just had him in order to collect the welfare checks. They'd never treated him like they did their own son. And when the other soldiers, his family, had pinned up photos of their loved ones Alex had never been able even to look at the crumpled photos of his parents. Which was why he'd never let anyone close to him since they'd died. Because he had never wanted to feel that way ever again.

Alex looked out the window.

He had to force Lisa out of his head. Just because he liked being here, liked feeling part of this little family, it didn't mean he had a right to be attracted to her. Didn't mean she had a right to be attracted to him.

All he knew was that he wanted her. And that she was forbidden.

It would take a stronger man to pull away from her again, though. And he didn't think he could be any stronger. Alex had fought it for so long. Thought he could go without love. Without family. Forever.

But the pain in his chest, the pain that had been there suffocating him for most of his life, told him he was wrong. That no matter how hard he tried to forget, to move on and not think about the past or what could have been, he would do anything for a family to call his own. To recreate what he'd lost. And that was why he hated the fact that William had saved him and not thought about himself instead. Because family was everything in this world. It was the reason why Alex felt he had nothing.

Now he knew more than ever how much he really craved what he'd lost. How much he wanted what could have been. And it was killing him that he was yearning for the family that William had sacrificed to save Alex's life. How twisted was that?

It was time to move on. Or at least to get this cabin fixed up as soon as possible so he didn't look like he was running out on them. And then he'd leave as fast as he could.

* * *

Lisa wanted to curl into a ball and never emerge. What had happened out there?

Oh, she knew. She knew because she'd been the one to go out there searching for him. She'd known that there was something between them, and she'd gone out there hoping to find out exactly what it was.

It had certainly been an emotional day.

First she'd had to deal with the therapist, not to mention her mother on the phone. Then she'd seen her mother-in-law in town. And Lilly had curled up on Alex's lap, and then... Well, she didn't quite know what had happened with Alex in the cabin. What it was they'd shared.

She only knew that they'd both acted on it.

And it had been Alex who'd pulled away. When it should have been her.

Alex. Just thinking his name sent tickles through her veins. Made them jump beneath her skin.

He was handsome. He was strong. And yet he was also vulnerable. So unlike her husband it scared her. William had been so together. So controlled. Yet at the same time like a wide open book. Alex was mysterious. Hard to read.

Yet sexy as hell.

She was beyond confused.

There were people who'd like her to be a grieving widow forever. Her sister was one of them. William's friends fell into that category too. She had no desire to be miserable and alone for the rest of her life. No desire at all. But then she didn't exactly want to move on yet either.

She thought of William's mother. Her in-laws were possibly the only people in her life who were allowed to make judgments. She wouldn't blame *them* for wishing she stayed a widow forever. She had been married to their only son. She was the mother of their only grandchild. Of course it would hurt to see her moving on with her life.

But even though William had been dead only eight months, to Lisa it felt like an eternity some days. And like yesterday at other times. Yet she'd hardly ever seen him. She'd been a single mom in many ways for most of their marriage. It didn't mean she hadn't loved him—she still did—but she wasn't going to be made to feel like she didn't care about his memory just because she was a little attracted to Alex.

Truth be told, if Alex hadn't come into her life she might have taken years to date again, let alone think about another man the way she was thinking about him. But he was here now, and there was something between them, and she wasn't going to let what other people thought get in her way. She was the only one to make decisions about her love life. And right now she didn't know what she was thinking!

She lay on the sofa and closed her eyes. It felt good. Relief washed through her as she stayed motionless. Her eyes stung from having cried, but she felt surprisingly okay. If she could just sleep it off maybe she'd feel better. Lilly was having a power nap, so why couldn't she?

Lisa woke with a start. How long had she been asleep?

She stretched out her limbs and combed her fingers through her hair before retying her ponytail.

Lilly.

Lisa hurried up to her bedroom and pushed open the door. She was up already, but Lisa knew where she'd be.

Less than a week ago Lilly would have been tapping her on the shoulder to wake her up. Now she wouldn't have had a thought for her snoring mother as she skipped out to find their guest.

Alex. She didn't particularly feel like seeing him right now, but she didn't have much of a choice.

She rounded the corner. Sure enough, there they were, standing side by side at the lake. Boston lay nearby, but he rose to greet her. The other two didn't bother to turn. Lilly might not have heard her, but she knew that Alex had. If he'd been a dog his ears would have twitched he was so alert.

"Hey, guys," Lisa said.

Lilly swiveled. She nearly took Alex out again with her hook. "Mommy, look what Alex gave me!"

She gave Lilly a beamer of a smile and went forward to inspect it. Now she had pointed it out Lisa could see she held a pint-size rod. Perfect for her little hands. "Wow! Your own rod, huh?"

Lisa acted like everything was normal, even though hearing Lilly talk in front of someone else still stole her breath away and made her want to jump for joy. But, just as the therapist had instructed her, she ignored it. For good measure she kept her eyes away from the lure of Alex.

Lilly had excitement literally dripping from her.

And Lisa couldn't help but look.

Alex still had his eyes trained on the water, his line out. But she knew he was listening. "I hope you said thank you to Alex, sweetie?"

Lilly nodded. Smugly.

Lilly turned back to the water and put the line over her shoulder. Lisa could tell there had been some practicing going on.

"Cast it back in the water like I showed you, nice and steady," Alex said quietly.

"Watch, Mom, watch!"

Lisa couldn't not watch, although half her gaze was focused on Alex. He stood with his feet spread shoulder-width apart, arms raised slightly from his sides. He looked as if he would be comfortable standing like that all day.

"Alex! Alex! Something's pulling!"

Lisa jumped at her daughter's excited train of words.

Alex calmly put down his own rod. "Stay still. Keep your hands steady."

Lilly did as she was told.

Alex moved to stand behind her and placed his hands over hers. Lisa couldn't hear what he was saying, but he was whispering in Lilly's ear as he guided her.

A splash indicated the line had emerged from the water, followed by an excited squeal from Lilly. "It's a fish!"

Lisa knew what would come next.

Alex helped her bring it in, then placed it on the grass. He worked to unhook it as they watched.

"Don't hurt it!" Lilly exclaimed.

Lisa tried not to laugh.

Alex looked confused. Lisa watched in amusement as his eyebrows formed a knot. "Aren't we going to have the fish you caught for dinner?"

Lilly shook her head. At rapid speed.

He sighed. "Shall we throw it back in, then?"

She nodded this time. A big grin on her face.

Alex threw Lisa a wry look over his shoulder—the first time he'd looked at her since what had happened between them earlier. "Here goes."

He let the fish go. Lisa knew as well as he did that it might die anyway, but Lilly looked happy.

"Bye, Mr. Fishy."

Alex shook his head in mock dismay.

"Let's catch another one, Alex!"

Lisa thought she could listen to her daughter talk to Alex all day. Now that she was speaking to him she'd probably never stop.

Lisa knew something was wrong the moment she walked inside. The light, happy feeling bubbling inside her from hearing Lilly talk turned off like a tap.

Something was wrong. Then she heard it. A soft rasp at the front door, only just audible. She went to see who it was. Her sister or mother would have just walked in. She knew it was unlocked because she'd been too caught up in her thoughts to go and lock it earlier.

Lisa swung it open. The person standing there took her breath away. It was William's mother.

"Sally." She tried to hide her discomfort. "I…ah…it's good to see you."

The woman looked like a shell of a human. Her eyes had lost the freshness they'd once enjoyed. Lines tugged at the corners of her eyes where before her skin had been seamless.

Lisa knew how she felt. That hollow feeling, and then the desperate barrage of grief-stricken emotion. It was what she'd experienced herself when the messenger had come. It still gripped her late in the night, when the cold sweat on her skin told her that William was gone for good.

For Sally, the torment was written all over her face. She would never see her son again. Just like Lisa was never going to see her man again. But at least Lisa had Lilly to keep her going every morning when she held her in her arms.

Sally had her husband and her grandchild, but she had lost her only son.

Lisa ignored the guilt tugging within her belly. She wasn't trying to replace William—she could never do that—but today she had for the first time wondered if she could actually start over. Give herself another chance while at the same time not forgetting William. The guilt she felt now told her that maybe she wasn't ready yet. She might never be. Not entirely. But Alex had at least made her want to find out.

"Lisa, I'm sorry, I shouldn't have come," the other woman said tremulously.

Lisa stepped forward and pulled Sally into her embrace. "Yes, you should have."

They stood like that, wrapped in one another's arms, not moving.

"Sally, about before—" Lisa started.

The older woman stepped back and dabbed at her eyes with a handkerchief, a shaky smile on her face.

"You've nothing to explain," Sally insisted.

Lisa appreciated not being judged. "But I want to."

"It's just—well, people were talking. After seeing you. I wanted to know for myself," Sally said.

Lisa nodded. Oh, she knew how the town would be gossiping. They'd all have her dripping in black and a grieving widow until the end of her days if they could. But deep down she didn't care about them. Or anyone. Except her husband. And her family. And Sally was family, even if they were no longer connected by her marriage.

She linked her arm with Sally's and led her into the kitchen. "There's someone outside who I want you to see."

Sally looked confused.

"The man you saw me with." She paused as Sally's face took on a hue of uncertainty. "He is—was—a friend of William's."

She sensed relief in the other woman. Her shoulders suddenly didn't appear so hunched, so shrivcled.

"He served with William. He's just returned home."

Sally's eyes looked hopeful. "Was he with William...at the end?"

"Yes."

Sally closed her eyes as Lisa held her hands even tighter.

"He's—well, he's troubled," she warned. "He doesn't like talking about what he saw over there."

Sally nodded. "Not many do." She gave Lisa a brave smile. "Not like our William did."

"I do want you to meet him,' Lisa reiterated. "But I want the time to be right."

"I understand," Sally said.

Lisa beckoned with her hands and stood up. Sally did the same and Lisa put her arm around the older woman and led her to the window.

Alex was visible. He was still with Lilly. They stood side by side at the edge of the lake.

"Are you two...ah..." Sally cleared her throat "...seeing one another?"

Lisa shook her head slowly. "No." She wasn't lying. There was nothing between them. Yet. If there was she would have said.

But she *had* thought about it. Had wondered if there was

any chance of something happening for real between them. Although after his reaction earlier…

Sally leaned into her. "Do you want there to be?"

Lisa didn't answer straight away. She'd known this woman for years. She'd been a fantastic mother-in-law. And she wasn't about to start lying to her—not when she'd never done it before.

"I think so." It felt strange saying it, but it was the truth. If there was a way to be loyal to William, keep her family happy, *and* attempt to develop something with Alex—well, she would do it. The thought made her bones rattle.

Sally started to nod, and as she did she also started to cry. Tears pooled in Lisa's eyes too, but she fought them. She didn't want to hurt this woman—or herself.

"Would William approve of you being with him, do you think?" Sally asked.

Lisa knew the answer to that. She'd wondered that in the night. This afternoon too. Hadn't wanted to think about it, but she knew the answer without even pondering on it. William had been kind, open and loving. He would have wanted her to be happy.

"Yes." She hugged Sally tighter. "In his absence, I can honestly say that, yes, he would." Tears stung her eyes once more.

Sally still had her gaze trained on Alex. Lilly was leaning against him, like she was tired. "Then you have my blessing," she said quietly.

Lisa's shoulders almost rose to the ceiling. It was as if the heaviest of weights had been removed. Not because she definitely wanted to move on, or because she was sure about her feelings for Alex yet, but because it was one less thing she had to battle with. To feel guilty about.

"You know this doesn't mean I didn't love William," Lisa said urgently.

Sally turned damp eyes on her and put both hands on her

shoulders. "You were a good wife to him, Lisa. And we'll always love you."

The Kennedys were good people. But she'd never thought they could be so understanding. Not when she wasn't even sure about her feelings or whether she forgave herself for being attracted to someone else so soon.

"Would you like to come around on Sunday night? That will give me some time to…get some things organized," Lisa suggested.

"That would be great. Why don't you come to our place, though?" Sally offered.

Lisa wasn't sure how happy Alex would be about going, but she knew he'd make the effort. Maybe it would help him. Just maybe. And maybe it would also help her to finally figure out her feelings.

CHAPTER NINE

"WHAT do you say we go for a picnic today?"

Lisa looked up at Alex as she asked the question. He was sitting eating his breakfast. There were kitchen facilities out in the cabin, but Lisa had made a habit of asking him in for meals.

She liked the company—although he was nothing like William had been in the mornings, up before her, chatting up a storm, planning their day. She enjoyed Alex's company even if he was quiet. There was something about him, about his presence, that appealed to her. And he seemed to have forgiven her for seeking him out and precipitating their kiss yesterday.

Besides, there was no fridge out there, so he wasn't exactly going to keep milk, was he?

He chewed his toast. Thoughtfully. Lilly sat beside him, slurping at a bowl of cereal.

"Okay," he said.

Lisa stifled her laugh. He didn't get a very good score in the enthusiasm stakes. "I thought it would be nice to take a walk through the National Park. Boston can come with us on a lead."

Alex nodded. This time he didn't take so long to make a decision. It was like something had changed between them yesterday. Even after what had happened, they seemed to have silently moved on. He was more open. Different. And there was even more of a closeness between him and Lilly. Lisa could sense it. Perhaps they'd been talking more than she realized?

"Do you walk the same track each time?" he wanted to know.

Lisa enjoyed a ripple of excitement as she saw she'd piqued his interest. One of the reasons this property was so special to her was its connection to nature. It was a nice feeling to think he was going to share it with her.

"I'll meet you outside the cabin in an hour. You'll find out all about it then."

Alex went back to eating his toast and Lisa rifled through the fridge for the makings of the picnic. Lilly loved going on excursions, but she knew better than to rush off empty handed.

And it helped keep her mind off Alex. There was a spark, a flame that traveled between them when they were close, but he was so hard to get to know. The barrier he'd built around himself was made of something strong.

Lisa loved being outdoors. Loved hanging out with her daughter and enjoying the weather. She hoped Alex would too. Anything to bring him a little further out of his shell. Right now it was like they went two steps back for every one forward.

She wanted to know more about the demons he fought. She wanted to know if she could help him. Yesterday, she'd never thought it would be possible. Not when she still loved William so much. Not when Alex had pushed her away.

Now she was wondering if maybe, just maybe, something real could develop between the two of them. If they both took a big leap of faith.

Lilly was dancing along the edge of the river as Lisa attempted to haul the rowboat from its makeshift house. She heaved hard, but it was only moving an inch at a time.

"Hey!"

She turned at the sound of the voice and watched as Alex crossed the yard.

"Let me get that."

She stood back. Grateful. She didn't much mind rowing it, and it usually wasn't so hard to get it out, but it had sat dormant since William's last visit home and then gone back wet the other day after it had been capsized. She should have told Alex to just leave it out.

He made it look easy, though. Alex hauled it behind him, the thick rope looped over his shoulder.

"You want to launch here?" he asked.

"Perfect."

She passed Alex two packs, which he placed in the boat. Then he reached for Lilly.

"Need me to do anything else?" he said.

"Grab the dog." That was the part she hated. Boston usually leapt and toppled them out, or she had to pick him up already wet.

Alex chased the dog and tackled him. "Come here, you filthy mongrel!"

Lilly laughed. Alex was trying his best to look stern.

Lisa decided not to point out how dirty Alex's T-shirt had become. He manhandled Boston into the boat, but the dog didn't seem to mind. He'd taken to Alex almost as quickly as Lilly had.

"Sit!" Lisa used her sternest voice.

Boston surprised her by obeying for once. She wondered if it was her command or the dirty look Alex gave him that had him sitting still.

Alex took up the paddles. "Where to?"

"I can row," she offered.

Alex looked her up and down before shaking his head. "I could do with the exercise."

That suited her just fine. She sat back with Lilly. Besides, it meant she got to admire him while he pulled the oars. Today was the first time she didn't feel quite so guilty about admitting she liked the look of him. Didn't feel quite so sinful.

"Head upstream. We go maybe ten minutes up, then get out to follow a trail," she instructed.

He started to row. She watched his arms flex back and forth. Her ten minutes might not even make it to sixty seconds, given the speed at which he was propelling them!

"Just watch out for ducks," she said slyly.

He slowed. Then gave her a pointed look.

"Boston tends to jump." She grinned.

"You think I don't know that?" he said.

Lisa laughed. "Just reminding you."

Alex shook his head and glared at the dog. "Not again."

Boston looked up at him like a sweet little lamb. Lisa knew that look well, and didn't trust him one bit.

"It's beautiful here," Alex commented, looking around.

"Take us in over there, by the outcrop," she said, pointing.

He slowed his paddling and expertly guided them in.

Lisa reached out to catch the edge and tie the little boat to it. She looked back at Alex. He was holding both packs. She took one and strapped it to her back.

"Ladies first," he said gallantly.

She climbed out carefully, and then put her hand out to take Lilly. Alex helped guide her. Boston was long gone.

"I thought we had to have him on a lead?" Alex said.

"We do. He got away from me, lead attached." Lisa grimaced. "Boston!" she called.

He emerged, flying out from between the trees, and came to a flying halt at Lilly's feet. Lisa grabbed him by the leash.

"Want me to take him?" he asked.

She threw Alex a grateful look. "Please."

They walked along in a comfortable silence that strangely made her feel closer to Alex than ever before. Lilly skipped behind them and inspected spiders' webs and bugs attached to the trees. Lisa kept up a steady pace, which had her lungs blowing after a while, but she didn't give up. Alex looked like he hadn't even walked an inch. His breathing was steady. No sweat. Just loping along. It was driving her crazy. Maybe she needed to do some army-style training to get her body up to speed.

He looked like he was chewing something over in his mind. She didn't pry. From what she'd seen of him so far, he needed to walk it off. Think. Not feel pressured. And he seemed relaxed despite it.

Lisa had already learnt the hard way not to expect too much in the conversation stakes. She was a compulsive talker, so it wasn't easy, but she could appreciate his pain. The way she felt about William wasn't exactly something she knew how to talk about. What he was feeling she guessed was on par with her pain.

"Tell me about Lilly."

Just when she thought he'd gone and lost his tongue, Alex surprised her by talking.

She slowed down. Lilly had fallen behind anyway. So much for a punishing pace! If she went any faster she'd lose her own child.

"What does her therapist think about her progress?" he asked.

She still hadn't figured out why he had bonded so well with Lilly. What it was in her that resonated with him. Why she'd chosen him to talk to after all these months. Lisa was too scared to ask either of them in case she rocked the boat. But what was it that her daughter's eyes had seen that had made her want to connect with him so strongly?

"That she's doing okay, but she's taken William's death incredibly hard," Lisa told him.

He stopped. His hand fell to Boston's head as he looked back at Lilly.

"Has she been prescribed any medication?"

Lisa thought that was an odd question for him to ask. "No. There were things offered initially, but one school of thought says time and routine is enough. I'd rather go for the non-medicated option."

"Good."

Good? What did he know about therapists and medication?

Did he go to one himself? If only she was brave enough to ask him.

"You're lucky to have a therapist in a town this size," he commented.

Yes, they were. "She travels in every other week. Does the rounds of a few small towns."

She sensed Alex had moved on. He seemed focused on the path ahead now.

"Where do you want to stop?" he asked.

"We keep following this path, not much further, then there's a small pond and a clearing. A few picnic tables."

"Mind if I run ahead?"

Boston looked ready to go too. "Go for it," Lisa said.

He surged into action. A steady rhythm that he seemed to find from his first stride.

She couldn't steal her eyes away.

His calves were bare, shorts ending just above his knees. His back stayed straight. Then he disappeared.

Alex waited for them at the clearing. The run had done him good. Boston lay sprawled out beside him, still panting.

Lilly came into view first, followed by her mother.

They were a pair, those two. Lilly had her hair tied into pigtails, but a handful of the hair from each had escaped. She gave him her usual grin and collapsed beside him. Lisa—well, he didn't even want to look at her too closely.

"Have you seen anything yet?" Lilly asked him.

He wasn't sure what she meant. Should he be keeping an eye out for something in particular?

"Mommy always says to keep your eyes peeled for moose and bear and caribou and elk and even wolves!" Lilly elaborated.

Lisa was shaking her head.

"Well, that's one very informed mom you have there," Alex teased.

Lilly smiled proudly.

"Let's have this picnic before any of the above find our stash, shall we?" Lisa said.

Alex ignored the niggle in his chest as Lilly sat beside him and Lisa fiddled with the food. Getting too close to these two would mean more pain. Emotions that he couldn't deal with again. So why did he suddenly feel prepared to risk his heart for the first time since his parents had died?

They sat on a rug beneath scarcely waving branches as sunlight filtered through to warm their skin. Lisa was conscious of Alex's leg close to her own. So conscious that if she as much as wiggled her leg her thigh could be pressed against his.

She hadn't brought up the kiss, but then neither had he. They'd skirted around the issue, and she had a feeling it wouldn't ever be spoken of if she didn't bring the subject to the table. Literally.

Right now it was like she'd been released. As if she'd realized that she could be happy again. That she could be a woman and enjoy the pleasures of another man's company without disrespecting her husband.

But she needed to understand this man. Know more about him.

"Alex, you've never mentioned anything about your family," she murmured.

Other than implying he didn't have one.

A wary look danced across his face. She recognized that look now. Knew it meant for her to back off. Fast.

"You don't have to tell me. I was just curious," she said reassuringly.

He lay back, his hands finding a spot beneath his head. Lisa held her breath. He was going to talk. She could feel it. To her it seemed like a major breakthrough. As if they were finally connecting. What they had, the bond between them, meant he could finally trust her.

"My parents are both long-dead. It's just me," he said tonelessly.

So there was a reason he'd never mentioned them. A reason he'd kept them close to his chest. "You lost them young?"

"Yup."

She drew her knees up to her chest and hugged them. Maybe if she offered him something of her own past he'd keep communicating. "My father died of a heart attack when I was pretty young. So then it was just me, Mom and my sister."

He propped himself up on one elbow. "You were close to your father?"

She gulped. It still made her feel sad, thinking about her father. "Very." She might have been eighteen when he'd died, but it had still hit her extremely hard.

Lisa watched Lilly where she sat with Boston less than a few feet away. She was sprawled out with him, stroking his fur. They often spent hours like that. "Where do you live, Alex? I mean before your term away where did you live?"

A shadow over his face told her she'd probably asked enough questions for the day. But she needed to know. Wanted to know more about him.

"California. Originally."

She nodded.

"But I haven't exactly had a place to call home for a long, long time," he admitted.

"That must be hard. Not having somewhere to go."

They sat silent for another few moments. Lisa looked up at the trees, her head snapped right back, and Alex plucked at the short shoots of grass.

"Alex, are you going to be deployed again?"

She sensed him tighten.

"No."

Lisa could have leapt to touch the highest branch! She had been fighting that question for days, hours, and to hear him say no was the best news she'd received in a long while. Relief shuddered through her. She didn't need to pine for another soldier. Not ever. Losing one was enough. She wasn't even sure if she could ever truly let another man into her life. Even Alex. She certainly could never, ever cope with losing another one.

He drew up to his full height and brushed off his shorts. "Shall we get back to the boat?"

Lisa didn't push him. There was nothing else she needed to ask. She put out a hand for him to help haul her up. He did. His hand clasped over hers and pulled her upright. His fingers felt smooth, firm against hers.

She didn't want to let go.

She was starting to read him. To understand him. To put all the pieces of the jigsaw together slowly. He might have stopped talking, but he hadn't closed himself off. His eyes were still light, open. He wasn't shutting her out. Alex's lips hinted at a smile. Hers were more than hinting, but she was trying to keep herself in check.

He's not going back. He's not going back. The words just wouldn't stop ringing in her ears. Did it mean she could let something happen between them? That if something special developed she could find room for both William and Alex in her heart?

She let go of his hand as he pulled back. Reluctantly. He started to scoop up their belongings and she helped him to pack.

What she needed was to keep him talking without pushing the wrong buttons. They'd covered enough heavy stuff for today, but it felt good to just talk openly without him being guarded.

"Do you cook?" Was that a silly question for her to ask, given the years he'd probably spent in the army?

"I do a mean lasagna, and that's it," he replied.

"One signature dish?"

He nodded before swinging a pack in her direction. A wolfish smile turned the corners of his mouth upwards in the most delicious arrow. "Just the one."

She'd bet it tasted good too. It had been a while since anyone had cooked her a meal, but she'd like to try his lasagna. Might even pick up a few tips.

"I'll do it for you one time before I go," he promised.

A drum beat a loud rhythm in her ears. She'd almost forgotten their being together was coming to an end soon.

"Come on, Lilly." She forced her voice to comply with her wishes. To not show him how upset she was.

Lilly stretched like a kitten, then stood up. She grinned at Alex. Lisa didn't miss the wink he gave her.

"Let's go."

Alex fought to keep his pace slow and steady. He liked moving fast, but he wanted to enjoy walking beside Lisa. He'd had fun with his army buddies, his makeshift family, but times like this were a rarity for him. Once he'd enlisted he'd volunteered for every deployment and opportunity he could to stay overseas rather than come back to America. Because he'd had nowhere to go, nowhere to call home.

When others had gone home for even a few days if they could, jumped at every opportunity to come back, he'd stayed away. When the army was your only family you didn't have anything else or anyone to turn to.

Which was why this felt so special. This was what he imagined all those men loved about being back home with their loved ones. Just walking side by side with another human being, with a woman who made you feel happy and light. He could only imagine what it would have been like to come home to his parents—to his own family, even. Children.

For years he'd told himself he didn't want that kind of life. That he liked being a loner and didn't want to risk losing anyone close to him again.

But maybe he just hadn't realized what being loved, being part of a real family, would be like. Just what he'd sacrificed by closing off that part of him to any possibility of finding that kind of happiness for himself.

"Why are we stop—?" Alex's sentence died in his mouth.

Lisa turned to him. She motioned him to step backward. *Bear,* she mouthed frantically.

He obeyed instantly. "Quiet, Boston," he growled, only just loud enough for the dog to hear.

Lisa watched as Alex wound the lead tight around his fist, twice, then reached down to half his height to gather Lilly up to him.

Lisa felt a tremor of fear run through her body, gather momentum, and then explode within her. She'd never experienced it before. She was usually so careful, so aware.

They were still edging away, and the bear hadn't noticed them. Not yet.

"She's fishing," Lisa whispered.

Alex nodded.

"She hasn't seen us," she added thankfully.

Alex pulled them away behind a thick cluster of trees before stopping. "But she knows we're here," he warned.

Lisa's body shook again. Did she?

He must have seen the question in her eyes. "She knows. She just doesn't see us as a threat. Yet," he clarified.

They could still see her. Only just. If Lisa hadn't been so afraid she would have found it beautiful. This huge black bear, female, flipping her paw into the water and expertly tossing fish out.

Lisa glanced at Alex. He didn't look at her, but just like the bear she knew he had seen her. He'd just chosen not to look back at her. Yet.

"We need to move. If she has young we could be in real trouble," he murmured.

Lisa agreed. But she wasn't volunteering to move. Not with the bear right there.

"Can we walk back if we have to?" he asked.

She nodded. "It would be tricky, but it's possible."

He looked uncertain.

"They feed often at this time of year," she told him. She was angry with herself for being careless and stupid. Her head had been filled with ideas of a picnic, and yet if she'd thought—really thought—she'd have known this was a real bear time of year. They were still hungry—plenty hungry—and they were always out fishing.

"I don't think she'll hurt us—not if she doesn't see us as a threat—but she might not take kindly to Boston if he starts to bark," Alex said.

They were in serious danger. And for the first time in all her years of being an Alaskan, Lisa was worried that another animal was going to sneak up on them while they sat in wait. That she was going to make headlines in the local *Herald* about a trio eaten by a bear.

Alex met her eyes as his hold on Lilly tightened. She might not have known him for long, but seeing the grip he had on her daughter made her realize that he'd risk his own life to save Lilly. That she could trust him to get her precious daughter to safety. No matter what happened, he wasn't the type to let anyone down in a moment of crisis.

Boston let out a low whine and she dropped to her knees to comfort him. She buried her fingers in his long fur.

"So we're just going to wait?" Lilly suddenly asked.

Lisa sucked in her breath. "Shh, sweetie."

"Stay quiet, Lilly." Alex pressed his lips tight together to show her. "Quiet as a mouse, okay?"

Lilly tucked her chin down to her chest. Her blue eyes looked double their usual size as she clung to him. Lisa wished she was in his embrace herself, being held safe, but she banished the thought. Now was definitely not the time to think about why she wanted to be in Alex's arms.

He gave her a nudge with his leg and indicated with his head. Lisa followed his steel-capped gaze and found herself wriggling closer to him. She stood against him, their bodies skimming, and she had no intention of moving away.

The bear fell back to the bank, on all four legs now, and looked around. She sniffed at the air.

Lisa's heart thumped.

The bear finally turned her nose down and loped off into the forest.

"Let's go—in case she heads back this way," Alex said authoritatively.

Lisa knew not to run, she knew it instinctively, but still she moved faster than she should.

"No." Alex's voice was no more than a whisper but it held as much command as a shout.

She slowed obediently.

"We need to move fast, but carefully. When we get to the boat I need all three of you in so I can push off quickly," he said.

Lisa understood. She was just glad that today wasn't one of those days when she'd elected to head out with Lilly alone. Although she never would have taken Lilly and Boston on her own this far. They only ever pottered around the lake in the boat or strolled down the bank close to home when it was just the three of them.

They reached the boat.

"In," urged Alex.

She took Lilly from him and he threw the dog in. They sat tight together as Alex pushed them out and jumped in. He took the oars from her.

"Hold that dog," he muttered.

Oh, she was holding him all right. And Lilly. There was no chance at all she was going to let go of either of them.

Alex steered the boat toward the little jetty. He had eyed it up the other day, and realized he should have tied it there all along instead of putting it back in the shed.

A shudder hit him as he finally slowed. They could have been mauled by a bear today. Actually mauled. Or worse. Thank goodness the bear had stayed put. He didn't want to think about what could have happened out there.

He didn't want to think about being responsible for losing

someone he cared for again. For allowing another person he loved to die on his watch.

His parents had died taking him somewhere he'd begged to go. William had died protecting him. And now he'd been close to losing Lilly and Lisa because he had been less than aware of his surroundings.

Alex leaned forward to catch the side of the jetty and almost collided with Lisa. "Sorry," he said quickly.

She flushed slightly, but he noticed it. Alex tied the rope and turned back to help his passengers out. Boston first, since he was moving from paw to paw, then Lilly.

He looked at Lisa, then offered her a hand.

She took it, but not before turning a smile his way that sent a *ping* straight through his skin. There was something about her, something that made him want to touch her and look at her and talk to her. But he couldn't. He was torn between want and guilt. Every bone in his body wanted her, craved her, but it was guilt, worry, responsibility that held him back.

"Thanks for what you did back there," she said.

He didn't know what answer he could give her. He'd done nothing. Just acted like any man would have. Looked out for a woman and her child. He'd just been lucky the bear hadn't turned on them.

"It was nice knowing you were there for us," she went on.

"Just doing what I had to," he answered.

She stepped out onto the timber jetty, then turned, her hand raised to shield her eyes from the sun. "Don't think so little of yourself, Alex. Not all men can trust their instincts like that."

She walked off before he could answer, with her hips swaying and hair swishing. Maybe if they'd met under different circumstances—if he hadn't caused her husband's death—then he'd have been able to act on his feelings. Maybe if he didn't feel like he'd already caused too many people close to him to lose their lives, then perhaps he could have given in to his feelings.

But he'd never have met her if he hadn't been the cause of

William's death, been there by his side when he'd lain there dying. He'd never have made his way to Alaska if he hadn't been fulfilling his promise to his friend.

And what a place it was. Wilderness to satisfy even the most enthusiastic of campers or nature-watchers, and water to soothe a man's soul. Or at least he hoped that would be the case. He had his pack in the car, ready to go camping, fishing—anything so long as he was with nature. When he moved on from here, getting to know the terrain was exactly what he'd thought about doing.

"Hey, Alex?"

He looked up. Lisa was walking back toward him.

"I might take you up on that dinner offer."

A grin tugged at his lips. He couldn't help it. "Yeah?"

"Yeah." She laughed and shuffled from foot to foot. "If you like you can cook up a storm in the kitchen while I send my book off to my editor."

He shook his head, torn between laughing along with her and crying out loud like a baby. This was starting to feel too real, this thing he felt for her. Far too real. Despite his inner struggle, despite knowing it was dangerous, he wanted it all. To cook for her. To be with her. To laugh with her.

He should be packing up and moving on, not coming up with reasons to stay, to be closer to them. Trouble was, Lisa and Lilly were getting to him. They were under his skin and it was starting to feel good.

CHAPTER TEN

THE smell of food hit Lisa's nostrils and made her mouth fill with hot saliva. She hadn't realized quite how hungry she was. She penned a brief message to her editor, then hit 'send'.

Relief washed through her like a welcome drizzle of sunlight on heat-starved skin. Her brain and her creativity were zapped. Energy depleted. For now.

Lisa was grateful to have Alex downstairs. Having William home had always meant a happy, relaxed household, but he'd never cooked. Not in all their years together.

She didn't exactly know what she and Alex had. She just knew that being cooked for gave her a tingle of pleasure.

Lisa went into her bedroom and changed out of her walking clothes and into a favorite pair of jeans and a soft cashmere sweater. She eyed a pair of earrings but decided against them. Alex was cooking dinner in her own home. It wasn't like it was a date.

She squirted a spray of perfume in the air and walked through it, then decided to brush out her hair before twisting and pinning it loosely on her head.

Another waft of cooking tickled her nostrils and she followed it down the stairs. This was just too tempting.

Alex could possibly be her favorite person ever—for now.

Whoever had said that the way to a *man's* heart was through his stomach obviously hadn't met her ravenous appetite.

* * *

Alex looked up as Lisa appeared. He liked the look he found on her face. Even though she was laughing at him. Part of him had put the garment on just to see if he could make her smile.

"I see you found my apron?" she said, giggling.

He looked down and shrugged. "Seemed to fit, so I thought I would wear it."

She slipped past him and sniffed at the air. "That does smell like good lasagna."

He wasn't going to deny it. It felt good. Cooking again felt good. Being in Lisa's company felt wonderful. Just talking to another human being without having to look over his shoulder. Without having to jump at every bang. It all felt fantastic.

Without wondering if he might have fallen in love with her too.

Enjoying her company was one thing, but it couldn't be anything more. Not when it was his fault her husband had died. He had to remember that.

"Anything I can do?" she asked.

He snapped out of it.

Lisa leaned against the counter, her palms pressed flat behind her on the stainless steel. Her tummy peeked at him, her top riding up to reveal it.

"No." He said it more firmly than he'd wanted, but she didn't seem fazed.

He forced his eyes back to the oven. He stared hard at the lasagna. *No* to being attracted to her. *No* to wanting her. *No* to anything that involved her in an intimate way.

He growled. A low rumble in the back of his throat.

"Sorry?"

Alex turned. "I didn't say anything." He tried not to cringe.

She looked puzzled, but she didn't press the issue. "Wine," she announced. "I can pour wine."

She reached for the glasses—he hadn't known where to find them—and he saw a glimpse of lightly tanned skin again. This time he swallowed the groan. The growl. Not wanting her was a fight his will was struggling to push back against.

"I hope you don't mind but I found a bottle. I opened it to let it breathe," he said unevenly.

She turned that supersize grin on him again. "You *are* domesticated, soldier. Who would have thought?"

He didn't know whether to be flattered or offended. He decided to go with flattered.

Lisa twirled with the glasses and set them down. Then she held the bottle in the air, looked at the label, and poured it. "So tell me—who taught you how to make this world-famous lasagna?" She smiled as she held out the wineglass to him.

He took it. But he didn't exactly want to answer. "Just something I've learnt somewhere in my years."

She didn't need to know that he'd sought to replicate his mother's signature dish as soon as he'd been old enough to cook, or try to.

"Ah," she sighed, before sniffing delicately at the wine, swilling it and then taking a sip. "Just what I needed."

He couldn't take his eyes off her. Couldn't stop staring at her no matter how hard he tried. For once desire was overpowering his guilt. The knowledge shook him. There was obviously a first time for everything.

Alex took a sip, a much larger one than she had, then forced the glass to the counter. His fingers were in danger of crushing the stem.

"I see you managed to keep Lilly entertained." Lisa took a few steps so she could look into the lounge at her daughter.

"I guessed I was being had when she told me you *always* let her watch movies before dinner," he said ruefully.

Lisa winked at him and swilled another sip. "She's already figured that you like to say yes to her."

"I guess."

Lisa looked back and watched Lilly some more. *"Lady and the Tramp?"*

Even Alex knew it was an old movie. "She likes the greats, does she?"

He leaned on the counter—close to her, but not too close. He could smell her perfume, the light, fruity spice lifting up to fill his nostrils. She smelt divine. And his willpower was so diminished it was non-existent.

"I think it's the dogs slurping spaghetti together that gets her." She looked at him. "That was what made it my favorite movie."

Alex found it hard to swallow.

"Are you sure there's nothing I can do to help here?" she asked.

He shook his head. Firmly. "Nothing at all."

Lisa shrugged gracefully, then gave in.

What he hadn't expected was for her to wiggle up on a stool and rest her elbows on the counter to watch him.

He found it awkward. Exciting. Knowing she was sitting there behind him. He also found it unnerving. He'd never cooked for a woman before—never felt so intimate with another human being.

"You sure look good in an apron," she commented as he bent over to peek in the oven at the bubbling lasagna.

He cringed again and straightened hurriedly. Did that mean she was looking at his rear end? Now he felt really uncomfortable!

Lisa watched as Alex moved about the kitchen. If he wasn't so nervous he'd look perfectly at home there. He kept himself busy, finding ingredients and chopping.

She liked to watch a man work. Make that *loved* to. And she particularly liked to see a man in the kitchen. Or she now realized she liked it. She'd never actually had a man cook in her kitchen before.

Only problem was that she was starving. Her eyes flitted over Alex's body, up his chest and to his face. If she had a few more glasses of wine she'd be tempted to admit she was starving hungry for more than just food.

Alex cleared his throat. She made her mouth shut. Any wider open and she'd have dribbled the wine right down her front. It felt naughty. But somehow so right.

"I think we're almost ready," he said.

Lisa dropped her glass to the table, then went to retrieve his. It was almost empty. She reached for it, and the bottle. Then she went back for the salad. She attempted to steal a piece of cucumber, but her hand froze mid-move.

"Huh-hmm." The rumble of his voice made it impossible to steal anything.

She looked over her shoulder. Alex was holding the spatula at a very ominous angle.

A giggle rang out. Lilly was standing by the table, watching them.

"I didn't take you to be so protective of a salad." Lisa said the words dryly, but inside she felt weak. Not witty at all.

"Out of the kitchen, woman. Out now," Alex ordered.

He hadn't moved or changed his stance. Lilly was still in hysterics.

Lisa put her hands up in the air like a criminal caught in the act. "Okay, okay. Guilty as charged."

Having a man in her kitchen felt as intimate as having one in her bedroom. It had been her private space for so long, her domain, and yet here he was, taking charge and looking so... at home.

It scared her. And excited her.

Butterflies started to tickle their wings inside her stomach. She sincerely hoped food would appease them.

"No laughing at your mother." She gave Lilly her sternest look before falling into the seat beside her at the table. Lilly ignored her, as she'd known she would.

Alex came over with the lasagna.

"Yum!"

Lisa met Alex's gaze as Lilly banged a fork on the table in

excitement. Lisa would usually tell her off for bad manners, but tonight she was less about manners and more about living in the now.

Would this feel more like a date if Lilly wasn't here? If they weren't in the house she'd shared with William?

Resolutely, she turned her mind back to the food. She needed to focus on safe thoughts. Happy thoughts. Like eating. Like her daughter. Like the weather…

Who was she kidding? It felt like the first date of her life, even though it was neither her first, nor anything resembling a date.

"I hope it's okay." Alex drew her attention back to reality. "It's been a while since I've made it."

"It smells delicious," Lisa said with honesty. She nodded at Lilly. "And this one doesn't lie."

Alex served Lilly first, but when he went to serve her salad she shook her head. He angled his. It was like they were speaking in a secret language.

Lisa wondered for the umpteenth time what it was they had between them. And she wondered exactly what had been said that day they'd been in the boat alone, before it had capsized.

It was no surprise to Lisa that Lilly won the dinner battle.

"She does usually eat greens," explained Lisa.

The look Alex gave her said *yeah, right*, but it was true. Although there was nothing usual about tonight, so she was throwing caution to the wind. For once.

Tonight she wasn't a widow. Or anybody's wife. Tonight she was just a single mother, enjoying dinner with her daughter and a friend. That was as far as she was going to let her mind go, for now.

She passed her plate to Alex and watched as he ladled it with lashings of lasagna and a pile of salad. Her perfect meal.

Lilly was already tucking in, despite how hot it was, picking around the edges. Lisa was ready to do the same. Anything to distract her from Alex.

"Bon appétit." She raised her glass in the air.

He did the same, but they didn't clink them. Instead they watched one another. Slowly. Letting their eyes drink their fill. She didn't dare hope that he was thinking the same as her. Didn't even know what *she* was really thinking.

Lisa reached for the wine. "Another?"

"Please."

He looked away then, and it took her a long time before she could brave a look back at him.

Her toes were wriggling. Her tastebuds were alight.

"You're going to have to share the recipe for this tomato sauce with me," she said.

Alex tapped at his nose. "Family secret."

She felt the pain of that comment. That made him the last person to hold that secret. But it was the first time he'd made a joke like that. It felt as if he was, in a way, finally letting her see the true him.

"I could trade you for the secret of pink macaroons?" she offered.

He grinned at her. Really grinned. "Rosewater macaroons don't sound very manly. Besides, everyone can have your recipe. Your book'll be on the shelves when?"

"Maybe a year. Maybe longer."

He laughed. "My point exactly. You can't trade something secret for something that will be public knowledge."

"I'll have you know that my recipes are not available for *public knowledge*, Alex." She stared him down. "The privilege of that will set you back at least twenty bucks."

Lilly pushed her plate in. "Finished."

There was not a lick of pasta or sauce left.

Alex reached across the table and tickled at her hand. "Did you slip that to Boston while I wasn't looking?" he teased.

She shook her head. Her just-grown top teeth bit down on her lower lip.

"Promise?"

"Promise."

She slipped away from the table and Lisa refocused on Alex.

They sat there in silence, finishing off their meal.

"What do you say I put Lilly to bed and we go for a walk outside?" The question burst from her. It felt like a big risk, blurting that out.

Alex's eyes looked hungry. Eager. She couldn't mistake it.

"I'll clean up while you put her to bed, if you like?" he suggested.

"Deal."

Lisa didn't like the cook having to clean too, but it was only once. She didn't like putting Lilly straight to bed on a full stomach either. But sometimes rules were made to be broken.

Alex wasn't sure whether to sit, stand, or just go wait outside. The two glasses of wine had started to help, but now they were just making him even more nervous.

Of what? He wasn't sure. All he knew was that there was something about being in a space alone with Lisa that made him feel in equal parts terrified and excited. Exhilarated, almost.

He stood, awkward, in the middle of the room. He could hear her upstairs, probably saying a final good-night to Lilly.

Alex decided on the sit option. He dropped to the armchair. It wasn't as comfortable as the sofa, but it did the trick.

Then he locked eyes with William.

His whole body jerked.

The photo of William in its frame just stared at him with an empty gaze. Guilt stung his body once again, with the ferocity of a blizzard of wasps.

A noise indicated that Lisa was descending the stairs.

He closed his eyes, counted to five, then opened them, looking in the other direction. William was not going to haunt him now. Alex wasn't doing anything wrong. They'd just had dinner, they were now going for a walk, then he'd wish her good-night.

His thoughts might not be pure, but his intentions were. He knew his place, what he'd come here to do. That he had to be careful.

He *knew*.

"Hey." Lisa stood there, looking like an angel descended from heaven before him. Her hair was loose about her shoulders. All reason left his mind as blood pumped through his body.

Alex noticed her legs, slender beneath her jeans, and her arms, hugged tight by the jersey. He noticed everything about her.

He was in way over his head.

"Hey." He answered her greeting softly.

Sorry, William. He sent a silent prayer skyward. He'd dealt with guilt all his life. But now...now he just felt like a man who was attracted to a woman. Drawn to a woman like he'd never been before in his lifetime.

If he could have done it without Lisa knowing he would have turned William's picture face-down to avoid those eyes. For once he didn't know if he could control his feelings, his emotions, his desires.

The cool night air snapped at their skin. Even though it was spring, the evening temperature still fell. Lisa skimmed her hands over her arms.

They walked along the bank, where grass fell down to the water. It was magical at this time of night. The water endless, the moon shining her white light down low. Lisa always wanted to walk after dinner, but it wasn't something she liked to do alone. Wasn't something she'd ever thought she'd enjoy with a man again. Not after so many years of sharing it with her husband. Not after believing she'd never fall in love again.

With Alex, right now, it was perfect.

"Let's hope we don't come across any bears."

She laughed at Alex's joke. Sometimes he was so quiet, yet other times he made light of a situation and made her feel completely at ease. She could only imagine what he'd have been like had he not been haunted by war.

"Did you miss this while you were away?" she asked cautiously.

He slowed his walk so that he was just swinging one foot in front of the other at irregular intervals. She slowed too.

"I missed the feel of earth that wasn't sand. I missed the wave of trees, the smell of the country. The comfort of being somewhere no one wanted to take your life," he replied.

She closed her eyes. She had no idea what it would be like to be in active combat, and she didn't want to know. William had always tried to skim over it, tried to make her think it wasn't that bad, but the honesty of Alex's words was precise. Real. He was saying it like it was.

"You never did say how long you were over there?"

He didn't hesitate. "I volunteered for back-to-back tours."

She looked out toward the water. It sang to her like a lullaby. Did it have the same effect on him? "How did you do it, Alex? How did you stay over there?"

There was a raw-edged honesty to his voice. "I had nothing to come back to. Nothing to want to come home for. The army was all I ever had for years." He paused. "When my parents died there was no one to take me in. So I ended up in foster care. The army was my chance to get out. Make something of myself."

She had no idea what it would be like to be an orphan. To have no family to care for you. The thought, to her, was unconscionable.

"So why have you left the army after all these years?"

He glanced at her. "Because I couldn't do it anymore. I felt like I'd seen too much, been there too long."

Alex stepped closer to the water. Closer to its silky depths.

She watched him. The breeze sent another shiver across her goosepimpled arms.

She couldn't deny it anymore. She wanted him in her life. Wanted to reach out to him, to tell him they could have a chance together. That they had nothing to feel guilty about.

Lisa walked up behind him. She stood there, so close she

was almost touching him, before placing her hands one on each arm. They settled over his forearms—strong, muscled forearms that clenched beneath her palms. Her fingers curled slightly, applying pressure to let him know she wasn't letting go.

"Alex…" She whispered his name.

He didn't react. Didn't move. He just stayed still.

Lisa started to move her fingertips, so lightly they barely made an imprint on his skin, until he made a slow half-turn toward her.

Alex met her direct gaze with his own. His eyes engaged hers with such intensity she felt a flicker of something unknown unfurl in her belly.

"Alex." She murmured his name again, but this time her fingers traced a path up his arms.

He raised a hand to her face. Touched her with his forefinger, running it down her cheek, while his thumb nestled against her chin.

Lisa felt a quiver that ran the entire length of her body. The softness, lightness of his touch sent a tremor across the edge of her skin.

"Alex." His name was the only word she could conjure. The only word she wanted to say.

He acted this time. Didn't answer her, didn't say her name, but answered her with his body.

Alex crushed her mouth hard against his. His lips met hers with ferocity, so different from that first time their mouths had touched.

Alex's free hand moved to cup the back of her head, pulling her against him as if he couldn't fit her body tightly enough against his if he tried.

Lisa felt her way to his torso, then ran her hands up the breadth of his back, up to his shoulders and down again.

"Lisa." His eyes looked tormented, wild.

She took his hand, slowly, carefully, and turned. He resisted. For a heartbeat he resisted. Before clasping her fingers tight, interlocking his own against them.

They walked back to the house in silence. This time it was not a comfortable silence. Lisa could have cut the tension with a blunt knife it was so acute.

She didn't even know if she could be with another man. But she wanted Alex so much it hurt. He was never going to be William, but she didn't want him to be. All she knew right now was that she desired Alex. Period.

Alex wasn't sure he could do it.

Lisa reached out to touch his face, just with one finger, and he resisted the urge to pull back. To turn on the spot, flee, and never look back.

But Lisa's eyes stopped him. The soulful depths of them, the honesty and trust and worry he saw there, made him reach for her hand again. She only stopped moving to lock the door.

The click of it hit him in the spine. He was inside for the night, and he'd never felt more apprehensive in his life.

Lisa turned those eyes on him again. She was so honest he couldn't bear it. So trusting.

She was waiting for him to make a move. Waiting for him to do something to say it was all right. But he didn't know if it was right. Couldn't tell her that it was.

The only light that was on was in the kitchen. He let go of her hand and went to turn it off. Darkness set its heavy blanket over them. Only a hint of the moonlight that had guided them outside let him find his way back to her.

"Lisa." This time it was him saying her name.

He could make out the tilt of her chin even in the dark. So defiant, so brave. He also saw the light quiver that made it tremble. She was scared. Not brave. As scared as he was.

He let his lips find hers, then he kissed down her neck, deep into her collarbone. Forgot everything and just focused on her.

"Upstairs." She choked out the word at him.

It felt wrong, yet at the same time it felt so right. He stomped on his inner demons and trusted her. Trusted that they were doing the right thing.

"Upstairs," he repeated.

She obeyed.

Lisa wished she could take a tablet to quell her nerves. A lamp provided some light, but she would have preferred darkness.

She'd only been with one man before, and it had never felt like this. The quiver in her stomach was back with a vengeance, her skin felt like acid was dancing along the surface of it, burning the tiny hairs on her arms. With William it had been kind, comfortable. With Alex the intensity of her own desire frightened her.

Alex shut the bedroom door behind him.

She looked at him.

He looked back at her.

Then he crossed the room like the strong, determined soldier he was. His long legs ate up the carpet before he pressed into her and walked her two steps backward until she felt the wall touch her spine.

Alex's touch was like fire. His mouth found hers. His hands seemed to search every inch of her. He bent to trace her collarbone, her neck, like before, then nibble lower, so slowly it tormented her.

Alex dropped to his knees. He ran a hand down one of her legs before slipping her foot from her ballet flat. He did the same with the other.

His hands found a trail up her legs as he stood up slowly once more, his mouth back to press hard against hers.

"Are you sure?" He mumbled the words against her skin, his lips talking into her neck.

"Yes," she whispered, her back arched with the pleasure of his touch. *"Yes."*

There was an unspoken nervousness between them. But Lisa wanted this like she'd never wanted anything in her life before. Her skin was alive. Blood was pumping with adrenalin through her body as if she was about to plunge from a cliff for the first time.

Yes, she was sure. She wanted Alex. She could no more put a stop to it now than she could stop breathing.

Lisa didn't know if he was asleep or not. His chest was rising in a steady rhythm, and she could hear the soft whistle in and out of his breath, but she didn't know if he was asleep.

She didn't think sleep was ever going to find *her*. She was exhausted, mentally and physically, but sleep wasn't searching her out.

Lisa felt incredible. She was tired, but her senses still felt ignited. In a way she felt brand-new again. Tonight had been about being brave despite her fears, pushing through her own personal barriers and Alex's too.

Tonight she had said finally goodbye to her marriage. She kept William in a part of her heart, but accepted she could be with somebody else and not taint the memory of him. It was like she'd become a woman all over again.

She moved closer to Alex. Anything to feel his body hard against hers again, to feel the planes of his skin and muscles beneath her fingers.

"Go to sleep." He spoke without moving an inch.

So he wasn't asleep.

"Alex?"

He didn't move. But she knew he was listening.

"Good night," she murmured.

His grip on her arm tightened, ever so slightly. Lisa settled her head on his chest and closed her eyes.

She hoped he had no regrets. She didn't. And she doubted she ever would. Never in her life could she have believed that another man would touch her heart the way William had for so many years. Yet here she was, with Alex, knowing that maybe—just maybe—she had enough love, enough room in her heart and soul, for both men.

She didn't ever want to forget William. But she also didn't want to push happiness and love from her life.

Love might just have come looking for her, and admitting it made her feel a whole lot better. For the first time she didn't expect nightmares. Instead she closed her eyes with a smile on her face.

CHAPTER ELEVEN

THE smile she'd given him, the closeness of her body before she'd fallen asleep, had made Alex stiffen in alarm. Even more so than when he'd first set eyes upon her that day on the porch.

It had been dark, and he'd mostly had his eyes shut, but he had seen that look. Seen the way she'd been watching him. It wasn't right. Not with Lisa. He was meant to be giving her a hand with the cottage out of loyalty to William. What he'd done was inexcusable. Weak. Wrong.

As William Kennedy's widow, she was forbidden to him. If he didn't know better he'd think he was falling in love with her. Actually falling in love with a woman who was so very much out of bounds to him.

He should be banged head-first into a tree for even thinking it, let alone admitting it to himself. Love was not something he'd ever seen in his future. The life of a soldier's wife was no life for a woman, and now here he was thinking about absurd things like love. The only people he'd ever truly loved were his parents, and he'd determined never to feel like that again in his lifetime. Never to be in a position to feel grief.

He couldn't ignore Lisa, though, or the effect she had on him. It had kept him awake nearly all night, that smile of hers. Haunting him with its power. Teasing him with its honesty. Making him question himself.

He looked up at her bedroom, at the curtains still shutting

the early-morning light out. He should have stayed with her. Should have been there for her when she woke up. Should have nurtured her like she deserved to be the morning after making love to her.

What had he done?

His mind skipped back to the night before. He couldn't not have done it—couldn't have pushed her away.

But why?

He had resisted beautiful women before. Not often, but he had. So what was it about this one? What was it about Lisa that haunted his soul more than any horror image of what had happened at war? What was it about her that made him push the boundaries, disrespect his friend's memory, and go back on his vow to keep his heart guarded forever?

He didn't need to soul-search to locate an answer.

She was different because she was a real woman. Not just some girl he'd met on a night out. Not a girl who had the same idea in mind as him, which consisted of one word. *Fun.*

Lisa was the kind of girl most men searched for. The kind that you took home to Mom because she would please even the most demanding of parents.

Lisa was the type of woman you wanted to love. To see mothering your children. Lisa was the type of woman he'd always avoided in the past. To protect himself.

But he had no family to take her home to. He had no one. He wasn't the type of guy who deserved a girl like that. Especially not her. Not when he'd taken her husband from her, ruined her chance for a family life.

Even with William's smiling face watching him from the hall and framed in the lounge he hadn't been able to resist her. He couldn't control himself, stop himself, when it came to Lisa.

And now he felt even more guilty than before. She was not the type of girl you made love to and then left in an empty bed alone. He'd been foolish last night, and had acted like an idiot this morning.

If he'd had the courage he would have crept back up those

stairs and crawled in beside her. Pretended like he'd never been gone. Pressed his body into hers and felt the warmth of her as she woke from slumber. Held her in his arms and kissed her eyelids before they opened for the day.

But he couldn't.

She hadn't been his to begin with, and there was too much keeping them apart to pretend she was. Or ever could be.

They had no future. It was impossible.

He had to tell her the truth. That if it wasn't for him William would still be alive.

He'd slept with the wife of the man who'd saved him. What kind of thanks was that? All he'd had to do was deliver William's bag of items to her. Comfort her, perhaps, if he'd really wanted to do something helpful. But take her to bed?

That was just unforgivable.

He'd taken advantage of a widow. Of a woman he should have vowed to protect. He'd taken from her, disrespected William, and there was nothing he could do to change it.

Being here with them, being part of their lives, had drawn him in. He'd run from it his entire life and he didn't want to be part of it now. Couldn't. Not after what he'd done. Not after holding William as he died, with a bullet in his chest that had been intended for Alex.

His friend. The man who'd talked about his family, told him and everyone else who'd listen how much he loved his life and what he had back home. So how was it fair that Alex was the one here and William was buried in the ground?

He heard a noise in the house.

It was now or never.

Alex kept his eyes open to avoid the memory or war, of what had happened, and focused on the porch to keep from seeing William lying in his arms. Looking up at him that day. Talking to him with such love in his eyes despite his pain.

To stop seeing scenes of his childhood that had started playing over and over in his mind. Of his family before they'd been taken from him. Of what he might have had to come home to if they were still alive.

When Lisa appeared he was going to tell her the truth. It was what he had to do.

A smile lit Lisa's face as she walked. Last night had been incredible. Even her skin felt as if it was still alive beneath Alex's touch. There was no guilt. Or remorse. She still loved her husband, but what she felt for Alex was great. Different, but wonderful all the same.

Lisa was pleased Lilly was still asleep. It wasn't often she slept in, but this morning it was welcome. She wanted to spend some time with Alex alone before they were interrupted. Talk to him, kiss him, taste him. Reassure herself.

She scanned the living room and the kitchen but there was no sign of him. He must be outside already. She hugged the blanket tighter around her and tried to dull down her smile. Just because she was happy it didn't mean she had to go around grinning like a cat who'd caught a rabbit.

Lisa pushed open the door and stepped onto the porch. Her eyes hit his. She could tell he was watching, waiting for her. So why hadn't he just waited for her in bed?

He looked every part the soldier this morning. His eyes were steady, chin tilted, stance at ease. So different from William. More serious, more like a soldier even when he was off duty.

She noticed the change in his face, though. Recognized it from the man who'd arrived here, not the man she'd been with last night.

It worried her.

She could tell before he spoke that something was wrong. That something had changed from when she'd said good-night to him. What had happened between now and then?

"Alex, what are you doing out here?" she asked.

She slipped into a pair of flip-flops that were resting on the porch and walked the three steps down to the lawn. A touch of wet hit her toes—the ground was still damp from the night—but she barely felt it.

"Alex?"

"I haven't told you the truth." His voice was filled with grit.

She reached for his arm but he stayed still. Too still. She let her hand drop. He was pulling away from her. Emotionally, she knew that she'd lost him. That wall had gone up again. Even more so than before, if that were possible.

"There was a reason I came home and William didn't. You asked me if I saw how he died, and the answer is yes."

She wasn't sure where he was going with this, but she stayed silent. He'd already said yes when she'd asked him that question before, but there was obviously more to the story. Alex looked angry, and she didn't want to interrupt him.

"We were on a mission when he died. We'd finished. Thought it was over. But it wasn't."

She kept her eyes on his. He was hurting and all she could do was listen. His jaw was clenched so tight a stranger might guess it was wired so. A vein she'd never seen before strung a line down his neck.

"I was out in the open. William saw the enemy before I did. He called my name, distracted me, then threw himself over me." He walked backward a step but didn't break his stare. "I was meant to die that day, Lisa. They were aiming for me. He didn't have to do it—save me—but he did."

She didn't know what to say. It didn't make any difference. Not now. It didn't matter what he said. Her hands started to shake.

"He had everything to live for, Lisa. And I had nothing. It should have been me who died that day, me who came home in a body bag. Not him."

His eyes were tortured, flashing. His hurt stabbed her in the chest but she didn't let him see it. Kept it hidden, tucked away, not wanting him to see her emotion.

"If it wasn't for me your husband would still be coming

home. He'd still be alive," he reiterated, as though torturing himself with that truth.

"Alex." His name came out strangled, broken. "Alex, please…"

"Don't you see, Lisa? It's all my fault. Everything that's happened to you, what's happened to Lilly, it's *my* fault."

He punched out the words with such fury she didn't know what to do.

His words stung—not because they hurt her, but because they were so raw. Emotion cut through his body, his face, visible for all to see. Every angle, every plane of him was angry. Hurting.

A sob choked in her chest.

She had woken up this morning thinking it was the start of something fresh. That she and Alex had something special between them. Now he was ranting at her like he'd deliberately taken something precious from her, like he'd done something unforgivable. When all he'd done was be a soldier at war. A man. He'd done nothing wrong. How could he not see that?

"If you'd known this you never would have let me stay. You never would have invited me into your home."

He spat the words out and she didn't want to answer him—not when he was like this.

"If William hadn't been such a hero and I hadn't been so careless he'd be here right now. Not me."

And with that Alex spun around and started to march off.

"Don't you *dare*, Alex. You *cannot* walk away!" Her voice was tearful, but she fought to keep it strong.

He turned, his eyes wild, almost glaring at her. "Damn it, Lisa! I've wanted a family all my life. Dreamed about being brave enough to recreate what I lost as a boy."

She stared at him. Unblinking. Questions in her eyes.

"And you—you and Lilly—you've shown me that it's worth fighting for. That family does mean everything."

She nodded mutely.

"I'm sorry that I ruined your family. I am, Lisa. That's two families I've mucked up now."

"No, Alex." She glared back at him, incensed at what he was saying. "You were a boy when your parents died. A *boy*. You had nothing to do with it."

"If I hadn't asked them for an ice cream—if I hadn't begged them to take me for one—they'd still be alive. If William hadn't—"

Lisa reached for him, and this time he didn't fight her. He let himself be pulled into her arms. She held him like she would comfort a child.

"You know William would have done the same for any of his men. You *know* that, right?"

He stayed ominously still.

"You can't keep blaming yourself, Alex. You're an intelligent man. You know a child cannot take responsibility for death. For fate. Lilly wanted to go for a picnic the other day, but it wasn't her fault that we came across a bear."

Alex pulled back and watched her. She saw recognition in his eyes, but he still looked angry.

"Alex?"

He took a deep, shuddering breath.

"I understand, Alex." She kept hold of his arms. "It doesn't mean you stop hurting. It just means you need to let go of the blame you feel. The guilt. Don't let your past stop you from…"

He watched her intently.

"From a second-chance family."

He looked at her long and hard. Then he carefully detached her hands from his arms and turned around.

He started walking.

And he didn't look back.

Lisa's eyes were too filled with tears to watch where he went.

She fell down onto the porch step. Her legs folded, buckled and refused to hold her up. Her hands shook like they had received an electric current that had torn every thread of her skin. Her muscles felt weak, bones liquid.

She had gone through every emotion possible when William had died, when the messengers in uniform had knocked on her door to tell her the news in person. They'd asked her if she had someone to come and be with her, watched with doom-filled eyes as she'd dialed her sister with a shaking hand and asked her to come over.

When they'd told her, as Anna held her hand, she'd sobbed with the uselessness of the situation, knowing that he'd been dead how long—maybe hours? An entire day?—and she'd just gone about her business with no idea that her husband had been gunned down. Then she'd been angry, beaten at the sofa with all her might.

Then she'd felt relief. A sickening wash of relief that there would be no more days of worrying, of hoping he was okay. Because he'd already gone.

Up until the day Alex had arrived she had still been heaving with different emotions, feelings. She still was.

But this? This was equally bad.

Because she'd finally pushed through her sadness, her grief and her anger, and she'd been ready to start over again. Comfortable with the choice she'd made last night.

How wrong she'd been.

And now Alex was going to leave for good. She could feel it.

He was going to leave and she'd never see him again.

The man she had been slowly falling in love with was going to leave her, and there was nothing she could do about it.

A few months ago she'd felt like the black widow. As if life was over and she'd never be able to claw her way back to normality. Well, she had. She'd forced her head above water, gotten on with life despite her pain, and then found Alex on her doorstep.

The man had been a stranger to her then, but now he was real. And she wanted him to be there beside her as she started this life. She'd chosen to love Alex without guilt in her heart. But instead of returning that love he was going. Blaming himself for something he had never had the power to control. Holding on to pain from the past that she wanted to help him say goodbye to.

She loved him. If she hadn't loved him she never would have invited him into her bed last night.

Alex walked. He walked like he'd never walked before. As if there was a demon after him that wanted his life and if he stopped it would grab him by the throat.

He'd grabbed his pack from the car on the way past and it thumped rhythmically against his back now as he moved. What he needed was a night out in the open to clear his head. He couldn't care less if it was illegal to camp in the National Park. The place bordered the property, and it was surrounded by thousands of miles of forest. No one was going to bother about a single man minding his own business.

His feet pounded, ignoring the tug of roots as they tripped at his boots. The aroma of pine trees that he usually found so alluring did little to appease him. To tease the thunderous mood from him.

He'd told her the truth. The whole truth. He'd never forgive himself for what had happened that day, for not being alert enough to notice the snipers, for not screaming *no* at William as he'd moved to save him. For not acting fast enough himself and preventing the situation in the first place. Just like he'd never forgive himself for asking for ice cream that day of the crash. For putting his parents in the car that day.

Alex stopped. He stopped walking and braced one hand against a tree trunk to steady his breathing. And his mind.

It had all happened so fast. Too fast for him to do anything about it. Too fast for him to realize what was going on around him. Too fast for him to stop William from sacrificing his own life. Just like he'd been powerless as a boy.

His mind flashed to Lisa. To the torment on her face. He'd hurt her.

He should have told her right at the start. Should have explained what had happened and asked for her forgiveness that first day as they'd sat on the porch. Instead of letting things get this far before admitting his guilt. Instead of taking her to bed and letting her become intimate with the man she should be blaming for the way her life had turned out.

If he could take it back he would. If he could go back in time and take the bullets that had been destined for him he wouldn't hesitate. Not when it meant giving a woman her husband back and a child her father.

Because who would miss *him*? Who would even care that he was gone? Wasn't that why he had joined the army? Why he had always been so good at his job? Because he'd had no fear.

All his adult life he'd never had anything to live for, and it had made him fearless in the field.

Until now.

He had done his time in the army and he was finally putting that chapter of his life away. He'd never thought the day would come, but after William had died something inside him had had enough. He'd finished his tour and then asked to be relieved of his duty.

He might not have any plans, no idea of what he wanted to do yet, but it didn't involve the army. Not anymore.

The only thing he *was* sure about was that he couldn't stay here. Not now. He had to leave.

Lisa would probably have his stuff packed. She'd probably already chucked his belongings in the back of his car and was waiting to bid him farewell.

A knife stabbed at the muscles of his stomach, but he ignored it as he would a hunger pang.

Then he started marching.

The demon was after him again and he wanted to lose it.

* * *

He'd crossed the spot she'd mentioned that time they'd all been out together. Close to the neighbor's boundary. Then he'd followed the river until he'd come to a trail, and then he'd walked until he was exhausted.

He should have brought his rod with him. A man could only walk so far. Even he knew that. And yet his anger, his determination and guilt, had seen him pound out miles even he hadn't known he was capable of.

If he'd brought a line with him at least he could have eaten.

Alex guessed it to be about two o'clock. He squinted up at the sun. Yes, at least two. He fell in a messy heap to the ground and dragged his pack off his back.

He'd thrown the bag together before he'd left the mainland, thinking he'd be camping his first night out, but it still didn't hold everything he needed.

There was a box of wax matches, a few snack bars, his sleeping bag, and a tall bottle of water. He pulled off the lid and sculled a few deep mouthfuls.

It was stupid, his being out here without preparing properly first, but it wasn't as if his decision to march off into a national park had been made via logical conclusions.

He knew how to survive, could fend for himself for a decent amount of time out here if he had to, but he didn't really fancy being this far from civilization. Not at this time of year, when the bears were still hungry. Not to mention the wolves he'd heard call out in the night from the cabin.

He jumped back to his feet. What he needed was enough wood to start a fire. At least that would keep predators and any four-legged foes at bay.

Alex started to work. He scouted the site for timber, and his search didn't take him far. But he still worked up a sweat. Wet heat clung to his forehead and neck. He removed his shirt and wiped his skin, before tucking it into the back of his jeans. Then he sought out stones for the fire's perimeter, which proved harder. He marked his trail, lightly, and headed back out to the river-edge. It took him at least half an hour to walk in and out with the first load of stones, but the next two trips were shorter.

By now he'd only counted one sign of wildlife. Two elk drinking greedily from the river. They'd scarpered fast when they'd seen him.

The loud twitter of birds had built to an almost deafening crescendo. He was pleased they were only just starting to sing like that. It meant he still had time to get this fire belting out heat and a steady flame glowing before darkness fell like a consuming blanket.

He pushed away the thoughts that niggled at his mind. He might have been stupid coming, but he was here now, and if anything he could punish himself by sleeping rough for the night.

He tinkered with the fire, blowing on the dried leaves he'd built up in the centre, cupping his hands to stop the wind dispelling the lick of flame that tickled the base of the leaves.

It only took him one try to get the fire breathing back at him.

Alex reached for a second snack bar and chewed each mouthful slowly. It had to last him until morning.

He had a feeling he should rest now too. When the wolves started their nightly ritual and sang to the forest, or the rustle of animal moved between the trees, he wasn't going to get any shut-eye. Plus he wanted to keep that fire stoked all night, to make sure he didn't become part of the food chain.

Alex took the waterproof sheet from his pack and strung it between the low branches of three trees that surrounded his spot. It was close enough to the fire to allow protection and a glimmer of heat, and the way the trees met with thick brush meant his back would be partly protected.

He dragged his T-shirt back over his head as the air began to cool around him, threw another few branches on the fire and slipped into his sleeping bag.

On second thought... He unzipped the end so his feet poked

out. At least he'd be able to run quickly if something did happen. The idea of being stuck helpless inside a bag was not one he wanted to entertain.

It was dark, and still he hadn't come home. Lisa was starting to worry.

The trouble was, she didn't want to call her mother or her sister. What would she tell them? That the man she'd kept insisting was just a visitor had left, as he was entitled to, and not returned? It wasn't like she was wanting to keep tabs on him, but walking out into the forest and not coming back before dark was not something she had expected him to do. Even that angry, she hadn't expected him to do that.

Alex never would have left the rental car sitting in her drive if he wasn't coming back, and his things were still in the cabin. She didn't have to check to know that.

Right now all she cared about was seeing his large frame walk back up her lawn. Seeing his shadow move behind the blind in the cabin. Or hearing his knock at the door.

She'd locked it, for safety, but she was ready to open it if he arrived home.

Home. It was a word she knew well. But she knew the same could not be said for him. It hurt her knowing that he had no one and nowhere to call on.

This was a man who had turned up on her doorstep looking for her. A man who had seemed so traumatized that there was no hope for him. But she'd seen a transformation firsthand. Seen the change in him when Lilly started to talk to him. Felt the change in him when they were together, just like she'd felt it within herself.

As Lilly had found her words, so Alex had seemed to start finding himself. Whoever that might be. She liked him whatever way he came, because she knew that deep down he was a kind, brave, honest person. He was just hurting. And she wanted to help him.

Her heart continued its steady thump against the wall of her chest. She tried to swallow but her mouth kept drying out.

She went to check on Lilly again. Her little girl was snoring, ever so lightly. Boston raised his head, then tucked back into her.

Before William's passing Boston hadn't been allowed on the bed. Now he slept with Lilly every night. If it brought her daughter comfort she was happy to turn a blind eye to the hair he left behind.

Lisa walked to the window one last time. She pressed her forehead against the glass and conjured an image of him. Of Alex.

He was a soldier, she reminded herself. That meant he could survive.

And when was the last time a human had been taken by a bear in these parts? Plenty of people camped in the National Park.

She quickly rid her mind of thoughts of camping. The average tourist stuck to the camping grounds. They didn't just take off and set up camp wherever their feet stopped walking.

Lisa pulled her eyes away. It was so dark out she couldn't see a thing anyway. The lights on her porch didn't filter light out that far.

She went downstairs and pulled her wheat bag from the bottom drawer. She put it in the microwave to heat it.

Lisa watched as the numbers counted down from four minutes. That was as long as she'd give herself. Four full minutes until the bag was hot, then she was turning in for the night.

There was nothing she could do to help Alex except try and make him see reason when he eventually turned up again.

She was no use traipsing off into the forest with a torch. She couldn't even call the local park ranger. Their trainee had left a few months back, and the ranger who had served the area for two decades had suffered a heart attack. Right now it was just a group of townsmen who'd banded together to take turns until a replacement was found.

Her brother-in-law was one of those men. She wasn't going to wake her sister up at this time of the night.

All she could do was wait it out.

William. She called him in her mind. He would never have done anything silly like this—walking off into the forest and staying out after dark. But then William hadn't been troubled like Alex. William had been a talker. Had grown up with love and without pain.

She liked that both men were so different. It helped her to know she wasn't trying to replicate what she'd had with William.

Alex had shown her she did want to love again.

If only he'd come back and give her the chance to tell him that.

CHAPTER TWELVE

THE door to the cottage was open. Alex fought against the clench of his jaw and forced his feet up the steps. His entire being felt shattered. Exhausted. More emotionally wrung out than he'd ever been.

His back ached, his mind was drained, and all he wanted to do was have a hot shower and rid himself of any memory of the hours he'd walked or the night he'd spent sleeping rough.

He had expected a mess. He had wondered if Lisa would throw all his things in a heap or politely have them waiting for him in the car. Thought she would have become angry, furious with him for what he'd done.

He was wrong on both counts.

Lilly was sitting on his bed. So was Boston. He ignored the dirty paw marks and levelled his eyes at Lilly instead. "Hi."

She gazed up at him. He could see questions in her eyes, things she wanted to ask, but he didn't push her. He didn't want to. He didn't even think he wanted to know what the questions were.

"Alex," she answered.

He hadn't got off as easily as he'd hoped. His head ached—an insistent, dull drumming of pain that banged at his forehead. He dropped to the seat across from the bed and looked at the little girl.

The last thing he'd wanted was to get close to her. In some ways he still felt nervous about how to talk to her, what to say, what to do around her. But other times it just seemed so natural to hang out with her and help her through her not speaking. Like they were connected by what had happened. But when he looked in her eyes he still saw what she'd lost. And it hurt.

"Alex, I know you're not my daddy, but sometimes I wish you were," she said in a small voice.

His eyes snapped shut. No. No, no, *no.* This was why he couldn't be here. Shouldn't be here.

He *wasn't* her father. He could never fill that role. And here she was, saying words that she didn't understand. Not knowing what had happened over there. Why her father had died and under what circumstances.

"Lilly…" He could barely whisper her name.

"I think Boston would like you as his dad too," she continued.

Alex crushed the fingers of his left hand with his right, and tried to control the tic in his cheek and the pounding of his heart. It felt like his pulse was about to rupture from his skin.

She jumped from the bed with Boston in pursuit. "Want to come fishing?"

Alex shook his head. "Not right now, Lilly."

She shrugged and ran off.

He tried to put his mind back together, like a tricky puzzle missing some of its pieces.

A knife had just been turned in his heart, giving him a fatal blow, so how was it he was still breathing? Why was it that the idea of being a daddy to that little girl had fired something within him that he hadn't even known existed?

He heard laughter, and then muffled talking from outside. Alex rose to close the door, then lay back on the bed.

He had no idea what to do.

He'd fought getting too close to anyone, being part of a family for so long. Now he felt as though he was on a precipice, dangerously close to the edge. One wrong move and he was lost.

* * *

"Alex?" Lisa tapped at the door. Her knuckles fell softly against the timber as she called.

A noise made her step back. She didn't want to be too in his face—not after how he'd acted last night. Not when she didn't know what was happening inside his mind.

But at the same time she wanted to scream. To yell at him and tell him how worried she had been, how she'd lain awake all night and prayed that he'd survive the night and then come back to her.

The door swung open. Relief hit her in the gut and stole the breath from her lungs, left her throat dry.

He looked terrible. Like a man who'd been out on the town for nights on end. Only she knew he hadn't. The darkness under his eyes was from the never-ending cycle of guilt and anger that she was determined to dispel. Even if she hated that he'd walked away, wanted to shake him and curse at him, she still wanted to throw her arms around him and hold him tight and beg him never to leave her like that ever again.

No matter what happened between them she wanted to help him. And there was one way she could do that. Without telling him anything, without letting her emotions take hold and make her say or do something she could regret, what she needed to do was *show* him something.

"Alex, I wondered if you might come somewhere with me?"

He looked wary. She understood. He'd expected her to be angry with him, to blame him, to shout back at him, but she didn't. She'd known William too well for that. If he'd decided to put himself in the line of fire to save another man—well, that had been his choice and she admired him for it. When it was your time to go, it was your time. Alex had had nothing to do with that. Just like as a boy he'd played no part in his parents' death.

She also didn't want him to know that she'd noticed his absence while he'd spent the night camping. Noticed it as if one of her vital organs had been slipped from her body for an entire night.

He just stood, watching her still, his eyes unfocused yet looking at her.

"Please?" she said.

He shifted his weight, then went back inside. She waited. He emerged maybe four minutes later with his boots on, hair damp from the quick shower he'd managed.

"Where are we going?" Even his voice sounded husky, like he was hungover.

She smiled at him. "You'll see. Go get in the truck and I'll grab Lilly."

He waited. He let his forehead rest against the butt of his hand as he leaned on the door. It was as if all his energy had drained through his feet and left them heavy with the residue of it.

He saw movement and looked up. Lilly was holding her mother's hand as they crossed down and over to the car. She jumped up beside him and sat in the middle of the bench seat before Lisa jumped behind the wheel.

"No Boston today?" he asked, trying to make normal conversation.

Lisa shook her head. "He'll be fine here for a little while. We're not going to be that long."

He looked back out the window. He had no idea where they were going and he didn't much care. When they got back he was going to leave. He couldn't stay.

They rumbled along the road in silence. Even Lilly stayed quiet.

Alex sat there and observed. That was all he could do. There was nothing he could say, nothing he wanted to say, and Lisa had turned up the radio—presumably in an effort to avoid conversation.

They pulled up outside a nice enough single-level home. It

was set back off the road and sported a rustic feel, like most of the places they'd passed on their way here.

"We'll just be a minute," Lisa said.

Lilly reached out and skimmed her fingers against his, before smiling at him and following her mom out the door.

A lump formed in his throat but he pushed it away. He didn't want to watch them but he had to. Couldn't drag his eyes away if he tried.

He saw Lisa's sister emerge from the house. They embraced and Lisa kissed her cheek. Her sister placed her arm around Lilly and led her inside.

Lisa started to walk back to the car. He was pleased her sister hadn't acknowledged him—it was, after all, what he deserved—but then maybe she hadn't even seen him.

She got into the cab and started the engine. They pulled back out onto the road. He wanted to ask her where they were going but he didn't.

She could take him wherever she liked.

The silence in the car became knife-edged. Although she hadn't really needed confirmation to guess that he wouldn't like cemeteries.

Every time she came here she thought of the funeral service. Now she wished Alex had been there to say goodbye to William too. Maybe it would have helped him find closure.

The memory of the jolt that had run through her body when the guns were raised and fired in a final salute still hit her spine every time she visited, but it was less pronounced than it had been the day of the service.

Full military honors and nothing less, and it had been very fitting for her husband. She'd taken home the flag passed to her by his commanding officer and tucked it in a special box in Lilly's wardrobe, there for her to have when she was old enough to appreciate it. Along with his uniform.

She cut the engine and turned in her seat to face Alex.

"Come with me," she instructed.

Alex wouldn't look at her.

"Alex?"

"No." He threw the word at her.

"I need you to come with me," she said firmly. She opened her door and took a punt that he'd follow her. Eventually. She traced the path to William's headstone, standing white, tall and proud amongst many older ones.

Lisa came here every week. Every Sunday she usually came with Lilly, and they ran a rag over the stone to clean it and placed fresh flowers in the grate.

It didn't hurt her coming here—at least not the sharp pain it had been to start with. Now she just wanted to make William proud by looking after him, looking out for him even in death. To show him that she loved him still.

Lisa felt a presence behind her. She didn't turn to look. She knew Alex was there.

"William was a great man," she said, forcing her voice to cooperate. "But he had many different roles."

Alex stood still behind her. She could feel the size of him, the warmth of his body, as he stood his ground. This had to be uncomfortable for him, but she hoped he wouldn't walk away.

"William was a son, a husband, a father and a soldier. He valued each role, but his life was the life of a soldier, and we all knew and accepted that. *I* accepted that."

She studied the headstone and hoped William could hear them. He *had* been a good man. She wasn't just saying it because he wasn't around to defend himself. He'd been great at everything he'd turned his hand to, but the role he'd been most destined for had been that of a soldier. He'd been a patriot, had strongly believed in serving his country, and she had never, ever resented that. Even now that he was gone she wouldn't let herself feel that way. She'd loved that he believed in serving and protecting. Apart from missing him when he was away, he had been the husband she'd always dreamed of.

"William was a soldier because he believed in fighting for

what was right. He was the type of man who would jump into a lake to save another human even if it meant he could drown himself. And that's why he saved you that day, Alex. Because that's the type of man he was."

She turned then. Let her feet swivel until she was facing Alex.

He didn't look any better than he had earlier, but she knew he'd listened. He could look her in the eye now, and that was more than he'd been able to do earlier.

"What I'm trying to say," she said, slowly reaching her arms up until her hands rested on his shoulders, "is that he couldn't *not* have saved you. It wasn't your fault that he died. He would have saved whoever was in the line of fire, and that day it just happened to be you."

Alex looked like he was going to cry.

In all her years as a married woman she had never, ever seen a man cry. William had smiled, laughed, shown anger on the odd occasion. But not even when Lilly was born had he cried.

She pulled Alex into her arms and held him as tight as she could, as if he were Lilly and needed all the comfort in her mother's heart. Alex resisted for a heartbeat, before falling against her. Clinging to her.

He buried his face in her hair and held on to her. Hard.

"William wouldn't judge us, Alex. He wouldn't. If I thought I was disrespecting him I never would have let anything happen between us. I admit that it took me a while to feel that way, but I do honestly believe it now."

His hold didn't change. She had thought he might shed some tears, but he was holding them firmly in check. She almost wished he'd let it go. She knew that holding tears back did nothing to help. That to move on sometimes you had to let go.

Alex straightened and cleared his throat.

"I'm sorry you feel like William's death was your fault, Alex. I really am. But I don't blame you, and I never will. You need to stop blaming yourself too," she said.

She didn't wait for him to respond. Instead she turned around, closed her eyes, and whispered a silent prayer. It was the same one she said every time.

Alex still stood behind her. He hadn't moved.

"I'm going to go back to the truck now," she told him.

He nodded. "Give me a minute, okay?"

She walked one step toward him, stretched to whisper a kiss on his cheek, then left him.

This was what she'd hoped for. That she could bring him here, tell it like it was, and leave him alone to make peace with William.

She got in the car and watched him.

Alex had crouched down. His long legs buckled under him as he squatted in front of the headstone, reading the words, then he sat back on the grass.

Lisa wanted to look away, to give him privacy, but she also wanted the chance to watch him while he couldn't see her.

The night before last had been incredible. Even if he had woken up troubled about what they'd done it had been amazing. Being in Alex's arms, being caught up against his skin, had been more than she'd ever experienced. Made her realize how different he was from William and how much she appreciated that.

His touch had filled every vein within her body with fiery light, made her want to keep him in her bed and never let him out. But it had been more than just physical. For the second time in her life she had fallen in love. Truly fallen in love.

She almost felt guilty. How was it that she'd had the privilege to fall in love twice? To have two amazing men come into her life and be able to love them both? She felt incredibly lucky, so special. She'd thought it would feel wrong, that it would trouble her, but it didn't at all.

Alex fought the urge to sink to his knees. He wished the ground would open up and swallow him in William's place, but he pushed the thought away.

He needed this. He needed this so badly—to say goodbye and ask William for forgiveness.

While they had been friends in real life, after leaving the army their paths might never have crossed again. Yet now their lives had intertwined in a way that neither of them could ever have imagined.

I'm sorry, William. He closed his eyes and reached one hand out to the tombstone, the cold hitting his palm. *I wish I could make things different, but I think I've fallen for your wife.*

Alex's heart twisted at the silent confession. He still didn't want to admit it, but whenever he thought of Lisa, whenever he acknowledged what had happened between them, he knew something inside of him had changed irrevocably.

And it terrified him.

But William had loved his wife. And he'd also valued their friendship and what they'd shared throughout the years.

Deep down Alex knew what William would say in response to his confession. He'd heard the words himself as he'd listened to him gasp his final breath.

Tell Lisa I want her to be happy.

Alex knew he'd meant it, had seen it in the openness of his friend's eyes despite the pain.

If Alex truly believed he could make Lisa and Lilly happy, then William would give him his blessing.

He sighed and dropped into a crouch, sitting low to the earth once more.

Goodbye, my friend.

Alex caught Lisa's eye as he stretched to his feet.

She met his eyes through the windscreen and saw what she'd hoped to see. He smiled at her.

A tickle traced her skin like a feather. Had she finally managed to put a sledgehammer through that wall? That fierce, impenetrable depth of solid concrete that had kept his heart tucked away?

The dread that had traipsed through her like a spiky stiletto was replaced with a nerve-edged flutter of calm.

Maybe they did have a chance. Just maybe they did.

The cottage was almost finished, and the thought of him leaving early made her want to convulse in pain. Maybe getting through to him like this would make him hang around longer. Every pore in her skin longed for him to stay.

CHAPTER THIRTEEN

"Come in with me to get Lilly."

Alex didn't particularly want to go in to Anna's house, but he did.

They walked up to the front door together, side by side.

"Anna's husband is called Sam. You'll like him," she promised.

"Was he a friend of William's?" Alex asked dryly.

"His best friend."

Alex stopped. He couldn't help it.

Lisa grabbed him by the arm and tugged him. Firmly. "Come on. You've got that look about you that you had that first day on my porch. Sam's not going to bite, and neither is Anna."

He let himself be led.

He wasn't so sure she was right about her sister, though.

But Lisa had been there for him today when he'd needed her. When all he'd wanted was to run, to be alone, she had guided him from the darkness into the light.

For the first time since his parents' death he had finally let someone in.

The house was exactly as he'd expected. The hallway was slightly dim, but it led into a large living room that was filled with Alaskan sun.

"Yoo-hoo! Hello?"

No one had answered when Lisa had knocked at the front door, so they had just walked on in.

He saw Lilly first. She was sitting outside in the sun with her aunt, painting. They had a huge sheet of something, and Lilly had a paintbrush in one hand and a tube in the other.

A man he guessed was Sam sat slightly in the shade, with a bottle of beer resting on his knee.

"Want a drink?"

Alex looked over at Lisa. She had the door to the fridge open.

"Sure."

"Beer?"

He nodded.

She popped the top on two bottles and passed him one. He took a long sip before following her outside.

He had a feeling he was going to need the infusion of alcohol to make it through this afternoon.

Earlier, he had thought Lisa would be on the verge of kicking him to the curb. Now he was at her sister's place. With her. As if they'd moved on and were taking a giant step forward together.

He took another swig. Lisa had bent down to talk to Lilly, and Sam was looking at him.

He smiled. Sam smiled back before rising to his feet.

It appeared not to be a hostile situation.

The air had a faint tinge of night to it. Lisa could smell the hint of rain leaving a dampness in the air before it even fell.

"We might have to relocate inside for dinner."

Lisa watched Alex as he helped gather up some plates with Sam. It had gone down pretty well, having him here with her, even if Anna *was* a touch on the sulky side.

"Lilly." She called her daughter over. "I think it's time to go wash your hands."

Lilly bolted into the house and headed for the washroom.

Alex walked beside Lisa, juggling plates. She took some

of the load. Their eyes met, flashed at one another before she looked away.

Lisa was pleased he was enjoying himself. There had been a tension between them that she hated, and she had wanted to dispel it as fast as possible. Last night, which he'd spent goodness only knew where, had been one of the most painful, the most worrisome of her life. She liked him, had fallen for him, and she didn't want to see him hurt, alone, so lost ever again. She also didn't want him to leave. Not yet. Not until they'd figured out what was happening between them.

Anna called out to her from the kitchen. She went to investigate as Alex joined Sam back outside.

Her sister was tossing a salad.

"Want me to take care of the potatoes?" Lisa asked.

Anna nodded in their direction. "Dish—top right-hand corner."

Lisa reached into the cupboard for it and gently brought it down.

"So, you guys are out of the closet now, huh?" Anna sniped.

Lisa put the bowl down. That type of question didn't warrant an answer.

"Come on, Lisa. I can see the way you look at one another."

Her face flushed hot. She wasn't embarrassed. It was just...

"Lisa?"

She spun around and waved a spoon with all the fury she could muster. "Enough, Anna—*enough*," she snapped. "We are *not* in a relationship, but if we decide to be it won't be based on whether or not we have *your* permission. I'm sick of trying to please everyone."

Anna glared at her. Her eyes were angry, wild. Lisa had hardly ever seen her sister looking like that. Not since they'd been kids and she'd broken the head off of her Barbie doll.

"It's too soon, Lisa. William's only been—"

"I said *enough*! Don't ruin a perfectly nice evening by sticking your nose where it shouldn't be," Lisa said.

Both their heads snapped up when a deep noise rang out.

Lisa felt guilty when she saw Alex standing there. He'd cleared his throat—loudly—to alert them, but how long had he been there? How much had he heard?

She glared at Anna. Her sister just shrugged. Lisa knew what it was about. Her sister wanted her to be miserable, to stay a widow and never emerge. Well, she wasn't going to, and no one was going to tell her when it was okay to come out of mourning. No one. She wasn't trying to replace her husband. Never! But she also wasn't about to be guilted into not moving on.

"Alex, could you help me carry this out?" Lisa asked.

"Sure." He jumped to attention.

She grabbed him before he reached her, stopped him with a hand to his chest, and stood on her tiptoes to plant a smacker of a kiss on his lips.

He didn't move. The stunned look on his face was priceless.

"Thanks," she said. "Here." She passed him the dish.

Alex walked out, still in a daze.

"You'll catch a fly if you keep your mouth open like that," Lisa commented to Anna.

Her sister clamped her mouth shut and stared at her in disbelief.

Lisa just shrugged. Two could play at this game. It wasn't her style, but she was sick and tired of being the serious one, of trying to please others.

Lilly adored Alex, and so did she. Right now that was all that mattered.

Alex still couldn't quite shake off the memory of that quick kiss. Even now, after dinner.

He sat with Sam while the girls nattered. He hadn't missed the tension between the sisters earlier, but they'd obviously pushed past it. Or they were just ignoring it for now and leaving the arguing until later. In private.

"Did you serve with William for long?"

Alex turned back to Sam. He had completely lost the focus of their conversation. He angled himself so he couldn't look at Lisa in order to give Sam his full attention.

Not that he particularly wanted to talk about William right now, but it would be rude not to reply.

He thought about the cemetery again, and calm passed over him. If Lisa could forgive him, then he owed it to himself to do the same.

For some reason hearing Lisa say William's name held less punch. Perhaps because she talked about him fondly, but with finality. Everyone else seemed to talk about him like he was still going to walk back in the door.

"We served together a few times, but this last time we were in the same unit permanently for around two months—maybe longer." He didn't say it, but it would have been much longer than that if they'd both served out the full tour.

Their friendship had been the kind that could only be formed by trusting another person so much it was as if they were a part of you. Knowing how they reacted, how they moved. He and William had been like that.

Sam nodded and held up another beer. Alex shook his head and motioned toward Lisa. "I think I'll drive. She's had a couple."

Sam opened one for himself and sat back. "William and I went way back. We both started dating the girls our last year of senior high."

Alex had guessed they'd been friends a long time.

"I can see why William liked you," Sam added.

"Yeah?"

Sam grinned at him. "Lisa obviously doesn't mind you either."

Alex felt uncomfortable. Was he joking for real, trying to hint at something, or saying it was okay?

"Sam, I—"

The other guy held up the hand that gripped his beer. "What you and Lisa do is your own business. I'm not part of the gossip brigade."

"Your wife sure doesn't seem happy about it," Alex pointed out.

He watched as Sam smiled over at his wife. Lisa looked their way too. It was as if the girls knew they were being talked about.

"Lisa's her little sister. Anna's just looking out for her."

"What about the rest of Brownswood?" Alex said ruefully.

Sam shrugged. "Small-town life is what it is. It's whether you care about the talk that matters." He looked hard at Alex. "And I don't take you for the type to care what strangers think."

"Guess you're right."

His attention was back on Lisa. She had risen, and was rubbing at her arms like she was cold. He ached to go to her and warm her, put his arms around her, but he didn't want to do anything that might upset her sister. Not if it would upset Lisa too. He didn't know if she would be okay with it.

He had expected tonight, this afternoon, to be dreadful. Expected to be judged, to find Sam hostile, but it had been half good. Better than good. It had been nice to have a beer with another guy—one who didn't want to interrogate him about war—and just behave like a regular citizen.

But then if the guy had been one of William's best buddies he probably knew enough about war to have already satisfied any curiosity he might have had.

It just felt good to feel normal. Something he hadn't felt in a long time.

Alex drove home. Lisa and Lilly were tucked up close to one another across from him, and he navigated through the steady path of rain that was falling on the road. He was pleased he'd refused a third beer. The road was slippery and he wouldn't have liked Lisa to be driving.

"You were right about the rain."

Lisa just smiled.

"Your sister was—"

"Wrong." She cut him off. "My sister was wrong."

He smiled. Was she just being stubborn because she didn't like her sister telling her what to do?

"We don't often argue, but tonight she was most definitely wrong."

"Who was wrong, Mommy?" Lilly asked sleepily.

Alex shook his head at Lisa. He wasn't going to tell if she wasn't.

"No one, honey. Alex and I are just being silly."

He pulled up outside the house and scooped Lilly up to ferry her inside. The rain was coming down hard now, trickling down his neck and wetting his hair. He managed to keep Lilly mostly dry.

Whining echoed on the other side of the door and Lilly called out. "Boston! We're home!"

Lisa emerged next to them. Wet.

She thrust the key into the lock and turned the handle. Lilly disappeared with her dog.

"To bed, young lady!" Lisa called after her. Then she turned to face Alex, pulling the door shut behind her.

The look on her face was…open.

"Do you mind telling me what that stunt in the kitchen was about?" he asked.

She grinned. "Proving to my sister that she was wrong."

"And that's all it was?" he wanted to know.

Her eyes glinted at him. "Maybe."

He shuffled forward so he was only a foot away from her. He absorbed the sight of her wet hair, just damp enough to cling to her head, the lashes that were coated with a light sting of rain. Then his eyes dropped to her lips.

She parted them. Her eyes lifted to look into his.

"We have everything stacked against us, Lisa. Everything," he warned. Then he bent slightly, so their lips could touch. Just.

Lisa let her body fall against his.

"Not everything, Alex." She sighed into his mouth as she said the words.

He tried to pull back, but couldn't. She rubbed her lips over his, teasing him, pulling him in deeper than he had intended going.

"I just don't want you to feel guilty about this later. About *me*," he insisted.

She disagreed. "We are both grown, consenting adults."

"It's not enough," he argued. He wanted to resist. He really, badly, desperately wanted to resist. But this was Lisa. This was the woman who had already forgiven him his sins and still wanted him.

It was Lisa who pulled back this time. "It's enough because there is no one judging us—no one that matters." She looked up at him. "Lilly is the most important thing in my life, and she accepts you. William would have accepted you. And in my heart I know we're not doing anything wrong."

He nodded. He knew it was the truth, but he had needed to hear it from her.

"And your family?" he asked.

"My family only want to protect me. Don't want to see me hurt. It's not that they don't like you," she insisted.

They looked at one another.

"You're not going to leave, are you, Alex? Not yet?"

He shook his head. "No."

"You're not just staying because of Lilly, though, are you? You don't have to worry about hurting my feelings, and I can comfort her—honestly. You shouldn't feel like you're trapped here," she said.

What? He traced a tender finger from the edge of her mouth down to the top of her collarbone. *Never.*

"I'm not just staying because of Lilly," he said gruffly.

"But…"

He shook his head. He felt the sadness of his smile and forced it to lift. "I shouldn't be here at all, Lisa. But I'm here because of you."

She leaned heavily against him. He felt her relief.

His mind started to play tricks on him again. A cloud of doubt hovered over his brain. "Do you only want me here because of Lilly? Because I helped her?"

She shook her head. Vigorously. "No."

Relief emptied his clouds of worry.

"I trust you, so trust me," he said.

"We're going to the Kennedys' place for dinner tomorrow night," she mumbled into his chest, not looking at him.

He gulped. Please, no… That was too much.

She looked back up at him and gave him the sweetest of smiles.

"Time for bed, Alex." She gave him a brief kiss on the lips—nothing like before.

He still stood there, stunned at hearing they were going to William's parents' house.

"Do it for me, Alex. It's just dinner."

He kept his eyes on her as she swept inside and closed the door on him. He heard the lock twist. She was punishing him still, he realized. She'd forgiven him—she'd shown him that today—but was still punishing him for running out on her after making love to her, and then spending the night in the forest by himself.

He was just coming to terms with what he'd done, and now he had to face William's parents. Great. His boots felt like they were filled with the heaviest of cement. Eating a meal with the parents of the man who'd died saving him wasn't exactly his idea of fun. But if he was going to try to move on, to open himself up, then maybe it was something he had to do.

The cottage loomed in front of him. He wished he was up in Lisa's bed with her, instead of trudging in the rain to the cabin.

Lying there in her bed, stretched out on her soft sheets, waiting for her to join him.

But he wasn't going there. Not yet anyway. He needed time to think.

Especially about tomorrow night's dinner.

Besides, Lisa had already locked the door on him.

Seeing William's gravestone today had helped him. But seeing William's parents and answering any questions they might have? Well, that was something else entirely.

He hoped he was up for it.

CHAPTER FOURTEEN

"I UNDERSTAND your loss."

He watched the looks cross George and Sally's faces and knew what they were thinking. It was what he'd thought every time someone had said those words to him.

"My parents died when I was eleven years old. We were driving home from an ice cream parlour and a car went through an intersection. They were killed instantly," he told them.

He didn't look at Lisa while he said it. Couldn't.

Almost worse than the sadness of losing his parents had been the pity. That was why he usually kept it to himself. But somehow tonight, sitting with these people, he needed to say it.

Alex looked at William's parents. He didn't see pity there. Instead he saw understanding.

Lisa reached for his hand beneath the table. He was relieved to feel her touch, but he knew he was strong enough to continue. He knew Lisa accepted him for who he was, understood that now, but being here meant a lot to him. It was the final missing piece of the puzzle to allow him to move on and stop looking back to his past.

"Do you have any other family?"

He shook his head at Sally's question.

"I went into foster care, then I joined the army as soon as I was of age."

* * *

Lisa couldn't believe he'd opened up like that.

The connection he had with Lilly was very real, and hearing his story, the full version of it, made her realize why.

Alex knew pain and loss more than anyone.

All of her own life she had felt so loved, so nurtured. As a married woman she had again known love, of a different kind, and then with Lilly she'd known she'd never be alone again.

But Alex—he was trying to start over, to put past demons behind him, and she wanted so badly to be there for him.

Lilly burst into the room then. The smile lighting her face was infectious.

"Hello, darling." Sally smiled at her granddaughter.

Lisa held her breath. The expression on her daughter's face had taken her by surprise.

Lilly looked at Alex. He moved his head, only just, but Lisa didn't miss it. Lilly smiled up at him.

"May I have dessert, Grandma?"

Lisa suppressed a squeal of delight. Sally had tears in her eyes, but—bless her soul—she just got up as if nothing was out of the ordinary.

"How does ice cream with chocolate sauce sound?" Sally asked.

Lilly giggled and sidled up to her, before winking at Alex.

Sally stopped as she passed Alex and let her hand rest on his shoulder. "Thank you, Alex. You've done her the world of good."

Alex smiled back.

He had brought light back into their lives like only William had done in the past. He had filled Lisa's world with hope for the future, had helped Lilly to find her voice again, and brought comfort to William's parents. Sharing stories. Telling them how highly their son had been respected by his men.

"Lisa, do you mind if I steal Alex away for a single malt Scotch?" George asked.

She emerged from her daydream and nodded. William had

always joined his father for a Scotch after dinner, so it was nice that Alex could share in that for one night.

"I'll join the girls in the kitchen," she said.

She rounded the corner and found her mother-in-law and daughter curled in front of the fire in the lounge. She stopped to listen to them talk.

It was like Lilly had never lost her voice.

The therapist had said this might happen. That one day she could just start talking again to everyone around her.

She'd seen the look Alex had given her daughter, though. Seen Lilly looking to him for guidance. Whatever he'd said, whatever they'd talked about earlier, it had obviously worked.

There was nothing about this situation that seemed entirely comfortable to Alex.

He didn't think he'd ever pass the buck on the guilt that still kept him awake at night sometimes, but at least this family had found comfort in his being here.

"Son, it doesn't take a genius to figure out you're troubled," George said.

Alex took the just-warm Scotch thrown over a handful of ice. He raised his glass, a brief advance in the air, as George did the same. It tore a fiery path down his throat that didn't disappear until it reached his stomach.

"Lisa and Lilly are the only family we have," the other man went on.

Alex understood how protective George must feel over them, but he'd made peace with Lisa, been accepted, and that was what he had to hold true to.

"I'm sorry that I couldn't help bring your son back alive. As God is my witness, I'd have traded places with him in an instant. But if Lisa wants me here I'm not going to turn my back on her," he said.

George sat back in his chair. "I'm not here to lecture you, Alex. You've brought happiness with you that some of us thought was lost forever. I want to thank you."

Alex sipped at his drink. He didn't know what to say.

"If you want to be in Lisa's life, in Lilly's life, we say welcome to the family."

Alex's palm was filled with George's. With the hand of William's father. He'd thought it would seem wrong, would fly in the face of the guilt that had tormented him these past few months, but it didn't.

Warmth spread through his fingers, and it didn't stop there. It traveled up his arm. Shook his shoulders. Hit him in the head.

For the first time since the night his parents had died Alex felt a burning ball form in his throat. Tears bristled behind his eyes.

He couldn't have answered if he'd wanted to.

Not without letting another grown man see him cry.

"I'd like to hear some stories when you're ready. Hear more about William. About what you went through over there."

Alex jumped to his feet, glass snatched firmly between his fingers. He swallowed the lump and turned his head at an angle.

He couldn't see anything out the window except blackness. Nothingness. It suited him just fine.

Tears stung his skin as they hit. He sniffed. Hard. Then wiped at his face. He swilled the last of his Scotch, then slung it back.

It burnt, but not as badly as his tears.

Alex wiped at his face once more and forced them back.

He felt lighter. The guilt that had sucked him dry was now turning to liquid and hydrating him once more. He was powerless to stop feeling as if everything had been lifted from his chest, the pressure finally gone.

"William took a bullet for me, George. I'll forever be grateful for that."

Alex closed his eyes as memories played back through his mind. For the first time in a long while he wanted to talk about the friend he'd lost. About how much those wartime friendships had meant to him, and how he'd never give up those memories even if he could. It was time.

Lisa pulled the covers tight up to her chin and tried to shut her mind off.

Tonight had gone better than she'd thought it would. Much better.

Sally and George's blessing meant a lot to her, but it went deeper than that. The change in Lilly was extraordinary. Exciting. But it worried her. The therapist's words kept echoing in her head. What if Alex *did* leave and she became worse than before? The thought sent a crawl of dread through her body. They'd only agreed on a few weeks. But now he had said he'd stay longer.

Something in Alex had changed tonight too. And it wasn't just meeting William's parents that had affected him. She didn't know what. Couldn't pinpoint what it was. But there was a change deep in his soul even more than the difference she'd seen in him after they'd visited the grave.

It wasn't that she only wanted him around for Lilly's sake. Far from it. What she wanted was a chance to make a relationship work with him. A chance to see if they could be together, without William or anything else hanging above them and ruining it before they even started. Without second-guessing themselves.

But it wasn't going to happen. She wouldn't be surprised to wake up in the morning and find him gone.

And it wouldn't just be Lilly hurting if he upped and left. Lisa cared for him. Deeply.

She didn't let her thoughts go any further. Couldn't. Because if she did she'd start wondering if she was in love with him again.

Lisa heard a noise. A creak. She sat bolt upright in bed. Her back so straight it could have snapped.

There was someone in the house.

She crept with stealth from her bed and grabbed the baseball bat tucked in the wardrobe. She glanced out the window. Alex still had his light on. He was awake. She could call to him for help if she needed to.

Lisa moved on tiptoes out into the hall. Her ears strained in the stark silence. The noise below cut a just audible snap through the air.

She moved quietly down the stairs, conscious of the treads to avoid from years of not wanting to wake Lilly when she was young.

A shadow loomed.

"Lisa?"

Her heart fell in a liquid heap to the floor.

"Alex!" She dropped the bat, relieved beyond all measure. "What are you doing in here?"

He didn't answer her.

She could just make him out in the half-light. He had pajama bottoms on. They were slung low, the drawstring tied in a knot.

He walked toward her. His big frame purposeful, determined. Angry?

"Alex?"

He didn't stop. But he did act.

His hand cupped behind her head. His palm filled with her hair. She heard the gasp as it fell from her mouth, but she was powerless to stop it.

Alex's lips found hers before she could even catch her breath. He took her mouth, crushed it into his own, and pulled her hard against his chest.

Her hands found his shoulders, his back, clawed at him to get her body closer to his.

"Alex…" She whispered his name against his skin as he pulled away.

He took one hand from her head and tucked it under her chin. Made her eyes meet his. The other hand was pressed into her lower back, keeping her immobile, forcing her to stay still.

But she didn't need any chains. There was no way her body would move even if her mind told it to.

"I'm sorry."

She opened her mouth to answer, but he pressed his index finger across it to silence her.

"I'm sorry, Lisa. I know now there's nothing I could have done to stop William saving me."

She nodded. His fingers still fell like a clamp across her mouth. He had finally stopped blaming himself. Had released himself. That was the change she'd noticed. His battle with himself over taking this huge step forward was finally done.

"Can we start over?" he asked.

She shook her head.

Confusion made his face crease and gave her the chance to escape him. Just.

"I don't want to start over."

He frowned. His eyes lost the glow they had been casting. His hand fell from her back.

She reached for it and put it in place again. Pulled him against her and let her mouth hover back over his.

"I don't want to start over, Alex. I like you just the way you are."

A smile spread across his face, but she didn't wait to receive it. She caught his bottom lip between both of hers and kissed him, her skin skimming his. She wrapped her arms around him, feeling his muscles, loving the masculinity of his big frame.

Alex scooped her up into his arms, and only then did she let her lips fall from his. She tucked her head against his chest and let herself be carried upstairs to the bedroom.

She had loved William. Wholeheartedly. As much as a wife could love her husband. And now she felt a different but just as powerful surge of love deep within her for Alex. Like her heart had been refilled and she had been given the chance to love all over again. Given the privilege to bask in the glow of another man's feelings toward her without having to give up loving her husband.

Alex looked down at her. He stopped halfway up the stairs.

He kissed her nose, her mouth, then her eyelids as they fluttered shut.

"I love you, Lisa. I love you. *I love you.*"

She tucked tight in against him as he started to walk back up the stairs.

"I love you too," she whispered.

From the thudding of his heart against her ear she could tell he'd heard her.

Lisa woke to light heating her face. She let her eyes pop open, then threw her hand over her eyes. Had she forgotten to close the curtains last night?

She sat up. Last night.

She didn't need to look beside her to know she was in bed alone. There was no weight causing a sag in the mattress. No one's arm had been slung across her when she'd woken. She was alone.

Nausea beat like a drum in her stomach. She reached for her nightdress, discarded on the floor, and wriggled into it before standing. She forced herself to walk to the window.

Had he gone?

She wished upon wishing that he hadn't. But for what other reason would he have disappeared before she woke?

Lisa closed her eyes and felt for the windowframe. She held on to the timber, counted to three, then looked. She didn't know what to expect, but she didn't expect to see Alex.

She placed a hand on the window, the glass cooling her palm and calming her mind.

He was there. With Lilly.

They sat cross-legged on the lawn. They were talking. It looked serious.

Please. *Please.* Don't be telling her that you're going.

She forced herself away from the window and fumbled for

her dressing gown in the wardrobe. She tugged it on and ran fast down the stairs. Her toe caught, but she fought the pain.

He couldn't be leaving.

"Al..." His name died on her lips.

Lilly had run off to chase Boston. She had bare feet and her hair was sticking out around her head, fresh from bed.

"Is she okay?" she gasped.

"She's fine." He got up. A smile tickled the corners of his mouth.

Lisa's own mouth went dry. He was smiling. That was a good thing, right? He walked toward her. She had a flashback to the night before. When he'd stalked her in the same way.

He caught her in his arms and tugged her forward. She resisted. Or tried to.

"Lilly...?"

"Is fine," he said, dropping a kiss to her nose before moving down to her mouth.

Lisa wriggled in protest.

Alex sighed. "I was just telling her something. Something I wanted her to know first."

Lisa tried to pull away from him again, but he held her tight. She was powerless. As good as an insect caught into a spider's web.

"Don't you want to know what I told her?" Alex asked.

She stopped wriggling.

He leaned back, his upper body giving her room but his lower body holding her in place.

She nodded. She wanted to know. Badly.

"You do?" he pressed.

"Yes." She wished her voice wouldn't give out on her in times of need. It sounded no better than a frog's croak.

"I told her," he said, brushing the hair from her cheek, "that I was going to ask her mommy to marry me. I had to check she was okay with that first, before I did it."

Lisa stared at him. *Marry her?* So he *wasn't* leaving?

"I thought you were going. That you were leaving. That you were telling her..."

Alex stopped her. Covered her mouth with his and kissed the words from her.

"Did you not hear what I told you last night?" he said, when he'd kissed her into stunned silence.

She stared at him. She remembered plenty about last night.

He caught her in his arms, lifting her from her feet and tucking him against her just like he had the night before. "I love you, Lisa." He dropped a kiss on her forehead. "If you'll have me, I want to stay. I'm not going to run. Not now. Not ever. You've taught me that. Made me realize I need to believe in family, in love, in myself again."

She closed her eyes and burrowed into him. Smelt the tangy aftershave that had taunted her from day one. Touched the biceps that had called to her from the first time she'd seen him shirtless. Pulled at the base of his neck to steal a kiss from pillowy lips that had begged to be touching hers from the moment she'd started falling for him.

"So you want to marry me?" She breathed the words against his cheek.

"I thought I was the one who was supposed to ask the question?"

She laughed. A head thrown back, deep in the belly laugh.

"Well, hurry up and ask me so I can say yes," she teased.

He didn't put her down. Just kept her folded in his arms, holding her like he'd never let her go.

A little voice squeaked from behind them.

"Mommy?"

Lisa let Alex swing her around to her daughter. She couldn't wipe the smile off her face if she'd tried.

"Did you say yes?"

Lisa didn't say anything.

He hadn't officially asked her, but of course she would say

yes. How could she not? She loved Alex. As much as she'd loved Lilly's father. So much.

Alex dropped to one knee. He took Lisa's hand.

"I think it's time to make this official. Lisa, will you please put me out of my misery and say you'll marry me?"

"Yes, Mommy. Say yes!" Lilly squealed.

"Yes," whispered Lisa.

Alex stood to wipe away her tears.

"I love you girls, you know?"

"We know," chirped Lilly.

Yes, we know, thought Lisa. And we love you too.

Earlier this year—weeks ago, even—she'd thought her heart would never open to another human being. Hadn't ever wanted it to.

But now she knew otherwise. She loved Alex now, and she'd loved William then—and still did. But her love for William was in the past: a loving, vivid memory to hold on to.

Alex was now.

Alex was her future.

EPILOGUE

ALEX ran his fingers over the emblem lying flat over his chest. The khaki shirt felt nice against his skin. Felt right.

Two months ago he'd been lost. A man without a path. Without a destiny.

Now he was happy. He had a future, and he no longer lay awake at night in a sweat with the world at play on his shoulders.

He tugged on his boots and grabbed the paper bag resting on the counter. He took a peek inside. And smiled. Neatly wrapped sandwiches, a token piece of fruit, and two big slices of cake.

It didn't matter how hard he tried to suppress it, the grin tugging at the corners of his mouth couldn't be stopped.

Alex walked out onto the porch. The lake's water shone in the early-morning light; the trees were waving shadows around the far perimeter. He stood there and looked.

When he was serving, even before that in foster care, he'd never dared to imagine a life like this. A life where everything was possible. Where he had a chance to make his own family, where a woman loved him, and where he could be part of nature every single day.

He walked across the front yard, jingling his keys.

A tap made him look up.

Lisa stood in the window, her hair like a halo framing her face. Lilly was standing in front of her.

His two girls. His two beautiful girls.

He raised a hand and then blew them a slow kiss. His lips brushed his hand before he released it to wave softly up to them.

Lisa pretended to catch it while Lilly giggled. That infectious bubble of laughter that she was so prone to throwing his way.

Alex turned, his hand going up behind him in the air as a final goodbye for the day. He heard the flutter of the flag as it waved proudly in the wind. He didn't have to turn to know it was looking down on him. The same flag that he'd tucked in his bag when he'd first joined the army. It had seen him safely through plenty of hard times, and now it was flying high in the air as a tribute to the friend he'd lost during wartime. A symbol, an ode to William and to how they'd fought over there in the desert. He wanted to show William that he'd take care of Lisa and Lilly until the day he died—just like William had looked out for him at the end.

Alex unlocked the truck and jumped in the cab. Something gave him a feeling that the other National Park ranger would give him a rough time about driving a baby-blue Chevy, but he didn't care.

The rumble of the engine signaled he was on his way.

National Park ranger by day, husband and daddy by night.

Somehow life had finally given him a hand of cards he wanted to play.

He turned up the radio and sang along to the country and western channel Lisa had it permanently dialed to.

He would have preferred rock and roll, but if Lisa wanted country he didn't mind one bit.

A KISS TO SEAL THE DEAL *by Nikki Logan*

Grant is furious that conservationists plan to destroy his family's farm! So he confronts the woman in charge, researcher Kate, who touches his heart in ways he never expected!

THE ARMY RANGER'S RETURN *by Soraya Lane*

Jessica's best friend is pen pal soldier Ryan. Her letters have offered him comfort while he was away fighting for their country, yet is he ready to fight for her heart?

BABY ON THE RANCH *by Susan Meier*

Since losing his wife Cade's been wedded to his ranch, until Suzanne and baby Mitzi reawaken his heart!

THE ONE THAT GOT AWAY *by Jamie Sobrato*

Good friends are hard to find. In fact, they're priceless. And it's only after almost losing her that Marcus *really* begins to appreciate Ginger...

CHARLOTTE'S HOMECOMING *by Janice Kay Johnson*

Charlotte's got a good job and good life in the city...until a crisis forces her return to the family farm and leads her straight into the arms of Mayor Gray Van Dusen.

0611_BOTM

are proud to present

June 2011
Ordinary Girl in a Tiara
by Jessica Hart
from Mills & Boon® Riva™

Caro Cartwright's had enough of romance – she's after a quiet life. Until an old school friend begs her to stage a gossip-worthy royal diversion! Reluctantly, Caro prepares to masquerade as a European prince's latest squeeze…

Available 3rd June 2011

July 2011
Lady Drusilla's Road to Ruin
by Christine Merrill
from Mills & Boon® Historical

Considered a spinster, Lady Drusilla Rudney has only one role in life: to chaperon her sister. So when her flighty sibling elopes, Dru employs the help of a fellow travelling companion, ex-army captain John Hendricks, who looks harmless enough…

Available 1st July 2011

Tell us what you think!

millsandboon.co.uk/community
facebook.com/romancehq
twitter.com/millsandboonuk

Dating and Other Dangers
by Natalie Anderson

After being trashed on Nadia Keenan's dating website, Ethan Rush faces three dates with her! *He's* determined to clear his name. *She's* determined to prove him for the cad he is...

The S Before Ex
by Mira Lyn Kelly

World famous celebrity Ryan Brady's secret wife is filing for divorce! Unfortunately for Claire Brady, her soon-to-be-ex is *still* the only man her body wants...

Girl in a Vintage Dress
by Nicola Marsh

Lola Lombard, 1950s style siren, is petrified: she's got to organise a terrifyingly glam hen do! Worse still, the bride's gorgeous brother seems interested in the shy woman behind the red lipstick...

Rapunzel in New York
by Nikki Logan

When a knight in pinstripe rushed to the aid of this damsel, she declared she didn't want saving, even by a billionaire! *Yet sometimes even modern Maidens secretly need rescuing...*

On sale from 1st July 2011
Don't miss out!

Available at WHSmith, Tesco, ASDA, Eason and all good bookshops

www.millsandboon.co.uk

0611/01a

MODERN

THE MARRIAGE BETRAYAL
by Lynne Graham

Sander Volakis has no intention of marrying—until he sees Tally Spencer. He can't resist her…little knowing that one night with the innocent Tally could end his playboy existence…

Doukakis's Apprentice
by Sarah Morgan

Wanted: willing apprentice to handle incorrigible, womanising (but incredibly sexy) tycoon! Polly Prince is determined to make a lasting success of the position, but soon learns that her workaholic boss *can* put pleasure before business!

Heart of the Desert
by Carol Marinelli

One kiss is all it takes for Georgie to know Sheikh Ibrahim is trouble, Trapped in the swirling sands, she surrenders to the rebel Prince—yet the law of his land decrees that she can never really be his…

Her Impossible Boss
by Cathy Williams

Successful New Yorker Matt Strickland's sexiness is off the scale, but new employee, feisty nanny Tess Kelly, thinks his capacity for fun definitely shows room for improvement! Although he's *determined* to keep things professional…

**On sale from 17th June 2011
Don't miss out!**
*Available at WHSmith, Tesco, ASDA, Eason
and all good bookshops*
www.millsandboon.co.uk

MODERN

THE ICE PRINCE
by Sandra Marton

No opponent can penetrate Prince Draco Valenti's icy exterior...except high-flying, straight-talking lawyer Anna Orsini! They're at odds in business, but in the bedroom Draco's desire for Anna has the power to melt *all* his defences!

SURRENDER TO THE PAST
by Carole Mortimer

Mia Burton thinks she's seen the last of Ethan Black—the man who haunts her heart. But Ethan's returned in all his very real glory, and it's clear he'll do *whatever* it takes to win her back!

RECKLESS NIGHT IN RIO
by Jennie Lucas

Gabriel Santos offers Laura Parker a million dollars to pretend she loves him. But they've already shared one unforgettable night in Rio, and Gabriel's not aware he's the father of Laura's baby...

THE REPLACEMENT WIFE
by Caitlin Crews

Theo Markou Garcia needs a wife—or someone who looks like his infamous fiancée—so offers disowned Becca Whitney a deal: masquerade as the Whitney heiress in exchange for her own true fortune...but don't fall for her husband!

On sale from 1st July 2011
Don't miss out!

*Available at WHSmith, Tesco, ASDA, Eason
and all good bookshops*
www.millsandboon.co.uk

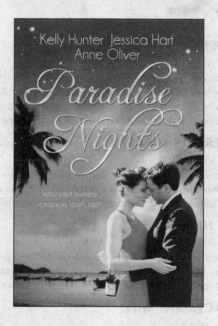

Intense passion and glamour from our bestselling stars of international romance

Available 20th May 2011

Available 17th June 2011

Available 15th July 2011

Available 19th August 2011

Royal Affairs – luxurious and
bound by duty yet still captive to desire!

Royal Affairs: Desert
Princes & Defiant Virgins

Available 3rd June 2011

Royal Affairs:
Princesses & Protectors

Available 1st July 2011

Royal Affairs:
Mistresses & Marriages

Available 5th August 2011

Royal Affairs: Revenge
Secrets & Seduction

Available
2nd September 2011

2 FREE BOOKS
AND A SURPRISE GIFT

We would like to take this opportunity to thank you for reading this Mills & Boon® book by offering you the chance to take TWO more specially selected books from the Cherish™ series absolutely FREE! We're also making this offer to introduce you to the benefits of the Mills & Boon® Book Club™—

- **FREE home delivery**
- **FREE gifts and competitions**
- **FREE monthly Newsletter**
- **Exclusive Mills & Boon Book Club offers**
- **Books available before they're in the shops**

Accepting these FREE books and gift places you under no obligation to buy, you may cancel at any time, even after receiving your free books. Simply complete your details below and return the entire page to the address below. You don't even need a stamp!

YES Please send me 2 free Cherish books and a surprise gift. I understand that unless you hear from me, I will receive 5 superb new stories every month, including two 2-in-1 books priced at £5.30 each, and a single book priced at £3.30, postage and packing free. I am under no obligation to purchase any books and may cancel my subscription at any time. The free books and gift will be mine to keep in any case.

Ms/Mrs/Miss/Mr _____ Initials _____

Surname _____

Address _____

_____

_____ Postcode _____

E-mail _____

Send this whole page to: Mills & Boon Book Club, Free Book Offer, FREEPOST NAT 10298, Richmond, TW9 1BR